RESCUING
A FALLEN

PART 1

VOLUME 3 IN THE RILEY SERIES

KELLY HOLLINGSHEAD

North Carolina

Rescuing a Fallen – Part 1
© 2024 Kelly Hollingshead. All rights reserved.

No part of this book may be reproduced in any form or by any means, electronic, mechanical, digital, photocopying, or recording, except for the inclusion in a review, without permission in writing from the publisher.

This is a work of fiction. All of the characters, names, incidents, organizations, and dialogue in this novel are either the products of the author's imagination or are used fictitiously.

Published in the United States by BQB Publishing
(an imprint of Boutique of Quality Books Publishing, Inc.)
www.bqbpublishing.com

ISBN 979-8-88633-034-2 (p)
ISBN 979-8-88633-035-9 (e)

Library of Congress Control Number: 2024912257

Book design by Robin Krauss, www.bookformatters.com
Cover design by Rebecca Lown, www.rebeccalowndesign.com

First editor: Caleb Guard
Second editor: Allison Itterly

To my pastor, Dennis Hudson, of Saginaw Park Baptist Church in Fort Worth, Texas. Thank you for your continuing patience and answering my barrage of questions through texts, phone calls, and conversations. You played such a vital role in helping me pull this one off.

As always, to my wife, Melissa, and daughter, Brynn. Thank you for putting up with me and believing in me when I doubted myself.

"Fate whispers to the warrior, 'You cannot withstand the storm.' The warrior whispers back, 'I am the storm.'"

Author Unknown.

And a great windstorm arose, and the waves were breaking into the boat, so that the boat was already filling. And He awoke and rebuked the wind and said to the sea, "Peace be still!" And the wind ceased and there was a great calm.

Mark 4:35–41, paraphrased.

CHAPTER 1

Riley and Maggie hid in the lake house with their bodies pressed against the front door. Riley prayed that the terror that had chased them into the house would be kept at bay long enough until he could figure out what to do next.

During the short time that Riley had known Jonathan, his guardian angel, they had battled demons and fought to stay one step ahead of the Devil. But now something far more sinister stood just on the other side of the front door. It was a mindless creature used for only one purpose: to kill.

Maggie stood next to Riley, breathing heavily, pressing herself against the door. Her expression was both fear and concern.

Maggie was the CEO of Gregory Portal Provider, a streaming company she'd started many years ago. She had been propelled into Riley's paranormal world because of her brief encounter with the fallen angel, Jonathan.

"Is it still there?" asked Maggie, referencing the unwelcome guest on the opposite side of the door. After Jonathan had been pulled into Hell, the hound immediately appeared, chasing them into the lake house. At first, Riley thought they had just been fortunate to have made it back inside, but now he wasn't so sure. The creature could have killed them when it had them trapped on the front porch. But thinking back on the way it happened, Riley realized it had only sniffed at them and never even attempted to follow them when they strategically moved around it to get inside.

The sun had put itself to bed as a full moon took up its vigilant watch in the night sky. Riley had turned off all the inside lights to conceal Maggie and himself in the darkness from the hound. But now the light from the moon shone through the glass patio door, playing tricks on his limited vision. Shadows appeared to take on a life of their own.

Riley peered out through the half-window at the top of the front door. There stood the colossally muscular beast with its glaring red eyes, and jet black, fur coat. It had the appearance of a black wolf, only it was the size of a bear. "It's still there," he whispered.

As soon as the words left his mouth, the hound turned its head, locking its menacing red eyes on Riley. The creature didn't just look at him so much as it seemed to stare straight through him. Riley was the prey, and it was the predator.

"Jesus, God," said Riley, quickly stepping away from the door.

"What?" asked Maggie.

"I'm certain it can see in the dark," Riley whispered.

"What?" Maggie asked again.

Riley shook his head. "It looked right at me when I spoke. One minute it's looking out at the yard, and the next its eyes are boring into me, as if it knew I was watching it!"

"What do we do?" asked Maggie.

Finally, having heard enough of the "what" questions, Riley turned the question around on her. "What do you think we should do?"

Maggie gave him a quizzical look. "What?"

Despite the intensity of their current situation, Riley laughed before immediately covering his mouth to stifle it.

Maggie frowned and delivered several hard punches to his shoulder. "Seriously, Riley, what are you, twelve?" she asked in an annoyed tone.

"Ow," said Riley, massaging where she had hit him. "Maggie, eventually that thing is going to grow tired of waiting, and it's going to walk right through that front door as if it were made of paper. This will sound crazy, but I don't believe it's actually here to harm us."

Maggie scoffed. "I think you have officially lost your damn mind!"

"Okay, but if it really wanted to harm us, then why didn't it do it when we were only a few feet away from it on the front porch? Do you honestly believe something produced by Hell could be kept out by wooden doors and walls? Or even the patio door that is made entirely of glass?"

Maggie's eyes widened as she looked back at the patio door. Riley didn't want her to worry, but he needed her to understand why he believed the hound wasn't here to harm them.

"I see your point," Maggie replied in an unsteady voice. "What do you suggest we do?"

Biting his lower lip, Riley couldn't believe he was about to go through with this next part. He spoke quickly, hoping that once he voiced his plan, he wouldn't be able to back out of it. "I'm going outside to test my theory. Don't try to change my mind. This was what Jonathan trained me for, to fight off and survive whatever the Devil threw at me."

Maggie looked at him dumbfounded and responded in a condescending tone, "Riley, you are absolutely correct. That's the dumbest thing you have ever said. Jonathan didn't teach you to fight just so you could fight off the paranormal!"

"No?" asked Riley.

"No, he taught you to fight to help keep yourself alive, not to put your life in danger just because you have a wild brain idea. We should just wait and hope the hound gets pulled back to

Hell. We have guns, ammo, and plenty of food. So, we need to wait it out, and if it does come inside, then we fight."

In spite of her making sense, Riley felt the urgency to track down the demon who had disappeared when Jonathan had been pulled into Hell. For some reason, Riley could literally smell the foul, rotting stench of the demon, but he was afraid if they waited too long, he would lose its scent and Jonathan would be lost forever. It had only been a few hours, but Riley didn't know how long this new gift would last.

"Maggie, I don't have time to play the waiting game to see who will make the first move. I have to find that demon. I'm not asking you to go with me, but Jonathan did something to me because I can now smell that rogue demon."

Maggie's expression changed from fear to understanding. "That was why Jonathan kissed and rubbed your nose."

Riley gave her a confused look before piecing together what she had said. The moment Maggie was talking about had occurred in the living room of the lake house. It was the last time all three of them had been together.

"Jonathan must have given me this gift so we could track down that demon and possibly be able to rescue him. I have to try, and I need to do it right now, with or without you."

Riley retrieved one of the handguns from under the kitchen sink and handed it to Maggie. When Jonathan had first entered Riley's life, they made the decision to leave Taupe City, where Riley lived, and move to Riley's lake house in Potogi. Jonathan had made several upgrades to the lake house and property, beginning with the construction of a large metal building a few feet away from the house. Riley referred to it as "the hole" because it was where Jonathan put him through intense and grueling daily workouts. An underground tunnel was next, starting in the garage and spanning the length of two footballs fields. Then they placed a small arsenal of various rifles, handguns, and shotguns in various spots around the house. Jonathan was constantly checking to make sure that Riley knew the precise location of each one.

Out of all the terrifying paranormal experiences Riley had lived through, from being attacked by demons, to meeting the Devil himself, none of those compared to what Riley was about to attempt, especially since Jonathan wasn't here to intervene or distract the hound if it did go on the attack.

Placing his hands on Maggie's shoulders, Riley gave her a weak smile and said, "This is going to work, Maggie. It is just another obstacle we need to overcome to rescue Jonathan."

As much as Maggie wanted to try and rescue Jonathan, she feared if she went along with Riley's quest, she could die and spend the rest of eternity in Hell, where her mother now resided.

Maggie didn't really want to believe it, but somehow knew it to be true: her mom was an occupant of Hell. The rogue demon they were after had conjured up dreams for both Riley and Maggie, revealing their deepest, darkest fears. Her worst fears were that there really was a God, but because she was raised not believing in such things, even if her and her family were all good people, they would still end up in Hell.

In Maggie's dream, she encountered her mother—not just a figment of her imagination, but her actual mom, who spoke to her, revealing facts only Maggie knew. At that time, Maggie wouldn't have the luxury of waking from the nightmare. This had only fortified Maggie's position in not wanting to believe in some kind of all-knowing God when it placed her in a lose-lose situation. On the one hand, she wouldn't be cursed to an eternity in Hell; however, it would mean accepting that her mother was in Hell, which was something Maggie could not and would not come to terms with.

Maggie had not realized that she had been crying until Riley said, "What's wrong?"

Wiping away her tears, Maggie couldn't make herself look at him. "I just don't think you should go outside. We should wait and see what happens. At least for a little while longer." But she knew Riley was not going to listen to reason.

"I'm going to sneak out the patio door and make my way around to the front where my truck is parked. If, for whatever reason, things don't work out as planned, then I want you to head immediately to the secret passage in the garage."

Maggie had been down there with Riley once before, and once had been enough. She would accept being mauled to death rather than subject herself to dying inside a small underground tunnel.

Riley went to the patio door, unlocked it, and stepped out into the night. Drawing his handgun out of the back of his jeans, he then pulled the door closed and disappeared out of sight.

Maggie hurried to the front door and stood on tiptoes to peer through the half window at the top of the door. The first thing she saw was a red pair of eyes looking back at her. It was just like Riley had told her; the damn thing could track their movements through walls. Now Maggie was merely a few feet from the hound with only a door separating them. If that "thing" truly wanted to get inside, then it could have done so at any time. The sheer size of the hound made her question if their handguns would do anything more than piss it off, like shooting a paintball gun at a grizzly bear.

This uneasiness of knowing that they were practically defenseless caused Maggie to grip the gun even tighter in her hand. As the intensity of their circumstances increased, Maggie raised the gun in self-defense. The hound issued a deep, spine-chilling growl, and Maggie immediately dropped the gun back to her side to deescalate the situation.

Maggie caught movement out of the corner of her eye, which caused her to break eye contact with the hound. As soon as she made this critical error, the hound disappeared. Without regard for her own safety, Maggie quickly pulled the front door open and stepped out into the night.

Once her eyes adjusted, Maggie saw the hound standing a few feet away from Riley. She raised her gun, putting sights on the back of its head, hoping the hound's skull would be its weakness.

Stiff as a statue, with both arms raised high above his head, Riley looked helplessly in her direction. "Maggie, whatever you do, don't pull that trigger. I want you to make your way slowly over to the truck and let me try to ease this situation."

Not wanting to tempt fate, Maggie walked backward away from them, keeping an eye on the hound until she bumped into the side of the truck. After blindly locating the door handle, she awkwardly climbed inside, pulling the door closed a bit harder than intended.

Staring out the passenger window, Maggie watched as Riley slowly reached back toward the massive head of the black hound, offering it his shaking hand to sniff. Instead, the hound issued a deafening bark, causing Riley to jerk his hand back and caused Maggie to involuntarily cry out in horror before she immediately covered her ears as it violently rattled the truck's windows.

After the ringing in her ears had subsided, Maggie opened

her eyes, surprised to find Riley still in one piece. *Just move slowly and get your ass to the truck*, thought Maggie.

As if sharing the same thought, Riley took one cautious step away from the hound and paused. When it didn't so much as move, Riley took another step, followed by another and another, until he was finally inside the truck, pulling the door closed quickly behind him. The hound had practically remained in the same spot, only turning its body ever so often to track Riley's movements.

Now that Riley was next to Maggie, she could see firsthand just how scared he truly was. "You're safe now, just breathe." She stuttered and then froze. Seeing movement in her peripheral vision, Maggie knew the hound had made its way into the back seat.

"W-w-what?" stuttered Riley.

Unable to verbally voice her concern, Maggie shifted her eyes toward the back seat several times, hoping Riley wouldn't make any abrupt movements.

Realizing the game of cat and mouse had come to an end, Maggie closed her eyes, hoping her death would be quick and painless. After what seemed like several minutes had passed, she forced her eyes open and glanced at the back seat. She gasped at the sight of the hound's red eyes boring into hers. Riley jerked and yelled something she couldn't quite understand.

"You can now call me crazy," said Maggie, her voice shaking. "But I agree, if this instrument of evil meant us any harm, then we would already be dead!"

Suddenly, her phone rang, causing a moment of chaos as she searched her pockets to answer her phone. "Hello?" she whispered.

"Maggie, is that you?"

It was her best friend, Stuart. "Yes, Stu, it's me," she said.

"Why are you whispering?" Stuart asked.

"Because I can't talk right now. I'll have to call—"

"You have to come back to Gregory Portal Provider right now," Stu said. "I know it's late, but I need you here as soon as possible. The feds have been here asking about you. If you don't come, then I have no idea what the feds will do, but I'm assuming they'll issue a warrant for your arrest. The agent in charge of the Miles Jackson investigation wants you to explain the million-dollar wire transfer that occurred between you two just days before his arrest."

Maggie said to Stu, "I'll be there in five hours tops."

Stu's voice took on a sense of pleading that she hadn't heard from him before. "Maggie, hurry. You need to be here no later than eight tomorrow morning so I can prep you. Call me as soon as you are in the office, no matter the time. Understood?"

"I promise," said Maggie. Not waiting for a reply, she disconnected the call. Riley gave her a hateful look because this meant they were being sidetracked from tracking the rogue demon and rescuing Jonathan. She knew that momentarily giving up the hunt for the rogue demon could potentially cause them to lose his trail, but she had to clear things up with the feds. Even if it was completely selfish because Jonathan's life hung in the balance, she said, "Riley, I'm so sorry. Just give me a little bit of time to resolve what's happening with my life, and afterward, I swear, I will help you find that rogue demon."

This was even news to her, as she hadn't known she'd completely made up her mind as to whether she was going to go through with this rescue mission or not.

Riley stared through the windshield in silence, and Maggie hoped that he would agree to the terms. She periodically kept glancing over at him, impatiently waiting for him to respond.

After what felt like an eternity to Maggie, Riley's voice cut the silent tension, "I will give you three days and then I have to leave," he flatly said. "I'm sorry I can't give you more time, but I have to locate that demon as soon as possible."

"Three days will be plenty," said Maggie, uncertain if she could really live up to her end of the agreement.

CHAPTER 2

Making the five-minute drive to church in complete silence, George Humphrey was aware that his wife, Miranda, had a drinking problem. He was also aware that he was likely the cause of it. Although she had always been moody and even downright rude on occasions, Miranda was now completely withdrawn after the move to Broken Falls. He wondered if she was experiencing a mid-life crisis and wished there were more he could do to lift her spirits. He stifled the thought when Miranda yawned, followed by a loud burp that stank of whiskey.

They had met on a blind date thanks to Brad, his old college roommate, who was dating Miranda's best friend at the time. Brad had been more than vague about the details. "Bro, she's drop-dead gorgeous. That's all you need to know. Besides, you haven't dated since high school, so enjoy getting out of your comfort zone for a little bit."

"If she is drop-dead gorgeous and single, what is wrong with her?" George had wanted to ask, but he shelved the thought. It was true that he needed to get out of his comfort zone instead of working himself to death in his office, hopeful for the day his hard work would finally pay off in the fast-ever-changing tech world.

George was sitting in the lobby of a restaurant staring at the one picture of Miranda that Brad had sent him. He couldn't understand how she was single. She had long black hair, dark mysterious eyes, pouty lips, and a perfect smile. He'd surmised that either his friend was having a joke at his expense, or there had to be something wrong with her.

When Miranda entered the restaurant, George immediately recognized her and stood, hoping to make a good first impression. However, what he got in return was a scrutinizing look before she tentatively accepted his outstretched hand. George could tell that she was ready to call the whole thing off and bolt out the door, but a young hostess had appeared, stopping her escape.

The dinner had been awkward and filled with small talk. Then Miranda abruptly stood when the check arrived. "Listen, George, I'm sure you really are a good guy, but this was a huge mistake."

Before he had time to respond, Miranda quickly walked away, turning several male patrons' heads in her wake.

After paying, George had started to leave, but then he noticed that Miranda was now at the bar talking to two eager men, both vying for her attention.

"Thanks for nothing, Brad," he'd mumbled.

Miranda made eye contact with him and waved, followed by a warm smile. Despite how badly their night had gone, George wondered if she wanted him to join her. That thought was instantly squashed once the three of them began laughing and pointing at him.

With a bruised ego, George ducked his head and proceeded to leave quickly when he'd accidentally barreled over a couple, which sent him flying face-first to the floor. Loud gasps followed by laughter poured over him as someone attempted to help him up. Too embarrassed to apologize or thank the onlooker for their assistance, George sprinted out of the restaurant.

Years later, Miranda reentered his life as a temporary employee at Code Creators, George's small software company. He wasn't the one who'd hired her, but he still would have given her the job.

He just didn't have the heart to hold a grudge. There was already too much hate in the world, and he didn't need to add to it.

When he'd walked into work that Monday morning, George stopped and did a double take when he saw Miranda seated behind the lobby front desk. Which is how they were reintroduced.

George pulled into the parking lot of the church and parked. Miranda could feel him scrutinizing her very existence. Her head buzzed from the alcohol she had consumed earlier this morning. "Do you ever feel like your life has just gone to hell, and all you're really waiting for is to take your final dirt nap?" It was a morbid thing to say, but at least it would change the narrative of him begging her to get some help.

When George's face changed from concern to pity, Miranda wished she would have said something uplifting so he would stop with his constant attempts to save her.

Her only reason she went to church with him every Sunday was so she could see the one attractive guy in this God-awful town that she desperately desired to have a fling with. They had never been properly introduced, but Miranda found herself daydreaming of taking this man for a good roll in the sheets, preferably in some sleazy back-road motel room. Besides, it had been far too long since she had the opportunity for a cheap thrill.

The only problem was that they were both married, which wasn't and hadn't been a problem for her in the past, since, in her opinion, it only generated more of a thrill. That was until they moved to this hellhole town and the limited participants it provided. Plus, the idiot she came to see each Sunday never picked up on any of her advances, even when she wore her blouse low, exposing as much of her ample chest as possible.

Maybe one day after church, she would lean in and whisper,

"Yes, they are real!" This thought caused her to laugh, making George scrutinize her even more.

"What, George? What?" she finally blurted.

Closing her eyes, Miranda knew he was working up the courage to give her an ultimatum, but instead felt him take her hand in his.

"You look very beautiful today, sweetie. Thank you for remaining by my side and helping me through this time. I know this isn't our ideal future, but I promise it's only temporary."

If she were being honest, she only had herself to blame. She was the one who'd pursued George all those years ago.

She had found a way to weasel herself back into George's life a year after their first date. She'd seen his picture in the newspaper with a headline that read: "Gregory Portal Provider considering merger with Code Creators." She knew George wasn't the wealthiest man in town but with his little software company, he was doing good for himself, and Miranda knew that anytime Gregory Portal Provider was mentioned, a large payout was sure to follow.

Boy was she wrong.

Miranda wanted to live a carefree life spending someone else's money, and with George's company being considered for a merger with the biggest streaming company around, she had made it her mission to do whatever it took to ensure she would run into George again. She'd called his office the next day to inquire about any open positions and lied about her qualifications just to get an interview.

She had watched as George's confusion turned into one of curiosity as he finally recognized her.

"Miranda, it's great to see you. How have you been?" George had asked.

She'd kept up the false persona and hoped that he didn't see through it. "I'm truly blessed, thank you so much for asking." When his expression changed from shocked to skeptical, Miranda elaborated. "I know, I was awful to you when we first met, and as cliché as this will sound, I'm no longer that person. That was a dark time in my life, and it took a lot of praying and soul searching to get me to where I am now. I just hope you can find it in your heart to forgive me."

George's expression softened. "Thank you for apologizing, Miranda. That was very thoughtful and kindhearted of you. I've never been one to hold a grudge. Though, my parents once told me that I was far too forgiving, and people would one day take advantage of me if I wasn't careful."

Miranda forced a smile.

"I just like to look for the good in people," said George. "In today's world, it's far too easy to judge someone just because we see them behave a certain way for even a brief moment of their lives."

Thank you for being so naïve, Miranda thought. She knew it was only a matter of time before he belonged to her. Months passed, and Miranda wooed him and got him to trust her. Finally, he'd asked her on a second date. Two months later they were married.

The big payday from Gregory Portal Provider never came because their merger with George's company, Code Creators, fell through. Although George made more than enough and she no longer had to work, Miranda wanted to travel and see the world, with or without him, preferably without.

A very depressing ten years later, which had felt more like a prison sentence than a marriage, George's parents' mental health took a turn for the worse.

"Fucking Alzheimer's," Miranda cursed under her breath when George told her.

The fact that both his parents were experiencing dementia

at the same time caused Miranda to believe that something in the universe was working against her, as if her quest for financial freedom would always be just out of her reach.

Against her wishes, George had sold Code Creators for a meager six figures. Then they moved to the small town of Broken Falls to be closer to his parents. Miranda would have filed for a divorce had it not been for the fact that she only had a G.E.D. and hadn't worked in a decade. She didn't want to end up following in her mother's footsteps, bouncing from one dead-end job to another, waiting tables and dreaming about a life that could have been. Instead, she was tied down to George, for better or worse.

Miranda did take comfort in the fact that they never had kids. At first, Miranda thought her infertility issues were because of George, only to later learn that she was unable to get pregnant. George had tried to console her, saying it was okay to not have children, but Miranda knew the truth: he really wanted to be a dad.

Later, when he brought up adoption, Miranda wanted to slap him senselessly. "Do you have any idea how that makes me feel? I can't have children of my own, and now you think adoption will make everything better?"

Truthfully, she never really wanted children. The only reason she had ever considered the topic of children was to lock down alimony, plus her half of everything when they got divorced. Except it never happened.

Damn that Gregory Portal Provider, Miranda thought. *If I ever meet the owner, Mary Allison Gregory, I'm going to punch her right in that perfect damn face of hers!*

However, now that the billionaire princess was having legal issues, and with Miranda contemplating divorcing George, maybe

Mary and Miranda would wind up waiting tables at the same restaurant one day. That would be justice enough in Miranda's mind.

"Honey, are you okay?" George asked, pulling her back to the present.

If she had any feelings for him whatsoever, she would have grabbed his face and kissed him long and good. However, Miranda only saw a weak, pathetic little man sitting next to her.

"George, I'm trying to refrain from telling you just how much my life is a living hell because of you! So, let's go into the church and receive our weekly lesson on how we suck at life. I'm sure that the good Priest Johnstone has a real gem up his sleeve to enlighten us with. Or maybe he'll just come right out and tell us how he prefers altar boys instead of abstinence!"

Not waiting for a reply, Miranda exited the Honda, slamming the door behind her, which caused her to teeter before regaining balance. Four older women passing by gave her a disapproving look as they whispered to one another. Miranda thought of grabbing her crotch since she was feeling so carefree, except George was now by her side, slipping his hand in hers.

As they began the death march toward the chapel, George took her by surprise and said, "I've had enough of your attitude! You treat me like I'm nothing more than a damn paycheck! If you ever speak to me in this manner again, I'll show you just how miserable I can make your life, beginning with cancelling every damn one of your credit cards!"

Strangely, Miranda found this side of him erotic since she had only seen him play the part of a submissive. Removing her sunshades, Miranda searched his face, which had turned a bright shade of red as the veins in his narrow neck protruded. She felt her cheeks redden when she thought about how rough he might be with her when they got home. However, the moment quickly passed when they made eye contact. The desperation and worry behind his eyes told her an apology would soon follow.

"Damn!" Miranda said. "I wanted so desperately to believe you. For you to force me back to the car, take me home, and slap me around till I learned my lesson." George's face went even redder from embarrassment, staring back at her in shock.

Once inside the cathedral, they found their usual seats. Not caring if she was being obvious about her intentions, Miranda scanned the crowd for her crush, spotting him several rows ahead of them. She let out a loud sigh, causing the man's wife to turn and look at her. She gave Miranda a knowing look, telling her that she was on to her game.

Returning the fake smile, Miranda mouthed "fuck you," except it didn't have the desired effect that she had anticipated. Instead, the woman's smile broadened before turning back around. Priest Johnstone walked to stand before the pulpit. *Here we go*, thought Miranda. *Serve me up an extra side of guilt and make sure not to hold back on the failure portion!*

CHAPTER 3

"**G**ood morning," Priest Johnstone said, receiving the appropriate mundane response.

Miranda let out a loud exaggerated yawn, followed by George giving her hand a hard squeeze. She leaned in to tell him that she would rip his balls off if he ever did that again, but her train of thought was interrupted by several people in front of her looking up at the ceiling. Following their gaze, Miranda found they were staring at the statue of the Virgin Mary. Shaking her head, Miranda couldn't understand why Catholics put so much faith in a woman who clearly hadn't been a virgin.

Priest Johnstone spoke in an authoritative I'm-right-and-you're-wrong tone. Miranda blocked him all the way out and resumed her focus once more on the statue. Water dripped down. She thought there must be a leak in the ceiling, but then she realized it hadn't been raining outside. Miranda stared more intently through her alcoholic gaze, finding that the water-like substance was coming from the statue's eyes.

Nudging George so he would confirm what she was seeing, only to be ignored, Miranda turned to glare at him, but he was also transfixed by the statue. *Guess I made that tequila sunrise a little too strong this morning*, she thought with a laugh.

Soft murmurs began to arise throughout the cathedral, as people noticed the same phenomenon.

Irritated, Priest Johnstone barked loudly, "Is there something more important going on than what God has asked me to speak on today?"

Unable to help herself, Miranda quickly stood and pointed up at the Virgin Mary. "Actually, good priest of ours, there is indeed something more important. You see, our dear old virgin appears to be crying because she finds you quite boring and thinks you're a hypocrite!"

The humor didn't find its mark as George jerked her back down.

Priest Johnstone gave her a condescending look, which Miranda answered by pointing at the Virgin Mary. Reluctantly, he gave the statue a quick glance, then did a double take and stumbled backward. Finding his balance, he made the sign of the cross over his chest with a shaky hand.

The entrance door then boomed open behind them as a large, dark haired man dressed in all black, strolled confidently down the middle aisle. He walked with an arrogance of belonging and although he was an attractive man, something about him resonated evil. He placed two fingers to his lips and held them up to the Virgin Mary, saluting her. The congregation went silent as they watched this stranger make his way up to the pulpit. He waved Priest Johnstone away like a nuisance.

"My good people of Broken Falls, it is my privilege to inform you that after today nothing will ever be the same in your little town, and I am the reason why. You see, I know who among you are worshippers of a false God and who are not. Come midnight, any worshippers of the false God that are left in my town will be executed on the spot, without question."

Miranda was intrigued by this strange man and enthralled with what he would say next. She leaned forward in her seat.

"I know most of you are probably thinking that I'm just some deranged lunatic saying utter nonsense to scare you. Some of you may even believe you can overpower me and turn me into your so-called authorities. However, be warned: If you challenge me, you will meet a quick and painful death, for I will show none of you, mercy. So, spread the word of my arrival and meet me back here at midnight, but only if you're ready to declare yourself to me."

Miranda and the rest of the congregation watched in anticipation as the stranger dropped to all fours and began dry heaving. His body rocked slowly back and forth, as if trying to spit up something lodged deep inside him, until at last he went completely still and faceplanted to the floor. The congregation was stunned into silence. The man lay in a heap, unmoving.

Suddenly, the man sprung to life, except he was no longer a man. He had transformed into a strange beast, with the body of a lion and an eagle's head. Down the length of the lion's body were scales of a snake that rippled, sending out currents of electricity. The eagle's mouth abruptly opened, revealing a long, slender snake in place of its tongue.

Chaos erupted. People screamed and pushed one another over as they made their way to the exit. Miranda remained seated, completely dumbfounded yet intrigued at what she was witnessing. George attempted to pull her to her feet, but she easily shook loose of him. He screamed at her, but Miranda couldn't understand a word he was saying, lost within her own thoughts. Again, he grabbed hold of her with a strength she didn't know he even possessed.

"Goddammit, George! Let go of me!" Miranda barked.

When he refused, she slapped the back of his hands until he cried out, releasing his hold.

"You can leave, but I'm staying."

Miranda was subconsciously aware that he was giving her

the exact same dumbfounded look he always gave her when he
found her passed out drunk on the couch. Except now she felt
stone sober, unable to take her eyes off this entity, not caring in
the least what her husband was thinking.

It wasn't until George resumed his seat that Miranda was
able to look away. "What in the hell do you think you are doing?"
she barked.

"If you're staying, then I am as well," George answered in a
matter-of-fact tone.

"George, did you not understand a single word this man, or
beast, or whatever the hell it is just said?"

George gave her a sympathetic smile, as if hoping to convey
that they were in this together. "Miranda, I have always loved
you, even from our first date when you blew me off. You aren't
easy to love, but I cherish every morning I get to wake up next
to you."

Miranda wasn't shocked by his admittance but felt the need
to make clear that he would only be throwing his life away
by staying. "George, I need you to listen to me—and I mean
actually listen—without thoughts of grandeur or belief in some
all-knowing higher God who will come rescue you in your time
of need." When he only responded with a defiant look, Miranda
grew a little more irritated with his self-righteous attitude. "I
know why you insist on bringing me here every week. You're
hoping I'll turn my life around and be the woman you think I
am, but I need you to understand that I don't believe in any kind
of deity and never have. What I do believe is that you will die if
you stay here."

Her words didn't appear to resonate as he looked at her with
complete defiance that his God would rescue him. "George, you
can put on a brave face now, but if that beast asks me, I know
without a doubt I'll do as I am commanded."

George's face finally softened as he replied in a softer tone, "Miranda, this may come as a shock to you, but I knew long ago that you never really loved me. I'm not as naïve as you make me out to be. I know you've cheated on me far more than once, and I know why you really married me. It took me awhile to come to terms with this. I just always hoped and prayed that one day you would realize I'm a good man, and you would learn to love me. So, with that said, if I must die to show you what true love is, then I will, but I will never abandon you."

Miranda closed her eyes, ashamed of how she had treated George. When she opened them, George gave her a sad smile, as if to communicate it was okay.

Looking around at the remaining congregation, Miranda was not surprised to find that the man she lusted over every Sunday was gone. However, his wife remained and was staring directly at her. His wife then mouthed, "Fuck you" to Miranda. Miranda just smiled back, knowing that his wife staying meant, whatever Legion had planned for them, it was going to be one hell of a ride.

Breaking eye contact, Miranda looked up at the Virgin Mary. The watery tears had now changed to a dark red. Even though Miranda wasn't a believer, she knew the Virgin Mary was crying tears of blood, warning all that death had arrived in their small town. Miranda grinned, then kissed her index and middle finger, just like the stranger did when he entered the chapel and held them up in an act of defiance.

CHAPTER 4

"We shouldn't be interrupted by the slaves for the next hour or so," Jameson informed Gideon and Barbados as they all stood crammed in Tristan's office. "However, we are all aware of the consequences if Savior unexpectedly drops in. So, let's keep this as brief as possible."

Savior was the name given to Lucifer by his assistant, Esperanza. Although Esperanza had only been in her current role for a short time, it was clear that Savior looked upon her with favor.

The three demons held their secret meetings in the tiny office where Tristan used to watch his slaves collecting the souls of the dead from Earth. Just as in all 666 regions, the Region Leader's office was furnished with a desk, three chairs, and an old couch. The size of the office varied from region to region, but this was on the smaller side. Tristan had paid no mind to the size of his office because his only concern was growing his region.

Tristan's territory was vast. Over a hundred slaves worked his region, as well as three Elder demons, Barbados, Jameson, and Gideon. The three began meeting secretly a lot more ever since Tristan had not returned from the assignment that Savior sent him on. The intent of their meetings was to devise the perfect plan to overthrow Tristan and claim the region as their own.

Out of all the 666 regions, Tristan was the only high demon to be rewarded with this many slaves. He had grown the region by scheming and causing problems for other Region Leaders. The leaders came and went, usually because of an uprising beneath their ranks, often caused by Tristan himself.

Savior seemed pleased by the turmoil in the regions, as he allowed Tristan to continue with his cunning ways and rewarded him by shrinking another region and expanding Tristan's. Tristan was the only Region Leader who had never been replaced. He was regarded as the closest thing to perfection in his job, second only to Savior.

However, now that Tristan had been out of the picture for quite some time, the region was in need of a new leader. The only question was, which of the three Elders would it be?

Savior only allowed 666 Region Leaders. He was, after all, quite fond of the number. Never had Savior allowed the other Elders to be in charge, no matter how small some regions had become. According to Savior, "The number is pure perfection," and he declared it to be his mark, which would live throughout all of time. Even humans both feared and loved the number, depending on whether they were a worshipper of the Devil or a worshipper of a false God.

"Where do you think Tristan could be?" Jameson asked the other two Elders, starting their little meeting the same way, they always did.

Jameson, the first Elder of Tristan's region, believed he was superior to Barbados and Gideon. The only reason they were now Elders was because of Jameson's recommendation. At the time, Tristan worried he needed two more Elders to help manage his ever-growing region. Jameson had gone out on a limb and suggested Barbados and Gideon, which Tristan eventually agreed to, except under one condition: Jameson was to train them, but if either one screwed up, Jameson would suffer the same punishment, which would result in all three being cast back into the pits of Hell.

"It's been far too long for him to be away," replied Gideon. "I just hope wherever he is, his worthless ass stays there!"

Gideon had an extreme hatred for Tristan due to a senseless punishment that had cost him his left eye. Tristan had ripped it out after Gideon supposedly gave him a questionable look. For further punishment and his own amusement, Tristan had cursed the missing eye so it would never regenerate.

The curse cast by Tristan caused the same worms that ate the damned in Hell to also reside in Gideon's eye socket. Tristan then fastened Gideon with an eye patch to cover up the gruesomeness. Luckily, the only punishment Jameson had ever received was a verbal tongue lashing.

Everything in Hell is always regenerated, with Gideon's eye being the only exception. The regeneration process was slow and painful as the bones, muscles, veins, and flesh grew back. Gideon was truly disgusting to look at; he was short but stout, his wavey brown hair was just long enough to be scruffy, and his face was scarred and weathered. Jameson couldn't help but shudder anytime he was around him. But he also couldn't stop staring, which earned a hard glare from Gideon's one good eye.

Jameson was the more handsome of the three, he was very lean and tall with short, curly red hair that matched the color of his wiry goatee. Barbados was the shortest, but he had a stocky body, his dark skin was covered in tattoos and scars, black buzzed hair sat atop his head, and his face always wore a scowl.

"You think that what I'm forced to endure is disgusting, don't you? If I could remove this patch, I'd show you what disgusting really is! I can feel every one of the worms crawling around, not just under this patch, but throughout my whole damn body. And you being squeamish like a—"

Gideon's brain short-circuited, leaving his mouth agape, his expression twisted in agony. He often lost his train of thought. The first time this happened was shortly after Tristan ripped out his eye. Jameson noticed these episodes had increased exponentially over the last few days.

After a few moments, Gideon came back around. Clearly confused as to what had just happened, he looked at Jameson and Barbados before he stuttered, "W-w-wait. W-w-was I just saying something?"

The reason Gideon remained one of the Elders was because Tristan loved how ruthless he was. Jameson overheard the slaves saying they believed he was even more unmerciful with punishments than Tristan. He would have made the perfect leader, if not for his memory being no better than a goldfish. Yet, both Jameson and Barbados feared it was only a matter of time until Gideon would become the new Region Leader. This had never sat well with Jameson since he was the one who had trained Gideon and recommended him for the role of Elder.

Jameson was aware of his own limitations and knew he couldn't compete with Gideon if they ever fought. Tristan must have also realized that Gideon was a legitimate adversary.

"What do you think we should do, Jameson?" Barbados interjected, not bothering to answer Gideon. "Should we just declare you as the new Region Leader? Or do you think we should wait for Master to make the announcement?"

"Don't be naïve, Barbados," said Jameson. "You know we can't declare me as leader just because we feel like it. First, there must be an uprising, followed by a leader being overthrown."

"True," Barbados replied, "but our leader is gone and hasn't shown his face for a month. What if Master is just waiting for someone to take the initiative and claim the territory?"

Gideon, still confused, said, "W-w-what are we talking about?"

Because of Gideon's ability to fight so well and his ruthlessness, Jameson knew that his first action as Region Leader would be to appoint Gideon as his enforcer. In doing so, he wouldn't have to worry about the other Region Leaders trying to take advantage of his new status as Region Leader. They, too, feared Gideon, as Tristan only used him to stir up trouble in other regions.

Barbados looked at Gideon. "You were saying that we shouldn't wait to declare Jameson as leader."

Jameson started to laugh, only to hide it by coughing into his hand.

"That's right, now I remember," said Gideon. "So, why don't we just make an announcement that you're the new Region Leader?"

This time Jameson couldn't suppress his laugh. With that, Barbados walked around Gideon to position himself closer to Jameson. Barbados crossed his eyes and circled his pointer finger around one ear as if saying that Gideon was indeed crazy. Jameson laughed again, earning a suspicious look from Gideon.

"What's so funny?" asked Gideon.

"What do you think would be the best way of making me the new leader?" Jameson said. "After all, it's not as if we can start an uprising when there isn't a leader to overthrow. Sure, the slaves will just follow along with whatever we say, but that means nothing when we all know that Savior is the only one who can declare it."

Without missing a beat, all his senses now fully intact, Gideon replied, "That's true, but we can always ask for an audience with

Savior. Nothing prevents us from doing that. Besides, the only two things Savior really cares about is that the territory continues to run smoothly, and the number of Region Leaders remains as 666."

Jameson and Barbados exchanged surprised looks, realizing that Gideon had just told them a perfect solution to their problem. "Even a blind squirrel finds an acorn every once in a while," Barbados softly whispered to Jameson. This time, however, Jameson did not laugh.

"Contact Esperanza at once!" Jameson ordered Barbados.

Esperanza was Savior's right-hand advisor and had the privilege of determining whether or not someone's situation warranted an audience with him.

Smiling broadly at Gideon, Jameson placed both hands on his shoulders. "You are a genius, Gideon. Seriously! An absolute genius!"

CHAPTER 5

Tamara and her father were just making it back to their small town of Broken Falls after a short visit to the neighboring town of Deadwater. They had headed out early on Sunday morning to take part in their yearly tradition of hiking the petroglyphs, a tradition they had done ever since Tamara was a toddler. When they began the hike, Tamara had tried to put on a brave face for her dad, but her mom wasn't there this time and more than likely never would be again.

Tamara was no longer able to keep up with the charade, breaking down at a part of the hike where small handprints had been painted on a rock. Her mother had always stopped at this location to admire the paintings. She would place her hand next to one of them and say, "It's so strange to think this three-hundred-year-old painting is the representation of a child's hand, which quite possibly touched this very spot I am now touching. Tamara, can you believe you used to be this small?"

That put a damper on things. Seeing the pain on her face, her dad had wrapped her up in his arms. "I'm sorry for being so inconsiderate. I just wanted to keep this tradition alive, but in hindsight, I can see that I was wrong. Please forgive me."

As his words poured over her, Tamara had clutched her father, fearful of what the future held for their little family.

They'd cut the trip short and headed back into town for greasy tacos and nachos. They'd just arrived at Taco Haven, Tamara's favorite fast-food joint, where she spent a lot of time with her friends. She was surprised at how empty the parking lot was, especially for a Sunday night. After receiving the food from an annoyed older male employee, they pulled out of the parking lot and back on to the main street. Several cars went around them on the two-lane road, ignoring the signs of no passing.

They exited off the main road and entered their neighborhood. Something was off. Families rushed back and forth carrying their belongings to their vehicles. Her father, however, appeared to be oblivious of the odd behavior as he pulled into the driveway of their home.

When Tamara got out, she saw her neighbor, Mr. Gentry, aimlessly throwing items into the back of his minivan. "Mr. Gentry, what is happening?" she asked, walking away from the car without bothering to help her father with the food.

Without stopping from loading the van, Mr. Gentry answered through sharp breaths, "Everyone has to leave by midnight. If not, then I pray that your family is ready for what is coming." Without elaborating, Mr. Gentry ran back into his house, yelling something that Tamara couldn't distinguish.

Hurrying around the front of the car where her father was aimlessly retrieving bags of food from the back seat, Tamara said, "Dad, something strange is happening. The whole damn town appears to have gone crazy!"

This comment pulled her dad out of whatever planet he was currently visiting. "Tamara, don't you ever use that kind of language. People who talk that way only show their ignorance." He then handed her a bag of food and reached into the car to retrieve the backpack he had carried on the hike.

Tamara placed the bag of food atop the car, then spun her dad around. She placed her hands on her father's face, forcing him to see the chaos occurring all around them.

Stepping out of her grasp, her father scolded, "Tamara, there is no need to treat me like a child. Now come inside and let's eat these greasy tacos before they fall apart even more."

Her father then pushed past her, leaving Tamara confused as to what she should do next. Something was going on. All of her neighbors were rushing around and loading their cars. There was an eerie silence. She spotted Mrs. Cafferty across the street loading items into the back of her SUV; Tamara hurried over to her. "Mrs. Cafferty, what's going on?"

She was a middle-aged woman who allowed Tamara to use her swimming pool whenever she wanted. She had also been Tamara's favorite teacher when she was in middle school. When Mrs. Cafferty didn't answer, Tamara asked again.

"Tamara, I heard you the first damn time!" Mrs. Cafferty snapped, which was so unlike her.

Immediately, Tamara saw the remorse on Mrs. Cafferty's tear-streaked face, except she offered no apology for having spoken to her in such a manner. "Our town is no longer safe. Everyone has to leave by midnight. A strange man interrupted the service today at the Catholic church, declaring that anyone who remained in 'his town' would be killed if they didn't become one of his followers."

Tamara's eyes widened in dismay, feeling as if she had just stepped into an episode of *The Twilight Zone*, which she sometimes watched with her father.

"Listen, Tamara, I know that your mother is on hospice and can't be moved, and as cruel as this will sound, you need to consider your own livelihood at this point." Mrs. Cafferty then placed her hands on Tamara's shoulders and squeezed.

With only a couple feet now separating them, Tamara could see just how frightened the woman was, as her voice took on a manic, high-pitched tone. "Tamara, this man is supposed to be able to turn himself into some kind of beast. He morphed into a demonic beast in front of the whole congregation. You know me, and you know I would never tell you to leave your mother unattended for any reason, but death has come to our town in the shape of a man. Come midnight, the streets will run red with the blood of those who worship God, and these heinous acts will be carried out by those who have formed alliances with the individual who calls himself 'Legion.'"

Gooseflesh appeared all over Tamara's body after learning the stranger's name.

"With or without your dad, leave this town and block it out of your memory. Don't bother packing anything or saying goodbye. My husband is insisting we take a few things, but I have given serious thought to just driving off and leaving!"

If Tamara didn't know Mrs. Cafferty, she would think she was talking to a madwoman. Glancing back at her house, Tamara wished her father was standing next to her, shielding her from all the chaos being spewed at her.

Mrs. Cafferty grabbed Tamara's cheeks, forcing her to look directly at her. "Leave this town, now!" she shouted, spraying spittle onto Tamara's face. Her eyes were fierce and bloodshot.

Tamara slapped Mrs. Cafferty's hands away and took a step back. She didn't know this woman at all.

Mrs. Cafferty burst into hysterical laughter, placing both hands on her knees for balance. Her laughing soon turned to sobs as she screamed, "Where is our God now, Tamara? Where? Just remember if you stay, you were warned!" And with that, Mrs. Cafferty got into her SUV, started the engine, and peeled away, spilling the contents of the vehicle all over the yard.

Mr. Cafferty ran outside moments later, screaming for his wife to come back, then collapsed to the ground sobbing.

CHAPTER 6

The drive back to Taupe City felt much longer than five hours since it had been in complete silence. Not long into the trip, Maggie noticed that the hound didn't breathe or so much as move. Not that she expected something of the paranormal to breathe, but the way it remained perfectly still creeped her out even more. When Riley had to brake or turn, the hound still didn't move, as if centrifugal force had no effect over it.

Taking the exit off the highway to Gregory Portal Provider, Maggie finally broke the silence. "Pull into the parking garage and park next to the valet."

Doing as instructed, Riley followed the marked arrows that led to an empty podium and parked. Seeing no one around, Maggie and Riley stepped out of the truck. Just when they thought they were alone, a man wearing a red jacket appeared out of nowhere. It was Spencer, the parking attendant for the building.

"It's so good to see you, Spencer," said Maggie, offering her hand. "I know the last time we saw one another it wasn't on the best of terms, and I would like to apologize for my behavior and treating you so awfully."

When Maggie was making her first trip out in public after the year of isolation she'd took to search for Jonathan, she had treated Spencer unusually harsh and as a replaceable employee in an effort to keep him from so much as mentioning that he'd even seen her. She wasn't ready for all the attention that would surely come if anyone else found out and reacted poorly.

Spencer started to reply, but his expression changed from a warm smile to one of terror. He took several steps backward.

Confused by the sudden change in his demeanor, Maggie started to ask what was wrong, but then the hound stepped in between them, growling. Riley was now standing next to her as well, breathing heavily.

"Why didn't you leave it in the truck?" Maggie hissed through her teeth.

Riley gave her an exasperated look, which Maggie immediately understood. The hound could obviously walk through walls, much like it had done getting into the locked truck.

"I'm so sorry, Spencer." Maggie positioned herself in front of the hound and gave it the foolish command to "sit," only to be ignored.

The hound once more started to make its way around her. Maggie held up a hand and gave it a stern look, and, surprisingly, the hound stopped. Even more surprising, its eyes had changed from red to brown, almost resembling a normal dog.

"Sorry, Spencer, he's brand new so I haven't had the chance to have him properly trained, but I can assure you that he is harmless."

Understandably, Spencer's nervous demeanor didn't change even after her reassurance. "Th-that is one intense-looking dog! What breed is it? Wolf?" His voice shook.

"You know, the shelter didn't tell me, and I never even thought to ask. He just looked so sad, stuck all alone in a cage, that I just had to bring him home. I just wish I would have bought a leash before I went to get him." Maggie spewed. It seemed to work because Spencer relaxed and offered an outstretched hand.

The hound induced the same ear-piercing bark it had made at the lake house, only now the noise was amplified as it echoed off the concrete walls of the parking garage. The three of them covered their ears and had the same painful expression on their faces. The hound stopped barking, but now the car alarms were responding to the threat, echoing their disapproval.

Still covering their ears, Maggie and Riley stepped between Spencer and the hound. When Maggie could finally hear herself think, she exchanged a brief look of relief with Riley, both thankful the situation hadn't escalated any further.

"Oh, Spencer, I'm so sorry for my dog's behavior. As I said, he's brand new, and I don't know much about his past or how he was treated." Maggie then leaned in and whispered, "To make up for how I treated you when we first met, to now placing you in harm's way, I just want you to know you will definitely be getting a significant pay increase."

Maggie reached into her purse and pulled out her personal business card. "If you ever decide to apply for a different position that you feel better suits you, contact me directly and I will make certain you are taken care of. My personal cell phone number is on the back of the card."

Maggie was afraid how the hound would react to Spencer reaching out to take the card from her. So, instead of tempting fate, Maggie quickly tucked the card into Spencer's jacket pocket and flashed him a warm smile. "Thank you for your discretion and for being such an amazing employee. Would you mind putting the truck in my part of the garage? The keys are in the ignition. I need to get this troublemaker upstairs and fed. But you remember to call me, understood?"

Wanting this ordeal to be over, Maggie said to Riley, "Shall we?" Not waiting for a reply, she gave the hound a nudge with her leg in the direction of the elevator. The hound obeyed. However, it never took its eyes off Spencer, walking backward the entire time.

Maggie pressed the up button for her private elevator and found Lady Fortune smiling down on her as the doors separated almost immediately, allowing them entrance. Maggie swiped her employee badge on the card reader until the doors finally closed. After the elevator began ascending, they both let out a loud exhale.

"Well, that could have gone a little better," said Riley. "Then again, it could have gone a lot worse. All I know is, we were lucky."

"Riley!" Maggie gave him a frustrated look and rolled her eyes. "Shut up. I don't know what to do with this freak of nature. I'm out of my depth here, and that isn't helpful."

"Okay, but you seriously need to take our current situation into account before you just go doing normal everyday things. Like, having me pull into a parking garage with a hellhound as a passenger and an innocent attendant who is to valet our vehicle. I admit, I also need to think less rashly before acting, but the fact of the matter is, we have no control over this hound. It does have all the control over us, though."

The hound's ears perked up at Riley's comment, indicating that the beast appeared to have understood what they were saying. The elevator doors opened, and the hound hopped out, sniffing the air and the carpet several times. Then it froze as its eyes met the door to Maggie's suite, and its hackles raised as it crept toward the door, issuing a deep menacing growl as it drew closer.

Afraid that her personal assistant, Victoria, might be standing just on the other side of the door, Maggie yelled, "Stop!" She hoped like hell to prevent another Spencer incident.

"What's wrong?" asked Riley.

Ignoring the question, Maggie pushed the hound to move him away from the door. When he didn't budge, she looked at Riley for help, only to see that he'd drawn his handgun. Maggie groaned in frustration. Riley was absolutely useless with a handgun. If the target were just a few feet in front of him, he would be lucky to land even one shot. When he'd taught her how to shoot, she was surprised when she could hit more targets than he could. After that, he stuck with either the shotgun or rifle.

"Riley, put that away! I think we have all the protection we need right here. Besides, I'm not worried about our protection. I just want to make certain that Stu or Victoria aren't waiting on the other side of this door."

As Riley slipped his gun back into his waistband, Maggie addressed the hound. "Listen, mutt! I don't know if you can understand me, but I need you to obey me and not enter unless I tell you to. Understood?"

The hound tilted its head to the side.

Maggie reluctantly put her key into the lock, turned the knob, and pushed the door open just a crack. "Victoria? Stu? I need you to answer me if you are inside." When silence was all that followed, Maggie breathed a sigh of relief. "Whew. Thank your God for small miracles."

Riley flashed her an annoyed look.

"Well, that's strange."

"What?" asked Riley.

"The beast actually obeyed me. I thought for certain it would have torn past me as soon as I opened the door."

"That's a bit odd, but it's a supernatural being. Do you really believe a little lock or even your door would have been able to keep it out? The damn thing has the ability to teleport itself to wherever it wants. No one is safe until we can figure out how to control it. Besides, I have reasonable doubts about it being here to protect us. It could only be here to keep track of our movements until the Devil gives it the order to kill."

Looking down at the hound, Maggie knew that Riley was correct to be skeptical of what its actual purpose was. However, for whatever reason, she no longer shared his skepticism, which was strange, since Riley had initially told her that if the hound wanted to harm them, it would have already done so. Even more strange was that Maggie began to feel a sense of belonging with this hellish hound.

"Well, go make sure everything is okay," ordered Maggie. The hound tore off into the dark room before she could even finish.

"Lights on," said Maggie, entering her suite. She couldn't help but smile at the disbelief on Riley's face as he stopped just inside the entryway.

The media had referred to her suite as "the ominous thirteenth floor" stemming from the old superstition that the number thirteen is bad luck, and most buildings omit the 13th floor. Several publications had even reached out, offering ridiculous amounts of money to take a few pictures and interview her. However, no matter the allure it had to others—this was her home and the one place where she felt safe after the night Jonathan had saved her from those men.

CHAPTER 7

The entryway opened into a large living room, and Riley was astonished at what he saw.

"Welcome to the ominous thirteenth floor of Gregory Portal Provider," said Maggie. "You are officially among a handful of people, outside the builders and myself, to ever step foot inside it."

Unsure how to respond, Riley shrugged his shoulders, earning a soft laugh from Maggie.

"I'll be right back. Make yourself at home," Maggie said, then disappeared down a hallway, leaving Riley to explore.

A plush leather couch with matching recliners sat atop a Persian rug. An oversized abstract painting hung on one wall, which had matching glass bookshelves on either side of it. A strange chrome statue of a man kneeling, arms stretched out to either side of him, palms up, held a large, curved TV. The entire back wall was a rock structure, with water trickling off it that fed into a koi pond.

Taking a seat on the couch, Riley leaned his head back, and just when he thought he couldn't have been more impressed, he found the ceiling was alive. Clouds rolled lazily across it, accompanied by occasional lightning, illuminating the outlines of the clouds. Distant star constellations could be seen when a cloud wasn't in the way. It appeared so real, Riley felt like he was in a planetarium instead of a living room.

The glass bookshelves held various items. A baseball-sized

bluish green rock resting atop one shelf caught his eye. He walked over to the shelf and was about to pick up the rock when a photo of three people laughing distracted him. He immediately recognized a much younger Maggie, who had her arms wrapped around an older man he presumed to be her father. The older woman in the photo Riley had seen before, only under worse conditions. At the time, he was trapped inside the Devil's home, in a dream-like state imposed on him by the rogue demon. In the picture, the woman was happy, smiling broadly up at Maggie. Riley reached for the photo when Maggie's voice stopped him.

"Don't touch that!"

Riley immediately dropped his hands to his sides.

"The cradle that it sets upon is pressure activated. If you pick it up, the room will lock down, alarms will go off, and there will be a lot of security coming through the front door. Plus, the police will be alerted, and I'd have to explain how you were an uninvited intruder," she said with a smirk.

"I wasn't reaching for the rock," said Riley.

"No?"

"No, I was reaching for the photo. I couldn't care less about your stupid precious rock!"

Coming to stand next to him, Maggie gave him a look as if he were dense. "Riley, that stupid precious rock is an uncut blue-green jadeite. It goes for three million dollars per carat on the open market! I've thought of donating it to a museum, but I'm kind of attached to it."

If the amount was meant to impress him, it didn't. "Maggie, I don't care about your rock. I just wanted to get a better look at the photo because I can tell that the little girl is obviously you with your parents. What was the celebration? You all appear to be so happy."

Maggie looked as if he had just struck her, then said in a matter-of-fact tone, "Well, looks can be deceiving." She then placed the photo face-down, putting an end to the conversation. "Are you hungry?"

From Maggie's pained expression, Riley knew not to push the topic any further. "What sounds good to you?" he asked.

"Well, I know everything in the fridge has been thrown out, as I've been MIA with you at the lake house for a few weeks now. I'd suggest pizza, but I don't think any pizza places are open at this hour. What do you think the hound eats? Or do you think it even eats?"

"Speaking of our friend, where did it wander off to?" asked Riley. "I figured it wouldn't want to let us out of its sight." Riley turned and called out for the beast when a loud, sharp whistle startled him. He looked at Maggie, who had two fingers pressed to the corners of her mouth. "What in the hell was that?"

Maggie burst into laughter.

"Oh my God! Seriously, you scared the hell out of me. Warn me next time!"

This only earned him another round of laughter, until finally she wheezed out, "Then you whistle. I don't want to scare you again."

Riley never learned how to whistle. He pressed his tongue against the bottom row of his teeth and blew out hard, but no sound came out. This brought on another round of laughter from Maggie. She was now bright red in the face and tears escaped the corners of her eyes.

Embarrassed and frustrated, Riley said angrily, "Okay, so I never learned how to whistle." Maggie's laughter grew louder, making him more frustrated. "Come here, you, stupid, wretched, mangy hound of Hell."

Finally able to compose herself, Maggie said, "Riley, that attempt to whistle was just pathetic. Seriously, how does a grown man not know how to whistle?"

"I'm going to look for it," said Riley. "Stay here if you want."

"W-wait," Maggie said. She punched him lightly on the shoulder. "I'm sorry for mocking you, but you seriously make me laugh."

"Ha-ha," said Riley in a mocking tone.

Riley followed Maggie down a hallway strewn with photos and strange artwork and arrived at Maggie's bedroom. It was decorated with cherry wood furniture and a massive saltwater aquarium set into a wall behind the sleigh bed. Newspaper articles were framed and hung on the walls, showing successful milestones of Gregory Portal Provider. There were two glass bookshelves, same as the living room, holding various colorful rocks.

"Your place is amazing," he said, "minus the useless rock collection. I know they're priceless, so don't bore me with the details because I really don't care."

Giving him a queer look, she ignored his snarky comment. "Amazing as my home may be, I spent a year locked away in here while I was searching for Jonathan, and it almost drove me insane. The walls eventually made me feel as though I was trapped inside a cell. When I finally decided to leave, I found myself quite literally afraid of the outside world."

On the evening Jonathan entered Maggie's life, she decided to walk home from the office. Despite the rain, she had been looking forward to the solitude of her ten-minute walk after having board meetings all day.

The rain had let up halfway through her walk home. Maggie thought the storm was passing, but then the brightest bolt of lightning lit up the night sky. It was as if the sun had been turned on for a few seconds and then right back off, illuminating everything for miles. The thunder roared with an anger Maggie had never heard or felt before. Being distracted by the beautiful chaos of the storm, Maggie had not noticed the two men until they were crossing the street and heading in her direction. Maggie knew what their intentions were. Although her company, Gregory Portal Provider, was located in a beautiful section of downtown Taupe City, crime was on the rise, especially at night. It had gotten so bad as of late that Maggie was forced to increase security for her company.

Maggie had turned away from the two men and picked up her pace. Their footsteps matched hers, and her heart pounded as she quickened her pace to a sprint, but it was too late—they had caught up to her. Maggie gasped as she felt the pair of hands grab her shoulders, abruptly jerking her to a stop, and then forcing her into a nearby alley.

Maggie was frozen in terror as one of the men tore her purse away while the other man held her from behind. Maggie's mind raced, knowing that once they had finished going through her stuff, she would be next, and she began to plead for her life.

Then the largest man she had ever seen entered the alley, silencing her. His hard expression, intimidating stature, and confident yet calm demeanor could humble even the evilest of men. He was a giant of a man, and although he had on clothes, his muscular stature was hard to miss. He walked straight over to the two men, causing them to abandon Maggie's purse as they attempted to get away but without much effort, he overpowered them. Maggie was still uncertain of this strange man's intentions, so while he was distracted, she grabbed her purse from where it had been dropped by her attackers, and she fumbled for her pepper spray, pulling it out in case he got closer. Jonathan left the men beaten but alive, and the moment he turned to check on Maggie, the men ran. As soon as Jonathan got too close for Maggie's comfort, she sprayed him directly in the face. He was stunned and held up his hand as if to say "stop." He looked curiously at her.

His fierce blue eyes softened when she began sobbing. "I won't hurt you. I am only here to help. My name is Jonathan," he had said, and all her fears faded away. Maggie not only felt safe but pure peace washed over her. At first, Maggie thought the feeling might be from the adrenaline of having just survived a traumatic experience. However, she suspected there was something more to this feeling and that Jonathan may be behind it. Before they went their separate ways, Maggie gave him her business card with her cell phone number on the back.

After a frustrating yearlong search for Jonathan had yielded no results, Maggie was desperate for answers, and was reduced to call upon the one man who could help her. At the time, Miles Jackson, a corrupt politician, had overseen all the Texas penitentiaries and held the keys to what she needed, which was to speak with the two men who had seen Jonathan that night too. They were the same two men who had tried to mug and rape her before Jonathan had stopped them.

Now, however, the price she was forced to pay was more than she had originally bargained for. She was risking Jonathan's life in order to get this mess cleaned up.

It pained Riley to hear the mention of Jonathan's name. He didn't know how much time they had left or how to save him. The stench of the rogue demon, which had been so strong before, had begun to dissipate. To hide his hurt, he walked over to the aquarium, taking in the ease and flow of the coral and fish housed inside it.

"Lights on," Maggie said when she entered the bathroom, then immediately jumped backward in fright. The room lit up, revealing the hound, whose eyes had turned back to their original red. It was staring into the vanity mirror with a fierce intensity.

Riley was instantly at her side. "Think it's seeing itself for the first time and realizing how ugly it is?"

Maggie didn't reply as she watched the hound staring at its reflection in the mirror. She knew exactly what the hound was seeing. This was the place where she had her second and most terrifying encounter with the paranormal. A demon materialized in her mirror before issuing a warning to stop looking for Jonathan and then breaking her finger to show he was serious. The first paranormal experience being her encounter with Jonathan.

"What?" Riley asked.

Maggie took several quick breaths until she was finally able to answer, but in a voice not her own. "This hound will be able to find our rogue demon."

"Maggie, you can't know that for certain." His tone sounded dismissive.

"Riley, you can laugh my intuition off if you want, but I believe this hound is somehow seeing where I first encountered that rogue demon of ours. I stood at that mirror and saw a reflection that morphed into a man who promised me a great deal of pain if I continued my search for Jonathan. The figure then somehow reached through the mirror and snapped my pinky like a toothpick to make sure I wholly understood the message."

Riley's eyes widened and his jaw dropped, but he remained silent. Maggie shivered at the memory. The hound's hackles were raised, mouth partially open, revealing rows of razor-sharp teeth. For the first time, Maggie saw the hound for what it really was: a cold-blooded killer who cared for no one, not even the one who had created it. Its only reason for existing was to inflict pain and to feed upon what Maggie and Riley fought so hard to stay one step ahead of— the demons.

CHAPTER 8

Lucifer was amazed as he watched from his chair in the middle of the viewing room as Jonathan fended off four of his hellhounds. The angel was powerful. If Lucifer could indeed break Jonathan, he had no doubt it would be the key to once more being able to step foot in Heaven.

Lucifer thought that by this point he would have broken Jonathan with one of the many different methods of torture he'd used. He desired nothing more than to feel the powers that the false God had given the guardian angels. Although Lucifer couldn't physically take a fallen angel's gifts, he hoped that if he inflicted enough pain, the angel would willingly hand them over to end the torture.

Lucifer had once been an angel—although not a guardian angel—since before humans had even been spoken into existence. No, the title he had held—Head Angel—was of much more importance, as he oversaw all the angels. According to the false God, he was the definition of perfection, until he was cast out for wanting more from his existence.

Lucifer was disgusted when thinking back on that tumultuous time. He hated the role he'd been forced to play, the hopeful and obedient angel for the arrogant false God. He did the work and put in the time just to be rewarded with nothing more than the title—Head Angel. He wanted more than a meaningless title. He wanted to be seen as God's equal.

Besides, why had God given the angels powers and free will

if they weren't allowed to use them except to love one another? It all changed that dreadful day when God informed the angels that he was making a new creation in his image, and they would be called humans. His chosen angels were expected to serve and protect this new creation. Humans were mortals and could do the one thing the angels never could: taste death. They had replaced the angels in the hierarchy, or at least that was how Lucifer remembered it. The details became a bit fuzzy after he had been cast out of Heaven over two thousand years ago.

The few followers who had supported his views were treated to the same punishment. God banned them from ever again being able to step foot in Heaven. However, Lucifer now had bigger plans, altering his destiny, believing he was truly a god. If he wasn't, then why had the false God been so quick to banish him for his opposition?

Lucifer felt that eventually the angels who were kicked out of Heaven with him would turn against him, and he had no choice but to deal with them accordingly. He tricked and forced them one by one into the depths of Hell, hearing them beg and scream as they were tortured beyond their breaking points. That being his first act as God, still brought a smile of delight to his face.

Lucifer then remembered that he had much more important things to think about, like the final battle between good and evil that drew closer every day. He needed to break Jonathan in order to possess the powers of a guardian angel.

Any idiot fallen angel would have been sufficient for his plans to work. Unfortunately, an angel falling rarely occurred, which meant he had to capitalize on this opportunity. Besides, he had not waited for over two thousand years to squander this chance at getting the upper hand.

Which brought Lucifer back to his current predicament as the once proud fallen angel, Jonathan, now sat beaten and exhausted. Syrupy thick strands of blood hung from Jonathan's lips after he endured the latest round of torture Lucifer had put him through. His muscled body glistened with sweat as he leaned his head against the wall, gasping for air.

"Jonathan, you fascinate me with your loyalty to a God who has clearly forgotten about you," said Lucifer. "Yet at the same time, you disgust me with how pathetic you are, having such devoted loyalty for a fake God."

Jonathan scoffed and tore off part of his shirt sleeve. After wiping the blood from his face, he balled the material up and pitched it at Lucifer's feet.

Several minutes passed, but Jonathan remained silent, praying that it wouldn't be much longer until God intervened. Oddly, he thought about Riley. He'd given Riley a temporary gift so he could track down the rogue demon by smell. At the time, Jonathan thought he was making a calculated decision when he bestowed the gift to the human. Now, as Jonathan endured torture after torture, he realized that he had inflicted Riley with a curse that could potentially lead to not only Riley's death but Maggie's as well.

Just before Jonathan had been pulled into Hell, the demon had revealed its true name: Legion. Immediately, Jonathan knew who the demon was, and it caused fear to touch his soul. Jonathan had heard rumors from the other guardian angels to watch out for Legion, as he possessed the same abilities and attributes as Lucifer. The only difference between the two was that at one point in time, Lucifer had trapped Legion and held him in restraints, forcing him to serve as a lackey.

Legion had been turned loose for one reason only: to capture

Jonathan. Now the job was complete, and Legion was causing destruction on Earth.

Lucifer snapped his fingers until Jonathan finally looked at him. Until now, Lucifer had worn a dark maroon hooded robe and his features presented as neither male nor female. However, he had changed his appearance to a strikingly beautiful middle-aged man, with a manicured goatee, and his sleek salt and pepper hair was closely cropped. He was dressed in dark slacks, a gray button dress shirt, and a black blazer.

"You do realize I was once of your kind? Worshipping like a fool, hoping one day I would be treated as an equal. Only to be rewarded by being cast out and forced into this role I now play as nemesis. I know that it's hard to believe, but I was once Head Angel, and the only reason for your existence.

"You see, Jonathan, I'm an experiment gone wrong, all because I chose to question certain decisions, in turn making me an outcast. My curiosity has been piqued, and I wonder why you don't want more out of your existence. Kneeling to a god is one thing, but having to kneel to a human we are sworn to protect is another. Angels were spoken into existence first for a reason. Why should we have to serve those who came after us?"

Jonathan remained silent, partially from the pain, but also knowing that engaging in a debate with the ultimate deceiver would only breed frustration.

"I remember when your God grew tired of it being just us angels and found another project to satisfy him. He told us that he wanted to create something in his image, and we would now serve and protect this new creation. Which is ironic when you think about it, for bowing to another god or individual is forbidden. It's even written in scripture and became one of the Ten Commandments: 'There shall be no other God before me.' Only for God to turn right around and command angels to serve humans, elevating them to a godlike status. And yet I'm the hypocrite?"

Even though Jonathan was trapped in Hell, he could still choose to block out the ramblings of this madman. Nevertheless, Jonathan was surprised to find himself intrigued by what Lucifer was saying. Not that he would ever doubt God the Father's wisdom, but he saw it as an opportunity to learn more from his adversary. To see if he could understand why the Devil had made the choices he had. Besides, the more the Devil said, the easier it was to defeat him.

"Jonathan, just so you are aware, I can hear every manipulative thought rolling around in that dumb head of yours."

Taken aback by this statement, Jonathan tried to think of something else, wondering how he was going to gain the upper hand. He looked down at the ground, then up at Lucifer, who flashed him a sadistic smile.

"Those foolish thoughts will not help with your current situation. You already know I can inflict whatever pain I want, and eventually you will succumb to me."

Jonathan scoffed. "You honestly believe that with all this torture, you can take my powers? You're not a god, just a Fallen, same as me. The only real difference is that one day I *will* be able to return to God, and you'll still be stuck in this place. So do your worst because I do not fear you. I only have pity for you."

If the comment stung Lucifer in any way, Jonathan couldn't tell. Instead, his captor leaned back in his chair and looked up at the ceiling as an awkward silence settled between them. He couldn't believe Lucifer didn't pounce on him right then for the insult. The tortures he had endured so far would be nothing compared to what he believed Lucifer would now do to him. Jonathan then reminded himself that this was only a trial he had to overcome, and God would never forsake him.

Lucifer chose not to act upon Jonathan's insolent utterance, knowing it was what Jonathan expected from him. Besides, Lucifer refused to allow the Fallen to get the better of him by painting him as predictable. Lucifer was sad to admit that his torturous methods hadn't worked. Jonathan had simply rejuvenated, same as the rest of the inhabitants of Hell.

The only part of Jonathan that hadn't fully healed was caused by a single black tear Lucifer had produced from his soul. The small scar started at the bottom of Jonathan's throat and spider-webbed across the left side of his face, stopping right below the hairline. Lucifer found it pleasing to look at, knowing Jonathan would carry this mark for the rest of his short life.

Lucifer had only used the black tear twice. The first time was when he had captured the idiot Legionaries thousands of years ago, and the second time was when he created the hounds. Lucifer would have used it more often if it didn't leave him severely weakened afterwards and completely vulnerable for six minutes. Six minutes seemed like a trivial amount of time, but if he wasn't careful, an idiot demon could start trouble and cause an uprising, which Lucifer would not be able to defend against. He could then easily be overthrown by one of the sociopaths who now served him, and Hell would have a new God.

What to do, what to do? Lucifer pondered.

Jonathan was more resilient than Lucifer had anticipated. Frustrated, Lucifer pressed the palms of his hands on his eyes until he saw purple spots. Then a sudden thought of clarity came forth, reminding him of something he had clearly overlooked. His perfect seven little deadly allies.

If he couldn't torture Jonathan into handing over his powers, then maybe he could manipulate him into doing so. The seven deadly sins—pride, greed, wrath, lust, envy, gluttony, and sloth—only existed because of him. Lucifer would simply start with pride and work his way through them all if needed. Eventually one of them would have to break Jonathan. Lucifer just didn't know which one it would be.

Why he had never thought of using seven deadly sins before quite literally baffled him. Deep down he knew they were the key to unlocking the abilities of the guardian angels, a secret code the false God must have overlooked when creating them. If the seven sins weren't meant as a key to unlocking a guardian angel's powers, then for what purpose had they even come into existence? Besides being used as guidelines for what the human race should avoid, they have to have a purpose, a use. The only way to know for certain was to test his theory and see what happens.

Returning his seat to the upright position, Lucifer put on his best poker face to hide his enthusiasm to begin his new games. Any idiot could physically harm someone, but to dip into someone's emotions and play with them like a hand in a stream creating little pools of chaos was invaluable. This was a skill that Lucifer had perfected over thousands of years but had never used it on a Fallen. The time had come to find out just how skillful he really was.

CHAPTER 9

Maggie and Riley sat on opposite ends of the couch in the living room. Riley wasn't sure what to say after Maggie's assumption that the hound would be able to locate the rogue demon. He was skeptical until the hound had growled at the mirror, replacing all doubts that it could indeed do what Maggie had said.

The topic of food was clearly the last thing on both their minds, but Riley heard his stomach offer up a complaint that he tried to ignore. The hound glared its red eyes on Riley, as if he had just threatened it.

"Calm yourself, mutt. I'm just hungry."

The hound took two steps toward Riley, its red eyes boring into him. Doing his best to ignore it, Riley asked Maggie, "You think we should give it a name? I think it believes we are degrading it by calling it whatever name we want, triggering its animosity toward us."

Maggie scoffed at his suggestion, then mumbled something that Riley couldn't understand. "I don't think you name something that belongs to the Devil. Its animosity doesn't worry me right now. It hasn't eaten us yet, so call it 'hound,' 'dog,' 'mutt'— whatever your heart desires."

Riley knew it was a dumb thing to even bring up, especially since Maggie was already at her breaking point due to all the stress. However, this new stress was not just related to the prior dealings Maggie had done with Miles Jackson. This new irritation occurred right after he made an innocent comment about the photo of her parents. Riley had only wanted to open the lines of communication between them with the little quip. Unfortunately, it had the opposite effect.

His mind was set on finding the rogue demon, with or without Maggie, but preferably with her. Having grown tired of the tension, Riley angrily said, "You're right. Naming the hound was a stupid suggestion, especially when we know what it is and who it actually belongs to."

Ignoring his comment, Maggie spoke in a monotone voice. "I need to let Stu know I'm here so he can prep me on what I need to get done for today." She then stood and began to walk out of the living room.

Riley knew that if he didn't get away for a bit, he would say something he would later regret. "I'm going to get something to eat."

Maggie turned to face him. "Really, Riley? Do you think that's wise given our circumstances?"

The way Maggie had asked the question, insinuating he was an idiot, was the final straw. "Maybe not, Maggie, but I'm hungry! Can you tell me what's close, or should I just Google it?" He pulled out his phone to prove how serious he was about leaving to get something to eat.

"I can order whatever you want and have it brought up. That way you can just stay here where you are needed most," she said in the same condescending voice.

Riley sighed. He knew his time would be better spent tracking down the rogue demon instead of babysitting Maggie. However, he did promise he would give her three days to accomplish everything that she needed. Still, the way she was speaking to him, as if he were one of her subordinates, pissed him off.

"Hmm...tell you what, Maggie. Let's really give some thought on where I'm actually needed most." Riley paced back and forth, as if weighing the heavy topic, then stopped and snapped his fingers. "Ah-ha! I got it! How could I be so shortsighted? I mean, it's obvious that I need to wait around here until you get your affairs in order, not out searching for my best friend, who is only in this current predicament because of you and the decision I was forced into making!"

It was an extremely low blow, but Riley was pissed and had no intention of sitting around catering to her feelings if she was going to act this way toward him. Maggie quickly closed the distance between them, her face filled with anger, but she took him by surprise when she threw her arms around him, burying her face in his chest.

Riley held her as the wave of emotion broke and she sobbed. It was strange to think how far they had come in such a short amount of time. They had learned to trust and value one another despite him trying to push her away at the beginning of their relationship.

"Riley, I am so sorry for only thinking about myself when we should really be worried about Jonathan. Just remain by my side for a little while longer, and I will help you find that rogue demon, even if it means we have to venture into Hell itself to save Jonathan. Just please don't leave me. Not right now."

Feeling horrible for acting like he had, Riley said, "I'm sorry, Maggie. It's not your fault that Jonathan isn't with us. It's mine. I'm so worried about him and took it out on you."

They held each other for several minutes until Maggie pulled back, wiping her eyes. "I'll order us something to eat. Just give me a few minutes. I need to contact Stu first."

"Take all the time you need," said Riley.

Maggie headed back toward her room, then turned. "Please be patient with me. I promise I will hold up my end of this agreement." She then disappeared down the hallway before Riley could reply.

Sitting only a few feet away, the hound's menacing eyes locked onto him. Strangely, Riley felt like it was judging him for how he acted, but it could just be his guilty conscious.

"I already feel horrible, so turn your judgmental eyes elsewhere before I name you Sophie!"

Even though Riley had concerns regarding their new companion, he started to feel a sense of belonging toward the hound, then quickly pushed the feeling aside. If Jonathan did have something to do with the hound's sudden appearance, then only time would tell, and until then, he would treat it as an outsider.

"I have no idea what your intentions are. I guess I'll eventually find out whose side you're really on."

The hound stared at him, then its red eyes softened to a dull brown, confusing Riley.

CHAPTER 10

As night finally subdued the town of Broken Falls, Tamara watched the sun kiss the horizon. Eventually, the sun and its light were slowly devoured by the darkness. She positioned herself on the couch in the living room, drawing the window blinds closed, hoping this small act would prevent evil from finding them.

This small peaceful neighborhood she had grown up in used to be her safe haven. Neighbors were as close as family members, sitting in their front yards discussing what was happening in their lives, all the while keeping a watchful eye on the children playing games.

The block barbecues throughout the summer that lasted long into the night now felt like distant memories, replaced by dark homes and the remnants of hurried departures of strewn items littering streets and driveways.

A door opened and closed behind her, pulling Tamara's attention away from her watchful perch on the couch. Her father was leaving the room where her mom's hospital bed had been set up, the same room where he ate his dinner most nights.

Without saying a word, Tamara watched him walk into the kitchen to discard the trash and frowned when he noticed Tamara's untouched food on the counter. After dropping the lid on the trash, he turned and jumped when he saw her sitting on the couch in the half-lit living room.

"Goodness gracious, Tamara. You just caused my heart to shift into overdrive. Was there something wrong with your dinner?"

Tamara wanted to scream at him for being so naïve, but she remained calm, reminding herself that he was one of the kindest people she knew. The absolute perfect father, having not once ever raised his voice or lost his temper with her. A couple of years before her mom got sick, she was going through her rebellious teenage phase, and whenever she had acted out by pushing the boundaries, he would simply tell her, "Tamara, I'm extremely disappointed in your behavior. I know you can make better choices." Then he would turn and walk away, which was far worse than any other kind of discipline she could receive. It caused her to consider her actions and the consequences more carefully.

Her father owned a successful business, Bob's TechWorks. Year after year, the business didn't just flourish but would outperform any large electronic chain that moved into the area. They would all shut down after only a year of operation. Not only did the service his company provide outperform the competition, but how he treated people—even going so far as replacing items free of charge if the customer couldn't afford them—was exceptional. He would always say, "It's only money. You just pay me when you can. Besides, I really do appreciate you bringing your business to me. It gave me the opportunity to introduce myself." Not only would the customer leave feeling valued but also seen and heard, and they would always return hours later to pay for the prior services and purchase more items.

"If you don't like what you ordered," her dad said, interrupting her thought, "I don't mind going back out and getting you something else. Or I can cook you something."

Tamara smiled; he was such a horrible cook. Any attempt he made to cook usually involved burning whatever it was. She wiped the smile from her face, knowing it was time to force him to acknowledge what was happening all around them. "Dad, I need you to look out the window and tell me what you see."

Giving her a halfcocked grin, he said in a poor imitation, "Sweetie, are you going to make me peer through a half-parted blind like I'm some character out of an Alfred Hitchcock movie?"

Again, Tamara had to contain her smile because she loved that her father referenced and quoted old movies. Tamara tried to picture him like Jimmy Stewart in the movie *Rear Window*, then forced the thought aside. "Dad, would you just look out the damn window and tell me what you see!" A pained expression crossed her father's face, which made her vision blur. "Please, Dad," Tamara pleaded, her voice breaking. "Please, just do this for me." They both silently stared at one another for several minutes. Tamara had never spoken to her father in that way before. She dropped her head, and the tears that had built up in her eyes had finally broken free and streamed down her cheeks.

Dropping his head in defeat, Bob knew it was time to level with his daughter and give up the act of being out of touch with reality. He slowly made his way to the couch, every step bringing him closer to a final goodbye that he wasn't ready for. Exhaling slowly, Bob sat on the couch and mentally tried to prepare himself for what was to come next. Time appeared to have sped up as he gently placed his hand on top of his daughter's leg.

"Sweetie, I don't need to look out the window. I already know fear has come to our town, creating chaos in its wake. On one hand, I don't want to believe it, because your mother can't be moved in her condition and I will not leave her. On the other hand, I believe in God and believe He will not forsake us in our hour of need. So, yes, my sweet girl, I'm aware of what is happening, and no, I'm not as naïve as you think I am."

Grinning, Bob leaned over and gently bumped shoulders with his daughter, letting her know that he hadn't missed the sideway glances she gave him anytime he went out of his way to help a complete stranger. Then, just as quickly as the smile had appeared, it was gone. Bob realized that, depending on the next few days, those special moments could soon become a distant memory of a past long forgotten.

God save us, Bob thought to himself, looking at his daughter, seeing the tears had finally won out and were streaming down her face.

Putting an arm around her, he prayed with everything he had that he would always be able to protect her. In that moment, tears filled his eyes and he cried softly.

"Tamara, this may sound strange, but you know how strange your dear ole dad can be. I always knew that if I were ever given the chance to be a father, I would make sure I was a better father than my father ever was to me. My father was a hard disciplinarian and always short on praise. I wanted to take a different approach as a parent and teach you to always love without limitations or expectations, be kind whenever possible, and to always try to find the good in people, even when it seems impossible. The only thing that truly terrifies me is my passive nature. I've failed you and your mother when it matters most. I'm not even adequately prepared to defend either one of you."

Tamara fell into his arms and sobbed. "I love you, Dad. So much."

Bob broke down as well, kissing the top of his little girl's head, stroking her hair with one hand as the other clutched her tighter to him. "I'm sorry for my shortcomings, sweetie. If given the choice, I'll gladly give up my life to protect you and your mother. I need you to know I am so proud of the young woman you have become. Couldn't have asked God for a more perfect blessing."

A thunderous knock pounded on the front door, informing Bob that his time was up. Aware that this could possibly be the last time he saw his daughter in this world, Bob clutched her in his arms, praying that God would spare her and take only him.

When the knocking became more persistent, Bob gave her one final squeeze. Wiping the tears from her eyes, he leaned in and kissed Tamara's forehead, fearing it would be the last time he'd be able to perform this act.

"Tamara, I want you to go kiss your mom, hug her tight, and tell her goodbye." Before she could protest, Bob looked directly into her eyes, gently cupped her face in his hands, and said more forcefully, "Please, just listen and know what I'm doing is out of love."

He hated how forceful he had to be with her. As fresh tears spilled down Tamara's face, Bob hurriedly whispered, "Leave through the window in the bedroom, run to the creek, and then lie down until you can no longer hear anyone. Water carries voices and noise, so you'll know when it's safe to move again. Do not cross the creek. The cornfield on the other side has too many acres, and you'll only get lost in it. Instead, follow the creek out of town, but stay off the road until daylight comes. Understand?"

Tamara nodded in agreement as she was too choked up and emotional to speak.

The knocking at the front door was replaced with men's distorted voices, followed by someone attempting to kick the door in.

"When you were born and the doctor placed you on your mother's chest, she made you a promise I will always remember. 'You are safe, little one. We will always protect you.' Tamara, I love you, but this is the moment I make my declaration to add to your mother's promise all those years ago. Know that I will always protect you. Now go and be brave. Go now!"

Bob could see from his daughter's pained expression that she was reluctant to leave, but finally she stood, gave his hand one final squeeze, and walked away.

In that moment, Bob watched as his daughter changed from teenager to adult within the span of a few steps. When she stopped to look back at him, Bob knew it was useless to put up a false persona to pretend that everything was going to be okay.

Instead, he signed "I love you" with one hand. She responded in kind before disappearing into the room where his wife lay.

CHAPTER 11

Legionaries took his time walking around the town's courtyard, considering all the events he had put into motion and why he had chosen the small town of Broken Falls.

Outside its secluded location and small population, the real reason Legionaries had chosen Broken Falls was because a backdoor was tucked into the crest of the neighboring mountains. It led straight from Earth to Hell, and no one knew about it except for Lucifer and an old relic known as the Ferryman, who was tasked with guarding the entrance. This entrance was perfect for Legionaries to recruit more demons, ensuring he would remain out of the confines of Hell until he was its new god.

Legionaries had no desire to rule Earth. This was a foolish way of thinking, and he would leave those moronic notions to his former master. No, for now, all he desired was to quietly build an army. It would be small at first, but hopefully it would make it more difficult for the Devil to come for him before he was ready.

He would not allow himself to fall victim to complacency. He would never believe he was safe or untouchable. What Legionaries had seen and learned throughout human history was that every great leader eventually fell because of their arrogance, ego, and false sense of immortality, believing they were all powerful. Legionaries was determined to never let that happen to him.

Continuing his lazy stroll around the courtyard, Legionaries marveled at the mayhem he had caused with his declaration that the town now belonged to him. As soon as he entered the town, Legionaries blocked all communication to the outside world. Every cell phone, computer, TV, and even the radio was now useless.

Legionaries had the foresight to know that word would travel fast, especially when the exiled fled from the town. He'd put up a perimeter which, once crossed, would cause everyone to forget about this town and anyone who remained in it. It would become like a black hole in their mind, and they would never be able to remember. Even the outside world would cease to remember Broken Falls ever existed. Maps would still show its location, of course, but it would be seen just as many other small towns that had died off because of the lack of jobs or tourism.

All the once brightly lit shops around the town square were now dark and abandoned. Windows were broken, and tire marks were left on the pavement and across manicured lawns.

With his demonic eyes, Legionaries looked through the walls, not having to stop at each shop and peer inside, hoping to find someone who had been dumb enough to stay behind and defy his decree. He could see through anything within a certain distance, and if his eyes weren't able to locate someone, his nose would. His keen sense of smell could detect non-worshippers but also the scent of fear emanating from anyone who tried to deceive him.

As he grew in power, Legionaries discovered little things here and there about his abilities. The most significant was his ability to stop Lucifer from listening in on his thoughts, which was why he was now free. Amusingly, this all happened after he had learned what free will was and how to use it to his advantage.

Leaving the town square, Legionaries walked back to the cathedral where this had all started, wondering what size crowd awaited his arrival. He could have looked through the cathedral walls, but he didn't want to ruin the surprise. Rumors spread around town about a strange man who transformed into a beast. Both worshippers of the false God and non-worshipers would want to know if Legionaries was who he claimed to be.

Humans are far too easy to manipulate. Give them something to put their faith in and watch them consume one another to prove they are worth more than the next individual. And for what? So they can be anointed as a higher . . . whatever? Simply pathetic!

However, Legionaries could work with the pathetic humans as long as it suited his needs. When he arrived at the cathedral, Legionaries saw an overweight man and a thin woman standing outside the entrance doors, dressed in all black except for the red bandanas wrapped around their heads.

"Fucking idiots," Legionaries muttered to himself as he ascended the steps, stopping several feet away from the pair guarding the doors.

The three studied one another for several long seconds until the woman spoke in a loud authoritative voice, "If you're affiliated with any sort of religion, you need to leave this town at once! If you don't value your life, by all means, stay."

The man, feeling the need to enforce his own dominance into the fold, spat a dark-colored substance at Legionaries, which landed on his dress shoe. Frowning down at the disgusting stain, Legionaries made a tsk-tsk sound before looking up at the man, who was now grinning a brown-toothed smile at him. The man used his tongue to reposition a large wad of tobacco from one cheek to another.

"Why, exactly, are you two imbeciles dressed alike? Are you under the delusion this is what will be expected of you?"

The man's smile slid off his face as he exchanged a look of uncertainty with the woman.

Legionaries ascended the steps and stopped directly in front of the woman, breathing in her wonderful scent of soon-to-be rotting flesh. He then smirked as he stood upright, and his eyes shifted from golden brown to a blood red.

"Ah yes, you are in fact, one of mine." Legionaries looked over to see the overweight man's mouth agape and the wad of chewing tobacco hung to the edge of his bottom lip. Looking at the man with disdain, Legionaries said, "However, your kind is not welcomed here. You have exactly"—he grabbed the woman's wrist and looked at her watch—"sixteen minutes till midnight to try and escape. But since you're so fat and out of shape, I surmise you won't make it to the town limits before you are caught. How about you stick around and become the first of many to be sacrificed on this night?"

In a blur of movement, Legionaries stood directly in front of the man, which sent the guy sprawling backward. Catching him by his shirt, Legionaries lifted him effortlessly with one hand until they were nose to nose.

"As tempting as it is to just snatch the life right out of you, I'm going to restrain myself from crossing the lines made centuries ago that dictate what my kind can do to you disgusting worshippers. However, every rule has a loophole. For instance, do you see this person that you've thought of as a friend? Should I order her to kill you, you would still be dead at my behest. Now I can see you thinking, 'it's frowned upon and carries a heavy sentence by the authorities,' but who will ever find out? Who is left in this town except for those who now belong to me?"

Legionaries loosened his grip and dropped the man to the ground. Eyes wide, the man scrambled to his feet and darted off in an odd, slow run, pumping his arms and legs as quickly as he could.

The woman started to taunt the man for not being one of

them, but Legionaries put a finger to his lips, silencing her. "There will be a time for gloating, but this is not that time. Now take me inside. I want to see how many of you there are."

As they stepped forward, the cathedral doors flew open and out came a middle-aged woman. She froze and her eyes widened when she saw Legionaries. Quickly regaining her composure, she turned to the woman who had been walking in with Legionaries and said in a dismissive tone, "Samantha, join the others inside. We will be in momentarily."

Without arguing, Samantha nodded and went inside.

"My name is Clara," the woman said to Legionaries. She held out her hand, then dropped it back to her side when Legionaries only looked at it in a dismissive manner. "Upon anticipating your return, a few of us followers took up leadership roles to ensure the church would not be burned down. Minor scuffles had broken out after people began protesting, but it was easily managed. My husband, who I am no longer with, was one of those disgusting Bible-thumping maniacs. You see, I was here earlier when you addressed the congregation. I only attended church to make sure this other woman didn't try to steal my husband out from under me. It was foolish of me to even care now that you are here to please me."

Legionaries backhanded Clara, sending her crashing into the side of the cathedral and falling to the ground.

"I am not here to please you! As one of my followers, you are here to please me and will do whatever I command of you. If you disobey, I will make an example out of you. The rest of my followers will then know what to expect from any kind of insubordination. Do you understand me, slave?"

Clara gingerly touched her split lip, winced, and looked up at him with a new understanding of her role. "Yes, Master."

"Good. Now open the door."

Without hesitation, she quickly stood, pulled one of the doors open, and bowed her head as he entered.

CHAPTER 12

L egionaries was surprised at how large the crowd was because he had expected no more than a handful of individuals. Shockingly, the auditorium was more than half full.

As he proceeded down the middle aisle, the crowd quickly silenced, knowing exactly who and what he was. Legionaries didn't bother making eye contact with any of them. He was too preoccupied with admiring the statue of the Virgin Mary, who was still shedding her bloody tears of joy, in his opinion. Just as he had done earlier, Legionaries placed two fingers to his lips and lifted them in the air, acknowledging the mother of the false God. "Glad you are here to witness my greatness, dearie."

Taking up occupancy behind the pulpit, Legionaries smiled at his followers. They returned the smile, believing they were in the presence of greatness. Legionaries only smiled because he had accrued more followers than he expected, and he was going to use each one of them as pawns to benefit himself.

A curvy woman in a tight, low-cut top sitting in the front row cocked one eyebrow and winked at him. The man seated to the right of her looked nervous but still frowned at Legionaries in disapproval.

"Before I begin, I want you all to move down to the front. I will not raise my voice to be heard, and I will never repeat myself. Now move."

Although his voice remained calm, people hurriedly took up occupancy in the first six rows.

After everyone was seated, Legionaries continued. "You are here because you finally saw what a god looks like. After seeing my true form, you remained because you want to be one of my followers. Any among you who do not want to be one of my followers should have left with the rest of the non-worshippers."

The man seated next to the curvy woman abruptly stood up. "You are not a god but a false profit!" he said angrily.

Without acknowledging the statement, Legionaries said, "Can someone tell me what time it is?"

The curvy woman next to the man answered, "Eleven fifty-seven."

The man's defiant look changed to shock as he looked over at the woman. Legionaries smiled as it registered that the two were a couple, a strange pair who held very different values regarding the context of their beliefs, but a couple, nonetheless.

"I gave you fair warning. Your kind is not welcome in my town after midnight," Legionaries growled at the man. "I made that quite clear when I addressed this very church earlier today. Now, unfortunately for you, time has just about run out on your life. Tick tock! Tick tock!"

"I'm not afraid of you, Serpent," said the man. "And I pity anyone who is foolish enough to cast their lot in with you." Although his outer appearance projected confidence, Legionaries was intoxicated with the fear pouring off him.

"Ah," said Legionaries. "You've mistaken me for my former master, who is associated with the name 'Serpent.' Trust, I am definitely not him, but if you want to stick around for another two minutes, I'll tell you about me."

Legionaries couldn't have asked for a better way to kick things off. It was like a dark comedy being played out, with one of the main characters finally realizing his wife never loved him and only used him to her own benefit.

"I will not abandon my wife, despite her being enamored by what you truly are. So go ahead, do your worst, false prophet. I am *not* afraid of you." The man then turned to his wife and said just loud enough for Legionaries hear, "If I've ever failed you or gave you pause as to how much you've meant to me, I ask for your forgiveness. I know you aren't a worshipper of my God. I just hope with my sacrifice you will come to understand. My God would never ask you to carry out the murder of innocents, as this false prophet will. I love you, Miranda Humphrey, and I always will."

Legionaries felt like applauding the man for delivering such a flawless speech.

The curvy woman, Miranda, whispered to her husband, "You are embarrassing me." She then held up her hand, giving Legionaries the zero sign, telling him time was up.

He hated to end things so suddenly, especially now when the theatrical display was finally getting entertaining, but it was time to put his plan into action.

"I'm afraid time is up," said Legionaries, annoyed. He nodded at two men in the front row. "Take this martyr and lock him into one of the empty secure rooms. And make certain he doesn't find a way to escape. We will deal with him shortly."

Without putting up a fight, the man went willingly, looking back at his wife one last time, but she refused to look at him. Minutes passed in silence before the two escorts returned, resuming their seats in the front row.

Legionaries paced back and forth until everyone was settled and quiet. "I am Legionaries, or Legion, but you may call me Master. You are here because you desire to be a part of something you can actually see to believe in. Not some all-knowing God who works behind the scenes, asking for too much and giving too little. Not long ago, I was once where you are now, a simple slave hoping for a morsel to fall off my master's plate so that I, too, could be fed. The real difference between us? My master tortured me unmercifully for millennia until I came to realize one simple thing. Do you want to know what this one thing is?"

Legionaries looked out at the faces in the crowd. He had them right where he wanted them. They leaned forward on the edge of their seats, anticipating his next words. He made eye contact with Miranda, who winked at him. She didn't even appear to be upset that her husband had so willingly thrown away his life for her. *Oh how simple-minded the female human race is,* Legionaries mused.

"My self-appointed master foolishly believes that he is God. Once I broke free from his control to suppress my mind, I realized I am actually a god."

In one fluid movement, Legionaries' hands and feet morphed into large cat paws. The rest of his body resembled that of a lion, and his human face was replaced with the head of an eagle, and a serpent for a tongue. Scales ran from the base of the eagle's head and down the length of his back, rippling with electricity. He noticed that this time hadn't taken as long to transform as it had in the past. His followers gasped at his new appearance. However, none of them attempted to leave.

Legionaries sent out a pulse of energy, calming his followers and leaving them in a state of mindless obedience. As long as Legionaries continued to pulse at least once an hour, his followers would do anything he ordered them to do without question. Changing back into human form, Legionaries was surprised to find his clothes had remained intact. Every time before this had left him naked.

"Every one of you is an outcast. You've been made to feel this way because you didn't fit the mold that your society expected of you. Well, that way of thinking is in the past. From this day forward, you will no longer care about anyone else's opinion or feelings, for I am the Alpha and Omega. Is that understood?"

"Yes, Master," his followers said in unison.

"Good. We will now play a game. You all like games, yes? You will go door to door to seek out all the vile unbelievers who refused to leave. You will drag them to the town square, where they will meet a swift and painful judgment. Am I understood?"

"Yes, Master," his followers said.

CHAPTER 13

Maggie stared at herself in the mirror. She had changed into dark business slacks, a blazer, and a silk buttoned-down blouse for the meetings that would surely take up the rest of her day.

She went into the living room and sat next to Riley on the couch. "I ordered a bunch of breakfast sandwiches from the deli nearby. I spoke with Stuart, and he said he would bring the food up as soon as it got here," she said with a polite smile.

Riley's stomach growled at the mention of food, and once again the hound didn't approve of it. As it took a step toward them, its eyes locked on Riley.

"Sounds great," said Riley. He, too, appeared to have noticed the hound's sudden change in demeanor but was trying to ignore it. "Has Stuart clued you in as to what the authorities are going to ask? Besides your past dealings with Miles Jackson?"

Maggie exhaled loudly in frustration, wishing this was all behind her. "He just said the FBI wants to talk to me, and they demanded that I meet with them today. If the feds force me to accompany them to their office, I'm sure the paparazzi will have a field day getting those photos of me." The more she dwelled on the topic, the more it depressed her.

The hound moved a bit closer, still staring daggers at Riley.

"Riley, you were right. We should just name the damn thing. I don't want to keep calling it hound, or mutt, or whatever."

Riley shifted uncomfortably. "How about just calling it Night or Darkness?"

The hound snorted loudly at the name suggestions, then issued a low growl.

"Maybe it's a female. How about Celestia?"

The hound grew visibly agitated and growled even more fiercely at the suggestion that it was a female.

It was strange to Maggie that one minute the hound appeared to want to kill them, and the next showed personality traits belonging to a golden retriever.

"I don't think it approved of any of those names, but especially not being referred to as a female," said Maggie.

She then studied the hound and oddly thought about the first dog she'd ever owned. Her parents had given her a black lab on her seventh birthday, and she remembered her father saying, "Give it a name that represents a trait you believe you lack. That way you can look at it and know it will imbue that trait." Maggie had named the dog Courage, which was eventually shortened to Curr.

Years later while Maggie was in college, she'd read Aeschylus's Greek tragedy *Prometheus Bound*. The story told of a god named Kratos who had been appointed by the God of lightning, Zeus, to act as his agent to bring down Prometheus. Maggie didn't remember the rest of the story, only that the name Kratos meant *strength*.

Since they would soon be hunting down a rogue demon and would quite possibly have to fight it, Maggie said, "What about the name Kratos?"

"Kratos?" Riley skeptically asked. "What does that even mean?"

"It's a Greek mythological name that means strength."

As if approving the chosen name, the hound's demeanor

changed. He let out a long howl, similar to a wolf's cry, except so ear-piercing that Riley and Maggie had to cover their ears.

After Kratos had fallen silent, Riley said in an annoyed tone, "What in the hell? I'm going to be deaf if he does that again."

Maggie's ears were ringing. "Kratos, don't ever do that again! It's okay if you need to warn us, but for no other reason are you to ever do that again! Do you understand me?"

Kratos's ears went straight up, and in a blur of movement, he was now standing next to the front door, his hackles raised, issuing a low deep growl.

Knowing Stuart must be close by, Maggie leapt off the couch. "Kratos, it's just my friend Stuart. Stand down, I promise we're safe for now."

When Kratos didn't move, Maggie kneeled down and timidly placed her hands on the side of his massive head, forcing him to look directly at her. "Kratos, I will not allow any harm to come to you as long as I draw breath. I'm afraid of what's to come, but for now I need you to be my strength and watch over me from the other room. Will you do this for me?"

Kratos's demonic red eyes softened into a dark brown. He then shook himself free and walked away, his large paws scraping on the hardwood floor until he was out of sight.

A sudden knock came at the door, causing Maggie to jump. Casting a quick glance at Riley, she gained her composure and opened the door. Stuart was standing there holding four bags of takeout, only to drop them to the floor and embrace her. They had only been apart a few weeks, which was the longest they had ever gone without communicating. Maggie had no other family or true friends, except for Stuart. So, the significance of the moment was not lost on Maggie as she fiercely hugged him back.

Maggie returned her best friend's hug, feeling safety in his embrace. The smell of his Azzaro Chrome cologne made Maggie feel like she was finally home, even if only in that moment, and she was grateful. Maggie only knew the name of the cologne because she had gone with his wife, Alyssa, to pick it up for his birthday nearly ten years ago, and Stuart still used it to this day.

Stuart released her, then took a step backward, leaving both hands atop Maggie's shoulders, his brown eyes holding back tears. "Do you have any idea how much I've been worried? You disappear one night and then only communicated with me when I made first contact with you. I told you not to let whatever you were searching for consume you. Which, of course, you gladly ignored because you're the most bull-headed woman I know. But to brush me aside as if I were no one and we haven't known each other since grade school . . ." He trailed off as tears fell from his eyes and, with that, once more wrapped her in a tight hug. After letting go, Stuart wiped his eyes and started to say something, but noticed Riley on the couch. "I'm sorry, I didn't realize you had company."

"Did you honestly think I could eat all these sandwiches by myself?" Maggie said in a joking tone. "Come, I want to introduce you to a friend who's played a big part in keeping me alive during my search."

Riley stood as Stuart came closer. He noticed the man was a good three inches taller than him. Reaching out to shake hands, Riley was stunned when Stewart wrapped him in a tight embrace.

"Thank you so much for keeping watch over Mags," he said. "It means so much to me that you protected her, and for that I will forever be indebted to you."

After they separated, Stuart's dark brown eyes remained on Riley, evaluating him further.

Wanting to make a good impression, Riley gave an honest smile. "I promise I'll always do my best to protect Maggie. She means a lot to me as well."

Maggie interjected herself into the conversation, "How about we eat, and you can fill me in on everything that has taken place since I've been gone."

As if finally satisfied Riley could be trusted, Stuart broke eye contact before saying, "Well, a lot has happened in your absence, and your remaining board members are extremely disgruntled with the negative publicity the company has obviously taken despite my best efforts in trying to persuade them into believing you're only under investigation due to an unfortunate misunderstanding. However, I think we should start with why I asked you to come back so abruptly."

Riley went to retrieve the bags of food Stuart had dropped in the hallway. He peeked out the front door, doing a quick sweep with his eyes to make sure Kratos hadn't snuck up on them. Seeing no trace of the hound, he picked up the bags and took them to the kitchen table. He then busied himself with sorting through the sandwiches until he found the one that had steak, cheese, and potatoes. Shortly afterward Maggie and Stuart joined him at the kitchen table.

"The one million you transferred into Miles Jackson's account was of course flagged," Stuart said. "Prosecutors aren't involved as of yet, but I'm guessing it's only a matter of time. After the fast-food employee posted selfies of you two on her social media pages, it brought the press out tenfold trying to locate you. The headlines got even juicier after they learned of your ties with Miles Jackson, making you once more the number one national news story. So, as your best friend and the person you left in charge of your company, I need to hear your side of the story."

Maggie flashed Riley a troubling look. He thought about the

consequences of telling their story and what would happen if they opened Pandora's box. He concluded that Stuart needed to know everything if he was going to help Maggie. He nodded at Maggie, hoping she understood she should tell Stuart everything and shouldn't hold back a single detail.

However, seeing the reluctancy on Maggie's face, Riley quickly swallowed his food and attempted to make light of the situation. "Good thing you ordered a lot of sandwiches."

Maggie offered a weak smile, then stared at Stuart for a long moment. Riley could tell she was still weighing out the options of how much to say. "Stuart, so much has happened since I last saw you. My thoughts are jumbled, and I'm not sure how or even where I should begin."

Wanting an excuse to step away, Riley noticed they hadn't had anything to drink, so he got up to go make coffee but after seeing Maggie's futuristic coffee maker, he headed for the fridge, only to be disappointed to find it empty. He was about to begin the search for cups because tap water would have to be sufficient, when Maggie came over to help.

"The coffee is probably stale, but I'll make us some anyway," Maggie said to Riley, as she opened one of kitchen cabinets. Would you like a cup, Stu?"

"Sounds good to me. I can always use the caffeine even if it is stale," Stuart said with a bit of a chuckle.

Riley sat back at the table while he waited for Maggie to get the coffee brewed. He gave Stuart a shrug, hoping to imply he was sorry for having interrupted. Stuart returned a warm smile. "What kind of work are you in, Riley?"

It was small talk, but Riley welcomed it over sitting there in awkward silence. "I have a small landscaping business in the lake town of Potogi. Have you ever been there?"

Finishing a bite of sandwich, Stuart nodded. "Indeed, yes, I have. Me, my wife, and two daughters head up there as much as possible. That's if the boss lady ever allows me to take back-to-back days off," he said with a smirk.

"I'm standing right over here," Maggie teased.

Riley liked Stuart even more for his candor. Not only was he very protective of Maggie, but he was relatable and didn't appear to be the type of man to look down on someone for their social status.

"Are you originally from Taupe City, like Maggie?" Riley asked.

"Well, actually, I'm originally from a very small town in Louisiana you've probably never even heard of called New Iberia. However, I'm sure you have heard of Tabasco sauce, which was birthed on Avery Island, a twenty-minute drive from where I spent my early childhood years. Wasn't until I moved to Taupe City in the second grade before I met Mags who, believe it or not, on the first day of school—"

"Here comes the first lie of many!" Maggie interjected.

The corners of Stuart's mouth went up as he continued. "As I was saying before being rudely interrupted, on my very first day of school at Taupe City Elementary, Mags came over and introduced herself. And do you know what she told me?"

Riley couldn't hide his smile. "What?"

"Maggie told me that one day I would be working for her, and if I ever wanted back-to-back days off, I shouldn't have ever shaken her hand. Apparently, that handshake sealed my fate, and to this day I wonder what my life would have been like if I had just ignored her and walked away."

Riley burst out laughing, and Stuart followed suit with his deep, booming laugh. Maggie placed three mugs on the table, careful not to spill them as she, too, was laughing. Taking her seat, Maggie wadded up a napkin and threw it at Stuart, who effortlessly dodged out of the way.

"I see. I need to restructure Gregory Portal Provider and appoint a new acting CEO now that I know for certain that my supposed best friend has lost his mind."

"Well, good luck with finding someone who doesn't mind eating Prozac as meal replacements. Especially after they learn what exactly this job entails and how sleep is just a fairy tale told to children. Speaking of no sleep, do you know if they have finally reinvented caffeine in the form of an IV, or do you still just have to swallow it the old-fashioned way?"

This brought another round of laughter. The mental image of Stuart popping Prozac like candy and washing it down with energy drinks and coffee made Riley laugh so hard it brought tears to his eyes. Managing to gain a bit of control, Riley noticed Maggie was trying to catch her breath.

After the laughter had finally subsided, Stuart reached across the table and took one of Maggie's and one of Riley's hands into each one of his. His smile remained but he spoke in a serious tone. "Where two or more are gathered in my name, I am there in the midst of them."

"Matthew eighteen, verse twenty," Riley answered.

Stuart gave Riley's hand a gentle squeeze. His expression then turned to sadness as tears brimmed in his eyes. "Mags, I'm your oldest and dearest friend. When our paths first crossed in the second grade, you frightened me with your kindness. The physical and mental abuse which I endured at home caused me to be mistrustful of people and taught me to believe at an early age that it was just how the world was. I was certain that kind of love and compassion only existed in stories and movies, or, according to my father, for kids who were extremely well behaved.

Yet no matter how hard I tried to please my father—hoping he would just love me like the characters on screen—he only saw disappointment and did his daily best to make sure I knew it.

"Then you came storming into my fragile little world and broke down every notion I had about the way life was supposed to be. You made sure I was your partner in every school activity, not once ever leaving me out or making fun of me for the way I dressed. You didn't know it then, but the way you saw the world bled into the way I saw it, and for that I thank you. I love you, Mary Allison Gregory, and I will protect you with every fiber of my being, because you are not just my best friend or my boss. You are my sister, and I thank God every day he was kind enough to have placed you in my life. If he hadn't, I'm not sure I would have survived my childhood, let alone turned out to be the man I am today."

Closing his eyes, Riley let the warm tears roll down his face, knowing Maggie must be feeling the same way. But when he opened his eyes, he saw Maggie looking down at the table, biting her lower lip.

"Please, Mags, open up to me," begged Stuart. "I have always been here and always will be. Just trust me enough to allow me back into your life. At least tell me everything that's happened since we last saw one another so I can try and help."

Stuart paused, and sadness spread across his face because of Maggie's silence. "If you won't talk to me, then I'll take it as losing my sister to an obsession that has consumed her and alienated me, in spite of how hard I've tried to hang on."

Maggie pulled her hand free from Stuart's grasp and placed her hands in her lap. Riley studied Maggie for a moment, unable to understand how she could remain so cold while the man she had known her entire life, and referred to her as family, was begging her to open up to him.

CHAPTER 14

Barbados couldn't comprehend how that idiot Gideon had been the one to come up with a solution for selecting a new leader. *Must be more than one marble rolling around in that useless head of his!* Barbados snickered at this thought, then became frustrated at the role he was being forced to play. He was the brains out of the three Elders, yet he was reduced to being the messenger after being outwitted by the two fools. *Why in the hell didn't I come up with the solution instead of wasting my time entertaining that useless ass Jameson?* The whole scenario was screwed up, and he was now standing outside Savior's home like some damn errand boy.

None of the Region Leaders or any other working demon was allowed to step foot in the Savior's home unless permitted. Only Esperanza and the hounds were given free access to come and go as they pleased. Barbados shivered at the thought of the hounds. In his opinion, they were the definition of cruelty, far worse than the fires of Hell or the worms. They were mindless individuals who didn't feel pain and couldn't be reasoned with after they were given an order.

Barbados had witnessed their merciless ways. Savior had ordered all Region Leaders and their elders to watch as he sent out six hounds to rip apart over a hundred demons. It was their punishment to an uprising, which was supposed to have been controlled by a Region Leader by the name of Mikell. The turmoil had lasted for over a month until Lucifer had enough and stepped in. The six hounds quickly restored order in a matter of minutes. As for Region Leader Mikell, he had been put back in charge, but his punishment was that his region would never grow, and he would never be sent out on any special assignments.

Barbados started to wonder if he should proceed any further. The black marble doors seemed to mock him and, at the same time, dared him to ring the doorbell. He shuddered at the thought of not knowing what fate awaited him on the other side of the doors once they opened.

I'm being silly, Barbados assured himself.

Gaining his composure, he pushed the doorbell, wincing at the gonging sounds playing throughout the house. The black marble doors were no longer mocking him but appeared to be flat out laughing at him for his stupidity. He thought for a quick moment of fleeing back to his region and telling Jameson that if he wanted an audience with Savior then he could do his own damn bidding. Unfortunately, before he could fully make up his mind, the door creaked partially open, revealing Esperanza. She gave him a knowing grin, as if she had been waiting to find out if he would follow through with his plan.

Under her gaze, Barbados was so entranced that he almost forgot why he had come. He wanted to start by explaining that this had not been his idea and he was sorry to have disturbed her.

"What do you want, Barbados?" she snapped.

The fact that she actually knew his name shocked him. He almost looked down to see if he was wearing a name tag. She cleared her throat and tapped her foot impatiently.

Her scrutiny of his very existence propelled Barbados onward. "Esperanza, this may come as a shock to you, but I'm the future Region Leader of what once was Tristan's! I have come requesting an audience with Savior because I think he would be anxious to move forward now that Tristan is missing. After all, the number of Region Leaders is to stay at 666, and we are now down by one. Furthermore, I'm sure you are aware and understand the significance of this number and why Savior—"

"You are absolutely correct," said Esperanza, cutting him off. "I better run to Savior's viewing room, interrupt what he's doing, and tell him that Barbados has a revelation that could upset all of eternity if a Region Leader isn't appointed immediately. So, stay here and I will be right back!"

She turned as if to go, causing Barbados to realize his mistake. "Wait, don't do that. I think he, ah—"

"He?" Esperanza asked in a reprimanding tone.

"I mean . . . Savior. I'm sure he knows he's down a Region Leader." He was now backpedaling, hopeful that Esperanza would show him mercy.

Barbados was confused at how quickly the situation had gotten away from him when all he meant to do was relay a message. A message which now carried grave consequences and could send him back into the fires of Hell. Or worse, be left to the mercy of the hounds who would gladly consume his flesh while tearing his body to shreds.

Esperanza watched with amusement as Barbados shifted from foot to foot. As stupid and easily manipulated as he was, Esperanza was surprised Barbados had informed her of something she should have already been aware of. Tristan was missing, and the region he oversaw was being run by his Elders. Esperanza stared at Barbados, her expression giving nothing away about her being unaware of what was happening in Tristan's region.

"Barbados, are you certain I shouldn't go get our Savior? I mean, after all, the future Region Leader is at the door."

Barbados raised his eyebrows in horror, then quickly looked away. "Could we start over? This conversation hasn't gone as I planned. Besides, this wasn't even my idea to come and disturb you. I'm just playing the part of errand boy for that useless idiot Jameson."

Esperanza bit her bottom lip to keep from laughing at how pathetic Barbados was acting. His story changed from him wanting an audience with Savior to blaming Jameson for why he was here. The power she had at her fingertips was intoxicating. However, she would never act upon it since she only lived to serve and please Savior.

"I tell you what, Barbados. How about we forget you were even here? But, if Savior asks who was stupid enough to ring his doorbell, I will then inform him it was you. Understood?"

Barbados looked relieved, and before he could respond, Esperanza closed the door on him. Walking back to her spot outside of Savior's viewing room, Esperanza wondered if she should broach the subject with her master that they were one Region Leader short. After all, it was her duty to keep track of these things, so Savior didn't have to.

As she continued to wrestle with the thought, Savior unexpectedly walked out of the viewing room and looked directly at her. Her eyes immediately went to the floor, hoping to prove her obedience. Anytime she was in his presence, she was unable to understand or comprehend the complexity of his perfection. He was perfect and pure in her eyes, and she would do anything he asked of her. Even if it meant sacrificing herself just so he would remain in glory.

"My child," Lucifer sneered. "I will be focusing all of my attention on the Fallen and will be unreachable until I break him. While I'm preoccupied, you are to handle all my affairs. If you feel something needs to be addressed, then do it. However, do not disturb me for any reason. If you do, I will show you no mercy, despite how fond I've grown of you."

"Yes, my Savior," said Esperanza.

Esperanza shelved the idea of informing Savior of Tristan's disappearance because he had enough to deal with. Besides, Savior had put her in charge, so she would handle the Tristan situation as she believed Savior would. There needed to be 666 Region Leaders, and that would be the first task she dealt with.

As he turned to go, Savior stopped and looked at her. "Oh, and Esperanza, the hounds can either be your greatest ally or be the key to your undoing. Keep that in mind as you go about my business. And if you ever get the foolish notion of replacing me as God, you will regret it."

"Never, my Savior." said Esperanza. Looking up, she found she was responding to a closed door.

CHAPTER 15

Legionaries led his followers to the middle of the town square and waited as they gathered around him. He turned slowly in a 360-degree circle, making eye contact with every individual.

The martyr George was kneeling, and although a certain death awaited him, he remained confident while praying silently. Two followers rested their hands on his shoulders, making sure he didn't try to flee. But if Legionaries were being completely honest with himself, he knew George was unafraid of what would happen to him after death.

Seeing George's confident demeanor reminded Legionaries of one of the more fascinating people he'd first encountered upon coming back to Earth's surface: a pastor named Beth. She hadn't known who he really was, as he had taken on the appearance of a man who attended her church. She had explained to him in detail about free will, and he'd felt a sense of gratitude along with the normal feeling of distain he felt for those who worshipped the false God. As he listened to her speak, Legionaries began to understand that free will applied to every living being, which in turn helped him achieve his freedom. Furthermore, it put him on this journey and helped him realize he was in fact a god.

However, armed with a new understanding of what free will really entailed, Legionaries now realized there may be even more to it, and he had only come to this revelation because of George.

Legionaries simply couldn't wrap his mind around how the man just knelt in prayer, already accepting his fate. He wanted the man to struggle, followed by lots of begging, pleading, and sobbing for his life to be spared, only for it all to fall on deaf ears. Instead, the man was compliant and completely silent, further confusing Legionaries as to why he would remain loyal to a false god who was allowing this to happen to him.

A distant cough broke his thoughts, bringing Legionaries back to reality. His followers were exchanging worried looks. He quickly let out a pulse of energy, and a moment later, the faces of the crowd returned stoic, waiting for his instructions.

George remained kneeling, his hands clutched, his head bowed as he prayed. Legionaries decided it was time for this martyr to prove just how loyal he really was to his god.

"You two." Legionaries pointed at the men standing on either side of George. "Bring forth the martyr."

In the middle of the square stood a large statue of a man riding a horse and holding his sword out in front of him. Finding this to be a fitting way to lead off with the executions, Legionaries reached up and broke off the sword. To Legionaries's delight, the sword was made of solid concrete. This meant the person wielding the blunt sword would need to have enough strength to lift it.

The two gentlemen escorting George appeared to be confused as to what to do once they brought the prisoner before Legionaries.

George, however, was not confused. He pushed the men away. "You've done your jobs and brought me face to face with my death. I'll take it from here. Retake your positions with the rest of the spectators for a far better view of my fate, but never forget what you are about to witness."

Without being prompted, George knelt and positioned

himself over the plaque next to the statue, leaving his neck exposed.

Legionaries wished he could be the one to end this overzealous ass. *What kind of fool would freely offer up their life so others could learn from him dying?* he wondered.

Oddly, this made Legionaries remember a distant and all-but-forgotten memory, which felt like lifetimes ago. His former master, Lucifer, had forced Legionaries to forget all about his past and who he was, but now, after having broken free, he was slowly regaining the lost memories. He closed his eyes and focused on the memory.

He had met a man on the shoreline of Gadarenes who proclaimed to be the son of God. In the end, the man sacrificed his own life, delivering a powerful statement right before his death, "Father, forgive them, for they do not know what they are doing." A powerful statement, that Lucifer despised.

Legionaries opened his eyes, infuriated by the memory. The so-called son of God had sentenced him to a life in Hell when he cast Legion into a herd of pigs before running them off a cliff, killing all of them at once. When Legionaries had awoken after the incident with the pigs, he had no memory of his life or who he was, and he was forced into the servitude of Lucifer for a millennia. Lucifer had created a split in Legion's personality by locking him away inside his own mind. After Legion, was able to extricate himself from the confines of his mind, he informed Legionaries of what and who he truly was. The disdain he now felt for the do-gooder worshippers of the false God was overwhelming, but his thirst for vengeance would soon be quenched by the blood his followers would surely spill this night, and it would begin with this first sacrifice.

"Who will be the first volunteer to draw blood for their God this night?" Legionaries hissed at his followers.

The curvy woman, Miranda, raised her hand without hesitation. Despite the anger his memories had caused, Legionaries was amused by how powerful and persuasive he had become. This was George's wife, after all, and he was certain he could now make family members practically eat one another alive if he commanded them to do so.

"Come, my slave, and reap your reward for truly declaring yourself to me."

Miranda rushed toward Legionaries, a large smile spread across her face, completely unaware he was poisoning her thoughts.

Returning the smile, Legionaries scoffed to himself. *How pathetic these worshippers of mine are!*

Out of breath, Miranda knelt before him. "My God, I am honored to do as you ask."

Looking down at her weak and frail human body, Legionaries wondered what it would feel like to stomp on the back of her head, smashing her brains across the ground, but seeing how submissive and eager she was to please him, he dismissed the thought.

"Take up the sword and prove your loyalty to me."

Miranda stood, walked over to the concrete sword, and attempted to lift it. When she failed in doing so, she dropped to her knees and managed to maneuver the sword onto her lap. After getting it under the crooks of her arms, Miranda struggled to her feet just before gravity won out, forcing it to free from her grip and back to the ground. Clearly embarrassed, she looked at Legionaries in utter defeat.

Although he had knowingly given her an impossible task just to see how far she was willing to go, Legionaries gave her a look of disgust in return. "Since you are too weak to carry out the task being asked of you by using this sword of stone, then we shall use mine."

Legionaries conjured up a sword out of thin air. It was perfectly balanced, impossibly light, and so sharp it could cut through bone like a hot knife through butter.

Tossing it to the ground, Legionaries said with distain, "Should I call upon someone else, or do you think you can manage to carry out this one simple task I have asked of you?"

Wanting to prove her loyalty, Miranda quickly retrieved the sword. It looked to be only three feet in length, and the blade was so skinny she wondered if it would break. As she held the blade a few inches away from her face, it suddenly produced a soft, eerie red glow. Uncertain of what she was seeing, Miranda looked out at the small crowd of followers for confirmation. They all looked to be in a dreamlike state and wouldn't be of any use to her. Focusing her attention back on the blade, Miranda noticed the soft red glow was growing into a bright beaming light, and she fought back the instinct to drop it and shield her eyes. Just then, the sword seemed to have taken on a life of its own, forcing her grip to tighten around its hilt. Miranda wanted to cry out for help, but the other followers seemed to have disappeared, leaving just her and the sword.

Legionaries spoke in an authoritative tone. "Be still my slave and know I am your god. Carry out what I have commanded, and you will be rewarded for your obedience."

Miranda gave a light shake of her head, for the voice sounded as if it had come from the sword itself. She thought she had imagined the voice until it returned with booming authority.

"If you want to truly be free, raise me above your head and cut the flesh of the man who has been holding you back."

The outside world came roaring back as the blade of the sword also appeared to return to normal. To Miranda's surprise, she was able to loosen her grip and again flex her fingers. As the confusion set in, she thought she had just imagined the whole ordeal. She then looked to Legionaries for some kind of conformation about what had just happened. However, he merely sneered at her, grunting in disapproval.

"Miranda, it's okay," said George, drawing her focus to him. "I'm willingly doing this because I believe my sacrifice will set you free from this false god who is poisoning your mind."

Again, Miranda looked to Legionaries for guidance.

"The choice is yours. If you want to be set free from the shackles of this mundane life, you know what must be done. If you choose not to go through with it, you are then wasting my time and I will find someone else who desires absolute freedom."

Miranda knew what she wanted, but she was confused about why she had to kill someone to obtain it. Before Legionaries showed up to their small town, she had thought many times about how George's death would free her. Her thoughts now swirled in her head. Could she be the one to end his life? He had been good to her and was never cruel, no matter how mean she became toward him. If this were the only way, could she really murder George?

As if knowing her internal debate, the sword once more took on a life of its own, causing her to tighten her grip and raise it above her head. She'd once again lost control over her actions and was unable to drop the sword. But now she knew for certain that she didn't want to kill her husband. In desperation, Miranda looked out to the other followers for help, but they were still in a dreamlike state. Nobody was going to help her out of this situation she'd so carelessly put herself in.

The sword then sent a shock down her arms as a voice screamed out, "Now, Miranda! Swing the sword and do it now!"

Fighting to keep the sword above her head was useless as her arms grew weary, causing them to fall under the impossible weight of the blade. Miranda cried out for mercy as the blade landed on the back of George's neck. His body remained draped across the plaque, but his legs and arms began spasming as blood ran down the plaque like a river. She watched in horror as his head rolled several feet away before coming to rest face up. His eyes met hers and blinked a couple of times as the light faded from them. His now lifeless eyes bore into hers.

Disgusted with the gruesome act that had been played out by her own hand, Miranda dropped the sword and clumsily staggered away from the chaos. Finally unable to take another step, she dropped to her knees and violently started vomiting, each wretch causing her body to shake uncontrollably.

Legionaries addressed his followers in a somber tone. "Do you see the anguish she's having to endure now? All because of a would-be righteous martyr. They fill your head with promises of love and understanding, only to immediately turn their back on you the moment your path deviates from theirs."

Miranda could vaguely hear what Legionaries was saying, but she was too consumed with her own thoughts to care. Where was the promised peace she was supposed to be feeling now? Where was the new sense of belonging? She only felt depraved and vile, wishing she had the strength to stand and tell everyone that Legionaries was a false god and George had been right all along. Unfortunately, the thought of George and what she had done proved to be too much, and she keeled over, losing what was left in her stomach.

"This road we now travel will be a difficult and painful one," said Legionaries. "Especially while you come to terms with the fact those you once called friends and family are now your enemy. Take comfort in knowing that I am your God, and I promise to never forsake you. I will fight this fight with you to the end. Put your trust in me and know I have your best interest at heart."

The crowd, despite having just witnessed the murder of an innocent life, let out a thunderous roar. Miranda couldn't believe it, but after seeing the rest of the followers in a dreamlike state, she figured they didn't understand this path they chose would lead to their doom. Innocent blood couldn't be simply washed away, as it now stained the souls of those who had willingly taken part in it. If there was ever a cross to bear, Miranda had found hers, and it was more than what George's god would have ever asked of her.

CHAPTER 16

Riley, Maggie, and Stuart remained seated around the kitchen table trapped in an uncomfortable silence. Maggie looked down at the table, refusing to make eye contact. Riley knew she was hellbent on protecting Jonathan but wondered at what cost? Stuart was practically a family member, and although Riley had only known him for less than an hour, he wholeheartedly trusted the man.

Finally, Maggie spoke. "A little over a year ago, I left the office late one night and, for whatever reason, I decided to walk home instead of driving. Because of that foolish decision, I was mugged and almost raped by two men. Then, out of nowhere, a stranger appeared and rescued me. Afterward, the stranger accompanied me to the hospital to assure that I got there safely, and during our short walk, I felt real peace for the first time since the passing of my parents. It was so overly intoxicating to feel so at peace, but I chalked it up to the severe adrenaline from surviving the near-death experience. When we finally said our goodbyes, I gave him one of my business cards. I assumed, or maybe more so hoped, that he would eventually realize who I was and would just show up asking for some money or a favor. The waiting turned into weeks, then months. After that night, I converted this floor into my own personal living suite. I figured if I eliminated all distractions and cut myself off from the outside world, I would be able to locate the mysterious man who'd saved my life."

"Now I understand why you made me acting CEO of Gregory

Provider," said Stuart. "Did you finally locate your stranger, or did I interrupt your quest by asking you to return?"

"Yes, I finally located him," Maggie flatly said. "His name is Jonathan."

Stuart leaned back in his chair and looked down in defeat. Maggie had basically divulged nothing, which was unacceptable in Riley's opinion. Stuart deserved the whole story, and Riley refused to sit here in some futile act of secrecy just because Maggie wanted to be overly cautious.

Looking Stuart directly in his eyes, Riley said, "From what Maggie has told me, you believe in God, which means, hopefully, what I'm about to tell you won't sound too unbelievable. I promise everything I'm about to say is the absolute truth. You see, the stranger, Jonathan, entered my life later that same night that he rescued Maggie. The thing is, he came here to find and protect me. I can confirm Jonathan was my late wife's guardian angel."

"Riley!" Maggie scolded, clearly shocked at his admittance.

Riley glared at Maggie. "This is not just an employee sitting across from you or some random person. This is your childhood best friend who has remained loyal to you when most people would have already bailed. So, forgive me, but I will not remain silent and simply sit here because you feel you are betraying Jonathan if you tell the truth about him. Besides, Stuart needs to know the whole truth about everything because, unfortunately for him, he became part of this situation the moment he walked through the door, and you know this."

Visibly stunned at how cavalier he was being, Maggie's demeanor softened under his intense gaze. Riley understood Maggie's reluctancy regarding who they told about Jonathan, but Stuart was now involved. There was no backing out, and he needed to be prepared.

"You're right, Riley, I am being unfair." Maggie reached across the table, and without hesitation Stuart did likewise. "What Riley said is true. However, I didn't mean . . . or at least, I should have realized I was placing you in harm's way by coming back here. I can't even imagine what I would do if you got hurt because . . ."

Maggie started crying, removing her hands from Stuart's embrace, and covering her face. Stuart stood and wrapped his arms around her. Stuart then whispered something Riley couldn't hear, which he didn't mind one bit, as this was a private and special moment between two close friends, and he didn't want to intrude on it. Eventually giving in to Stuart's hug, Maggie stood up and returned the embrace.

Stuart said in a loud whisper, "Do not allow your heart to harden under this burden you are determined to carry. This was all part of God's plan, and he is in control of everything that will happen. I have faith that everything will work out, and I will be just fine. I know you don't believe as I do, but I'm not worried and you shouldn't be either."

Maggie's eyes were still full of tears. "Regardless," she said, "whether you are afraid or not, I am sorry."

After Maggie had calmed down, Stuart returned to his seat, and the three of them fell again into an uncomfortable silence.

Pulling a napkin free from its holder, Maggie dabbed at her eyes, then spoke in a soft voice. "Jonathan is indeed a guardian angel. He chose to fall from grace when he felt he'd failed to protect his charge, Riley's late wife, Allison. He had been by Riley's side since the day he fell, helping to save people like him and myself along the way. Serving as our protector. Then he was pulled into Hell to save us, but before he went, he gave us two gifts."

Riley was taken aback that Stuart remained so calm and silent. If he were in Stuart's position, he would have interrupted several times and still would have had a hard time believing what he was hearing. Stuart, however, clearly possessed a talent for patience, as he remained sitting casually with one leg draped across the other, both hands resting in his lap.

He offered Riley a polite smile, as if to say, *Okay, what are these two gifts?*

Riley returned with a polite smile of his own. "Before Jonathan was pulled out of this world, he touched my nose several times, even went so far as to kiss the tip of it. As odd as this may sound, at the time I thought nothing of it until Jonathan was gone. Then I noticed a horrible stench in the air, I can only describe it as warm, decaying meat. Jonathan had told me when demons were close by, they emanate an odor. There is only one demon remaining in this world that I know of, and this particular demon had worked with the Devil to orchestrate the fall of Jonathan. Unfortunately, because of this new gift—or curse—of mine, it's up to me to locate this demon and figure out a way to force it to tell me how to find and rescue Jonathan."

Riley paused, anticipating Stuart to finally break his code of silence. But Stuart remained silent, his dark eyes studying Riley, as he stroked his perfectly groomed goatee.

"And the second gift?" Stuart finally asked.

"Truthfully, we have no control over this so-called second gift, and I have no interest in telling you about it," Maggie said. "I fear it would only put you in further danger."

As if knowing he had become the primary topic of the conversation, Kratos entered the kitchen, his red menacing eyes locked on Stuart. Kratos stopped at Maggie's chair, breathing in her scent, and then, like a predator stalking its prey, dropped his head close to the ground, taking slow, steady steps toward Stuart. Stuart stiffened as he pushed his body back a little further in his chair with every step Kratos took toward him.

Seeing the panic start to set in, Riley quickly reached across the table and grabbed Stuart's hand. "Stuart, I know you are afraid, but I need you to just listen to me and try to remain calm. Do not make any sudden movements. Just focus on me and try to block out him even being there."

Stuart's eyes grew wide. Under different circumstances, Riley would have laughed out loud.

Now invading Stuart's personal space, Kratos began the thorough process of determining whether Stuart was friend or foe, sniffing his legs at first and working upward until, finally, they were face-to-face.

Having enough of the ordeal, Maggie spoke sharply, "Kratos, come!" When the hound didn't budge, Maggie spoke even more forcefully, issuing a threat of her own. "Kratos, either listen and come to me or leave and never return!"

This time Kratos obeyed but did so on his own terms by walking backward, the way he had done in the parking garage.

"Breathe, Stuart. I promise you are safe," said Riley. Stuart exhaled loudly and wiped the sweat that had built up on his face with his hands. "I'm so sorry for having put you through this ordeal," Riley said sheepishly. "In case you were wondering, that is our supposed second gift, Kratos."

"It has a name?" Stuart asked, clearly disturbed.

"Well, yes, we gave him a name because we have no real control over Kratos. We were hoping he'd feel more accepted by us if we gave him a name, which I know sounds completely nuts. Maggie seems to be the only person he'll actually listen to."

Stuart took several deep breaths, slowly relaxing with each one. "I'm guessing Maggie came up with the name?"

"Yes, she did. What gave it away?"

A smile played at the bottom of Stuart's lips but disappeared when he looked at Kratos. "Well, Riley, I'm not a psychic, but when I first heard Maggie say the name, our time spent at Taupe

City Community College came flooding back. Our English 1301 professor had us read some mythological story. I don't remember much about it, except one of the main characters was named Kratos and the meaning of the name is *strength*."

"My father once told me naming an animal was a task not to be taken lightly," said Maggie. "They deserved our respect because they were placed in our lives for a reason, and they would now be a part of the family. To give them a silly cartoon name would be disrespectful because of the role they would play in our lives."

Riley thought back to his first dog, which he had named Scuffy. The name was from his favorite children's book his mom used to read to him before bed. Now Riley felt like maybe he had been disrespectful toward the animal for giving him such a silly name and all the other pets who came after.

Maggie laughed, breaking the seriousness of the moment. "You both are wearing the same guilty expression, so I should just clarify: I, too, have given plenty of animals silly names."

Riley chuckled, followed by Stuart.

Knowing there were more important matters to discuss, Riley said, "Stuart, I know we just met, but I want you to know that you can trust me when I tell you Kratos is okay with you being here. If he wasn't, well, we would be searching for bleach and trash bags to get rid of whatever remained of you!"

Stuart, still a bit shaken by his encounter with Kratos, offered a polite chuckle. "Somehow, I knew you were telling me the truth about Jonathan. However, if I had any doubt at all, it was instantly erased from my mind the moment Kratos revealed himself. I'm guessing since Jonathan gifted him to you, he is on our side, but he's terrifying. Do you know where he came from?"

"Well, believe it or not, he actually belonged to the Devil," said Riley. "I first encountered several of his kind after becoming an unwilling guest in the Devil's home."

Stuart held up a hand, stopping Riley from continuing. "Riley, this is almost too much for me to process. If I didn't believe in God or thought anything you said was false, I'd immediately leave and call a therapist for the two of you. This whole situation just keeps getting weirder and more bizarre by the second. I'm trying my best to keep up, but the more you tell me, the more it causes my head to swim from all the questions piling up. I mean, Riley, you're telling me that you've met the Devil and somehow survived? That sentence alone has me questioning my own faith. No one just goes to Hell and returns to talk about it. A guardian angel being your best friend is one thing. The Devil allowing you to leave Hell is a completely different thing."

Riley knew Stuart was right. Both his and now Maggie's life had become so complicated it would take a lifetime to try to explain everything. Although Riley had come to terms with the fact that his life would always be this way, it saddened him to think about how he could never have another normal relationship or a friend he could be completely honest with outside of Jonathan and Maggie.

"I'm sorry, Stuart. I've grown so accustomed to this now being my life that I've never considered one day I might share my story with anyone other than Jonathan and Maggie. I have developed a respect and fondness for you in this short time I've gotten to know you today. You are a good man. I can see this by how you treat Maggie and stand by her side. I look forward to the day when I can tell you my full story. For now, I will just conclude one thing. Yes, I have met the Devil on more than one occasion. As for Kratos, he is an instrument of the Devil, and I'm not sure if he is loyal to his master or not, and therefore don't really know if he is here to protect us or to keep a watchful eye over us until he's ordered to kill. More and more I believe the latter not to be the case, but I'm still hesitant."

Stuart cast a quick glance at Kratos, as if to make certain he was still next to Maggie.

"Tell you what," said Maggie. "I have three days to correct everything that has gone wrong in my life. During our downtime, I will tell you as much as I can and do my best to answer every question you have."

"I will do likewise," said Riley. "You will just have to learn to excuse the mutt for acting the way it does."

Kratos issued a low growl, which made Riley smile. Stuart appeared to be a little less apprehensive as he returned the smile. "That's acceptable, and thank you, because I know the questions will come non-stop once we begin. Now as for your situation, Mags, we are going to need a whole lot more coffee!"

CHAPTER 17

Tamara softly pulled the door closed behind her and took a seat on the bed next to her mom. She offered up a quick prayer that this wouldn't be their final time together, but in her heart, she knew it was. Her mother's vulnerable condition angered Tamara, making her want to lash out by simply marching back into the living room, stand shoulder to shoulder with her father, and vow to fight off anyone who meant to do them harm.

However, it was a futile thought, and she would only be throwing her life away. Besides, if she were caught, her captors would be her neighbors and possibly even people she had once considered friends. This realization caused her to shudder at the madness of what was happening.

Her dad had made the impossible decision by telling her to leave and get as far away from the city as possible. Tamara hoped she could find refuge in the neighboring town of Deadwater. The trip by car would take less than an hour, but she knew it was more than likely she would have to walk it. Doing a quick calculation, Tamara felt defeated, realizing that she wouldn't arrive in Deadwater until tomorrow morning at the earliest, if she survived the hike.

"Mom, our town has gone crazy, and God seems to be okay with it. I just wish you weren't sick so you could protect me and give me guidance through this darkness that has consumed our small town."

Tamara immediately wished she could take back the selfish comment. Her mom was fighting her own internal battle with lung cancer, which was strange since her mom had never smoked a day in her life.

The first symptom had been a light cough, which grew worse in the span of a few months, followed by lack of energy and appetite. Having tried every over-the-counter cough and sinus medicine in existence, she'd finally caved and went to their primary care physician. After several rounds of bloodwork and a CAT scan, the doctors confirmed she had stage four lung cancer, which had metastasized into her lymph nodes.

Tamara remembered the day her parents told her the news. It was her favorite time of year, when winter was at its peak providing soft blankets of snow. She had just returned from school, and as soon as she had walked through the door, Tamara knew something was wrong. Her parents were seated side-by-side in the living room, their expressions masquerading behind smiles, which never even reached the corners of their mouths.

"Sweetie, we need to speak with you. Could you come sit with us?" her father had asked in a shaky voice. His eyes were puffy, as if he'd been crying.

Pressing two fingers into the side of her head, Tamara had massaged her temples until dark spots clouded her vision, hoping that if she pressed hard enough, she would return to a reality where everything was back to normal. When she finally opened her eyes, the spots had dissipated. Her parents were no longer trying to put on a brave face.

"How can this even be possible?" Tamara had asked. "Mom doesn't even smoke. Lung cancer only happens to people who smoke. What am I missing? Or did the doctors screw up the results?"

Her mother had begun to speak, only to then drop her head in defeat, clearly struggling to find an answer to the same question.

Tamara quickly fell to the floor in front of her mother, wrapping her in a firm embrace. "I'm so sorry for my selfishness. I'm just afraid of what comes next. Please forgive m—"

The rest of what Tamara intended to say was muffled, as all three held on to one another.

When enough time had passed, her mom took hold of Tamara's face and gently kissed her forehead. "This is in God's hands. I hope you will not think I'm being selfish, but I refuse to become some lab rat to be experimented on. All while doctors continually argue over which treatment might possibly work."

Wanting to argue why she wanted her mother to seek treatment, Tamara remained quiet, respecting her mom's decision. The new silence allowed for the nightmare to take hold in Tamara's mind. Her future was more uncertain than ever.

The aggressiveness of the cancer had surprised her doctors. Home nurses moved in much sooner than anyone expected, transforming her parents' bedroom into a hospital room.

During one of their final talks, before the pain became too much, it was her mom consoling her instead of the other way around. "Tamara, no one sheds a tear in Heaven. So don't you worry about me. I'm not afraid of what comes next for me. I'm just sad I won't be here for all the milestones still to come for you, or that I won't be here for you when life gets too hard." Soon after this conversation, the pain meds took her mom to a place Tamara didn't have access to.

The pounding on the front door grew louder and more vigorous, bringing Tamara back to the present. "Mom, I need you so desperately right now. I just wish I had your strength, so I knew I'd survive and overcome whatever comes next. I'm so scared, Mom."

Tamara stretched out next to her mom on the hospital bed, wrapping one arm across her middle, and laying her head on her mom's chest. She listened to her steady heartbeat, wishing for more time. "You are the most selfless person in the world, and I know one day we will see each other again. On that blessed day, I will fall into your arms, and you will hold me like a child. You are and always will be the woman I will strive to be. I just hope what I do in life brings you joy and makes you proud."

The banging from the front door became even more intense, warning Tamara she was out of time. She took her mother's hand, wishing to feel a gentle squeeze, then kissed her mother's cheek for what she hoped would not be the last time. Then Tamara went to the open window and climbed out. As soon as her feet touched the ground, she heard the front door give up its fight, and the voices of the intruders filled the space.

CHAPTER 18

Now that the first martyr was dead, Legionaries led the followers from the town square and into the first neighborhood, declaring that it was time to rid the city of those who opposed him. Miranda found refuge in the back of the crowd, hoping she wouldn't have to participate in the madness for much longer. There had to be an opportunity to flee.

The crowd marched through the neighborhood, eerily silent as Legionaries pointed to random houses and said "non-worshippers." Without hesitation, a small number of followers would storm up the driveway, gain entrance, and drag the homeowner outside. The people were usually elderly, so the struggle didn't last long, as they were then hauled to the town square to await their execution.

Miranda was disgusted at how eager everyone was to commit such heinous acts of violence, all in the hope of gaining favor with their new supposed god. *Ironic,* she thought. *Only a few hours ago, this supposed god had told us, "At one time I had been where you are now, a simple slave hoping for a morsel to fall off master's plate so that I, too, could be fed."*

When she heard this proclamation, it hadn't even registered with her. She had been so consumed by this stranger's ability to turn himself into a beast that she felt like she had been living in a fog. Now she was able to see clearly, and she wished for a way out of this nightmare. She walked slowly with the rest of the followers, innocent blood now on her hands.

His followers all shared the same blank stare. Miranda felt like the only sane individual remaining. She couldn't explain how Legionaries was doing his tricks or why everyone looked to be in a trance. She only knew for certain that he wasn't who he was claiming to be.

Lost in thought, Miranda was not paying attention to what was going on around her until she walked straight into the back of someone, sending her stumbling backward to the ground. Gaining her composure, Miranda looked up to see Legionaries towering over her, eyeing her suspiciously. His eyes faded to a soul-piercing black. Magic trick or not, Miranda found herself unable to meet his gaze.

"You dare touch me without my permission?"

Stunned by what she had done, Miranda opened her mouth to explain herself, but nothing came out. No sound at all.

Legionaries leaned down until his face was only a few inches from hers. He breathed in deeply as if taking in her sent. "You appear to still be one of mine. However, your scent reeks of doubt. Let's remedy this, shall we?" Legionaries easily pulled her to her feet and dragged her toward a vacant house.

Miranda was still too afraid to cry out, to beg for help or mercy, but took solace in the fact that if he was going to kill her, he would have already done so. At least she hoped this was the case. Then a worse thought poured into her consciousness: a quick death would be better than what some men take pleasure in doing to frightened and vulnerable women behind closed doors. She tried to resist this thought, but as many rape victims had experienced, herself included, fear only fueled the desire of men seeking dominance over someone.

She struggled to free herself from Legionaries's grip when

they stopped at the front door of a darkened house. Legionaries waved his hand once in the air, causing the door to open, then jerked her effortlessly inside. The interior lights flooded the room, casting out the dark, and revealing an unruly scene created by a sudden departure.

A loud bang echoed off the walls, causing Miranda to freeze. She thought Legionaries had just shot her, until he let her go and viciously threw her to the ground. The sound had only been the front door slamming shut. Miranda waited a moment to see what Legionaries was going to do to her. When nothing came, she hesitantly got to her feet. Legionaries stared at her with such a ferocious intensity, and Miranda shrank under his gaze.

"Sit," Legionaries demanded, pointing to the couch behind her.

When she was seated, Legionaries abruptly fell to all fours in front of her, followed by coughing and dry heaving, just like he had done in the chapel. His body methodically rocked back and forth, as if willing his stomach to regurgitate whatever was inside him. After several more heaves, followed by a steady rocking pattern, a soft white glow began to pulse inside Legionaries, illuminating the outline of a mass inside his stomach.

Miranda was horror stricken, yet unable to look away from the madness playing out right in front of her. Legionaries's stomach doubled in size, giving him the look of a pregnant woman. This was nothing like what had taken place at the church service. Something far different had occurred when Legionaries morphed into a beast in front of the whole Sunday congregation. Miranda knew that what she was witnessing now had never been seen by anyone else, making her feel special and entitled.

An exhausted Legionaries dropped his head to the carpet, making himself completely vulnerable. Seeing him in this vulnerable state, Miranda felt drawn to him. Unsure whether it was the power that was coursing through his body, or the importance she would feel from being by his side, she gave in to it. Feeling a thrill from it all, her thoughts darkened, causing any guilt or remorse to fall away.

In anticipation of what would happen next, Miranda remained perfectly still, going so far as to hold her breath. If she so much as moved, it would disrupt everything, and she would be forced back into being ordinary.

Legionaries lifted his head and let out a violent scream but was quickly silenced when his bottom jaw became unhinged and his mouth widened, taking on the appearance of a snake when feeding. His facial features continued to stretch until they were no longer recognizable. Both eyes now resided on the sides of his misshapen head, with only the whites of the eyes visible.

Without any further preamble, the mass began making its way out from Legionaries's stomach, moving to his throat, and stopping halfway out of his overstretched mouth. Shaking his head side to side, and making a choking sound, Legionaries leaned forward and vomited the entire mass onto the living room floor.

In complete disbelief, Miranda watched in stunned silence as the mass took on a life of its own, quickly taking the form of an infant male.

"Holy shit," she heard a female voice say, too enthralled by the situation to realize those words had emerged from her own mouth.

The newborn turned its head in Miranda's direction and frowned. She wanted to laugh, but the strange glow that originated in Legionaries was now coming from inside the baby's stomach.

Unexpectedly, the baby began shaking violently until the glow from inside its stomach became so bright she had to shield her eyes from it. When Miranda could tell the light had faded, she looked down to see a small child no older than the age of five staring back at her. Too overwhelmed at what she was witnessing, Miranda could only stare at the child in disbelief. Within seconds the glow returned, this time much faster than before.

The child screamed in pain, and Miranda had to shield her eyes from the light. When the process was complete, the small child had now transformed into a teenager. The process cycled again, and in the span of seconds, a full-grown naked man was kneeling in the middle of the living room, sobbing.

Legionaries, having changed back to his human appearance, stood, and smiled down at his creation. "Open your eyes, slave. It's time for you to make good on your promise by serving me."

Sharing the same confused expression as Miranda, the man blinked several times. He made eye contact with Legionaries, then quickly looked away.

In that brief exchange, Miranda thought she had witnessed pure terror in the man's eyes. Clumsily getting to his feet and taking in a deep breath of fresh air, the man doubled over and vomited, then collapsed face first into it.

Laughing at his new creation, Legionaries grabbed a handful of the man's hair and said in a mocking tone, "Oh, how the mighty have fallen." Legionaries dropped the man's head back into his vomit and directed his attention to Miranda. "Allow me to introduce you to the former Region Leader of the largest region in Hell. His name is Tristan, but he now holds the same title as you: slave."

CHAPTER 19

Pride (noun)
1. : the quality or state of being proud: such as inordinate self-esteem: conceit
2. : a reasonable or justifiable self-respect
3. : delight or elation arising from some act, possession or relationship

Lucifer stood from his chair and walked out of the viewing room. When he didn't immediately return, Jonathan allowed himself to relax a bit. It was his first moment alone since having been dragged into Hell. He still had a long road ahead unless God found it necessary to intervene. That wasn't likely, for just as Granny had gone through her own trials when she had chosen to fall to save her human, Cristal, Jonathan was now experiencing his trials without Riley by his side.

Granny had also been an angel, and like Jonathan she made the decision to fall to protect her human on Earth, long before he had. He was not aware of all the details of Granny's story, but he loved her for helping guide him through this endeavor. In the end, she gave up her life to heal Jonathan after he had become sick.

The trials weren't a form of punishment from God the Father, but more of a change in perspective that he had to learn from.

This way, the fallen angels could better understand and empathize with the daily struggles of the humans' lives, to be almost human but possess abilities that most humans would never comprehend. Jonathan believed this to be the case with most humans, except for when it came to Riley, his best friend loved him unconditionally. He knew Riley was coming to rescue him even if it cost him his life, and there was nothing Jonathan could do to stop him.

"God, what have I done?" Jonathan said to the empty room. "Please, Father, intervene. I failed my beloved Allison. Don't let my actions also lead to the death of Riley."

It was only the second time Jonathan had spoken out loud since being here. The burned skin, which now covered the left side of his neck and face, strained from the pull of his facial muscles. He tenderly touched the side of his throat where Lucifer's black tear had landed, methodically tracing the outline of the marred skin to figure out just how large the seared scarring was.

He determined that the scar started out small at the bottom of his neck, then spread out like a strange spiderweb across his left cheek and ended just below his hairline. *Just one more scar in the long list of many*, he thought.

Jonathan looked around the viewing room, observing dark stains on the floors, walls, and somehow a large spot on the ceiling. He decided the reason Lucifer called this his viewing room was because of the damned he tortured here for his own amusement.

Unable to bear the thought of resting where others had cowered, Jonathan started to get to his feet. Then Lucifer abruptly came back into the room, closing the door softly behind him.

Giving Jonathan a knowing smile, Lucifer walked over and knelt in front of him. "Trust me, Jonathan. I took great delight in every tear shed, every drop of spilled blood, every scream, and every plea my victims ever made to me to stop from hurting them.

You look at these stains and feel sadness, and you are disgusted with how I treat those who belong to me. But I see the beauty in the story told behind their origins, telling of how a wrong was made right. For instance, did you get a good look at the one spot in the corner of the ceiling?"

Lucifer, still crouched next to Jonathan, pivoted on his heel to look at the stain. He then turned back around to face Jonathan; the smile erased from his face.

"That's where one of my hounds defied gravity and ripped apart the woman I'd grown to love," said Lucifer in a somber tone. "Before she could regenerate enough to explain why she lied to me, I banished her back to the depths of Hell. I already knew the truth, and anything she would've said would've just been another lie. I know love seems like a strange emotion for me to speak about, to wholly love another being, to give all of yourself to that person and ask for it to be reciprocated. In some cases, it works out, but in most it never does. I imagine you find it ironic to hear me even say the word *love*."

Jonathan remained silent, not daring to take the bait. Besides, nothing good would come from engaging in this conversation. It would be just another story Lucifer would spin so Jonathan could understand his point of view and maybe even feel sorry for him. Lucifer's smile returned, reminding Jonathan his thoughts weren't private.

"You see, Jonathan, after being banished to live out the rest of eternity forever stuck between the worlds of Hell and Earth, the loneliness can grow quite tiresome. Especially having no real companion to share it all with. My first thought was, 'What is a man's best friend?' To which I answered, 'A dog.' So, I created my hounds, but as you have learned, they're not much of conversationalists and are only happy when I snap my fingers."

Jonathan frowned at Lucifer for insinuating that he may call the hounds, and when nothing happened, Jonathan blew out a breath of relief.

"This is ridiculous," said Lucifer with an amused look. "Me talking about a stain as if to convey my betrayal by a woman who was nothing more than a foul human who deserved to be punished. Besides, why would you care or be interested in anything I tell you of my past? It's not like you'll ever believe me anyway, and that's according to your own thoughts. We are, after all, sworn enemies and will never have a common ground to stand on, no matter how much I try to help you understand me. You were taught to hate me and supposedly I am to hate you as well."

"That's not exactly true," Jonathan replied, his worried look replaced by one of compassion. "I don't hate you; I more so, feel pity for you. From my viewpoint, I can't understand why you would choose this path you are now on. You had it all. You were the Head Angel, and for whatever reason, you threw it all away for greed. It completely baffles me."

Lucifer chuckled. "Well, after years and years of doing the same routine day in and day out, I grew not only bored but lonely. Which led to me reminisce about my time in Heaven and remember how God kept preaching about family and how we were all brothers and sisters. That's when I came up with the plan to start my own family. With the countless numbers of women who were either damned or slaves, I began entertaining some of the women who are now part of my world, hoping to eventually find one who could bear my child. However, I was disappointed time and time again, learning after months the chosen woman was not pregnant. I'd then simply cast the wretched failure back into Hell, where I should have left her to begin with. I'd then start all over with another one."

Jonathan shook his head in disgust.

"Jonathan, I really would've preferred not to force them back into Hell, but I simply couldn't just keep them around like trophies. Besides, I needed the next potential prospect if I wanted this to work. I know it sounds awful to tell it this way, but I thought you'd at least appreciate me telling you the truth. If you will listen without judgment until the end, then I will continue. Is that fair?"

Jonathan hesitated for a moment, but reluctantly gave a single nod of his head.

"Eventually, I did find a woman who appreciated me as much as I did her. We shared such an amazing time together, I completely forgot about wanting the child. I wish I could look back on it fondly, but everything was shattered because of a single lie. She told me she was pregnant in an attempt to solidify her position at my side, which only caused our time together to come to an abrupt halt. She wasn't aware I could hear her every deceitful thought. I was filled with such an anger, so I allowed my hounds to do what they do best. It really was a horrific thing to watch, and after she was gone, I realized I would always be alone. I refuse to ever put myself through that kind of pain ever again."

Jonathan watched as Lucifer dramatically wiped his eyes before continuing. "So, my loneliness continued for several long, agonizing months until I had an epiphany. I was at a bistro in Marseille, enjoying a cup of espresso, when I noticed a young couple a few tables away from me, clearly frustrated with one another. While listening in on their conversation, I learned the frustration stemmed from the woman announcing that she was pregnant. Clearly, this had not been what the gentleman had wanted to hear over coffee and pastries. 'How in the hell did you allow this to happen?' the man asked. When the young woman didn't answer, the man held up his left ring finger and shook it at her. 'You know my situation, and you told me this was never going to be anything more than just fun! You got pregnant on purpose, didn't you? You lied about being on the pill. I'll pay for an abortion, but after that, we are done!' Without waiting for a reply, he tossed several bills on the table, and stormed away."

Jonathan made a loud scoffing sound. "Let me guess, you came to the woman's aid, taking advantage of her misery, whispering sweet nothings in her ear until she was all used up? Then you talked her into taking her own life? Is that about the gist?"

Lucifer replied in an annoyed tone, "Do you want to hear the story or not?"

The tension between them was palpable, until at last Jonathan gave a nod of his head.

"To answer your snide questions, I have no idea what became of the couple. However, their argument made me wonder how many unwelcome children are brought into the world every day. Hundreds of thousands would be my guess. Every one of them doomed from birth and labeled as a mistake. Which made me think about all my beloved in Hell would welcome the opportunity to have a strong father figure in their life. So, I spent weeks pouring over the files of the occupants until I found two, I believed, were perfect. Their names you should already know."

"Bryce and Abel," said Jonathan without a hint of remorse for what he had done to them. Lucifer had sent them to try and capture Jonathan and kill Riley. They had almost been successful, except God chose to intervene by allowing Jonathan to listen on Riley praying for Jonathan's safety.

"Yes, those were my sons whom I adored and cherished. They brought a sense of fulfillment to my life, until you believed it was your duty to rip them apart and in turn sending them to the depths."

"No, that was *not* my duty!" said Jonathan angrily. "Me tearing them apart was on you. You sent them on that mission in hopes of capturing me and killing Riley, knowing exactly what would happen if they failed. You want me to be disgusted with how violently I ended Bryce and Abel, but I'm not! I protected Riley because I am a guardian angel, a title you will never hold because of your own arrogance. So, answer me this, Devil. Where are your so-called beloved, cherished sons Bryce and Abel now? Did you welcome them back with open arms? Or because they failed you, are they suffering the same fate as the rest of the damned? Truthfully, it makes no difference to me what you have done with your spawns, Bryce and Abel. Just know, whoever you send to hurt those I have claimed as mine, I will take great pleasure in returning them to you in pieces."

Jonathan clutched his side and cried out in agony. Confused by what was happening, Jonathan looked at Lucifer, then around the room to see if Lucifer had called his hounds. Seeing that it was just the two of them, Jonathan pulled his hand away from his side, revealing a bloodstained palm.

Lucifer gasped and then spoke in a hushed tone, "Thank you, false god, for your short-sightedness. All the countless trial and errors made this moment all the more special."

Unable to focus on what Lucifer was carrying on about, Jonathan lifted his torn shirt, revealing a deep laceration on his right side.

"Two thousand years ago, I took on the likeness of a Roman soldier and ended a false prophet's existence. His name was Jesus. Ironic that after all this time, you will share the same fate as him," Lucifer said.

Dropping his shirt and regaining control over his breathing, Jonathan remained silent, yet his eyes begged for answers. What exactly did Lucifer mean when he said Jonathan would share the same fate as Jesus?

"One down, six to go," Lucifer gloated.

Jonathan looked at Lucifer, confused about what was happening. Before he could ask, Lucifer snapped his fingers, conjuring up his beloved hounds.

Lucifer then said only one word, "Feed."

CHAPTER 20

After the full pot of coffee was gone, Maggie showed Riley how to make individual servings so he could make more for just himself. After the tutorial, Riley declared himself to be an expert barista. He then experimented by making a new flavor with each cup, while Stuart brought Maggie up to speed on everything that had gone on in her absence.

Finishing off the last of his fifth or sixth cup—having lost count with the different flavors of coffee—Riley felt amazing and completely rejuvenated. Even his feet agreed, as they danced away to some unheard rhythm of their own under the table. Stale coffee or not, Maggie's coffee maker was worth every penny in his humble opinion. Never in his life had he tasted coffee so amazing, even compared to the big chain coffee shops he used to frequent.

Looking disappointedly into his empty mug, Riley noticed his fingers, much like his feet, appeared to have a mind of their own as they tapped on the tabletop. Even though he had clearly surpassed his normal daily consumption of caffeine, Riley still wanted another cup, only a different flavor this time.

Weighing the question out carefully about whether he should have another cup, Riley finally concluded, *Why in the hell not? Your life is always going to be in shambles. You are always going to be on the run, and peace is a word found in the dictionary that only applies to those who haven't encountered the Devil. So indulge away and enjoy it while you can.*

Feeling justified by his logic, Riley went to stand, but Maggie stopped him by taking his hand in hers, giving him a questionable look.

"I think you've had enough caffeine for now, maybe even the day," said Maggie. "Let me get you some water instead."

Riley hadn't even noticed he had been sweating until he felt a bead of water slide down the side of his face. His heart was beating rapidly. He placed his index and middle fingers next to his windpipe and tried to count the beats per minute.

Stuart smiled. "Are you hearing colors conversing among one another yet?"

Maggie laughed as she came back to the table and placed a cup of water in front of Riley. "Drink this. It should help level out the insane amount of caffeine that you just inhaled within the last hour."

"How much did I drink?" Riley asked, then took a long gulp of water.

"Well, you practically consumed the first pot of coffee all by yourself," Stuart said. "Then you concocted every flavor the 'futuristic coffee maker,' in your words, would produce."

"I called it what?" asked Riley, wondering if they were teasing him.

He was answered by another round of laughter from Maggie and Stuart.

Riley thought he had been acting perfectly normal. Apparently, he hadn't been. Wondering if Kratos had also noticed his strange behavior, he looked down to find the hound's dead eyes already locked on him.

Ignoring the damn useless hound, Riley drained the cup of

water, hoping when he came up for air his body would return to normal.

"I don't think you have any clue how funny you can be without even trying," Maggie teased, giving his shoulder a playful punch.

"What in the hell is wrong with your coffee maker?" asked Riley sharply, the irritation rising in his voice.

"You mean, my 'futuristic coffee maker'?" Maggie mockingly replied, earning another deep laugh from Stuart.

Angry at being used as a punchline, Riley began to stand, but he stopped when Kratos issued a low, threatening growl.

"Oh, shut up, you damn mutt!" Riley spat.

Kratos let loose his signature ear-piercing bark, causing Maggie and Stuart to cower in their chairs and cover their ears, while Riley just glared at Kratos. Kratos then moved directly in front of him. Kratos's ears were plastered to the sides of his head, his mouth partially opened to reveal several rows of sharp canines. The deep growl altered into a sinister sound not made by any normal animal.

Seeing Maggie and Stuart's helpless, frightened expressions, Riley decided Kratos had just threatened him for the last time. "Enough!" screamed Riley, kicking his chair backward and bouncing it off the wall ten feet behind him. "You want me to be afraid? Well, fuck you! What do you think you could do to me that hasn't already been done? I've lost my wife, Granny, and Jonathan because of your creator!"

Kratos continued to growl, even snapping at Riley, but then strangely backed away. Too enraged to care of the repercussions, Riley hovered over Kratos, matching him step for step.

"You want to end my life? Well, I'm standing right here, so do it, you worthless piece of shit!"

When Kratos's back legs met the wall, it startled him, sending his body into a blur of movement as he turned to attack whatever had snuck up behind him. What followed was a loud crunch and tearing sound. He'd bit a large hole in the wall.

Riley held his ground. "You ever threaten me or my friends again, and I will find a way to send you back to Hell myself! I don't care what it takes. Even if it costs my own life, I will end your miserable existence!"

Kratos was now poised to strike if Riley advanced any further. The two came to a stalemate, both staring daggers at one another, clearly wanting the other dead. After what felt like minutes, Kratos at last acquiesced and slowly bowed his head to the floor in submission.

With that, Riley felt his anger begin to subside, only to immediately be replaced by embarrassment from how he had just acted out. Slowly stepping away from Kratos, Riley kept his eyes averted from Maggie and Stuart. He retrieved the chair off the ground, finding it had left a large dent in the wall where it made contact. He wondered what they would say now that everything had calmed down. *How could you be so careless? We were joking around, and you flipped out just because Kratos intimidated you! Seriously, Riley, what was the purpose of your action except to scare us and put our lives even more in jeopardy?*

Clutching the back of the chair, Riley closed his eyes and hoped Maggie would just tell him to leave and put an end to this debacle. He could no longer smell the demon, but with a little luck, maybe he could still locate it.

A hand tentatively touched his shoulder, accompanied by Stuart's soft voice. "Riley, I want you to know I will never judge you. I can't even begin to imagine what you have lived through. I still have trouble wrapping my head around what you've already told me. I would, however, like to offer you some advice, something I usually shy away from doing. Although now I believe it would be beneficial in regard to this crazy little scenario, we find ourselves in."

Still turned away from Stuart, Riley gave a single nod of his head.

"Riley, you know a little about the abuse I endured in my childhood, but what you don't know is what helped me survive it. You see, in eighth grade at youth camp, I found God. Becoming a Christian completely changed my life. I still struggle daily, just as everyone else, but what helps me during my struggles is something you're already familiar with. God grants peace to those who are humble enough to ask for it. I know I'm only a stranger to you, but we are brothers in Christ. You are loved and valued, Riley."

Stuart's words flooded Riley with comfort, when only moments prior he had been so quick to speculate what Stuart might say to him. Taking even himself by surprise, Riley wrapped Stuart in a tight embrace. The pent-up anger and contempt he had toward Kratos, losing his wife, Granny, and now Jonathan, plus everything else going wrong in his life in that moment—it all came flooding out of him and left Riley sobbing into Stuart's shoulder. He realized he was truly among friends.

"You are going to be okay, Riley," said Stuart, returning the embrace. "You've been through a lot, and it can't be easy dealing with a creature created by the Devil. The hellish mutt needed to be put in its place. I'm just glad you had the courage to do it, because if I would have tried, right now you would be searching for bleach and large plastic bags to take care of whatever remained of me!"

Just as quickly as the tears of frustration had burst forth, tears of laughter now poured down his cheeks. Riley felt accepted and comfortable with Stuart. Even if he had only known him a short time, he couldn't imagine going through the rest of his life without Stuart being a part of it. He had no judgement, but rather an easy candor about him, where he could turn something negative into a positive with just the right amount of dry humor.

Stuart stepped back. "I'm sorry for my flippant remark about hearing colors. I have a tendency to goad someone when I find a situation funny. Which gets me in trouble, especially when I'm trying to make a good impression on someone who appears to have a special place in Mags's life."

Riley wanted to clarify to Stuart that he and Maggie were just friends and were only together because of Jonathan, but instead replied, "Thank you." He then quickly added, "If you and Maggie have finished going over everything, I can try to answer your questions and tell you anything you want to know about Jonathan and the rest of the paranormal events I have been through and survived."

Stuart looked down at his watch and made a face. "I want to hear your entire story. However, if we don't leave right now, we are going to make some FBI agents very unhappy. How about tonight after we are finished putting out fires? Unless, you have other matters you need to take care of."

"Believe it or not, my schedule is completely clear," Riley said.

"Perfect, because I have so many more questions, but I need to stay by Mags's side. Hopefully, I can keep her from screwing up her life any more than she already has."

"Still sitting right over here," said Maggie. Her body language—arms crossed—showed how frightened she was by the outburst.

This made Riley feel even worse about adding to her uneasiness. "Do you need me to leave so you can have this floor to yourselves?"

"No, just make yourself at home. We're going down a couple of floors to the boardroom," said Stuart. He then hugged Riley and whispered, "Later, let's pray together, and then I want to know as much as you can tell me."

Riley smiled, unable to believe how lucky he was to have met Stuart. "I look forward to it."

Stuart gave Riley's shoulder a squeeze, then said to Maggie, "I'll be right outside." He left the two of them alone.

"Don't give the damaged wall another thought," Maggie quickly said. "I will get it taken care of immediately. Besides, Kratos needed to be put in his place and I'm thankful."

"Maggie," Riley interjected. "Slow down. You have more important matters to take care of, and you don't need to be afraid. Just tell the FBI the truth but leave out the part of Jonathan being a guardian angel."

Maggie offered a polite smile, so Riley took both of her hands in his for assurance. "You couldn't have asked for a better friend to be by your side than Stuart. Just lean on him when you feel too overwhelmed, and everything will work out fine."

Maggie blew out a hard sigh. "He is pretty amazing. Happy that you two got along so quickly."

"If I didn't know any better, I would think he isn't from this planet. Like, maybe I just met another guardian angel," said Riley.

Maggie laughed. "If I hadn't known him practically all my life, I would think the same thing. I do know one thing for certain, and that is I definitely don't deserve him." She broke eye contact for a quick moment. "Um . . . I do have one small request, if that's okay."

"Name it," said Riley.

"Would you mind staying in the suite for the time being? I will try to make it back as soon as possible so you don't feel trapped but having you walking around will lead to more questions than I have answers to right now. And then there's the matter of Kratos."

Looking around the massive kitchen, Riley made a disgusted

face and shook his head. "Well, I guess I can try to make do, but this will be highly uncomfortable. Do you at least have someone who can draw me a bath?"

This earned him a smile. "I better go, so wish me luck," Maggie said.

Riley gave her a quick hug and watched them leave. After the door closed, he glanced at Kratos, who hadn't moved since their altercation. Having been too caught up in the moment to care, Riley now saw the damage Kratos had done to the wall with one ferocious bite. Not only was there a three-foot gap of sheetrock missing, but two of the wood support beams had been snapped in half.

What in the hell was I even thinking threatening one of the Devil's hounds? thought Riley.

Shuddering at the realization, Riley looked down at his dirt-smeared jeans. The stains held the harsh reminder of how he had failed at his attempt to save Jonathan after being coerced into betraying him. Lucifer had orchestrated the outcome perfectly, presenting Riley with the impossible choice between the fate of Maggie or Jonathan. If he had chosen Jonathan, then Maggie would have suffered for the rest of eternity in Hell, and since she wasn't a believer, there would be no way to rescue her. That thought alone would have driven Riley insane, which left Jonathan having to pay the price for Riley's choice.

Closing his eyes, Riley said a quick prayer for Jonathan, hopeful that his friend could hold on to his sanity until they could rescue him and not submit to what the Devil desired.

Seeing the complexity of the situation, Riley at last acknowledged he was preparing to lead them both on a suicide mission. Maggie would follow him either out of guilt or because of a foolish promise she'd made to Jonathan, believing that Riley would keep her safe. A task he wouldn't be able to do on his own.

Swallowing his pride, Riley stared down at Kratos in defeat. "I'm sorry I've been so hostile toward you, but I don't see how we could be more than enemies when the being who created you has stolen my world from me. I can't comprehend why you're even here, but I'm taking a leap of faith you're here to protect Maggie and me. If not, I think you would've already killed us. I may be wrong, because your previous master uses manipulation and pain to get what he wants. But I'm going out on a limb and choosing to trust you."

Riley considered everything he had learned from Jonathan, with the most important lesson to always be prepared. Such a simple motto, even Boy Scouts were taught it at a very young age, and yet here he was, a full-grown man who still couldn't grasp it. What Riley thought he knew regarding good and evil, didn't equate with his current predicament. His fate was now tied to the unlikeliest of allies.

"Even if I don't fully trust you, I will never force you to do something that could cause you harm. And I will never force you to do anything on purpose to hurt or betray you just to benefit myself. But I'm asking, will you help me?"

In the blink of an eye, Kratos stood directly in front of him, staring straight into his eyes. The eerie quickness the hound possessed was faster than anything Riley had encountered of the supernatural, including Jonathan. Without giving it a second thought, Riley stretched out his hand to Kratos in a sign of trust. After several sniffs, Kratos produced a large black tongue and licked his hand once, his red eyes never wavering from Riley's. His upper lip pulled back again, revealing a mouthful of long, razor-sharp canines.

"Thank you," said Riley, finding solace in the cold, menacing dead stare of Kratos. "I'm coming, Jonathan, and I'm bringing a part of Hell with me."

CHAPTER 21

S till seated on the couch, Bob prayed silently for the safety of his wife and daughter, willingly offering himself up for sacrifice in their stead. The loud knocks from earlier were replaced by the sounds of what Bob assumed was someone kicking the door. Moments later, the wood frame gave way to the disturbance of three men and a woman. Bob knew each of them by name since they all had gone to his electronic store for one reason or another.

"Patty, Mitch, Chuck, and Justin, I wish I could say it's good to see you, but I know why you are here."

They all wore the expressions of grizzled veterans who had seen too many acts of violence. But when they heard their names, they snapped out of their trance.

"I'll willingly come with you without any resistance," Bob said. "My only request is that you spare my wife. I'll gladly give you my life and soul in exchange for you to just turn a blind eye and forget she's even here. She is lying completely helpless in the other room. Her fight with cancer is almost over. I selfishly held out hope that she would recover. It's only a matter of time now, which is why I stayed. I couldn't bear the thought of abandoning her to die alone."

Patty collapsed into the chair opposite of Bob and dropped her head, clearly disgusted with her new role as henchman. Chuck, Justin, and Mitch were also silent, as though they were uncertain with how to proceed. Bob capitalized on their silence by standing and walking to the door, hoping they would follow and heed his request.

Reluctantly, the four followed him out into the night. A somewhat comical thought occurred to Bob. Usually, it was the captors telling the captive it was time to go, not the other way around. It wasn't as if an inmate on death row ever complained, "Hey, are we going to have an execution or not?"

However, Bob was just thankful to have gotten them out of the house, and his wife was safe for the time being. He turned and looked at them. "If you want to lead, I will follow, but I suggest two of you walk in front of me and the other two behind me. From all the old movies I've seen, that is usually the arrangement."

As the four took up their new positions, the house across the street suddenly caught fire, stopping them in their tracks. Black smoke poured out from the bottom windows as a large man nonchalantly walked out the front door, followed by a naked man and a woman whom Bob recognized. It was Miranda, George's wife, one of his favorite employees.

As they drew closer, Bob thought, *How had she gotten herself mixed up in all of this? And where is George?*

The handful of times they had interacted, she was pleasant enough but was always in a hurry. George, who was completely smitten with her, showered her with praise anytime Bob asked how she was transitioning to their small little town. He always said how supportive and unselfish Miranda was with her time, how she went out of her way to ensure George's ailing parents were taken care of at the nursing home.

George always needed Sundays off to attend church, which was something Bob knew wouldn't sit well with this particular group. Seeing Miranda with them now didn't fit George's narrative of her at all, and since he was nowhere in sight, a bad feeling washed over Bob.

Patty, Mitch, Justin, and Chuck knelt in front of the large man, while Bob remained standing. His thoughts were too preoccupied with what happened to George and the strange naked man.

The new self-proclaimed leader of the town stepped around them and stared down at Bob in disapproval. "My name is Legionaries, and apparently you are too stupid to follow the very simple guidelines I've set in place for those who don't want to worship me. You will serve as a martyr to all others who doubt me when I tell them the fate that awaits them should they choose not to follow me."

Bob's thoughts bounced to the safety of his wife and daughter and how surreal this all was. He wasn't afraid of Legionaries, nor did he fear death. His only hope was to buy enough time for his daughter to leave town unnoticed and for his wife to be left alone. If it meant he had to die to achieve this, then so be it.

"Take him to the town square for execution," said Legionaries.

Dropping his head in defeat, Bob hastily headed in the direction of the town square, hoping his body language appeared believable. He had always been a docile man throughout his life, avoiding any sort of confrontation and making sure to head off the problem before it arose. Unfortunately, this time he had made a crucial and very costly mistake. His only thoughts were for his wife and daughter's safety.

"Stop!" Legionaries thundered behind him.

Bob abruptly turned as fear coursed through every fiber of his being.

Legionaries grinned at him, telling Bob that his hidden intentions had been found out. "Are you certain there was no one else inside the house?" Legionaries directed the question at Patty, Mitch, Justin, and Chuck.

Bob foolishly hoped his four captors would help him, but to no avail. They all remained silent, unable to look at Legionaries.

"That's what I thought," Legionaries sarcastically said. "Patty, you are to go with Tristan. He will make sure you do the job right this time. Tristan, you know what I expect to be done."

"Patty, don't do this!" Bob screamed. Legionaries smiled at him with satisfaction. "Please, Legionaries, take my life but spare my wife. She's too sick to be moved or we would have left. We just aren't capable."

Legionaries just smiled at him. Bob's fear was replaced by anger he didn't know he was even capable of. He lunged at Legionaries but was blocked by the outstretched arms of Chuck and Mitch.

"You are supposed to be a god," he shouted. "But I know what your kind is most afraid of."

Bob hadn't even had time to realize what happened, but he was now lying flat on his back, looking up at a distorted view of Legionaries. A heavy taste of iron filled his mouth, and before he could locate the source, darkness fell upon him.

CHAPTER 22

Legionaries fumed as he watched Tristan practically drag Patty away. He then turned and addressed the three remaining followers. "If you ever disobey one of my orders again, you will suffer the same as those who oppose me. Do you understand me?"

In unison, Mitch, Justin, and Chuck responded, "Yes, Master."

"Good. Now take this non-worshipper to the town square."

All three jumped to attention and hoisted Bob onto their shoulders, then made their way for the town square. Five minutes into the walk, the three began to argue back and forth. Unfortunately for Bob, this was about the time he started coming back around.

"What's happening?" Bob asked with a thick tongue. He was quickly silenced by another devastating blow from the back of Legionaries's hand, sending the entire group crashing to the ground.

Legionaries said through clenched teeth, "First, you disobeyed a direct order from me, and now you feel you have the right to complain after I give you a second chance? There will not be a third. Tomorrow only one of you will wake. Which one of you it will be depends on who pleases me the most. Unless you want to die right here and now, pick up that filthy non-worshipper and do as I have commanded."

The three exchanged nervous looks before bolting upright, and to Legionaries's amusement, they lifted Bob onto their shoulders and began running. Chuckling at this, Legionaries resumed his casual stride, only to notice Miranda walking dutifully alongside him.

Legionaries assumed that the moment he had stopped paying attention to her she would sneak away, except here she was. Something he found even more odd was that after she executed her husband, she had not succumbed to his pulse like she once had or like the rest of the followers were. Instead, she had fallen to the ground and begun to doubt him. This was until he had off-handedly decided to share the birth of Tristan with her.

He was supposed to feel nothing for his followers. After all, they only existed to serve him. Yet when he felt her small hand slip into his, he didn't reprimand her or pull away. Instead, they continued like this all the way to the town square without saying a word. When they arrived, she let go first without him having to tell her to.

Such a small, simple action made Legionaries question why he was even allowing this follower to cloud his thinking and his vision for the future. Now, as he watched her disappear into the rest of his followers, he found himself caressing the hand she had been holding, wishing she were still by his side.

Throughout his two thousand years of existence, Legionaries watched the humans and wondered what it would feel like to have companionship. Even most of the damned had experienced some form of companionship before becoming residents of Hell, all except for him. He had been nothing more than just a simple lackey who was only kept around to be abused and tormented by Lucifer. He had no understanding of his past or where he came from, only that, according to his alter ego, Legion, he apparently once ruled a small kingdom in Gadarenes. Now having his first taste of companionship, he wanted more. Much more. This thought brought a smile to his face.

The town square was packed with his followers organizing the non-worshippers into a tight bunch. One female follower was attempting to light a large wood pile on fire that had been strewn together, only to stop when she made eye contact with Legionaries.

Letting the smile drop from his face, Legionaries ascended the small grass mound in the middle of the town square, stopping at the peak where the broken statue stood. Looking out at his followers, Legionaries found eager faces staring at him, anticipating his next order. They reminded him of Lucifer's hounds, just waiting to be told what to do next. The appetite for bloodlust consumed their thoughts.

The non-worshippers, consisting of mostly elderly men and women either too weak or stubborn to leave, were all bunched together in front, not a dry eye among them as they pleaded for mercy.

"We all know one another!" a short Hispanic woman was saying, her body posture projecting confidence, her wide eyes telling a different story. "I want everyone to stop this nonsense before it's too late!"

An older gentleman singled out one of Legionaries's followers. "Jimmy, this isn't right, and you know it! Hell, you have known me your whole life. I'm not just some next-door neighbor. Your parents trusted me to babysit you when you were younger. Now I want you to stop this right now! Do you understand me, young man?"

Jimmy appeared confused as to what was happening, until Legionaries sent out a pulse, bringing him back under his control. Giving a shake of his head, Jimmy offered a sympathetic smile, then landed a thunderous left punch to the side of the old man's chin. "Mr. Baker, you, old, senile bastard, I'm not a little kid anymore!"

The other followers, having witnessed this outburst, laughed at how Mr. Baker's unconscious body came to rest. Both legs shook from the nerves short-circuiting in his brain before going still.

Legionaries held up his hands to silence the crowd, all except for the soon-to-be martyrs, whose sobbing had now turned into fits of hysteria. Glaring down at them, Legionaries waited for several long minutes until they quieted into soft, incoherent whimpers.

"Jimmy," Legionaries coolly said. "Nicely done. Now take that lifeless corpse and place him on top of the woodpile as fodder for the bonfire we will be having later."

Without hesitating, Jimmy hoisted Mr. Baker over his shoulder, sauntered over to the wood pile, and with help from another man, placed Mr. Baker on top of it.

"I look around and see how happy you are with yourselves. You have cleaned out the first neighborhood and captured nineteen non-worshippers without any casualties on our side."

Legionaries clapped, and his followers joined in, several shouting triumphantly. After a while, the shouts died down and silence ensued. Legionaries's claps came slower and slower, mocking his followers for their overzealous behavior.

"When I walked the streets of this town before I ever made my presence known, do you know what I realized? Your town consists of four large neighborhoods, which inhabits a little under two thousand occupants."

Scanning their faces, Legionaries made eye contact with Miranda, who gave a simple nod of her head. Returning the nod, Legionaries didn't bother analyzing why her opinion even mattered to him.

"Slaves, I didn't come here with the expectation of being satisfied with overthrowing one neighborhood. I told you from the beginning, I'm here to claim this town for my own. If you want to find satisfaction in one small victory, then take it from this: we are all still here. No one from our side has been killed yet. However, notice how I said . . . yet?"

Legionaries pulsed, and the followers' faces went from uncertain back to determined. The martyrs were still sobbing, with a few of them saying a single word: "Mercy."

Curious if this time Miranda had been affected, Legionaries made eye contact with her, finding her eyes were clear but fiercely loyal. Then, as if to prove her devotion to him, she gave another nod of her head and a smile played at the corners of her mouth.

Not able to help himself, Legionaries returned the smile, then dared to think, *Maybe I can have it all. Power and companionship. Maybe, just maybe.*

CHAPTER 23

Greed (noun)
1: a selfish and excessive desire for more of
    something (such as money) than is needed.

Jonathan was both mentally and physically exhausted from trying to keep the onslaught of hounds off him. He hadn't gotten a moment to register what Lucifer had meant by, "One down, six to go."

"Enough," said Lucifer, causing the hounds to immediately disappear.

After Jonathan was sure this wasn't just a trick, he collapsed to the floor, his legs sprawled out before him, coming to rest where others had their blood spilled.

Lucifer came forth, staring hungrily at Jonathan's right side. The wound had healed but left a scar just as the black tear had.

Jonathan was covered in sticky, warm blood, his clothes hanging on to him in shreds. Tearing his shirt free, Jonathan wiped his face as realization came over him. *One down, six to go.* Had Lucifer been referring to the seven deadly sins, and if he had, what importance did they play in Jonathan's current predicament?

Lucifer squatted a few feet away, his black eyes still locked onto Jonathan's side. Jonathan could see Lucifer was bursting to share his revelation.

"One down, six to go," said Jonathan, wanting to draw the answer out of him.

Lucifer's mouth opened, as if to answer, but then closed.

Jonathan prodded him. "Want to clue me in on why you referred to the sins, which only came into existence because of your evil and deceitful ways?"

Lucifer smiled. "Oh no, Jonathan. I may have planted the seed of evil, sure, but it was the humans' twisted minds that nurtured it into the seven deadly sins. They've caused evil to grow so fiercely that it now runs rampant everywhere in the world, and no one really even seems to care. Sometimes, the human race surprises even me."

Realizing that he wasn't going to get a real response, Jonathan wadded up the remains of his filthy shirt and tossed it at Lucifer's feet. Resting his head against the wall, Jonathan looked up at the ceiling for a moment, then back at Lucifer. "This is just a guess, but you must believe if you can make me commit all seven sins, it will be the key to unlocking my powers. Am I right?"

Without confirming or denying whether he was correct, Lucifer asked, "How long do you believe I allowed this last torture session to go on?"

Jonathan knew what Lucifer's intentions were by asking the question. Instead of continuing to pry, he decided it was best to just play along, at least for now. Considering Lucifer's question, Jonathan honestly had no idea. Time worked in Hell the same as it did in Heaven, except a minute felt like an hour in Hell because there was no peace or love.

"An hour maybe, two at most," said Jonathan.

Lucifer flashed a broad, menacing smile. "Why don't you take one more guess. Maybe this time aim lower. And I do mean much, much lower."

Jonathan considered. All of God's creatures had a breaking point. He wondered just how much more he could endure, for his body was physically taxed and his mind was beginning to play tricks on him. What made it all worse was that the individual tormenting him appeared to have figured out how to use the sins to benefit his purpose.

"I honestly don't know, so just tell me," Jonathan said. He could hear the defeat in his tone.

Lucifer's smile slid off his face. "Well, Jonathan, I'm sorry to be the bearer of bad news, but you were only off by a little." He held his thumb and pointer finger an inch apart to show just how small of a margin. "Thirteen minutes. No, more. No, less. It was thirteen minutes on the dot. I told you to aim lower. I just hate to see you so disappointed and wish—"

Seeing how much enjoyment Lucifer was getting out of his misery, Jonathan looked away. The answer both shocked and mentally broke Jonathan, as he tried to wrap his thoughts around the minuscule amount of time that had passed.

"Just stop," said Jonathan. "The sound of your voice is both tiresome and annoying. Besides, we both know what you are after, and we both know I'm unable to give them to you. Torturing me will only bring you some form of satisfaction, but you know how this will eventually end, with you disappointed, frustrated, and wondering just how this all went so wrong."

Lucifer abruptly stood and peered down at Jonathan. "Perhaps, but only time will tell. For now, let's venture outside what you have come to call my torture room, and I will show you something that isn't written in any history book." Before Jonathan could answer, Lucifer grabbed his hand, and with one quick movement, jerked him to his feet. "I think you are going to like this."

Lucifer blew across the palm of his free hand, and shiny red and black dust particles suddenly appeared and danced across the room. When the room had filled, the dust particles slowly expanded in size, somehow capturing the light and blanketing it into a darkness with such intensity that Jonathan could physically feel the weight under the blackness. As eerie as it felt, Jonathan welcomed the change since it didn't cause him to feel pain.

A small stream of light crept its way into the darkness, growing until the light overtook the darkness and brought forth a memory of Lucifer's past. Jonathan could see that Lucifer's memory was when he still resided in Heaven. It started out with Lucifer speaking to another angel while walking down a street. Jonathan recognized the street, as he had walked it many times himself. The gold cobblestones couldn't be mistaken for anything ever constructed by humankind. It led up to a massive auditorium where angels met each night to spend time with God.

The meetings were not structured. However, they usually began with songs of praise, followed by angels sharing stories about their humans. Some were heartbreaking to hear, especially when an angel told of how their human had passed away, and they would never be able to see them again. Other angels shared stories of hope, love, and sometimes extreme humor. Jonathan missed those days now more than ever.

This made Jonathan wonder what occurred in the meetings during Lucifer's time, when humans hadn't been spoken into existence yet.

Suddenly, something slammed into the side of Jonathan's face, setting off an intense ringing in his ears. He pressed his hands to the sides of his head. When the ringing subsided and he could focus, Jonathan tasted the salty thickness of iron filling his mouth, causing him to spit several times.

Lucifer's black eyes bore into him. "I'm trying to show you what really happened to me and why I'm now forced to play the role of your nemesis. So, either stop letting your mind wander and give me your full attention, or we can return to the torture room. I'm sure my hounds would be more than happy to see you."

Although Jonathan felt physically capable now that his body had some time to regenerate, he knew he wasn't mentally up for the task of battling off the hounds. Spitting out another wad of blood, Jonathan dragged a hand across his mouth and focused once more on Lucifer's memory. He didn't recognize the angel who was speaking to Lucifer but could tell from his body language that he was clearly frustrated. He listened in.

"Lucifer, I can't believe God grew tired of us so quickly. Callously announcing he'll be creating some new being in his image and they'll be called humans. And as if that wasn't enough, we're to serve and look after these humans as their guardians even though we were created first!"

"Calm yourself, Nicholas," said Lucifer. "Our Father's design is perfect. We aren't expected to understand it, just to trust and—"

"Calm myself?" Nicholas snapped. "How am I to remain calm now that we're just being pushed aside? You're the Head Angel. Father gave you this title because he values your input. So, speak with him the next time you are alone or else!"

Lucifer grabbed Nicholas's arm. "Or else what? Are you threatening me? Or are you trying to start an uprising against Father? Do not ever speak to me in this way again. I will talk to Father and tell him of our concerns in due time. For now, I'm only interested in learning more about the creation of these humans and what exactly Father has planned for us and them."

Nicholas shook loose of Lucifer's grip, walked a few frustrated steps away, and stared out into the distance. Several moments passed, then Nicholas turned and smiled at Lucifer. His smile said everything was okay, but his eyes held the promise of a distant storm brewing.

Nicholas walked back to Lucifer, stopping only when they were nose to nose. He leaned in and whispered, "I'm not the only angel who feels this way. There are more of us who share these concerns." He took a step back. He had a smug look on his face now that he'd backed Lucifer into a corner.

"Nicholas, what have you done?" Lucifer said.

When Nicholas remained silent, new lines of worry etched into Lucifer's brow. "Are you telling me there will be an uprising if Father goes through with his plans?"

Instead of replying, Nicholas briskly walked the rest of the way to the auditorium, leaving Lucifer behind.

The scene faded, and with it came the same darkness from before, once again engulfing Jonathan and restricting his movements.

"Once we went inside the auditorium, the rest of this gets a little redundant, with the songs, stories, etcetera," said Lucifer. "So, let me fast forward to where things go awry."

Lucifer snapped his fingers, causing the darkness to release its hold as another memory came to life. God the Father was sitting on the steps that led to the podium in the auditorium. He wore the same silky white robe as the rest of the angels. However, his features were partially hidden by a shimmering light that offered pure peace. Jonathan immediately began to prostrate himself, but Lucifer jerked him back upright.

"I don't give a damn about you wanting to show your allegiance to your God," said Lucifer. "Last warning, and then it's back to the hounds. Now pay attention!"

Jonathan could vaguely hear Lucifer despite their proximity. Even though this was only a past vision, he was still completely unworthy to look upon the face of the one true God. Jonathan gave a single nod of his head to inform Lucifer that he understood.

The scene continued, with God the Father speaking calmly. "I have thought more about the creation of humans, and I have decided to start with just one. I will give him the name of Adam, which will mean *man*."

One of the angels in the auditorium stood and spoke loudly, "Father, have you grown tired of us?"

As shocked as Jonathan was to see one of his own behaving this way, he kept his eyes on Father God, who only smiled at the angel and called him by name. "Patrick, I could never grow tired of you or any of you. I cherish you all just as I always have and as I will cherish my new creation."

"Then why do you ask us to serve these humans?" Patrick continued, an edge in his voice.

Two other angels stood, voicing their agreement with Patrick, quickly followed by several more. Each one cried out for understanding as to why they were being cast aside.

Lucifer, seated in the front row, looked around, bewildered at how his fellow angels were behaving. He then locked eyes with Nicholas a few rows back, who wore the same smug look from earlier, as if to say, "I told you this was going to happen, and you wouldn't listen."

Nicholas stood and gave a single wave of his hand, silencing the auditorium. "Father, I think I can speak for everyone here when I say we love you and are grateful you have given us life. It is and always will be our honor to serve you. However, several of us now fear we no longer hold value in your eyes, especially if you go through with the creation of the human race. Why would you force us to serve and even bow down to this creation? Father, our allegiance is to you, and we will not bow to anyone or anything other than you!"

The boldness from Nicholas's statement started a buzz in the auditorium, which gradually grew to be thunderous.

"My special, beautiful, chosen children, I am not asking you to serve the humans," said God the Father. "As I said, I am starting with just one, whom I will create in my image, and I hope you will love him as I know I will. Always remember I value, love, and cherish each and every one of you, and I will never think of you as replaceable."

Clearly frustrated with God the Father's answer, Nicholas cut in. "I don't think you realize the awkward position you will be putting us in. At the very least, let us have dominance over humans instead of having us watch after them. Why do we need to look after them when they have you? I don't think it's asking too much."

God stood and held out his arms to reveal unblemished wrists, causing Jonathan to suck in a sharp breath. "Father," Jonathan said meekly, knowing one day soon the unblemished wrists would be pierced by the very creation currently being discussed.

Jonathan could feel Lucifer's eyes on him, knowing Lucifer could see the significance behind those unblemished palms. He was the very reason why sin existed in today's world.

"Nicholas, where is this frustration coming from?" asked God the Father.

"Him." Nicholas pointed an accusatory finger at Lucifer. "Your appointed Head Angel now remains silent and cowering behind a curtain of ignorance, when it was he who first voiced his concern. He began holding private meetings behind locked doors after you announced your plan for a new creation."

This brought Lucifer to his feet. "Nicholas, that is not true!" He then addressed Father God, "May I, please, have a quick word in private?"

Nicholas fired back. "Is it not true that just earlier you stopped me before we entered, telling me it was time for us to address the issue regarding humans in the hierarchy structure?"

Patrick, who had started this rift, now stood. "You also spoke to me in private, cornering me and asking if I understood the logic of our Father's choices."

This started an uproar, as angels now divided on both sides of the issue spoke angrily to one another. God looked at Lucifer, clearly concerned with how everything had transpired.

"Why did you not come to me first?" God asked.

The intense conversations all fell silent at once, having witnessed Father God's hurt from the actions of a few rebellious angels.

"Have I not always listened and encouraged you? Even going so far as to place you as the Head Angel because I believed you to be worthy?"

Lucifer looked at the faces of his fellow angels. Several were smiling amusingly at him, eagerly awaiting the fallout to occur, while the rest glared at him in disdain.

Turning to face God, Lucifer pleaded, desperation rising in his voice, "Please, give me a moment alone to explain. I don't—"

God cut him off, speaking with such an intensity it caused every angel in the auditorium to cower. "I will not grant you a private audience away from our brethren. That is exactly how this whole misunderstanding got started in the first place. So, Lucifer, you've been scheming behind my back? Your liar's tongue has done more damage than a blade ever could."

"Stop," said Jonathan, frustrated with himself for letting his guard down and almost believing what he was seeing.

Lucifer waved his hand, dismissing the vision. They were back in the torture room.

"You honestly expect me to believe God the Father, the creator of the heavens and Earth, not only didn't have the foresight to know what was actually happening, but would forever punish you based on the lies of a few? You're pathetic."

Under different circumstances, Jonathan knew how he would have handled this situation, He visualized pounding Lucifer into submission until he begged for mercy, then dragging Lucifer's limp body down into the pits of Hell so the damned could show him the true meaning of the word *pain*.

"You are fortunate that God is merciful," Jonathan said, "because I know I wouldn't be if I was in his position. I would not only take your kingdom away from you, but I'd make it my own. Just so I could watch the damned tear you limb from limb, ensuring God the Father would never have to deal with you ever again!"

Lucifer held up two fingers, and a large knowing grin spread across his face. "Your thoughts and words betray you with the sin called greed. Two down, only five more to go, Jonathan."

Before Jonathan could realize his mistake, an invisible blunt object pierced his side. As the object left him, Jonathan was overcome by an empty feeling, as if part of his soul had been stolen from him. The pain from before roared back to life with such a ferocity, and Jonathan released a scream so violent that white flashing lights danced across his vision. Each painstaking breath tore him down and exposed him for who he truly was a broken, fallen angel who had been reduced to pleading with his adversary for mercy. Jonathan thought he heard someone sobbing, but just before he passed out from the pain, he realized the sobs were coming from his own mouth.

CHAPTER 24

The elevator journey from Maggie's suite to the boardroom passed in twenty seconds of silence and without incident. Stuart knew that before any big meeting, Maggie would vomit from getting so worked up from the stress and overthinking the situation. No matter how prepared she was, it was her unusual ritual.

Today was different. Stuart was a little afraid for Maggie because "game-face ready" hadn't occurred. It was a phrase the two of them used when referencing Maggie's ritual.

When the elevator doors opened, Stuart stepped out into an empty corridor, praying that the time Maggie had spent away from the company with Riley and dealing with the paranormal had taught her business meetings were minor details in the importance of one's life.

"Just be as truthful and forthcoming as possible," said Stuart. After what he'd seen and heard over the past hour, he quickly added, "Just not too truthful." The last thing he needed to deal with was Maggie coming across as some crazed lunatic, proving to the FBI that the tabloids had been correct in saying she had a breakdown.

When Maggie didn't reply, Stuart glanced over his shoulder and found he was talking to himself. Hurrying back to the elevator, Stuart stuck out an arm to prevent the doors from closing. Maggie lay crumpled in a corner, trembling uncontrollably, looking as if she were on the verge of a panic attack.

Stepping back onto the elevator, Stuart pressed the "close door" button, followed by the red "stop" button. Opening the compartment housing the security phone, Stuart lifted it off its cradle just as it began to ring. After providing the safe words to the security officer on the other end, Stuart placed the phone back on its cradle, looked briefly at his distorted image on the elevator door, and whispered a silent prayer asking God for strength.

Having talked his mom through plenty of panic attacks after what they had lived through with his father, Stuart was confident he could help Maggie. He sat in front of her and took her hands in his. When Maggie tried to pull away, Stuart held firm until Maggie relaxed.

"Do you remember when I first transferred to Taupe City Elementary? We were in second grade, and after I'd been there for a bit, we sort of became best friends. At least you were mine. Then one day at recess, you asked me how come I missed so many days of school, to which I replied with what I had been programmed to say."

Maggie's breathing was returning to normal. Stuart continued, "I said, I suffer from intense headaches which keep me indoors."

Maggie made eye contact for a split-second before looking away.

"You then asked if I had ever tried headache meds. I hadn't been prompted on how to reply to this question because everyone else just took me at my word. You were the first person to actually show any kind of concern for my well-being, aside from my mom. I remember looking back at you completely dumbfounded, wondering why no one had ever taken an interest in helping me. When I didn't answer, you told me not to worry because you had plenty of headache meds at home since your mommy also had bad headaches, and that you would bring me some so I wouldn't have to miss anymore school."

Maggie finally looked at Stuart, tears in her eyes, telling him to finish the rest of the story, despite her already knowing what happened next.

"I didn't feel like playing with the rest of our classmates, so you took my hand and led me away. When we were finally alone, I could no longer stay silent from the war raging inside of me and opened up to you about why I missed school. I remember crying and shaking, much like you are now, when I said my daddy was a very mean daddy who hit me and my mommy. We were so young, Maggie, but you still somehow knew what to do and how to handle the situation. You embraced me and reassured me everything was going to be okay.

"Later that night, police officers came to my house and took my dad away. I had never been so afraid in my life when they wrestled him to the ground to put the handcuffs on him. I wasn't afraid because he was leaving, but I was afraid because of what he promised as he was being taken away. Yelling at me, saying how he wished I had never been born, and how I was a mistake he would remedy once he got out of jail. I couldn't sleep that night. I was too busy worrying that he would somehow escape and make good on his promise. When the daylight poured through the window shades, I felt relief until I heard car doors close outside. I pressed my back against the front door and prayed, 'Please, God, show us mercy. Don't let us get hurt anymore.' To which God immediately answered in the form of a familiar child's voice, 'Stu, it's me, your best friend, Maggie!' I don't remember what came next, but I remember your father telling me I won't have any more headaches. He gave my mom a job, and that same day he moved us away from where my nightmares had lived."

Stuart pulled a handkerchief from his jacket and handed it to Maggie. He waited until she had cleaned herself up. "You have done more for me than anyone else ever has. You have shown me what unconditional love really is. Do you think I would abandon you during your time of need? Mags, it is my turn to be your protector. You are not just my boss or my best friend. You are my sister, and I will literally do anything to make sure no harm comes to you."

Maggie had stopped trembling, kissed one of his hands, and gave him her million-dollar smile. "Thank you, Stuart. I love you so much, and I don't know what I did to deserve you."

"I love you too, Mags." Stuart then wanted to make her smile. "Just remember this come bonus time, and make sure I get stock shares and add enough zeros to my bonus check. Oh, and a raise! I mean, I more than deserve it after what you have put me through with having to constantly cover for you. Yes, I believe a raise, stock shares, and a large bonus will suffice."

Maggie reached out and embraced him, lingering for several minutes. Stuart was content with making the feds wait just a little longer. He needed to make sure Maggie had herself under control before walking into the boardroom and getting drilled with questions.

When they finally let go of one another, Maggie looked at her watch and sheepishly said, "Well, despite me being a mess, we better hurry to the meeting. I'm sure by now they are pissed beyond belief."

Without answering, Stuart pulled off his dress shoes, tossed them against the opposite wall of the elevator, and sprawled out, placing both hands behind his head. "Eh, let 'em wait. I say we just stay right here for a while." He then made overly exaggerated snoring sounds, forcing a laugh from Maggie. Taking hold of his hands, she attempted to pull him up, which he shrugged off. "Go away. I'm finally getting some rest. My boss is hell on wheels, and I just need ten more minutes!"

This brought more laughter from Maggie, as she once more

took hold of his hands and helped him up. "Well, since your boss is hell on wheels, then I demand you put your shoes back on and do your job by taking me to this meeting."

Stuart gave Maggie a serious expression. "This is your coming out party after being hidden away from the public eye for so long. You hold the power to either make or break yourself, not the feds. Do you understand?"

Maggie nodded to let Stuart know she was "game ready." Returning the nod, Stuart opened the doors with his keycard and proceeded to lead Maggie to the boardroom.

CHAPTER 25

E xiting the corridor and entering onto the floor where the employees sat in office cubicles, Maggie heard the soft murmur beginning to spread as she passed by. On any normal day, she would have made time to speak with as many of them as possible, but her life was now anything but normal. Stuart walked a few paces ahead of her, then stopped and opened the door to the boardroom, giving her a reassuring smile as she entered.

Two men and a woman were seated at the long rectangular table. They stood as she entered. "Ms. Gregory, I'm Agent VanPatten, and this is Agent Winters and Agent Peterson."

Maggie shook hands with each of them without exchanging false pleasantries. They were here to practically ruin her, and she was only here because she had to be.

"This is my vice president, Stuart Branch, who served as my acting CEO while I was away. I trust no one more than him, so he will be present during my questioning."

Without giving the agents an opportunity to respond, Maggie pressed on. "I would say it's nice to meet each of you, but under these circumstances let's forego the pleasantries. I will also be waiving my rights to have my attorney present."

After everyone had taken their seats on opposite sides of the table, Maggie had to suppress a grin as the three agents exchanged questionable looks. She assumed Agent VanPatten, the older of the three agents, would be asking the questions. However, clearly frustrated with Maggie already setting the tone for the meeting, he chewed at his lower lip in contemplation.

Maggie knew just as well as he did that if he was successful in proving her of any wrongdoing, it would set his career on the fast track with whatever came next inside the Bureau.

You are here to ruin me, and I'm here to prove my innocence, thought Maggie.

"This is just preliminary work so we can get your side of the story," Agent VanPatten said. "However, we would like to record it, unless you have any objections?"

"I have no objection," replied Maggie.

"Perfect, let's get started." Agent VanPatten's mood now changed to an aggressive eagerness. He chewed at his lower lip again.

Agent Winters removed a small recording device from her bag, placed it in the center of the table, and gave Maggie a sympathetic smile.

Instead of seeing it as a sign of weakness—something Maggie usually preyed upon during important takeovers of smaller companies that tried to compete with Gregory Portal Provider— she accepted it for what it was, a small gesture of kindness. Returning the smile, Maggie shut her eyes for a brief moment, letting her conscience argue over how she should proceed.

On one side Maggie heard, *If you show weakness, they will take advantage of it, sort of like the woman you used to be before you went soft. Remember exactly why they are here. Do not play into their mind games unless you want to lose everything you and your family have worked so hard for.*

On the other side, Maggie was reminded of something she heard once before, back at the lake house. A moment shared with only Riley and the God he worshipped. Maggie had rushed over to Riley, believing he was having a stroke. When she touched him, she heard a male voice mysteriously coming from inside Riley through their embrace.

For I know the plans I have for you. Plans to prosper you and not to harm you, plans to give you hope and a future.

When the voice was gone, Riley told Maggie it was a Bible verse, which meant nothing to her at the time. However, now Maggie understood the message behind the words.

Agent VanPatten was giving her a quizzical look, then he looked to Stuart and asked in a condescending tone, "Do we need to take a break?"

Stuart started to respond, but Maggie held up a hand. "Before we begin, I need to apologize for my rudeness and that you've had to wait for so long. It's not lost on me how this could do wonders for your careers if you are able to connect me to any illegal activity involving that slimy worm Miles Jackson."

This earned another smile from Agent Winters and a chuckle from Agents VanPatten and Peterson.

Maggie continued. "After the media learned of my dealings with Miles Jackson, I've had the most awful things said not only about me but also my company. It has been difficult and painful." She paused, realizing she was rambling and portraying herself as a victim. Steadying herself for a moment, Maggie smiled. "What I want to say is that there will be no further hostility on my part toward any of you."

Maggie had been certain it was Agent VanPatten in charge. However, Agent Winters answered on their behalf. "I have been with the Bureau for exactly twenty-four years."

This caught Maggie off guard, as the woman appeared to only be in her late twenties.

Agent Winters's smile returned, seeming to already know what was running through Maggie's mind, before continuing. "During my time I have worked on some strange cases, and as cliché as this will sound, this one is right up there. A corrupt public official who allows extreme punishment to take place inside the prisons he oversees, for one reason: money. We have located bank statements proving Mr. Jackson received large unexplainable deposits over the years, which we were able to link back to top-notch players housed inside his jails. During interviews, these men, who will remain nameless for obvious reason, all told us the exact same story, in which their group was allowed to operate without close supervision as long as they paid Mr. Jackson monthly dues."

Maggie had only met Miles a handful of times at local charity events, but she always came away with the same opinion: he loved doing favors if the price was right or if there was another benefit he could later capitalize on. It was why Maggie had eventually turned to him when her search for Jonathan hadn't yielded any results.

"And if they couldn't pay?" asked Maggie.

"Well, Mr. Jackson would make an example out of the leader, usually by having them transferred to another prison, which was run by a rival gang. Then the individual would be murdered. Or he would keep them in the same location and cut off the gangs' privileges to freely operate until a new leader was appointed. The old one would be killed off by one of his own crew so things could return to normal. The body count that can be linked back to Mr. Jackson makes him one of the most ruthless men to ever hold an appointed position."

Massaging her temples, Maggie cursed her shortsightedness. *Dammit, Jonathan, why did you ever have to cross my path in the first place?*

"What exactly do you mean by freely operate?" she said. "It's not as though these appointed prison leaders have much control outside the jail. Or am I just dumb and naïve?"

This earned a polite chuckle from Agent Winters. "I'm sorry to laugh, but no, you are not dumb for not fully understanding how the underground world works. If you did, we wouldn't just be here to get your side of the story. That topic will have to be a story for another day, though."

"Well then, at least tell me the second reason why this case is so disturbing to you."

"Mr. Jackson is a masochist," Agent Winters flatly said. "I won't go into much detail about it at this time. Just know he loves power and takes extreme satisfaction from hurting those whom he considers to be inferior to himself. Which brings you into this strange situation. Why did you approve a million-dollar wire transfer to a man you refer to as a 'slimy worm'?"

CHAPTER 26

Maggie looked down at her hands resting on top of the table, wishing she had more time to process what she had just been told about Miles Jackson. She suspected he played outside the lines. It was the reason she'd called him. However, she couldn't have imagined it was to this kind of extreme.

Aware that everyone was watching and waiting for her to respond to Agent Winters's question, Maggie allowed the silence to stretch. It was strange that Agent Winters had chosen to intervene and open the doorway to a normal conversation instead of playing good cop–bad cop with Agent VanPatten.

Maggie wouldn't say they were necessarily on her side since they were here to question her. However, the new direction of the conversation made her feel comfortable about her future, at least financially. Her future regarding Riley and her promise to help him find Jonathan was a whole other matter.

"Ms. Gregory?" Agent Winters gave her a genuine look of concern. "I know you're worried, but the best advice I can give is just tell the truth. I tell everyone I question, even my children and husband, the same thing. In the long run, it makes everything so much simpler. Sooner or later the truth will come out, and by then it's too late."

This made Maggie respect her, and she appreciated the

woman even more. It was the exact same thing Stu had told her, excluding the supernatural events that had set all of this in motion.

"Sorry, and you are right," said Maggie. "Telling the truth is so much simpler than lying. Stuart actually told me something similar on the elevator. It was his way of calming me down after my panic attack."

This earned a smile from all three agents.

"The reason for the wire transfer was that I needed to see two inmates, and I needed the meeting to occur after hours. After being absent from the public eye for as long as I had been, I wasn't ready to be seen out and about, so this was my only way of avoiding that."

Stuart shifted in his chair, crossing one leg over the other, but remaining quiet.

"I knew Miles Jackson was corrupt, which was why I called him. However, in my defense, I had no idea he played on *that* level of insanity. I just knew he was the Commissioner of the Department of Corrections and could make what I needed to happen. Which explains the million-dollar transfer, half a million per inmate."

Agent Peterson, who had been quiet throughout this whole ordeal, let loose a soft comical whistle.

"Agreed," said Maggie. "It is a lot of money. And seems it is still costing me beyond the money I already paid."

"What was so special about these two inmates?" asked Agent Winters.

"Well, they are part of the reason I disappeared from the public eye. They attempted to rob me, and who knows what else they would've done if it hadn't been for a passing stranger who intervened. Although I came away without being physically harmed beyond a few scrapes and bruises, mentally and emotionally, I was a wreck." This part was a lie, but Maggie knew it would raise less questions than the actual truth. "For me both professionally and personally, I knew I needed to confront these men if I wanted to stop living in fear and have any resemblance of a normal life again."

"We spoke with the inmate, Mr. Packton, but Warden Smart would not permit us to speak to Mr. Mahoney."

This made Maggie smile. She remembered how stern Warden Smart had been with her. She had even posed a question that opened Maggie's eyes to how selfish she was being.

"With it being so close to the date of Mr. Mahoney's execution, we decided not to push the matter."

It felt as though the air had been sucked out of the room as a wave of heat crashed over her, followed immediately by tears and incoherent sentences. "When is this to . . . happen? Why d-don't. I thought . . ." Maggie was overtaken by sobs of helplessness. It was the crimes against her that put him there and she felt responsible for him losing his life.

She had only encountered Mr. Mahoney the one time, a tragic night that would forever alter everyone involved and place each individual who had been a part of the assault on extremely different paths.

Stuart handed her a water bottle. She took several gulps, hoping when she came up for air her ability to speak would return. Handing the half empty bottle back to Stuart, Maggie noticed Agent Winters was now seated next to her.

"Sorry," said Maggie. "I imagine I must be coming across as exactly what the tabloids made me out to be."

"On the contrary, I think your vulnerability and compassion for another person's life, especially someone who intentionally attempted to harm you, tells me all I need to know about your involvement with Mr. Jackson."

Maggie exchanged a look of uncertainty with Stuart, then looked at Agent Winters.

"Yes, you're in the clear. As I said, we just wanted to get your side of the story involving the money transfer. Unless either of you have anything else to add?" Agent Winters said to her colleagues.

Agents VanPatten and Peterson replied in unison, "We're good, if you are."

Even though she had been cleared, Maggie wished there were something she could do to keep Mr. Mahoney from being executed. She dabbed her eyes with a tissue until she felt more in control of her voice. "When is Mr. Mahoney expected to be executed?"

"Well, if he doesn't have a lawyer submit any last-minute appeals—"

"He won't," interjected Maggie, earning a questionable look from Agent Winters. "When I spoke with Mr. Packton, he helped me understand why he and Mr. Mahoney had agreed to turn themselves in. He said that even though Mr. Mahoney knew that owning up to everything he had done in the past would put him exactly where he is now, and yet he still did it."

Maggie hadn't meant to allude to something supernatural having propelled the two men to turn themselves in, but then again, Maggie hadn't known Mr. Mahoney's execution date would be mentioned or that she would react so emotionally.

"Why exactly did they turn themselves in? This is another thing that makes this case so bizarre. What propelled a man to, quite frankly, throw his life away? Eventually, yes, they both would have gotten caught, but even the guilty ask for mercy at the end. And yet . . ."

Maggie let the questions hang in the air, desperately wishing she could fill in the gaps for Agent Winters. "You've been more than fair with me, and I'll never be able to thank you enough for it," she said.

Agent Winters nodded. "I go into every case already knowing I'll never have all my questions answered. As frustrating as it can be, at the same time it keeps me coming back for more. Guess I'm a prime example for the definition of insanity."

Maggie forced a smile and stood. Saying goodbye to the three agents, she leaned into Agent Winters while they shook hands. "I will tell you, Mr. Packton told me he heard God's voice in the alley that night, where he accosted me. As for Mr. Mahoney, I believe he must have come face-to-face with God, and that's why he turned his life around."

Agent Winters gave her a look of approval. Then, keeping up the conspiratorial tone, she whispered back, "What about you, Ms. Gregory? What did you encounter?"

Maggie wanted to reply truthfully that there may be such a thing as a God, but then the image of her mother suffering for the rest of eternity surfaced. If she did allow herself to admit there was a God, then she would be forever condemning her mother to an eternity of pain and suffering.

"Ms. Gregory?" Agent Winters softly said, pulling Maggie out of her thoughts.

"I don't believe in a God, and if I did, I would say he is cruel and unmerciful. My experience that night left me feeling the same as you when taking on a new case. That all of my questions will never be answered, and yet I still keep searching for the truth. So, Agent Winters, like you, I also am a prime example for the definition of insanity."

CHAPTER 27

Esperanza stood outside Savior's torture room, unable to comprehend the trust he had placed in her. Although time all but ceased to exist in Hell, Esperanza felt that only a few short days had passed since she had been summoned into Savior's home. That day, three other women stood next to her for only the briefest of moments before Savior quickly dismissed them because they were too incompetent to carry out one simple request.

"Draw me a bath," Savior had commanded. She had been the only one successful in carrying out the task.

Esperanza recalled how confused and shaken she had been, when only moments prior she watched as fire licked at the top of her skin with its red serpent tongue. How she would slap at the unending flames, sending up charred ashes of dead skin into the dark shadows of a ceiling that was not evident to the naked eye.

Hell was all but black, except for the occasional fire eruption which would show the outlines of individuals who appeared to be dancing inside the inferno. Only the dance wasn't a dance. It was actually just the other damned going insane from the pain being driven through them—a pain so intense they carried out unmerciful acts on one another in hopes the pain would subside. Some even descended into cannibalism.

Thinking back, her body appeared to float aimlessly in the air, her only means of movement limited by those around her. One minute they clung to one another seeking refuge, and then next they were lashing out in a panic.

Which brought Esperanza to now. Fate had somehow intervened and was showing her mercy because she was trusted enough to be left in charge. Even if it was only until Savior broke the Fallen, she was fortunate to be in this position and was going to do everything in her power to please Savior.

The real challenge would be keeping all the Region Leaders in line. They would scheme and do whatever it took to make certain Savior got rid of her when he returned. Casting her back into Hell, never to be heard from again.

Two hounds walked out of a room down the hall and came directly to her. It was a silly thing to wonder if they had picked up on her worried thoughts. Savior had warned her that the hounds could either be her greatest ally or the key to her undoing.

Testing the theory, Esperanza spoke in a flat tone, "Sit."

In unison, the hounds did as they were commanded.

"Stand."

Again, the hounds moved in unison.

Esperanza was amazed that the hounds were already aware they were now to serve her in Savior's absence. Any other demon who tried this would already have been torn to shreds.

As she vowed earlier when Savior had placed her in charge of the occupants of Hell, Esperanza would make her first priority to handle the Tristan fiasco. The last thing she needed was that idiot Barbados twisting her words to the other two Elders, Gideon and Jameson.

Another thought came to Esperanza. *What did Savior desire more than just the Fallen? The human the Fallen was supposed to protect. Riley.*

Even with her newly elevated status, Esperanza knew that only Savior could declare a Region Leader. So, she would use the three Elders—Jameson, Barbados, and Gideon—as pawns and send them out to kill Riley. She would promise that whoever was successful in carrying out the task would earn her recommendation for Region Leader.

"Heel," Esperanza commanded.

She led her two new companions from Savior's home and into Hell, where she would find the wormhole to transport her to Tristan's region. Once inside the confines of Hell, Esperanza stopped and gazed at the pleading faces pressed into the translucent wall that separated her from the damned. Unlike her predecessor Legionaries, Esperanza enjoyed spending time down here. It helped her appreciate just how fortunate her new situation was.

Her favorite part of being down here was running her hands over the faces of those who called to her for help. The wall could bend like a stretchy material, but only so far. There was no breaking through the wall, no matter how many of the damned pushed against it.

The first time she had touched the wall, Esperanza forced herself into doing so, fearful she may be pulled in. What a rush it had been! She was by no means a thrill seeker, but it had been a surprisingly fun thing for her to learn.

Reaching out, Esperanza delicately traced the face closest to her with her fingertips. She would not physically try to harm the damned, but she did find pleasure in mentally abusing them. Their pleas were even more enjoyable as she heard everything from false promises, to threats, to her personal favorite: when someone cried out to their mom for help.

Esperanza always answered the requests with the same line as she touched each face. "No one who cares can hear you, and no one out here cares how much you're suffering." It was the little mental push the damned needed to break them even more.

Knowing she needed to hurry, Esperanza started walking down the corridor that led to the wormhole. She kept her hand on the wall, as if to taunt them a bit more, until she came to the green swirling wormhole. She stepped into it with the two hounds, then looked back at the translucent wall, only to find one of the damned was actually smiling at her.

"Tristan's region," Esperanza coldly said.

Feeling bitter about one of the damned getting the better of her, Esperanza broke her usual calm demeanor and flipped off the smiling face before being whisked away. Her last image was of the individual returning the gesture with both hands, which infuriated her even more.

The wormhole had been designed with 666 regions, each featuring a point of origin where the Region Leader had a small office. These points of origin were spread out across Earth. However, they couldn't be seen by the human eye. The same was true for Savior's house, which sat between Earth and Hell. Savior taught Esperanza how it worked when he had taken her on as his assistant, but he had never again stepped foot in the wormhole. He was able to travel without it.

Esperanza had been in Tristan's office only once before when Savior sent her to retrieve him. At that time, it had been exceptionally tidy. Now, however, it was quite evident that Tristan was indeed missing. There were maps of the region piled atop the desk, with other items randomly scattered out across the floor. Jameson was sprawled out on the only couch in the office, snoring loudly.

Without having to say what she wanted, Esperanza looked down at the hounds and nodded. Their barks were so deafening even Esperanza winced from the ear-splitting pain.

Jameson reacted far differently than she expected. He curled himself into a tight ball and screamed, "Please, don't hurt me! Oh please, don't hurt me!"

Certain that the point had been made, Esperanza placed her hands on the back of each hound, silencing them. After Jameson came to his senses, his look turned to rage until the hounds issued a threatening growl.

"Where are the other two Elders?" Esperanza asked flatly. "Bring them here. I have a deal to offer, and I won't repeat myself."

She could see the contempt Jameson held for her but knew he would never act on it. To affirm she was the one in charge, Esperanza touched the top of the hounds' heads, making them growl.

Jameson stood and cautiously maneuvered his way around the hounds in the cramped office. Clumsily locating the doorknob, he quickly exited, slamming the door closed behind him.

Amused by her current situation and loving the power she possessed, Esperanza gave herself a mental kick not to overplay her hand. She took a seat at Tristan's desk. The hounds took up occupancy on either side of her.

Moments later Jameson returned, and now that he had reinforcements in Barbados and Gideon, he had a newfound sense of authority. The three Elders encircled the desk and loomed over it in an attempt to intimidate her.

In response, Esperanza waved her arm, sending all the maps on the desk into flight. The three Elder demons quickly stepped back.

"If I were Savior," she said, "all three of you would be in the depths this very instant. Fortunately for you, I'm only here to address the missing Tristan issue. Now be seated! Unless you want to continue your nonsense, and I'll prompt my two associates to put an end to your intimidation tactics?"

The hounds issued threatening growls until Jameson, Barbados, and Gideon conjured up chairs and sat.

"We asked for an audience with Savior to address the Tristan issue, not his—"

"Finish that thought, Jameson, and I promise it will be the last coherent one you ever have."

One of the hounds moved quickly behind Jameson, silencing him. Esperanza knew Jameson was about to call her Lackey, a nickname that was used to reference her predecessor, Legionaries. Esperanza had put an end to it by referring to Region Leaders as "replaceable." If she had to, she would address the matter with Savior behind closed doors when it was just the two of them. What the leaders didn't know was that she would never stoop to that level over something so petty. She would never bring Savior into a situation when she was more than capable of handling it on her own. After all, she was only here to please Savior, not the other way around.

"From what I understand, Tristan has been missing for quite some time, and only now it has occurred to the three of you that Savior needed to know this information sooner rather than later?"

Jameson opened his mouth to respond but stopped. His eyes darted to the side at the hound baring its teeth.

"Please accept our apologies, Esperanza," said Gideon. "You are absolutely correct. We should have brought this to Savior's attention sooner. You're disregarding the last time we saw Tristan, though. It was when you came to call on him at Savior's behest. So, we just assumed he was still out on a job."

Esperanza was taken aback at how softly spoken the short, stocky demon was, yet pissed at what he was implying. Going off his looks, one would assume he was just a disgusting brute with a tattered gray eyepatch.

Gideon continued. "However, I'm finding difficulty in seeing how we are the only ones to blame for this current predicament we seem to find ourselves in. If something had gone awry with Tristan's last job, wouldn't it have been one of your duties as our Savior's liaison to bring it to his attention? Especially since it is your job to keep . . ." Gideon's facial expression contorted into one of pain, his entire body stiffening under the strain.

Confused, Esperanza looked at Jameson and Barbados to fill her in on what was happening, but Gideon interrupted by letting out a long, loud sigh before going stiff all over again.

As the silence continued, Esperanza's frustration and anger boiled over. She lashed out. "Seriously? What in the hell is going on here?"

"Oh, well," answered Jameson. "Tristan punished Gideon for undermining him and tore out his eye, cursing it with the worms of Hell, making sure it would never regenerate. The worms have now spread from his cursed eye to the rest of his body. Lately, these episodes of paralysis and confusion are happening a great deal more often."

"By my calculations, he'll be a vegetable within a week," added Barbados.

Esperanza made a disgusted face at Gideon, who momentarily rejoined the conversation. But before he had time to speak, his body once again went rigid, and this time he didn't return.

"He may be down for a bit longer this time. Like I said, the episodes have been increasing," said Jameson.

"Fine," said Esperanza. "I'll leave it up to the two of you to fill him in later on my proposed offer."

Jameson opened his mouth to speak, but Esperanza held up a hand to silence him. "I know you will have questions, but just listen for now. Savior is currently busy attempting to break the Fallen. In the meantime, he has appointed me in charge and tasked me to make sure everything continues to run smoothly in his absence. I hate to agree with this imbecile, but I did fail at my job by not being aware that Tristan was missing before Barbados showed up to inform Savior. Which places all of us in the same predicament. You could go running to tell Savior how I screwed up, but I could also do the same to you. Then we would all be cast back into Hell and simply replaced with someone else. Do you agree with this statement?"

Barbados and Jameson exchanged brief looks before nodding.

"Good. This is what I suggest. Savior wants the human, Riley, dead. It's what he has expressed to not just me but to every Region Leader. So, whichever one of you can kill Riley, I will personally tell Savior that you should be the new Region Leader. As for Tristan, we're going to have to wait and hope that Savior will show us mercy for our lack of communication if we kill Riley."

Jameson and Barbados stared at her without voicing their opinions, clearly contemplating whether they could trust her.

Esperanza, on the other hand, knew that she had to trust them . . . for now. Sooner or later, Savior would ask why she hadn't mentioned Tristan's absence, and even though it was an oversight on her part, Savior would still discipline her the same as he would the others.

"All right," said Jameson, cautiously looking over his shoulder, making certain the hound was still seated. "We are bedfellows for now. But if you try to screw us, I will make certain you wind up in the pits right next to us."

"Agreed," said Esperanza.

"Given the time limit of only sixty seconds to take over a non-worshipper's body, how do you intend for us to kill this human, Riley? Unless you have a way of removing this restriction, the mission will be next to impossible to carry out. Furthermore, how do you even expect us to find Riley in the vastness that is Earth?"

"The time restriction I can remove, but your powers will be

limited," she said. Jameson and Barbados exchanged skeptical looks. Esperanza sighed in frustration. "If I could give you the use of all your powers, I would. After all, your success weighs heavily on the outcome of how Savior will judge us. I have no intention of returning to the pits, but that's exactly what will happen if we fail."

"And, specifically, what powers are we giving up?" Jameson asked, annoyed.

"Almost all of them. You'll basically be mortal," Esperanza replied. "In the past, Savior has allowed me to release demons to carry out certain jobs for him. And because he enjoys watching scenarios play out when there's lots of struggle and conflict, I can only release you without the fear of being pulled back within a specific time frame."

"Well, that's just perfect," said Jameson. "Wouldn't you agree, Barbados?"

Unable to control her temper, Esperanza stood and seethed. "Listen, you fools! When Savior is back in charge, and we have only hollow apologies for an oversight that happened on our watch, we will all be returned to the pits without so much as a second thought. So, get the job done and do it quickly."

"Okay," said Jameson, speaking on behalf of everyone.

Barbados looked irritated because he didn't have a say in the matter, while Gideon continued to stare off into space without so much as even blinking.

"Perfect. I have no idea how long it will take Savior to break the Fallen, so I suggest you leave immediately. As for locating Riley, he has partnered up with one of the wealthiest women in the world by the name of Mary Allison Gregory. She has a large corporate office called Gregory Portal Provider in Taupe City, Texas. I'd start there."

Not wasting anymore time, Esperanza stood to leave.

Barbados reached out and grabbed her arm to stop her. "Aren't you forgetting something?"

Esperanza jerked her arm from his grasp and stepped into the wormhole with the two hounds. "The time limit restriction has been removed. Now get the job done."

Just as the wormhole was about to transport her back to Savior's home, she heard Gideon ask in a slurred voice, "What happened?"

CHAPTER 28

After being dragged back to Bob's house by this new, strange, naked man named Tristan, Patty stopped resisting. She hoped she would be shown mercy after she completed what had been originally asked of her. Analyzing her situation was a foolish errand, especially after pledging her allegiance to Legionaries, a being who felt nothing but pleasure when it came to sacrificing those who opposed him.

"I assume since you are mortal you are unable to smell the rank, diseased stench these non-worshippers produce," said Tristan.

He had positioned himself at the end of the bed where Bob's wife lay helpless. Her chest rose and fell in rhythm with the machine pumping life into her.

Ignoring the comment, Patty focused on the woman she met only a handful of times when she had shopped at Bob's TechWorks. She recalled how this woman, much like Bob, shared the same over-the-top kindness every time Patty had gone into the store.

At first, Patty thought this overzealous display of attention had been just an act to ensure she would purchase something. But the next time Patty returned to the store, this kindhearted woman addressed her by her name and seemed genuinely interested in what Patty had been up to. It was as if they were old friends running into each other, which made what she was about to do even more painful. Patty wished she could remember the woman's name to show some form of respect to her, just as the woman had done for Patty.

Perhaps it was for the best, given the nature of her visit. Patty then immediately decided against it. If she was going to serve as executioner, then this woman deserved more than just to be referred to as Bob's wife.

Patty knew she could kill; she had hunted animals her entire life. It was an ethical way to harvest meat, and she took pride that she could be a provider, not just to her family members, but also to neighbors who enjoyed good game meat. Anyone could walk into a store, pick up a perfectly cut steak, pay for it, and leave. To Patty, that diminished the respect for the piece of meat having once been a living being. Yet now here she stood, ready to take a woman's life, and all she could think about was the dilemma of not being able to remember her fucking name.

Tristan sniffed the air several times, pulling Patty out of her useless thoughts. His look was hard to read, but Patty guessed he was going to enjoy what was about to occur.

"Patty, this human's shell of a body isn't long for this world. Perhaps a few hours at best until the long sleep takes her fragile hand."

He made eye contact with Patty, but instead of looking away from the soul-shuddering stare, Patty held Tristan's gaze. The expression was the same one her brother wore after he returned home from completing two tours of combat duty in the Army. The weary, war-torn shadows that outlined her brother's face had eventually gone away, but only after the light was snuffed from his eyes and his large frame had been squeezed inside a casket after he had taken his own life.

"What are you waiting for?" asked Tristan.

Patty was going to say she needed to remember Bob's wife's name before she could carry out the murder, but instead made an observation. "If you are correct with your assessment of how much time remains, why the need to hurry things along? She's dead either way. So, why not just leave and let nature take its course?"

Before Patty had time to register what had happened, the feel of grainy sand coated the inside of her mouth, and something heavy pressed on the back of her head. When the pressure subsided, Patty pulled her head away from the wall and began spitting splinters of wood paneling onto the floor.

Struggling to remain on her feet, Patty gave up and sat down when the objects in the room began to somehow shift and then move all on their own. Something warm poured down the side of her left cheek. When she went to wipe at it, she found herself too weak to even accomplish the small feat. She had experienced a similar feeling to this sort of vertigo on a hunting trip after stepping on a moss-covered rock, the end result being a broken arm and a nasty gash which required fourteen stitches to close.

Attempting to speak set off a loud ringing in her ears that continued to grow in volume until she doubled over and vomited into her lap. She absolutely loathed nothing more than throwing up and would usually struggle and do everything possible not to. With each wretch, the ringing quickly subsided. After everything inside her had been purged, Patty leaned her head back against the wall and shut her eyes, praying the ringing wouldn't return. Vomiting was one thing, but the ringing going off inside her head was beyond intolerable.

The sound reminded her of the time she had gone hunting with her father and he fired his rifle inside the deer stand without warning. She was a young kid at the time, and she'd fallen asleep waiting for a deer to show up. She had been jerked out of her sleepy consciousness when he fired the shot. She instantly pressed her hands to the sides of her head. In his excitement, her father hadn't noticed her discomfort. He was instead screaming incoherent sentences, a wide smile spread across his face.

Tristan knelt before her, and with one rough hand, grabbed the sides of her face, forcing her to focus on him. "Because, Patty, it doesn't matter how much time I believe this insignificant woman has left. Legionaries gave a direct order, leaving no room for interpretation. Now, are you ready to comply with the order, or do you need another lesson in obedience?"

Not caring what came next, Patty replied in a slurred voice that even she didn't recognize, "I can't even stand, you ass."

Again, before she realized what was happening, she was jerked upright, and a soft foreign object was forced into her hands.

"This next part I cannot help you with since lines would be crossed. Lines the false God put into place centuries ago."

Patty hadn't a clue what Tristan was carrying on about, but she realized the object in her hands was a pillow. She knew what she was expected to do with it. Even though her thoughts were jumbled, Patty desperately clung to the one that bothered her from the start: she couldn't recall Bob's wife's name.

The floor once more began to sway back and forth, causing Patty to close her eyes and stumble. Thrusting out both hands, she managed to catch herself from falling all the way to the floor. After what felt like only a few seconds, she regained control of her senses, opened her eyes, and found she had unexpectedly completed the task Legionaries ordered her to do. Tears clouded her vision as shame washed over her, bringing with it the rest of the long-forgotten memory she had tried to block out.

"Got her!" her father had said that day. "Let's go see just how big of a doe she really is."

Descending the six feet of stairs and hearing the crackle of

September leaves beneath her feet, Patty had looked after her dad in awe as he hurried toward the spot of his latest kill.

Drawing near, Patty noticed a young fawn close by. Her attention was drawn back to her father, who was waving his arms and screaming, "Not your time, so get your ass out of here!"

The fawn ran off a few yards, stopped, and looked helplessly back at them. The shot doe lay helplessly on the ground, attempting to raise its head. Then her father, without giving her warning, had fired off another shot, extinguishing the light from the animal's black eyes. The ringing sound from before returned, but not quite as bad as when her father took the shot in the confines of the deer stand. The fawn was now gone, leaving Patty shaken and sobbing from the realization. It was the last time the doe would see its fawn.

From that day on, Patty knew any ethical hunter would have never taken that shot. It wasn't just cruel but inhumane since the death of the doe would end up taking two lives that day. The fawn, now left to fend for itself, wouldn't survive on its own for long. One thought Patty did take refuge in was that nothing lived forever or died happily outdoors. Not even the predators of the mountain, because sooner or later, they, too, would become something else's meal.

From that day forward, she took pride in the fact that she was better than her father. She was an ethical hunter, a true outdoorswoman who actually appreciated her role in conservation.

Yet on this night, she was now far worse than her father had ever been. Here she stood, looking down, not the black eyes of the doe but the green eyes of the kindest woman she knew, whose only fault in life had been her kindness for others.

Although Tristan was standing behind her, Patty remained unmoving, not bothering to ask the useless question of "what will happen to me now?" She would not feign ignorance, nor would she beg for her life just because she had now become the prey. It was the same law the animals she hunted abided by any time they stepped foot in the clearing of the meadow. They knew, as well as she did, the dangers when it came to the unknown factors. And yet the temptation of what lies just out of reach could drive any living thing to cast aside their sanity and march recklessly into the void.

"Her name was Amy," said Patty, surprising even herself as the name fell from her lips upon the deaf ears of the life she had taken. Having regained use of all her faculties, Patty dropped the pillow to the floor, glad to be rid of it.

"Perhaps at one time you drew breath same as I do now. Shared similar feelings such as love, compassion, fondness, maybe even warmth for others. I'm certain the time period you once lived in is now long since forgotten, leaving you with only the feelings of remorse, contempt, and anger." Patty turned and faced Tristan. "I have a peculiar question, which most people wouldn't understand or see the logic behind asking. However, since I know I'm about to die, I will ask regardless."

When Tristan said nothing, Patty continued. "I have always been a hunter, not a killer, but a hunter. And yes, despite political correctness, there is a difference between the two words. Most people are just too ignorant to be able to distinguish between them. So, my question is this: What was your fondest memory before you passed from this world? When I take an animal's life, I've always wondered what they might say if they could talk. So, here I stand completely vulnerable, predator to prey, wondering . . . What was most important to you when you drew free air?"

When Tristan didn't respond, Patty accepted that either he didn't remember, or it was too painful for him to recall.

"Let's just get this over with," said Patty.

When Tristan still didn't move, Patty studied the man. His

expression had softened into one of great remorse and now he refused to meet her eyes.

CHAPTER 29

Tristan couldn't explain his current predicament. He was acutely aware of every passing minute, of the small chunks of his past life on Earth all dropping into place like building blocks. What he did know for certain was that Legionaries was now in charge, and he would do whatever Legionaries asked of him. The thought of even failing Legionaries made Tristan tremble.

His past god, Lucifer, had stirred a similar feeling inside Tristan's paranoia. Lucifer had only tortured him with his hounds and occasionally beat him. But even that only happened a handful of times and never made him feel as vulnerable as when Legionaries had reached inside of Tristan, ripping out his soul and swallowing it.

However, what he just lived through—being trapped inside Legionaries—hadn't been painful, just terrifying because he had no way to fight back. He was surrounded in a thick, heavy blackness, with no idea if he would ever be set free again. The longer the ordeal lasted, the more Tristan began to feel his mind atrophy. As his memories slowly slipped away with each passing second, he wondered what he had already forgotten.

Thinking back on it, Tristan was certain if Legionaries wouldn't have freed him, he would have eventually ceased to even exist, becoming just another clump of mindless cells making up the complexity that was Legionaries's body. Shuddering at the thought, Tristan hoped that all of his memories that were slowly falling back into place would stay intact, and Legionaries would continue to find use for him.

"Tristan, you know what I expect to be done," Legionaries had said, letting Tristan know his disobedience would not be tolerated and would be dealt with swiftly. Something even this strange mortal, Patty, seemed to comprehend with the expression, "Let's just get this over with."

Who was she to order him to do anything? She was a mortal, a lackey, a useless individual whose only purpose was to serve, and when she could no longer do that, she was to die. Nothing else was required of her, especially not to ask questions that would cause him to dwell upon thoughts of a life he had left long forgotten in the past. Yet she had, with what should have just been a dismissive question. "What was your fondest memory before you passed from this world?"

Never throughout his entire reign as the largest Region Leader, or before that, had he ever been asked such a question. His slaves and his three Elders all knew their places and respected his boundaries. If not, then he made an example out of them and dealt with them swiftly. Patty, however, neither cared nor feared what he would do to her. It was as if she had already accepted that she wouldn't be leaving this house alive and was strangely okay with it.

The painful memories Tristan thought he had forgotten— after his soul left his mortal body in this world—were slowly being resurrected. He was now a part of this mortal world once again, at least in some capacity. The pain of these past memories told Tristan of his many countless mistakes, a reminder that he would never be able to make them right. One in particular began to surface, as if a cruel, unseen artist was making large brush strokes back and forth across his mind's eye, pulling forth a scene Tristan was powerless to stop.

"Dad, please? The children's program only lasts an hour." It was his son, Troy, pleading with him from the back seat. Tristan ignored the pleas of his seven-year-old.

"Cats in the cradle," said his wife from the passenger seat.

Too frustrated to care about the traffic, Tristan removed his eyes from the road and glared at his wife. She had only been trying to make a joke to neutralize the situation, but it instead pushed him over the edge. She had been smiling, but after seeing his glare, she immediately cast her eyes downward.

"You know what? Maybe you're right. I'll blow off this mandatory meeting and watch my son play a donkey for the next hour!"

"Shepherd, Dad. Not a donkey," Troy quickly corrected.

"That's right, a shepherd. I offer my deepest apology," Tristan said sarcastically.

The offhanded remark hadn't registered with his seven-year-old. However, it had with his wife. "I'm sorry for making you feel guilty. It really wasn't my intention, but please don't belittle him," she whispered only loud enough for Tristan to hear. "He's too young to know you're making a joke or that it's at his expense. Besides, it's rude and disrespectful for no reason."

Not bothering with a reply, Tristan drove the rest of the way to the church in silence. He even ignored his son in the back seat making offhanded comments about the Christmas lights and decorations on neighboring houses.

The long eighty-hour work weeks he had been putting in at the firm for the last fourteen months were becoming more of a burden that wore his patience thin. He had been chosen to assist in a wrongful death case against Lizera Pharmaceuticals, which if he helped win, would open endless opportunities for his career.

Dropping his wife and son off in the church parking lot

without so much as a parting goodbye, Tristan sped away, not even bothering to ask how they would get home.

Twenty minutes later he arrived at the law firm of Muskraw, Phillips, and Fisk. He exchanged a brief hello with the night security officer and took the elevator up to the third floor. When the doors opened, Tristan hurried off, only to be caught by surprise by the loud music coming from the boardroom. Pulling open one of the large mahogany doors, Tristan stepped inside and was immediately handed a half-filled glass of light-colored whiskey. His boss, Franklin Muskraw, was standing on top of the boardroom table, red-faced and hoisting a bottle of gin in the air.

"Turn the damn music down for a minute!" he screamed in a loud, slurred voice. As silence encompassed the room, he continued, "Here's to Lizera Pharmaceuticals and the fifty million the bastards won't even lose sleep over."

This was followed by thunderous cheers as glasses were clinking and being drained and immediately filled again. The firm's two other partners, Mr. Fisk and Mrs. Phillips, were also enjoying the celebration, their usual permanent scowls replaced by large smiles, clearly adhering to whatever Mr. Muskraw wanted, given that he was a hard man to work for and was the senior partner.

After taking a long pull from the bottle of gin, Mr. Muskraw waved his arms in the air, asking for silence. Teetering for a moment but regaining his balance, he drunkenly said, "I want each and every one of you to take the rest of the week off. That's an order. If I so much as hear of anyone coming in, including you two"—he pointed at Mr. Fisk and Mrs. Phillips—"I will fire your asses for insubordination!"

Again, there were loud shouts and cheering, but Tristan noticed the two other partners' broad smiles had been replaced with "fuck you" grins. As the music started back up, Tristan sought out Daphne, a young female paralegal he had grown quite fond of.

"Looks like we won," Tristan shouted into her ear.

She smiled deviously at him and said something Tristan couldn't make out. When he only shrugged and gave her a look of confusion, she took him by the arm and led him out into the corridor.

"Looks like we won," Tristan said again. "Settling out of court shows just how screwed they really were with the evidence against them. Or they thought it was cheaper for them this way rather than risking a trial."

"Screwed indeed," she agreed in a sensual undertone, arching an eyebrow at him.

Understanding exactly what she meant, and knowing he wanted it just as badly as she did, Tristan placed a hand on the small of her back and escorted her to an empty, darkened office. Before he had time to close the door behind them, she was already all over him, sliding his slacks halfway down his legs, and causing him to stumble and fall. Within moments she was on top of him, kissing him with such passion and desire that Tristan thought nothing of the consequences.

Afterward, in the afterglow of their carnal passion and feeling exhausted from their erotic activities and the long, grueling work hours, they stretched out on the giant plush rug and cuddled into one another as sleep soon found and subdued them. Then Tristan was awakened by a voice, followed by bright lights that forced him to cover his eyes with his hands.

"Tristan, you need to get up, and I mean right now." It was a man's voice, and it didn't sound upset or offput so much as concerned at the sight of the two half-naked coworkers. "I'm dead serious. Something bad has happened. Get up!"

Believing something must have gone wrong with the

settlement, Tristan bolted upright, sending Daphne flying off his chest in the process. Her head made a loud thud as it made contact with the floor.

"What in the hell?" asked Daphne, her voice both slurred and angry.

Tristan frantically attempted to pull his slacks up and tuck in his shirt at the same time. "What happened? Was there a problem with the settlement?"

Through sleepy eyes, Tristan finally made out who the man was. Mr. Muskraw, who had been smiling and laughing earlier and made quite a spectacle of himself, now wore a serious expression through bloodshot eyes.

"What is the name of the church you attend?"

The question stumped Tristan since he didn't actually attend church. He may have said something off-hand at one time about his wife attending one. The fact that his boss remembered such a minor detail both impressed and worried Tristan.

"Harmony. Harmony Baptist," said Tristan.

"Oh God, no," said Mr. Muskraw, falling into a chair and covering his eyes with his hands.

"What?" Tristan blurted, wanting to shake his boss out of his theatrics.

"By any chance were your wife and son there tonight?" Mr. Muskraw asked. He cast a quick side glance at Daphne before looking accusingly at Tristan.

Under different circumstances, Tristan might have reminded the man that he himself had been married and divorced seven times. Each of his flings started in the confines of that very firm. "Yes," said Tristan, now unable to hide the worry building inside him.

"I am so sorry, Tristan. I am so damn sorry."

As he began to tell the nightmarish events that had occurred at the church, Tristan was unable to sit and listen to all the details after hearing "church shooting." He bolted, passed his boss and raced to the church.

Tristan was forced to stop a half mile away from the church because of the news vans and first responder vehicles. Without thinking, Tristan ran toward the church but was stopped after only a few feet when a police officer cut him off.

"My wife and son! Holiday program!" screamed Tristan at the young female officer. "I need to get to them!"

The police officer looked down for the briefest of moments, informing Tristan that he was too late.

In the following weeks, Tristan learned that three active shooters carried out the worst massacre to have ever taken place in the history of their town, taking the lives of over forty individuals, and injuring more than two dozen others. His wife and son were among the casualties who never made it out of the church alive. No one ever learned the reason behind the shooters' actions. In the end, they took their own lives without explanation.

There was a reason Tristan had buried these memories. Not only were they painful, but they didn't offer any help regarding his current situation. However, this conversation would end here between Patty and himself. Now that all of his past memories were falling back into place, Tristan didn't feel the need to answer, nor did he want to.

"I feel nothing for the human race, or even other demons, for that matter. Every one of you is merely a means to an end, which I freely use to benefit myself. Regardless, I will answer your question and tell you about my fondest memory from before my passing."

Feeling dizzy as the memories continued to come back to life, Tristan placed a hand on the wall to steady himself. When he was certain the process was complete, he stood upright and looked at Patty.

Tristan began, "I was once married and had a son. You might think I would say 'my family,' but you would be wrong. I believed I loved them, but in the end, I failed them in many ways. Truthfully, my fondest memory was my childhood. Although it was flawed and I was tormented, I found comfort from my sister. When I awoke each morning, I knew my sister—my best friend—would be there for me. We would play the same games and do the same activities together, but if any of my classmates ever found out, they would've ridiculed me for it. My sister was my constant, my love, and the only person I would do anything for. Eventually, as life does, our paths pulled us in opposite directions as we grew up. I can still recall holding my sister's first child and the two who followed with extreme pride as I looked at their innocent faces. As happy as I was for my sister and her new family, I felt hurt because time had moved on, and my childhood was forever put to bed. So, Patty, my answer is my childhood. My answer is my sister. My answer also causes me deep pain because I know I will never be able to see her again for the rest of eternity."

Patty closed her eyes and nodded, letting Tristan know their conversation would end and die here. Just as she began to speak, Tristan silenced her by quickly snapping her head to one side. She'd already wounded him so deeply with just a simple question. Letting go of her head, Patty collapsed to the ground.

As Tristan looked back and forth between the two women, he realized that despite their close proximity, one was being welcomed into Heaven, while the other was being tortured without an end in sight.

CHAPTER 30

Sloth (noun)
1: disinclination to action or labor: indolence
2: spiritual apathy and inactivity; the deadly sin of
sloth

Jonathan stirred from his pain-induced sleep. Voices cried out inside the torture room. He wasn't sure if his mind was still playing tricks on him. His only communication since arriving in Hell had been with Lucifer. Massaging his temples until his vision cleared, Jonathan could vaguely make out three people speaking to one another in the far corner of the room.

Wanting to get a better view, Jonathan attempted to push himself up off the filthy carpet, but the pain in his head roared back to life. Curling up into a fetal position, Jonathan clutched the sides of his head, hoping to ward off the pressure building inside it.

He equated the pain to how Riley described his migraines. At the time, Riley would treat them with medicine and rest in a dark, quiet room with a warm, damp washcloth over his eyes. That was before he allowed Jonathan to treat him. Jonathan would touch Riley's arm and send out an aura of peace that would put Riley into a deep, relaxing sleep.

As the pain subsided, Jonathan managed to open one eye and saw Lucifer grinning at him.

"Welcome back." Then Lucifer jerked him to his feet, which sent a crippling pain throughout Jonathan's entire body.

"Help me. Help me," Jonathan heard himself pleading as a pair of arms encircled him. Finally able to catch his breath, Jonathan managed a meek "thank you," unsure of who he was thanking or where he was at the moment.

As he regained some of his strength, Jonathan made sure his legs would hold him upright before stepping out of the stranger's embrace. He wasn't the least bit surprised when he found out it was Lucifer who'd both caused and eased his pain.

"You are most welcome, Jonathan," Lucifer said condescendingly. "However, you may not want to thank me just yet. I am going to put you through another trial."

Lucifer then placed an arm around Jonathan and guided him to the other individuals in the room. The pain in Jonathan's head threatened to come forth if he made any sudden movements, so he allowed Lucifer's arm to remain where it was.

Stopping in front of a glass-barred cell, Lucifer released his arm from Jonathan. Now that his vision had returned to normal, Jonathan exchanged helpless expressions with the cell's occupants.

"So, this contraption is my own design," Lucifer said proudly. "It works like this: If I use one of my servants in the depths of Hell, I draw them forth by speaking their name. Whatever is housed inside the cell cannot come out unless I allow it to, but anything outside the cell can freely enter."

To illustrate his point, Lucifer reached inside the cell and moved his arm back and forth through the clear glass bars. Withdrawing his arm, Lucifer wanted to further prove his point, so he gazed upon the cell's occupants. "James, come forth," he said flatly.

The frail middle-aged man gave the briefest shake of his head before looking at Jonathan for help.

Barely managing to hold himself upright, Jonathan pressed a hand to the side of his temple and said dryly, "No need for any further demonstration. I get it. Nothing can leave unless you allow it."

Ignoring Jonathan, Lucifer repeated his command, and when James still didn't move, Lucifer's eyes faded to black.

"Okay. Okay," said James, shaking uncontrollably. "I'll do as you ask. I'm just scared, and I didn't mean to disobey." He sobbed uncontrollably as he took one tentative step in front of another toward the cell bars.

Jonathan wanted to look away, but he knew Lucifer would just make the man repeat the same horrendous act over and over until Jonathan submitted to watching.

Helpless, Jonathan closed his eyes and flinched when James let loose a final violent scream before hurling himself through the bars. When he opened his eyes, Jonathan saw that James had landed unharmed outside of the bars.

"See? Nothing to be afraid of," Lucifer comically said. He directed his attention to the woman standing inside the cell. "Your turn, Samantha."

Like James, the woman was hesitant to comply. "Please, I'll do anything you ask. Just don't ask this of me. I know what happens, I've been here once before. Master, don't you remember me?"

Lucifer's eyes turned black, and Samatha silenced. Without any further arguing or hesitation, Samantha screamed and jumped toward the cell bars. Her body came to rest on the floor next to Jonathan's feet.

The cell bars were no more than four inches apart, each one an inch wide, and they ran from floor to ceiling, making up the confines of the cell. The parts of Samantha's body that had not made contact with the bars lay atop the blood-stained carpet, basically reducing the woman to long strips of meat.

Disgusted, Jonathan wanted to shake his head in disapproval, but the fear of the crippling headache returning stopped him from doing so.

"See? You foolishly proclaimed earlier to understand how the cell works when you clearly didn't know anything. Now you most assuredly do!"

Lucifer took Jonathan by the arm and turned him to face James. The man was curled into a fetal position, praying, asking God for mercy. The scene was more than Jonathan could take, as it reminded him of something Granny had said before her life ended in the process of healing him. "Do you think the souls trapped in Hell cease to pray?" she had asked him. At the time, the thought had made him shudder, but now he was witnessing it in real time.

"I have to feed my hounds several times a day to keep their strength up," said Lucifer. "Luckily for me I have an endless supply of food for them."

Lucifer snapped his fingers and a dozen hounds materialized in the room.

How many actually exist? Jonathan wondered.

"Great question," Lucifer said, listening to Jonathan's thoughts. "They total 666, the same number as my regions and leaders. However, they possess a callously savage mentality that even my most ruthless Region Leaders will never be capable of. You see, Jonathan, just one of these hounds can consume an entire human body in a matter of seconds."

Lucifer let go of Jonathan and stroked one of the massive hound's heads. "Everything in Hell, including you, Jonathan, possesses self-healing. No matter how much harm is inflicted on them, everything regenerates to what or who they previously were, including my hounds."

Lucifer grabbed the scruff of the hound's neck, gave it a hard jerk, and held up its decapitated head for emphasis, letting the blood stream down to the floor before dropping it.

"Feed," said Lucifer to the remaining eleven hounds.

The hounds immediately consumed the bodies of the dead hound and Samantha. Jonathan was going to ask what became of the two, but Lucifer had read his mind. "She is now back in the depths of Hell, practically brand new. Although, she is now a meal for someone else. As for the hound, well, it is standing just right over there."

Jonathan looked in the direction Lucifer was pointing. The hound had appeared. Its muscled pink meat was still going through the rebuilding process, its organs performing their normal functions. Moments later, dark fur covered the hound. Its predatory eyes locked onto Jonathan's.

Jonathan knew Lucifer was baiting him to commit the next deadly sin, and since he now had a better understanding of the game, he was cautious, especially after committing the first two sins so easily. The only obstacle in his way was not knowing which of the remaining five sins Lucifer was setting up for him.

The first sin had been pride and the second was greed. That left wrath, lust, envy, gluttony, and sloth. Even if Lucifer was listening to his thoughts, Jonathan knew he had to be more proactive rather than waiting for things to transpire. The Bible verse in the book of Proverbs came to him, which offered some solace. *Whoever trusts in his own mind is a fool, but he who walks in wisdom will be delivered.*

Deducing that lust, envy, gluttony, and sloth did not apply to his current situation, Jonathan reasoned the next deadly sin had to be wrath, and Lucifer must be anticipating him to lash out in a blind rage in an attempt to save James, the last remaining of the damned.

The only thing he was certain Lucifer had overlooked was Jonathan's job as a guardian angel, which entailed the protection of mortals who still remained on Earth. It did not apply to those who were damned. Unfortunately for James, he was now and would forever remain a lost soul. He had made the choice not to be a worshipper of God the Father, and for that he would always belong to Lucifer.

"My babies are still hungry," said Lucifer, coaxing Jonathan to make a decision.

James was still in a fetal position, and although Jonathan felt immense sorrow for the man, there was nothing he could do for him except to pray the whole ordeal wouldn't last long.

"I am sorry, James," said Jonathan. "I wish . . ." He stopped from saying more, realizing it was meaningless.

"Feed," Lucifer ordered the hounds.

Jonathan turned his head and closed his eyes. When the screaming ended and there were no more sounds of flesh being consumed, Jonathan opened his eyes.

The black hounds were covered in James's blood and were licking one another to get the last remnants of their meal. A large red stain was all that remained of James. *I'm so sorry*, Jonathan thought.

Lucifer's face held no expression, and for a moment Jonathan thought he might have won this round, but he had the feeling something was wrong.

"When I was an angel, we were taught love and compassion, to love and appreciate one another at all costs. That we were of one body and resided in God the Father, and love existed above everything else," Lucifer said. "I actually believed this whole heartedly until God pushed us angels to the side, forcing us into a life of servitude for his new creation: the humans."

Jonathan focused again on the remaining five deadly sins. *Wrath is extreme anger. Lust is sexual desire. Envy is resentful jealousy. Gluttony is overindulgence. Sloth is* . . . Jonathan realized his mistake.

His job, above all others, not only as a guardian angel but as a child of God, was to always show love and compassion. It even applied to those who were damned. He had even told Riley that God the Father felt and hurt for those lost souls who chose to never believe in him or worship him.

Lucifer's expression had been unreadable only moments prior. Now he was smiling broadly as he held up three fingers. "Your thoughts, although misguided before, are correct now. The sin you just committed is known as sloth. Spiritual inactivity to do nothing as those around you suffer. You couldn't have saved James and Samantha from their eternity as one of my damned. However, even I believe you should have shown a little more compassion other than a hollow apology. Might have done them some good. Instead, you put yourself above them, deeming them worthless."

Hoping to ward off the pain to come, Jonathan held his hands on his right side and waited. As minutes passed, he developed a false sense of hope, thinking everything was going to be okay. Then an unseen object pierced his right side, causing him to cry out and collapse to the ground, writhing back and forth from the pain until it became too much. He blacked out.

When he finally came to, Jonathan saw the splattered stains on the ceiling and knew he was still in the torture room. In his attempt to sit up, Jonathan realized that his body was numb. He couldn't move an inch except for his eyes.

Hearing what he thought must be Lucifer sliding something

heavy across the ground, Jonathan felt helpless as he tried to see what the noise was. A moment later, a large black snake slithered into his unrestricted view. From the size of the snake's head, Jonathan was terrorized and knew what would come next.

"Three down, four to go," Lucifer said in a taunting tone.

The snake's mouth moved in sync with the words of his adversary. Glad he still had control over his eyes, Jonathan quickly shut them and prayed, "Father, please hear my plea and grant me peace for just a little while."

As soon as the words left his mouth, Jonathan received his peace as God the Father replied, "Be strong and courageous! Do not tremble or be dismayed, for the Lord your God is with you wherever you go. I am with you, my beloved. Your trial is not bigger than me."

Still refusing to open his eyes, Jonathan could feel he was no longer lying on the ground as his feet were above him. He didn't want to think about what was happening, but he had no choice in the matter. Lucifer's new snakelike form was in the process of swallowing him whole. He heard his bones begin to snap under the strain of pressure as he slid further inside the snake's throat.

Father again spoke, putting Jonathan's mind at complete ease. "Your trial is not bigger than me, my beloved. It's almost over. Now rest."

And with that, Jonathan fell into a deep, peaceful sleep.

CHAPTER 31

Tamara knew that after tonight's events, no one would ever mistake the town of Broken Falls for a place of fairy tales. Evil now lived and breathed freely, roaming the streets, a living nightmare eagerly anticipating its next meal. Strangely, even the town's name, Broken Falls, was now living up to this nightmarish hell going on inside its borders.

Broken Falls had been a popular tourist location known for its hiking, hot springs, and the beautiful waterfalls coming off the surrounding mountains. Unfortunately, those days were long gone, and who knew if they would ever come again?

Refocusing her thoughts to the task of getting out of town as quickly and safely as possible, Tamara whispered a silent prayer, asking for God's mercy for the remaining inhabitants who might still be trapped inside the town's perimeter. She prayed for the strength she would need to carry out the task as her father had instructed her to.

Tamara hurriedly made her way across the backyard, finding relief once her hand found the back fence gate. She opened it gently so the rusty hinges wouldn't give her away. She slowly pushed the gate half open, just enough to ease herself through, and closed it softly before sneaking away.

Although the creek was less than twenty feet away from her back gate, Tamara was hoping it was close enough that the noise of the constant moving water would be sufficient enough coverage for her daring escape, even if she was to lose her footing and fall in.

The overgrown weeds and other shrubbery presented the real problem, as moving through them the entire way out of town wasn't going to be possible. To avoid the weeds, she needed to immerse herself in the cool water and walk the creek as her path. Although the creek was only a few feet deep, the constant pull from the current and the soft, sandy bottom would quickly tax out her legs.

Pushing these negative thoughts away, Tamara crouched down and pushed her way through the tall weeds, stopping just short of falling off the bank into the creek. The water had carved a deeper drop-off where she now stood. One more step, and not only would she have been drenched, but anyone in the area would have heard her and known exactly where to find her.

Thanking God for small miracles, she made her way around the drop-off to an area where she could get into the creek without too much noise. She pushed the weeds aside and eased herself into the water with a little less difficulty.

Shocked by the chill of the water, she stood there a second as her shoes immediately filled with sand from the creek's bottom. Taking her first step, she felt her right shoe begin to pull free from the suction of the sand and the weight of the water. Two steps later, the shoe came off completely.

She quickly reached down and pulled her shoe free from the sand but fell face-first into the water. After pushing herself upright, Tamara removed her left shoe. She grabbed the laces of both shoes, tied them together, and tossed one shoe around her neck to carry them.

Although the splash she made from falling hadn't been very loud, an eerie feeling washed over her that someone was watching her. No longer caring about how cold she was, she cautiously made her way to the closest bank of the creek, sat down in the water, and did her best to fully submerge herself to keep from being seen.

Tamara strained her eyes to see if someone was out there, not sure what she was looking for exactly. She looked behind her, then in the direction she had been going, but nothing appeared to be out of the ordinary. Only the light from the moon flickered off the waters. As the minutes passed, her body shivered and she decided she had wasted enough time. Just as she began to stand, a soft whistle in the distance forced her back into the water.

She pressed her back into the side of the embankment, taking refuge in the overhanging weeds and hoping she hadn't given herself away. As the seconds ticked by, the insects started to emerge, crawling across the back of her bare neck and moving quickly to her face and shoulders, even getting tangled up in her hair. All the while she was still refusing to move, knowing someone was stalking her.

After a moment, another short whistle came, but now it sounded as though it had come from right next to her. Trying to remain calm, Tamara told herself not to move and she would be fine. Her thoughts were interrupted by a large, winged insect that flew directly into her face. Unable to stop her natural reaction to the giant bug, she let loose a startled cry, then quickly dunked her face into the water. Holding her breath, she rubbed her face, neck, shoulders, and hair.

Realizing she may have just given herself away, Tamara slowly brought her head out of the water. Her heart raced when she saw two men sitting on the opposite side of the creek, pointing rifles at her. Not sure what else to do, she raised both arms above her head.

"Are you alone?" one of the men asked in a hushed tone.

"Yes," Tamara answered, hoping her quick response would let

the men know she was telling the truth. What followed was a long silence as the men whispered to each other.

"I want you to slowly make your way over to us."

Tamara was angry that she had been caught. It was foolish of her to believe she would have been able to get out of town safely on her own. The stakes had been piled against her from the beginning. No matter what she had done, or how flawless she had been, she would have failed. She dropped her arms and made her way through the creek over to the men.

"Whoa!" the man snapped, no longer whispering. "Do not drop your hands! Keep your hands in the air! Do you understand me?"

Frightened from the man's outburst, Tamara shot her arms back up in the air, reaching as high as possible. Too petrified to move, she waited for further instruction, but when none came, she took a cautious step forward.

The creek's banks were only ten to fifteen feet apart, but it felt like it was getting farther away with each step forward. With only a few feet separating them, Tamara could now see the men more clearly. One of the men was older than her father, and the second man was middle-aged. She still didn't recognize either of them.

"Tamara! Why in the hell are you still here? Where is your father?" One of the men clearly recognized her. He swore under his breath. "I'm sorry, Tamara."

Although the guns were no longer pointing at her, Tamara was frightened and kept her arms up in the air.

"You can put your arms down now," said the man. "You're among friends. Again, I'm sorry for scaring you, but I promise you have nothing to fear from us."

With this reassurance, Tamara accepted the man's outstretched hand, and he helped her out of the creek and up onto the bank. The night air mixed with her wet clothing, making her shiver.

"It's lucky it was us who found you," said the older man. "About a mile up the creek there are diggers just waiting to ambush those who are still attempting to leave."

"Diggers?" asked Tamara.

"Short for grave diggers. It's what we—those of us who stayed behind—are referring to those who've aligned themselves with the false prophet."

Speechless, Tamara looked back and forth between the two men, thinking how surreal this all was.

"We have been following the diggers ever since they left the church," said the younger man. "Seriously, Tamara, we're lucky we found you before they did. Come with us to where the rest of our people are held up. We can provide you with protection and dry clothes, and hopefully get you out of town with the other women and children."

"Forgive me, but I'm at a loss," said Tamara. "You know who I am, but I have no idea who either of you are."

The two men exchanged brief smiles. "Tamara, we both know your father," said the younger man. "We recognized you from the pictures your father would show to us. He talked about you all the time when we went to his store. This is my dad, Jasper Wear, and my name is Brian Wear."

She knew Brian hadn't meant to hurt her with his words, but the mention of her father brought tears to her eyes. Even if she survived this nightmare, the thought of her parents would be like pouring salt in an open wound.

Brian embraced her in a quick hug, then offered a sheepish smile. "I'm sorry, Tamara. Those who have cast their lot with that man who is claiming to be a god will one day be held accountable for their transgressions, either in this life or the next. I can promise you that much. For now, please come with us and I will make certain to keep you safe."

Thankful for the apology, Tamara wiped the tears from her eyes.

"Okay, even the slightest of sounds carries over water, which is why we were able to find you so easily. While we are near the water, I need you to do your best to remain as quiet as possible. Do you understand?"

Tamara nodded. Her father had said the same thing.

Mr. Jasper gave Tamara a sideways hug. "We're going to walk up this side of the embankment and enter into Mr. Hightower's cornfield," said Jasper. "Brian will lead, and I'll bring up the rear with you in the middle. This way you won't get lost, as we'll need to go pretty deep into the field to avoid any unwelcome guests. Then we'll cut over to my neighborhood. I have an underground fallout shelter where we will be safe. Brian used to tease me about it, always telling me I was like some doomsday enthusiast. But who's laughing now?"

In spite of the gloomy mood, Tamara couldn't help but laugh before stifling it with the palm of her hand.

"Okay, you were right, and I was wrong," said Brian, unable to hide the amusement in his voice. "Now let's get moving."

Tamara put on her wet shoes and followed Brian up the side of the creek's steep embankment. From the weight of her wet shoes, Tamara stumbled a bit as she fought to keep them on her feet while she trudged her way to the top of the embankment. She took a deep breath of relief when all three of them stepped safely into Mr. Hightower's cornfield.

CHAPTER 32

Since they hadn't really had a moment for Maggie to show him around, Riley went in search of a guest room and bathroom. He could have just used Maggie's, but he was curious and wanted to explore the rest of the living quarters. He had to be mindful if he came across anymore of her stupid, precious rock collection.

The set-up of the suite was pretty basic. Excluding, of course, the lavish furnishings and pricey décor. The entryway led into the massive open-concept living room and kitchen. There were two hallways that broke off from the living room. One led to Maggie's bedroom, and the other Riley assumed was where he would find a guest room and bathroom. So, he ventured down the hall, only to find a personal gym and a locked door.

"Strange," Riley said to Kratos. "It's hard to believe this entire suite is made up of just a kitchen, master bedroom, living room, gym, and whatever lies behind this door."

Kratos sniffed at the locked door and looked at Riley, waiting for further instruction. If Riley gave the order, Kratos would turn the door into splinters, but he decided against it. "I'm sure it's locked for a good reason. So, I guess I'll just have to use Maggie's bathroom. But before I do, how about we get you something to eat?"

At the prospect of being fed, Kratos's ears went up. Riley envisioned Kratos devouring whatever demon he was ordered to kill for nourishment. He forced the vision aside. "Now I seriously doubt there is any dog food in this museum Maggie calls home, but there are a lot of leftover sandwiches you're welcome to."

Riley hoped Kratos would rush past him toward the kitchen. Instead, he dropped his head and raised one paw, as if asking for permission to go eat.

Despite telling Kratos they would always be mortal enemies; this small act of obedience provided him with a little more clarity into Kratos's character. He hadn't asked to be created, but he had been created regardless.

Riley dropped to his knees and placed both hands on the sides of Kratos's face, just as Maggie had done, forcing the hound to look him in the eyes. "Kratos, I'm not asking you to submit to me. After we save Jonathan, I will not let go of you so easily, even if Lucifer demands that you return to him. So, hear me and know what I'm saying is true: your life is anew from this day forward. You are not what you once were, and my hope, as strange as this may sound, is for you to remain with us if you choose to. And not as a servant to a master, but instead as our equal."

They looked at one another for several moments, then Kratos stepped forward and placed his large head on Riley's shoulder. Wrapping both arms around Kratos's neck, Riley slowly stroked the hound, no longer fearful or worried of Kratos's reason for coming into their lives.

When Kratos stepped back, Riley stood. "Now, let's get you some food."

Riley felt Kratos move past him but never saw him. Only the scratching sounds of paws on the hardwood floor alerted Riley to Kratos's movements. *My God, it is far quicker than Jonathan.* Then another thought occurred. *And I thought it was wise to threaten him?* This realization made the hair on the back of his neck stand up as gooseflesh covered his arms.

Entering the kitchen, Riley found Kratos holding the bag of sandwiches in his mouth. "I said you're welcome to them."

Exhibiting a normal dog's behavior, Kratos cocked his head to one side as if asking Riley a question. Taking a guess as to what it might be, Riley smiled. "I'm full, but I appreciate the consideration."

In a blur of movement, Kratos devoured not only the sandwiches, but the bag and wrappers as well.

Riley filled a large bowl with water and sat it down next to Kratos, who instantly drained it. He then looked to Riley for more. Riley filled it two more times.

"There is a scripture which tells us how the occupants in Hell beg for just a drop of water to cool their tongue. You'll never be an occupant of Hell again. I don't know how this will play out exactly, but I do know I won't leave you there. That's a promise, and I will make you another promise. I will always keep your water bowl full, so you'll never have to ask again, but for now, unless you really are thirsty, let's show some restraint."

Riley could see Kratos was struggling with this dilemma as he allowed himself a few more laps of water before sitting back on his haunches.

"Good, because I'm beyond exhausted. I'm going to shower and try to get a few hours of rest. In the meanwhile, you are on your own, but please do not venture outside of Maggie's suite."

Riley rubbed Kratos behind his ears before disappearing into Maggie's room.

After showering and drying off, he realized he had nothing clean to wear. He didn't have any toiletry items, thanks to their hurried departure from the lake house.

He dabbed toothpaste on a finger and brushed his teeth the best he could. Then he threw on one of Maggie's bathrobes and walked into her bedroom. As comfortable as her bed appeared, Riley wasn't about to get into her bed and under the covers.

Riley stumbled down the hall to the living room and fell onto the couch recliner. He fiddled with the side control and was pleasantly surprised when the seat went completely horizontal. The live night sky was displayed across the expansive ceiling, making Riley feel as if he was being propelled into outer space.

Before allowing sleep to overtake him, Riley spoke around a yawn. "Kratos, would you mind standing watch while I rest?"

Riley hadn't seen the hound when he entered the living room; he just had faith that Kratos had heard him. Moments later, Riley felt hot breath on his outstretched hand, followed by Kratos's wet nose.

"Thank you," said Riley.

Then he unexpectedly coughed into the palm of his hand. Too tired to retrieve a napkin from the kitchen, Riley was about to wipe the residue on Maggie's robe when he coughed again.

"Allergy season," said Riley.

However, Kratos didn't appear convinced as he placed his two front paws on the chair and leaned into Riley's face.

Then Riley burst into a fit of coughing and was unable to stop for several minutes. Finally, he managed to take in a full breath before drawing a hand across his mouth. A new fear slid into Riley's thoughts as the taste of iron weighed heavy on his tongue and there was blood in his palm. Kratos issued a low, deep growl.

CHAPTER 33

Maggie stared out the window at the skyline of Taupe City from the boardroom on the eleventh floor of Gregory Portal Provider. She felt fortunate and blessed. The first obstacle to putting her life back together had been dealt with. The morning sun seemed to offer its approval, warming her skin with its rays as she gazed out at the busy streets.

The city itself, with its constant traffic and hurried occupants, never rested. Maggie could remember a time not long ago when Taupe City had been surrounded by farmland. That was until her company became the forefront in internet streaming and had birthed the rise in large corporations purchasing the surrounding real estate, causing a domino effect to the farmland owners as they were pushed out of the area one by one. Maggie felt like she was the primary cause for destroying a past that was now long forgotten, no remnants left of the once farmed lands. As she stared out the window at all the buildings and the people running around below, this realization saddened Maggie, but at the same time, she found some comfort in knowing the large corporations had paid the landowners four times what the land was actually valued at.

She had monopolized the market in streaming with her innovative way of thinking. Years ago, people needed multiple subscriptions to enjoy their favorite programs, from sports, to movies, to regular daytime soap operas. Her father had told her that everyone used to enjoy free television programing with just a pair of rabbit ears attached to their TV, usually adorned with aluminum foil.

This story was what actually inspired Maggie with the idea of bringing everything, once more, back together and making it more affordable for everyone. If you paid a monthly subscription to Gregory Portal Provider, you would have access to everything involved in streaming.

Even now Maggie couldn't believe how successful she was when she stopped and thought about it. She had taken a large gamble when she purchased bandwidth on an already established and owned satellite. Eventually it paid off, and she had enough capital to purchase thousands more satellites.

The boardroom door opened and closed behind her, pulling Maggie's attention away from her vantage point of the city. Maggie knew it was Stuart returning after seeing the three agents out of the building. She could still see the sad expression on Agent Winters's face after informing her she didn't believe in God.

Stuart walked over, and they looked out at the skyline of Taupe City. Maggie slipped her hand into his and gave it a gentle squeeze. "Thank you, Stuart."

When he didn't respond, Maggie continued with the next item on the agenda. "How soon can you schedule an emergency meeting with the remaining board members?"

Again, no response. Maggie knew Stuart had something else on his mind but decided it was best to wait until he was ready to tell her what was troubling him.

"I heard what you whispered to Agent Winters," said Stuart in an accusatory tone.

Removing her hand from his, Maggie felt the small relief

of the victory they had just achieved slipping away and being replaced by a slow building of anger. *Stay calm, stay calm*, Maggie mentally told herself. However, she'd be damned if she was apologizing for not believing in a god who would punish her mother for eternity and left her to an afterlife of nothing but pain.

"I don't understand. After all you've seen and gone through, how can you not believe there's a God? Every individual on the planet asks, 'Why?' 'Why do I exist?' 'Is there life after death?' And yet here you stand knowing firsthand not only of God's existence but the Devil's as well. Along with demons, angels, hellhounds, Heaven, and even Hell!"

"Hell?" Maggie asked sharply, no longer caring about keeping the anger at bay. She refused to be lectured about her beliefs when she had her reasons for them. "Maybe you're right about Hell and all the rest of the stupid supernatural crap being real. Regardless, if I allow myself to admit I believe in a god who would allow such cruelty, then it's like I'm personally condemning my mother to an eternity of torture and pain. You can think and believe whatever or however you want, but do not push me to believe the same or question why I refuse to believe in some all-knowing and loving entity the way you do."

Stuart was unable to hide his troubled, shocked expression.

Maggie fumed because she not only had to defend herself to her best friend, but also at the direction her life had taken. Taking in a deep breath and blowing it out, Maggie looked away out the window at the view of the outstretched city. Sooner or later, she would have to face a harsher reality than what had already played out over the past few hours. She may have even been welcoming death out of ignorance because her future involved tracking down a rogue demon.

"I'm sorry," said Stuart. "It just feels like hollow words when

I've never even considered that your parents could play a part in all of this. But for what it's worth, I truly am sorry for my ignorance."

Too angry to acknowledge the apology, Maggie changed the direction of the conversation. "How soon until you can get the board members together? I hope to have everything completed before the day's end."

Checking his watch, Stuart sighed. "It's a little after nine now, so I believe I can have everyone here by ten."

He left her side, took a seat at the table, and began typing up what Maggie assumed was an email to the board members.

No longer than twenty minutes after Stuart sent the email, the room began to slowly fill with happy voices Maggie recognized. She remained with her back to the room, looked out the windows, as she worked up the courage to ask everyone for forgiveness.

She had personally approved and promoted every single one of her board members, working alongside each one of them for countless hours, forming strong relationships that could rival any close-knit family.

Nevertheless, she had also put their jobs in jeopardy after the media learned of her dealings with Miles Jackson. Before that debacle, Maggie had brought unwelcome scrutiny upon them, taking a yearlong leave of absence in search of Jonathan without even so much as an explanation.

Stuart had smoothly handled the transition after she had placed him in charge, but that wasn't the point. She simply walked away to chase her new obsession, forgetting all about the sacrifices each and every individual had made in order to make Gregory Portal Provider what it was today. Maggie wanted to tell them she was sorry for what she had put them through, but only saying that much would be inadequate.

After what felt like too much time had passed, Maggie forced herself to turn and face them. She was caught off guard as each board member, including Stuart, was standing and smiling at her. Speechless, she smiled back at them, then gave a small shake of her head as she covered her face with her hands and began crying.

"I am so sorry for my actions," was all Maggie was able to get out.

One by one, her board members stepped forward and hugged her, offering her words of encouragement. Now that the hard part was over, Maggie took her seat, thankful to work with such amazing and kindhearted people.

"Thank you all so much for your dedication. During this tumultuous time, we have lost five amazing board members to my selfish actions. Nonetheless, I can assure you, those days are now behind us. I have cleared up the issue regarding the Miles Jackson fiasco and was told earlier I have nothing further to be worried about. Also, I think we can all agree that Stuart has done an amazing job in my absence, and I'd like him to continue in his role for the time being. That's if he agrees, of course."

Several members of the board nodded their heads in approval, while the others voiced their agreement. Stuart smiled, but Maggie could see the uncertainty he tried to hide behind. He was by far the smartest man she had ever known, and yet he carried a cloud of self-doubt that Maggie never could understand.

"I'm guessing you're leaving me no choice in the matter," said Stuart, "so I accept."

"Thank you, and you are correct. You have no choice in the matter," said Maggie, smiling at him and making everyone laugh at the easy candor. "The reason for this transition is because I have something I need to take care of before I return for good. I would rather not discuss it, as it is of a personal nature, but I do promise it will have no ill effect on any of you or Gregory Portal Provider."

The board members nodded their heads in approval, thankful for the reassurance.

"I hate to cut this short," said Maggie, "but that's all I have for now. Unless anyone else has something that needs to be discussed?"

"Just glad to see you're okay and hope you hurry back to us," said Mrs. Daniels, sweetly smiling at Maggie.

Returning the smile, Maggie nodded her head as gesture of thanks.

As the meeting came to a close, hugs and promises to remain in touch were exchanged. Stuart took his usual seat to the left of Maggie after everyone had gone. Opening his laptop, he gave her a genuine smile then began tapping away at the keyboard.

"Figured I'd get an early start on the companywide email. Your employees will be happy to hear their jobs are no longer in jeopardy now that you're in the clear," he said with a soft chuckle.

"I'm lost, Stu," said Maggie, ignoring his light banter. "I feel lost, and I'm terrified to submit to your God even though I do know he exists."

The typing ceased and Stuart looked at her. His expression didn't offer pity or reassurance, but rather great sympathy as his lower lip began to tremble.

He truly is my godsend, she thought. "I saw my mother. I know, it sounds strange, but I didn't just see her—I was threatened by her."

Maggie stared forward. Hot tears slid down her face as the pent-up anger dwelling inside her kept her strangely calm. "The rogue demon we're after put both Riley and me into what we thought was a form of deep meditation. What followed was more than just a living nightmare. It was a glimpse of what awaited me once I pass from this world."

Stuart took her hand, but Maggie didn't move or bother returning the grip.

Then, as if her anger had burst forth and now had control of her, she barked, "I hate your God because of this even being a possibility! How am I to submit, love, or respect a god that allows this kind of pain and turmoil to take place? My mom was the kindest person I've ever known. Her compassion and love for others taught me kindness. So, answer me this, Stu, because I respect and love you more than anything or anyone else in this world. Why would you ever ask me to believe in such a god? Furthermore, how could you even believe in this sick fuck of a god? At this very moment, my mother is screaming and crying out for mercy and yet receiving none. Instead, she is being fed upon by worms, flames, and others who are stuck in the same situation as her. So, why should I follow him?"

"Because I can't imagine you ever having to suffer like she is now!" blurted Stuart.

Maggie's jaw dropped. She sat there with her mouth agape, stunned. Not at what Stuart said, exactly, but because he had just provided confirmation her mother was in fact in Hell.

"I love your mother and I always will," said Stuart. "I also know your mother only wanted the best for you, even if it means you will never see her again. Parents will do anything for their children—and I mean anything—to ensure they never have to suffer the same hardships. Trust me, Mags. She does not want you to end up where she is. That's if she's even in Hell. So, you can rationalize and play all the mind games you want, but that is exactly what the Devil wants you to do. You know the truth, and as painful as it may be, you have a decision to make before heading out to find that rogue demon. Remain ignorant and be damned or open yourself to the possibility that my God is love."

Maggie pulled her hand free, frustrated that she was unable to make him see and agree with her logic. "Your god is the furthest thing from love," she said coldly. "No matter how you slice this scenario, my mother is still damned."

Stuart broke eye contact for a moment, then studied Maggie. "If it is possible, let this cup pass from me. Nevertheless, not as I will, but as You will." Confused, Maggie started to ask for clarification, but Stuart continued, "Jesus asked God to show mercy so he wouldn't have to taste death. Later in the scripture before he died, Jesus said, 'Forgive them Father, for they know not what they do.' So, yes, Mags, my God is love. If he wasn't, then he would have never allowed his son Jesus to taste death so we might have everlasting life."

Although Stuart was making sense, Maggie was done with this conversation. Before she had a moment to change the subject, Stuart did it for her. "If you would like to discuss more about this later, you know I'm always here for you. I don't want to overwhelm you, and I'm sorry if I made you feel that way. It's almost noon now, so how about we check in on Riley? Perhaps get some lunch?"

Maggie nodded, stood, and turned to leave, but before she could, Stuart embraced her in a tight hug. "Thank you for sharing with me. I wish I had the ability to take away your pain."

"Thank you," said Maggie. "I have no doubt you would if you could."

CHAPTER 34

Playing the part of the idiot to perfection, Gideon appeared to listen intently as Jameson explained Esperanza's plan, all in the hope that they wouldn't be judged too harshly if Savior found out. They were forgetting one major detail, which made them even bigger idiots than Gideon had been pretending to be since Tristan punished him. They served an unmerciful psychopath who didn't give second chances, which meant all of them were going to be punished back to the depths, or worse, after Savior learned the truth regarding Tristan.

That was, of course, except for Esperanza, whom Savior flat out adored. He was grooming her to be more than just another lackey as her previous predecessor had been. Savior saw her as he had Bryce and Abel, and he had a deep affection for her. So, no, her punishment wouldn't be nearly as severe as theirs.

Even stranger was that throughout Gideon's time of being an Elder, and even when he was just a mediocre slave collecting the dead in Tristan's region, Gideon couldn't ever recall anyone referring to Lucifer as Savior. It only began after Esperanza delivered her introduction speech before a trial to all the Region Leaders. Tristan later fumed over the idea because he hadn't thought of it first. And if memory served correctly, it was the same day when Tristan ripped out Gideon's eye and fastened him with the patch to hide the gruesomeness behind it.

After that atrocity, Gideon decided enough was enough

and began devising a plan to overthrow him. Now that Tristan was missing, Gideon's new mission was to locate him, not for retribution, but because he believed Tristan discovered a loophole to keep himself out of Hell.

In Tristan's absence, Jameson immediately asserted dominance and put himself in charge, which was predictable. His first act was instituting a schedule for all three Elders so they could, for the first time in their demon lives, experience some downtime to do whatever they wished, something Tristan would have considered as a sign of weakness.

Gideon knew why Jameson made this his top priority, and it had nothing to do with proving how much he valued either of the other two Elders. It was done as a bribe to ensure Jameson's position if Tristan were to unexpectedly show back up to reclaim his region.

If Jameson wanted to be in charge, then by all means he could be. Gideon's only purpose in this moment was keeping up the act and getting out of Hell. Thinking back on the series of events that had unfolded before this meeting with Esperanza, couldn't have come at a better time for Gideon.

Figuring out how to obtain that information had been an arduous task when only the Elders and Esperanza knew of Tristan's absence. Gideon couldn't let anyone catch on to his plans, so he would have to get the information from someone else.

Most demons assumed only Savior knew exactly how many occupants resided in Hell at any given time. The number grew so drastically from moment to moment that it would be impossible for just any demon to keep track. However, Gideon recalled the legend of the Ferryman.

The Ferryman was a relic, and at one time, humans had put their faith in him. According to the arrangement, the dead must pay two coins for the Ferryman to carry their souls safely across the lake of fire and into what they believed to be a perfect paradise.

Tristan had explained the legend of the Ferryman to four Region Leaders, so they'd assist him in his next invasion to expand his region even more. The only real currency in Hell were stories with veiled tips about how to escape the fiery inferno; and the Ferryman's story promised such freedom.

Tristan was a rarity because he was the only Region Leader who had never been replaced. He was the only one both slaves and leaders alike begged to have an audience with, willing to do whatever he asked of them. Regardless of the demon's status, they were ignored if what they had to offer didn't benefit Tristan. More often than not, Tristan would make up stories to get what he wanted from an individual. He would later laugh about how ignorant the fool had been, saying, "Greed is not just a deadly sin that only applies to mortals."

When operating outside the confines of Hell, even while gathering the souls of the dead from Earth, a demon only lasted a measly sixty seconds before being pulled back to Hell. But many demons believed there were workarounds to get past the minute-long time limit. Rumors spread of rogue demons who were permitted to walk the Earth without fear of being pulled back within any specific time limit.

The Ferryman's story was true, for the stakes had been too high for Tristan to be making it up. He had asked the four Region Leaders to help him overthrow the largest region at the time. If he were successful, Savior would reward him by expanding his own region.

After Tristan overthrew the new region, the four Region Leaders were never heard from again. Savior replaced them without any questions, which meant Savior knew they had escaped Hell and relished in the unknown chaos four escaped demons would bring. But Gideon was puzzled because if Tristan knew the Ferryman was able to grant safe passage out of Hell, why hadn't he abandoned his region long ago?

The answer was simple: Tristan had the foresight to know that all good things came to an end, and Savior would eventually pull back those who were foolish enough to believe they had escaped from Hell. The leaders did not return to their previous roles; instead, they were forced to the depths of Hell, never to be heard from again.

Still, what if they were truly free? The question weighed heavily on Gideon's mind, as there was no real proof, they had been caught. Tristan was now missing after going on an errand Savior ordered. Legionaries, Savior's previous lackey, was also gone, and all anyone knew was that he had been quickly replaced by Esperanza. Two very important demons basically vanished, and the only way to find out what had really happened to them was by seeking out the Ferryman.

In Tristan's version of the story, Savior was the one who had brought the Ferryman into existence. The Ferryman became known to humans because Savior had filled a corrupt king's dream with a deceitful tale of Hell and death. Savior played on the king's fear of what would happen to him in the afterlife. Savior made himself available when the king attempted to sleep. The king's dreams were filled with images of a dark-robed man pushing a small wooden boat across a lake, coming closer to him until at last arriving at the shore where the king was standing.

As moments of silence passed between the two, the king attempted to board the small boat, only to be stopped by a skeletal hand. Red eyes were set ablaze, but the rest of the Ferryman's features were hidden by his dark brown robes.

"Payment," the Ferryman declared in a low, gravelly voice.

He left no interpretation as to who was in charge of the

situation. Frantically, the king searched his pockets but only pulled out lint and loose threads. Helplessly, the once confident king was reduced to sobs and pleas, even falling to his knees as he begged for mercy, only for it to fall upon deaf ears.

The Ferryman sat back down in the boat, and without any compassion for the king, methodically made his way back to the open water. As his outline began to disappear in the heavy fog that covered the lake, the king's loud sobs resonated off the troubled water.

"Please?" the king begged.

As the helplessness of the situation began to set in, the king slapped at the sides of his face, pulling large clumps of his hair out.

The king yelled out, "Who are you to judge me? Even as a king I showed mercy to those I've conquered on the battlefield, for only the godless are without compassion for the meek!"

The fog was dense as the water interrupted the silence with its endless beating against the shoreline. The king dropped his head in defeat. Just as he was turning away, he heard the reply to his question.

"Two coins, king of nothing. No more, no less. For I possess no compassion for the dead."

The king's own screams startled him awake. That day, the king declared that every burial must include two coins being placed upon the departed's eyes. Even the king himself started carrying pockets full of change, ensuring he would never again be stuck in limbo.

According to Tristan, Savior targeted the king because he was a ruler, and his beliefs would trickle down to all those who served him. This, in turn, would drive out the false God's prophets who taught his ways. Those who refused to follow in the king's decree were branded as traitors and either met with an immediate death or fled the kingdom, further ensuring Savior's foothold would never waver.

Savior made the Ferryman the first lackey in charge of notating the number and names of the occupants in Hell, as well as keeping record of those who had found ways to escape and not be pulled back. Even though it rarely happened, Savior did find extreme pleasure when rogue demons would escape to roam Earth, creating destruction and havoc in their wake, but he also kept track of them.

The first day Gideon got downtime, he left his region to find the Ferryman. Based on Tristan's story, he had an inclination about where to start his search. The journey started by taking a wormhole into the depths of Hell. Once it opened up, Gideon found himself smack dab in the middle of a fight for his life, fending off the damned while they bit and clawed at him.

As he forged on in search of the wormhole to the Ferryman, he continued fighting through the damned. The madness of the depths threatened to overtake him. Finally, he saw a blue outline of another wormhole only a few feet away. According to Tristan's story, there was something different about this wormhole. It operated like a normal door with an actual knob, whereas all the other wormholes worked by stepping inside them and speaking the destination of where you wanted to go.

Fighting off the damned with a new sense of urgency, Gideon finally made it to the door. He located the knob and attempted to turn it, but he was only met with resistance. Cursing himself for believing anything that had slithered from Tristan's mouth, Gideon prepared to fight his way through the damned to the wormhole he had arrived in, only to find that they were no longer trying to get to him or fighting each other. Instead, they were staring at the Ferryman's wormhole with a new kind of hunger growing in their eyes.

For whatever reason, they'd been oblivious to the wormhole's existence until now. Maybe they were too distracted by their pain and anguish to have even noticed it before. However, now that Gideon had drawn their attention to the door, he saw their expressions change to curiosity.

Before any of them had time to even move, the door flew open, pulling only Gideon through, and dumping him face first into a new dimension of Hell.

After regaining his senses, it appeared he had sand in his mouth. He spit several times until the sound of water lapping broke into his consciousness. He quickly stood, only to stumble backward, falling back to the ground at the sight of the overwhelming landscape in front of him.

He pressed the palms of his hands into his eyes until dark purple spots danced into view. He was certain he was imagining it. Water did not exist in Hell. It was another form of punishment to drive all the occupants further into insanity, as they would plead for just a single drop to quench their thirst.

Opening his eyes once more, he awkwardly stood to take in the immense size of the crystal-blue lake. Without a second thought, he darted toward the water, dropped to all fours, and tediously reached out to feel the wetness in the palm of his hand.

Before he could scoop up the water, a dry, amused voice stopped him. "Touch it if you want, but your quench will not be satisfied here."

CHAPTER 35

G ideon froze and reexamined his plan. Everything he had done led up to this exact moment. He'd made Jameson and Barbados believe Tristan had cursed his missing eye with worms, enforcing the narrative that he was losing his mind. He played the part of the fool for so long, only to have it all come crashing down around him. Had he been too blind to realize that someone had seen through his act and reported him? Turning reluctantly around to face his judgment, Gideon let out a sigh of relief at what he saw. The gaunt figure of the Ferryman, dressed in a brown robe hiding his features, was resting on top of a hollowed-out log.

"You presume too much if you suspect I'm happy to find you upon my shores, Gideon, elder in the region once known as Tristan's," said the Ferryman.

Having been called out by his name, his title, and his region surprised Gideon. At the same time, it confirmed another part of Tristan's story to be true: Savior wasn't the only one who knew every detail of the occupants residing in Hell.

"I can see from your change in demeanor that I must have revealed something you were unsure of until now. Care for me to take a guess? Or shall we dispense with the pleasantries and get down to why you have come?"

Gideon nodded in response while taking the seat the Ferryman had gestured to.

"You seem to know all about me and my past. Well, at least

you believe you do. And although my story has been diluted from demon to demon for well over a century, there is one thing that has remained consistent in every telling."

Gideon knew what he was alluding to, but still cocked his head in mild curiosity. This had to be the first time in years the relic entertained company.

"You are correct, Gideon," said the Ferryman. "Also, much like Savior, I, too, can listen in on your thoughts, but my ability is limited to this wasteland I oversee. Or as I have come to call it, my forever, tucked-away, estranged paradise."

Gideon looked up and down the shoreline and noticed for the first time that it was indeed a wasteland. The blackened soil stretched limitless in both directions, adorned with sparse vegetation, either dead or on the verge of dying. Moments ago, Gideon was eager to dip his hands into the crystal-blue flowing water to quench his unending thirst. Now, he could clearly see that it wasn't fog resting atop the water, but smoke billowing up from the bubbles bursting on the water's surface. Acidic bubbles bulged through the surface until it was unable to sustain any more pressure, popping and releasing the smoke along with the strong smell of sulfuric acid into an otherwise clear blue and sunny sky.

"Now," said the smug Ferryman, "I know you're here because you want me to tell you how to escape and how to locate Tristan. However, you, Elder Gideon, have nothing with which to pay me. For you are only fifty-one years of age in eternity. Are you aware your mortal life was longer by thirteen years? Or have you already forgotten all the precious memories of your past life?"

None of the occupants of Hell had memory of their past life, whether it was erased from the daily excruciating pain they endured or because they chose to forget. Drudging up memories wouldn't help their current situation and would only serve to drive them further into insanity.

When Gideon had been unexpectedly rescued from the depths to work as a slave in Tristan's region, he rose from slave to Elder in a short period of time. During that time, he learned he was different from the other slaves and demons because he possessed the ability to remember his past life.

While collecting the dead souls, he'd cautiously began asking those he had worked alongside if they remembered any part of their life on Earth, only to be answered with stern looks and hard nos. Eventually he stopped asking, not wanting to draw any further attention to himself.

Gideon had actually benefitted from his inability to forget the past, as it provided him with memories to escape from the pain. Being able to block out physical pain was the only reason Tristan and Jameson had agreed to promote him to Elder. That was how he'd overheard Tristan's story about the Ferryman.

When Region Leaders unexpectedly showed up to accuse Tristan of any wrongdoings, he would summon Gideon to the small, cramped office to make sure things didn't get out of control. Although Tristan never knew Gideon's secret, he definitely reveled in the fact that Gideon could face several demons at once and always come out victorious. No matter how much physical damage he'd receive in the altercation, Gideon was able to keep going long after the Region Leaders had submitted.

As Gideon stared at the Ferryman, he realized he did have a way to bargain, his memories. He got straight to the point.

"What you say is true, for I possess nothing with which to pay you. I would share stories of what I've endured, but they would only bore you, for I am certain that all the demons who have come before offered similar proposals. To be fair, all you need do is simply breathe in our scent and you'll know every detail about us."

Even though he couldn't see the Ferryman's face hidden

behind the hood of his brown robes, Gideon knew the Ferryman was relishing in the power he held over him.

"Do you think of yourself as special?" asked Gideon. "You are nothing more than a relic, an irrelevant piece of the past, a character written into existence as a scare tactic to ensure our beloved Savior's kingdom continued to grow. You were a means to an end, and yet, embarrassingly, you still believe yourself to be of importance."

When the Ferryman didn't respond to the insults, Gideon remained silent too. Knowingly he felt he had made clear he was looking for a fight. Gideon believed if he was able to best the Ferryman, then he would at last obtain the answers he was seeking.

"Are you finished berating me? Gideon, now former Elder of Tristan's region, and soon to be new resident of the depths of Hell," said the Ferryman in an amused tone.

Picking up on the not-so-subtle threat, Gideon couldn't help but grin. "Glad we could come to a mutual understanding. If I best you, I only want to know what happened to Tristan. The rest of what I have planned doesn't concern you."

"And when you lose?"

Still smiling, Gideon reached out and offered a hand to seal the deal, which the Ferryman hesitantly took. "Then you won't have to send me to the pits, for I will go of my own accord. Unlike the rest of the damned, my word actually still means something."

Preparing himself for the fight, Gideon backed away from the Ferryman. He turned his back on him and closed his eyes. When he was in Tristan's cramped office, his opponents were more intimidated when they couldn't see what he was doing.

There were other reasons why he turned his back. First, it was easier to block out the loud voices in the room and focus on the sound of the small bell that sat on Tristan's desk. When it rang, the time for conversing was over and Gideon was to handle the rest. Secondly, and more importantly, he kept his face hidden because his past memories would surface more when his eyes were closed.

Gideon's memories were so real that he could taste the food; feel the touch of his wife; hear his children's laughter; smell the faintest of scents, like fresh cut grass; and recall every word said in previous conversations. He was at peace until the bell rang, tearing him out of his memories and ripping his loved ones away from him all over again. Then he would snap, not caring if there were a hundred leaders in the room. He would rip them all apart for stealing the only thing that kept him sane.

He kept his back turned to the Ferryman as the memory of his daughter's wedding roared to life around him. The DJ announced it was time for the daddy-daughter dance. Escorting her onto the dance floor, Gideon marveled at how cruel time was, how it felt like just yesterday he had been changing her diapers, bandaging her scraped knees, kissing away her nightmares, watching her become a young woman, and now a wife. As the music poured through the speakers, his daughter's smile widened.

"I thought you might recognize this song," Gideon said, moving slowly across the dance floor.

"It's perfect, Dad," said his daughter. "Thank you for choosing yours and Mom's song for this occasion."

Gideon held his daughter closer as he sang along to the words, trying to keep his tears at bay. Just then, a hand touched his shoulder, ripping his daughter out of his arms.

Gideon quickly tackled the individual to the ground. He unleashed a barrage of lightning-fast punches before the Ferryman had a chance to even react. "Yield, you bastard, or I will drag you to the depths myself!"

The Ferryman's hood had fallen askew during the attack.

What Gideon found looking back at him was a younger version of himself. In shock, he pushed himself backward, scrambling to get off the Ferryman. Gideon shook his head, unable to comprehend what he was seeing.

"What's happening?" Gideon managed to ask in a rough voice.

This younger reflection pushed himself up and answered in his own voice. "How can you remember your past?"

Still shocked and confused, Gideon could not answer.

"I can no longer remember what I look like. However, I can take on the appearance of any who comes to my shore as they currently look. Never anything from their past life before. So, how is it you can remember your past? Not just remember, but actually place yourself into your memories and experience them as if for the first time all over again?"

Although he understood the Ferryman's question, Gideon was distracted by the familiar face looking back at him. Without having to say anything, the Ferryman changed his appearance to an old man.

"I don't know how or why I can still remember everything about my past life," said Gideon. "It's both a curse and a blessing. For one, it allows me to turn off all effects of physical pain when I escape into my past memories. However, knowing these are only memories, and I will never really have a second chance to see my loved ones ever again, which is far more painful than anything anyone could ever physically do. If I had to choose between the two, I would choose the physical pain."

The Ferryman nodded his head in understanding, then resumed his seat back on the hollowed-out log. He motioned for Gideon to sit next to him instead of in front of him as before.

"Those who come to me with the hope that I will show them

the way to escape do not get what they bargained for. Tristan sends them to me knowing they are destined for the depths of Hell. Including you. Nevertheless, your ability to remember your past has intrigued me and saved you."

Gideon suspected as much when it came to Tristan. He was the most conniving and sly demon. After all, he was the only Region Leader to never have been replaced. The thought of this gaunt relic believing he could so easily force Gideon back to the depths without so much as a fight was comical.

"I can understand why you think it to be an unbelievable feat," said the Ferryman, who had been listening in on Gideon's thoughts. "But I assure you, I can. This is my domain, and it's remained mine for well over a thousand years. All I have to do is say your full name and Hell takes care of the rest. Pulling you back into her depths, never to be heard from again."

Worry etched its way into Gideon's thoughts, as he realized he was powerless to do anything if the Ferryman was being truthful.

"You truly are fascinating to me. I will give you the answers you are looking for. Obviously, I will want something in return."

Gideon nodded in agreement, knowing the alternative would be far worse than anything the Ferryman could ask of him.

"Savior will eventually realize what has happened to his missing demons and will pull you all back. That's one thing you can be certain of, so I suggest you enjoy your time on Earth as much as possible. Upon your impending return, I will bring you back to my shores, and I will take every last one of your memories and make them my own. I will then send you on your way back to the depths. Where you'll be just another absentminded and amnesiac demon."

Gideon's eyes widened. "Damn. All of them? Just gone?" He had said he'd rather deal with the physical pain than the mental pain he felt when remembering his past. But now that his memories were being used as a bargaining chip, he felt the overwhelming need to protect them.

"Gideon, it is your choice whether you hang on to them. I cannot take your memories unless you agree and freely give them to me. Nevertheless, if we don't come to some kind of agreement, then I will simply speak your full name and be rid of you."

"Why do you even want them?" Gideon asked defensively. "What could they possibly mean to you?"

"As I said before, I do not remember my own face. I can't even remember if I had a life before this one, I'm stuck. But—"

"You want my memories to claim as your own. But no matter how much you lie to yourself, you'll always know the truth," said Gideon.

"I'm not interested in the truth. I am merely looking for a way to escape this abysmal existence, even if it is only in my head," said the Ferryman.

Without more time to consider his options, Gideon just had to trust the Ferryman and his plan to escape Hell without a time restriction. After all, Tristan and Legionaries were able to walk freely without fear of it, hopefully this was the way he could too.

The Ferryman, growing impatient, tapped at his wrist where a watch would be, indicating Gideon's time was up.

"I agree to your terms. However, you should know if you double-cross me in any way, I will figure out how to open the wormhole between here and the depths. You will then find a never-ending onslaught of demons to your shores. You may be in control for now, but even you are aware time is limitless in Hell, and Savior enjoys a good uprising."

This revelation caused the Ferryman's right eye to twitch with concern. The Ferryman had revealed too much when he said he had never encountered another like Gideon. On some level, the Ferryman held him in higher esteem.

"Agreed," said the Ferryman. "Tristan is now working under Legionaries in a small, secluded town by the name of Broken Falls. He never returned after his last assignment, and as of now, is not a resident of Hell."

This didn't sit right with Gideon, for Legionaries was just a simple lackey to Savior. "You're lying." he said.

"You are still a very young demon, despite your title," said the Ferryman. "Legionaries is far more than anyone's lackey, for he possesses a secret that only Savior and a few others outside of myself know about. This secret has been kept dormant and locked away by Savior, until now. If you do make it to Broken Falls, you, too, will learn his secret. That is, if he allows you to stay and doesn't immediately send you back to the depths himself."

Gideon thought about Legionaries, and how Tristan would laugh when he told him what Savior had done to torture him. How he screamed and begged for mercy as the hounds tore into him.

"Gideon, believe what you want, but know this: I could end you simply by speaking your full name, and yet even as powerful as I am, I fear Legionaries. If he ever came to my shores, I would do whatever he asked of me, if only in the hope that he would show me mercy."

With that, the Ferryman ran the back of his hand down the side of Gideon's face, causing him to black out.

CHAPTER 36

Now that Gideon knew the truth, he put the second part of his plan into action to further manipulate Jameson, Barbados, and Esperanza. She was the key to traveling to Earth without the limitation of the one-minute time restraint. She was on board, and the rest was up to him.

Jameson snapped his fingers a few inches away from Gideon's face, pulling Gideon from his thoughts of meeting the Ferryman and grounding him in the office, where two morons sat looking back at him. One had a look of worry, while the other was simply amused by the whole ordeal.

"His mind went cuckoo once more." Barbados stuck out his tongue as a small grin formed around the corners of his mouth.

Showing great restraint, knowing how easily he could beat the two into submission, Gideon closed his eyes and counted backward from ten. Then, taking a deep breath, he opened his eyes.

"Welcome back, sunshine," said Barbados, no longer snapping at him as if he were a dumb animal.

"Barbados, do us both a favor and shut the fuck up!" screamed Jameson.

Gideon realized that this was the first time Jameson had ever spoken that harshly to either of them. The stress of the upcoming mission was beginning to weigh heavily on Jameson.

"I heard most of what you were saying before I blacked out," moaned Gideon. "When does Esperanza want us to leave?"

His question went unanswered for several moments. Jameson and Barbados exchanged looks of uncertainty. Given their expressions, Gideon knew he was going to have to be careful and convince them that he was indeed okay. If he had overplayed the fool, they would think he would be more of a hinderance than help.

"Well, we thought it might be best if you stay behind to keep watch over the slaves of the region," said Jameson in a soothing tone.

"Just in case Tristan does return, you'll be here to run interference," added Barbados.

No, you, fucking idiots, I will not be staying behind! Gideon wanted to scream at them. Instead, he said, "That's actually not a bad idea. I know something is happening to me and we can no longer ignore it. My lapse in memory and short-circuiting will only hinder you both."

Barbados grinned like the overconfident, holier-than-thou asshole. Jameson only nodded back at him with a look that almost appeared sympathetic.

"The sooner you get the job done, the less all four of us have to worry," said Gideon. "However, please hurry."

Gideon massaged his left temple, and, in turn, created doubt as to whether it was safe to leave him alone.

Not surprisingly, it was Jameson who once more put himself in the position of leader. "I'm afraid we can't risk leaving you here," he said, earning a disapproving snort from Barbados. "If Tristan—or worse, Savior—unexpectedly shows up and you are stuck in some catatonic state, it would only lead to questions Esperanza would willingly clear up. And I think we all know what that means."

Assisting Gideon to his feet, Barbados whispered so Jameson

couldn't hear. "If you blackout at any time while we are on this assignment, I will not hesitate to send you back to Hell."

Under different circumstances, Gideon would have laughed. However, on the verge of getting the answers he so desperately sought, he just nodded his head in understanding as the three Elders stepped inside the wormhole.

Because the human population was so vast, with thousands of them sharing the same name, the wormhole was limited in its ability to pinpoint a single individual on Earth. Jameson narrowed the search to the town based on what they had been told by Esperanza.

"Taupe City, Texas," said Jameson.

Moments later, they were standing in a half-lit alley when the sound of broken glass echoed to the right of them. The only light pollution came from the changing traffic lights. As the light changed from yellow to red, they spotted a middle-aged woman, her best years far behind her. Closing in on the woman, Gideon could visibly see the hardships of her life written prematurely into what could be an almost attractive face if substance abuse hadn't gotten the better of her.

"She's one of ours," said Barbados.

"I can see that for myself," Jameson said angrily.

The woman, dumbfounded by what they were saying, began to speak when a violent cough interrupted her. She rubbed the back of a dirty hand across her mouth and said in a strained voice, "If you want to claim me, then you better have cash. I don't give freebies, and I don't trade sex for drugs or alcohol."

"We'd honestly be doing her a favor," said Barbados.

When Jameson didn't answer, Gideon took the matter literally into his own hands. He grabbed the woman by her hair and repeatedly slammed her head into the wall. The first blow would have been sufficient, but Gideon didn't want to take any chances. When it was over, he released the woman's bloodied, crushed skull to the ground and glared at Jameson.

"Barbados, drag her deeper into the alley so she isn't discovered too soon," ordered Gideon.

Mouth agape, Barbados did as he was told without complaining.

"We can't afford to draw any unwelcome attention to ourselves," said Gideon. "That woman could have been a threat to us and our mission, regardless of her status in this world."

Rejoining them, Barbados slapped Gideon harder than necessary on the shoulder. "Guess we kept some of our powers after all," he said.

Gideon had had enough of this nonsense and decided it was time to reveal his true motives. "No, Barbados, you, fucking idiot. I'm just a ruthless individual who enjoys hurting those who pose any sort of threat to me."

Barbados looked stunned that Gideon had spoken to him in such a manner. Gideon capitalized on the moment, delivering several quick blows to the side of Barbados's head. For further emphasis, he drove a hard knee into his groin, crunching his testicles.

"Hey!" barked Jameson.

Jameson grabbed Gideon's shoulder and jerked him around. Allowing himself to be pulled, Gideon used the momentum to slam his elbow into the side of Jameson's head. The blow landed with more force than Gideon had intended, knocking Jameson unconscious.

Gideon took a moment to admire his work, feeling fully justified after having to put up with their underhanded remarks for so long. He smiled broadly and stepped over Jameson and

Barbados, leaving the alley to venture out into a world he was once a part of.

CHAPTER 37

Wrath (noun)
1: strong vengeful anger or indignation
2: retributory punishment for an offense or a
   crime: divine chastisement

onathan awoke on the stained carpet of Lucifer's torture room. His body was broken and covered in slimy mucus from being in the confines of the snake's stomach. He remained motionless until his body began undergoing the painstaking process of mending itself back together. He winced each time one of his bones snapped back into place.

This was a new experience for Jonathan—a different type of pain he had never encountered before. After being eaten by the snake, his body had been stretched and digested, reducing his entire body mass down to no more than a few inches in diameter.

Lucifer, having returned to his original form, now stood towering over Jonathan, watching his torment with an amused expression.

"It's okay if you want to cry out for mercy," taunted Lucifer. "I know how much this hurts; it is one of my favorite forms of torture to use on my damned. Odd though, when I actually stop and think about it. Being paralyzed before being consumed by an animal is what causes the human mind to break. I thought the flames would have done that already, but it is strange what you can grow accustomed to throughout an eternity."

Ignoring him, Jonathan waited until his body had fully healed before moving. Breathing out a sigh of relief, Jonathan placed a hand on the stained wall for support as he stood slowly.

"I know you believe God has not forsaken you," said Lucifer. "The pain and turmoil you are going through are just trials you must endure for you to better understand the human race. But do you wholeheartedly believe the end will justify the means?"

Jonathan just nodded his head in agreement.

He had given up trying to outwit Lucifer after failing to do so three times. Crossing his arms, Jonathan leaned back against the wall, curious as to where the conversation was heading. Lucifer cocked an eyebrow at Jonathan's relaxed demeanor and snapped his fingers. Immediately, Jonathan was filled with fear. Lucifer was summoning the hounds. Suddenly, a chair materialized, sweeping Jonathan's feet out from under him.

"I want you to be completely comfortable for what I have planned next," said Lucifer, snapping his fingers again, much to Jonathan's worry.

"Don't be so apprehensive." Lucifer sat in a chair directly across from him. "I snap my fingers for many reasons, not just to call the hounds and strike fear in my subordinates."

Jonathan would have argued that he was far from being under Lucifer's authority, but given his predicament, the statement was kind of correct, at least until his trial was complete.

"What do you remember about the Bible's teachings involving Job?" asked Lucifer.

"Well, I'm sure you know," said Jonathan, "all angels can quote the Bible word for word from Genesis to Revelation. I don't presume you know all the details, since you twist and bend them to fit whatever sadistic game you're playing at the moment, especially when you're trying to corrupt and ruin someone."

Lucifer held up his hand in a gesture to snap his fingers, this time leaving no room for interpretation as to what would come if he did.

Acquiescing, Jonathan answered truthfully, "I know you took everything away from Job. God allowed you to test him in order to prove his allegiance, and in the end you failed."

Shaking his head in amusement, Lucifer crossed one leg over the other, now taking on the look of educator. "Failed, you say? No, Jonathan, I more than succeeded in what I set out to achieve. I even surpassed my own expectations. The speculation and doubt I created has bled throughout time among those who consider themselves biblical scholars. From the average person's mindset—and yes, I do include you in this group after hearing your answer—when they read the book of Job, they only see how good supposedly triumphed over evil. That what poor Job endured did in fact justify the means. However, what they fail to see is the havoc I created behind the scenes with the scholars and philosophers because of the language used, and how I was still allowed access into Heaven even though I had allegedly already been cast out. Many argue that Job may have been the first book ever written in the Bible."

Strangely, Jonathan knew part of what Lucifer was saying to be true. The Bible was written by forty different authors, consisting of sixty-six books, and took a span of over fifteen hundred years to complete. So, obviously there was a lot of room for interpretation. But Jonathan had to shamefully admit that the way Lucifer had orchestrated himself into more than just the meaning behind the Bible's teachings was genius work. However, Jonathan did find some comfort in the fact that Lucifer would lose in the end, despite him ruining billions and billions of lives in the process.

"Glad to hear you think that of me," said Lucifer, listening in on Jonathan's thoughts. "After all, I wouldn't be much of an adversary if I wasn't a genius. As for me losing in the end, just because it's written doesn't mean it can't be changed. I would remind you, history is written by powerful men, and men are corruptible. So, how do you really know what is written in the Bible is actually true? Furthermore, how do you know I wasn't there poisoning the ideas of the very authors who wrote even the smallest part of the Bible? Because if you believe I wasn't, you're an even bigger fool than those who put their faith in the words that were written."

Debating Lucifer was pointless. Jonathan felt compelled to point out the obvious. "You're right about history being written by powerful men and how powerful men are easily corruptible. But if you are all-powerful and are in fact a genius, then why am I here? Why do you believe you will be able to step foot into Heaven if you can unlock a guardian's power? I mean, after all, Lucifer, you are all-powerful. Aren't you?"

Lucifer's eye twitched. Jonathan had struck a chord. "Perhaps," Lucifer said dryly. "You are correct, though. I did take everything from Job in the end. I had all ten of his children murdered, all of his servants killed, and all of his wealth stolen away. Yes, he was rewarded for staying true to his beliefs, but did the end justify the means? Your God allowed me to use him as a pawn so He could prove to the world He was indeed all-powerful. But merciful? I think not. I know you don't agree with my sentiments, but Job's wife, children, and even his servants may have a different outlook regarding the situation. They were the ones who ended up paying the ultimate price."

Again, Lucifer made a valid point. Jonathan also noted it had been the third time Lucifer said, "Did the end justify the means?" Jonathan wished he knew more about what had happened to Job's family to have some kind of response. It would be best to remain quiet, instead of speaking about a situation he didn't have complete knowledge of.

"How would you like to make a wager?" asked Lucifer. "Similar to the one that God allowed Job to go through."

"No," said Jonathan, unable to stifle his quick response, earning an amused look from Lucifer.

Suddenly, Jonathan and Lucifer's chairs swiveled around and came to rest with them facing a wall. The lights dimmed and soft mechanical sounds began to fill the air. As if out of nowhere, long heavy red curtains appeared and then separated to reveal a large screen. The torture room had become an exact replica of an old theater.

"What I'm about to show you is occurring in real time. You can either stand back and allow the events to unfold—the same as your God did with Job's family—or you can choose to intervene. Regardless, you will make a decision in the next few minutes."

The screen showed a large countdown from numbers five to one. Holding his breath, Jonathan moved to the edge of his seat. Suddenly, the number one was replaced with an image of Riley leaning back in Maggie's recliner. He had his hand outstretched, then smiled as one of Lucifer's hounds pressed his nose into it.

Jonathan was surprised it was the same hound he'd encountered when he was first pulled into Hell. At the time, Jonathan had to tear the hound's teeth away from his neck. He'd gripped the snarling hound by its massive head and ordered it to go and protect his beloveds, Riley and Maggie. To ensure it wouldn't hurt them, Jonathan had slipped a tiny part of his powers into the hound. Once it had shaken free of his grasp, it appeared disoriented for a second and then disappeared. Jonathan wasn't sure if it had actually worked . . . until now.

"What is he smiling at?" sneered Lucifer.

Ignoring the question, Jonathan put up a guard around his thoughts. He leaned even further forward in his chair as Riley began to cough.

The coughing continued for several minutes, turning Riley's complexion from red to a light shade of purple. Immediately standing, Jonathan reached out and touched the screen, wishing there was something he could do for his beloved friend. The screen suddenly flickered off and on. When Jonathan removed his hand, he saw Riley spitting blood into the palm of his own hand.

"Oh God, no," said Jonathan in a pleading whisper.

Riley exchanged a brief look of uncertainty with the hound. Then, in a weak attempt to stop the cough from returning, Riley placed his hands over his mouth, causing him to appear as if he was in prayer. Unfortunately, violent coughs once again overtook him.

"What are you going to do, Jonathan?"

Jonathan ignored Lucifer and continued watching the scene unfold.

Riley stumbled his way into the kitchen, frantically flinging open cabinet doors and pulling out drawers in search of what Jonathan assumed was a cup. Riley gave up his plight and vomited into the sink while fumbling with the faucet. After rinsing his mouth out, Riley rested his head on the counter for only a moment before he succumbed to another coughing fit.

"Are you willing to just watch Riley die?" Lucifer's voice once again interjected.

Again, Jonathan ignored the question, unable to take his eyes off Riley.

What followed were unrecognizable cries for help, before at last Riley collapsed to the floor. The hound was now barking so loudly that Jonathan worried Lucifer would become aware of its presence. The hound then exhibited the strangest behavior as it attempted what could only be described as CPR, placing both front paws directly onto Riley's chest.

"Stop. Stop. Stop!" screamed Jonathan.

Riley's eyes were bloodshot, staring blankly out into the abyss. His mouth slowly opened and closed in search of one last gasp of air, just as Granny's had done before finding solace in death.

"Ah, too late," said Lucifer.

The screen went dark. Jonathan closed his eyes in disgust at his limited abilities to act. He found refuge in the darkness, as rage unlike he had ever encountered before took ahold of him. In the silence that followed, Jonathan could only hear his labored breathing as it came and went, then at last he turned and faced his adversary.

"Summon all your hounds," Jonathan sneered through his teeth. "Call every one of the damned who are forced to serve you. No matter their numbers, it will not make a difference in the outcome. Because you will now see just how powerful a guardian angel really is."

A window into Hell came alive behind Lucifer, and instead of pity for the damned who were suffering because of their choices, Jonathan couldn't help but smile at their pained expressions. A dozen hounds then appeared and clustered around Lucifer.

"That's not going to be enough," smirked Jonathan.

Without warning, Jonathan turned into a blur of movement, laying waste to everything in his path. A continuous stream of hounds appeared in the hundreds. Jonathan tore through them all, leaving their broken bodies dismembered throughout the room. A sinister smile crept across his face as he stared at Lucifer, the gooey blood dripping off him and the hounds' flesh clinging to his half-naked body.

Jonathan then proceeded to lick the blood off the back of his hand before turning his rage on Lucifer. Stepping just out of Jonathan's reach, Lucifer snapped his fingers, causing the glass window to erupt, filling the room with hundreds of the damned. Moving through them, easily casting them aside, Jonathan attempted to find Lucifer amidst the madness, only to catch sight of him slipping out the one door of the torture room.

Following him, Jonathan felt his anger morph into a blind rage as he went from merely tossing the damned out of his way to biting and tearing their throats out. An immense pleasure overcame him as they begged him for mercy, only to become another body on the ground.

With this new taste of blood in his mouth, Jonathan laughed in a wicked tone. Finding such enjoyment in causing the damned pain, he forgot all about trying to catch Lucifer. Now that Riley was quite possibly dead, Jonathan found refuge in not having to care.

The two-dozen damned who remained cowered together against the walls in trembling fear. Others who had suffered his rage were strewn across the freshly stained carpet along with the hounds.

Their sobs and cries for God's mercy stopped Jonathan cold in his tracks. They were begging for God's mercy from him. He had only seen this type of fear in humans once before, and just like back then, he had been the cause of it. The incident had occurred in Taupe City when he was ill from being infected in the fight against the two demons. Both Riley and Jonathan had been trying to get back to the only other fallen angel they knew existed.

Her nickname had been Granny, which suited her good-hearted selfless demeanor. She had been an intensive care nurse who had remained by Riley's side as he went through the final days with his wife, Allison, but also freely gave up her own life to heal Jonathan. Before reaching Granny, he had lost control on the highway during a routine traffic stop. What followed left a path of destruction once Jonathan came back to his senses. The fear on Riley's face told him he had gone too far, similar to the look the damned now wore as they stared helplessly back at him.

Looking down at his bloodied hands and blood-spattered body, Jonathan knew without a doubt what was to come next. Just then, as if to interrupt his thoughts, someone began clapping to the right of him. Shaking his head, disgusted and disappointed in himself, Jonathan glared angrily at Lucifer.

"Wrath," Jonathan said in a sad monotoned voice. "The deadly sin I just committed is known as wrath."

Holding both arms out to his sides in the same fashion as Jesus once had, Jonathan then closed his eyes and grimaced as the excruciating, stabbing pain tore into his right side. It felt as if his insides had been set ablaze. Jonathan clenched his teeth, refusing to cry out or plead for mercy. He would not provide Lucifer with any further satisfaction than he already unintentionally had.

Feeling the warmth of his tears rolling down his face, Jonathan so desperately wanted to make a vow to God to do better, to not let Lucifer so easily play on his emotions, to stand true throughout the rest of his trials. Yet Jonathan also knew it would be nothing more than a false promise he could not live up to.

"Father, I know I am a sinner. It is in my nature to ask for much and give little in return. Angels and humans alike, although created in your image, now share imperfection because of sin's creation, and sometimes the line between right and wrong is blurred by emotions. I am so lost, please help me."

When there wasn't an immediate response, Jonathan grew frustrated, feeling the last bit of rage boiling just underneath the surface, begging to be set free. Pushing the anger aside, Jonathan whispered, "Amen," which was accompanied by an echo. Looking up, Jonathan saw Lucifer smiling at him.

"That was a beautiful, heartfelt prayer, Jonathan. Nevertheless . . ." Still smiling, Lucifer held up four fingers. "Four down, three to go. Then you will learn that just maybe you knew less than you thought, and the authors of the Bible really did get it wrong. So, I ask again, do you believe the end will justify the means?"

Warm tears streamed down his cheeks. Jonathan questioned if he even had the mental strength to survive his trial. He wondered how Granny had kept her faith all those years after failing her human, Cristal, and could no longer hear God. It wasn't until decades later, when Jonathan had shown up at the hospital, that she was able to hear God once more. Yet here Jonathan sat, struggling to even make it through the beginnings of his trial, each committed sin drawing him closer to whatever may happen if Lucifer were to succeed.

"Jonathan, I have something to cheer you up," said Lucifer. "I feel it's the least I could do, since it's only a matter of time until I'm finished with you."

Remaining quiet, Jonathan wiped the tears from his eyes.

"Riley is fine," Lucifer said. "He came back around after I whispered to his unconscious mind that you had committed the fourth deadly sin. You have only three more sins to go until I kill you. He practically bolted off the floor, as if he had some foolish notion of somehow coming to rescue you. I suppose even fools find a way to make themselves believe there is still a ray of hope amidst their darkest hours."

Squeezing his eyes closed, Jonathan hoped Lucifer wouldn't be able to listen to his thoughts as he prayed that Riley would give up his attempt to find him. He opened his eyes to see Lucifer giving him a quizzical look, which told Jonathan that his thoughts were his own in this moment. He assumed the reason Lucifer wasn't privy to his thoughts was because God was stepping in, or maybe Lucifer was too distracted by the scene playing out to listen in.

CHAPTER 38

Coming to, Riley felt as though a sledgehammer was being driven repetitively into his chest. He emerged from his haze, realizing Kratos was causing his pain. The hound was rearing up and dropping all of his weight onto Riley's chest.

Slowly turning over to his side, careful to avoid any further trauma from Kratos to his already bruised chest, Riley drew in short, ragged breaths, followed by tears of relief to still be alive.

Thanking God while resting upon the cool tiled kitchen floor, Riley's thoughts shifted to how dogs could be trained to save their owner's life by administering CPR. Even in some cases, dogs were trained to alert their owner before a seizure occurred. Dogs always had a reputation for being man's best friend, and maybe this included Kratos.

Kratos licked the sides of Riley's face until Riley reached up with both hands to stop him.

"Good boy. You're a good boy, Kratos," said Riley, his voice raspy from his sore throat.

Satisfied, Kratos stepped back to let Riley slowly maneuver himself onto all fours. Kratos's eyes then changed from bright red to a dull brown.

Riley thought he saw real concern in those eyes, and with that, he was unable to stop himself. He wrapped his arms around the hound and buried his face into the side of his neck.

"You are such a blessing, Kratos."

Riley kissed Kratos on the nose, causing him to release several loud snorts. Another thought seeped into Riley's mind, and despite the pain, he bolted to his feet. A disembodied voice echoed in his ears, "I just orchestrated a scenario that pushed Jonathan into committing the fourth deadly sin. Three more, Riley, and I will have no further use of him!"

Stumbling past Kratos to the kitchen counter, Riley placed his hands down and steadied himself. Why would Lucifer deliver such a warning? Lucifer had whispered directly into Riley's ear, as he was waking from his unconscious state. Riley's chest hurt. Maggie still wasn't here, and he feared that Jonathan would be lost forever if they waited any longer. He needed to call Maggie. He reached toward his pocket for his cell phone, then realized he was still in Maggie's robe.

He tried to sidestep Kratos but had no luck because the hound mirrored his every move. His gratitude to Kratos quickly slipped into frustration. "I don't have time for this!" Riley snapped, tossing up both arms. "Jonathan will be dead soon, and I need to get to him! You're supposed to be here to help me. So, either help or stay out of the way!"

Kratos finally sat back on his haunches, and Riley, for a fleeting moment, wondered about Kratos's intentions, then forced the paranoid thought aside when he heard the sound of a key being inserted into the door.

"Riley?" called Maggie from the other side of the door. "It's just me and Stu. Is it okay if we come in?"

"Yes, Kratos and I are in the kitchen in some sort of a standoff."

Maggie quickly pushed the door open to find Riley in her robe, leaning casually against the kitchen counter with both arms crossed over his chest. Kratos sat a few feet in front of him as if he were a normal dog begging for treats.

"You can't joke around like that," scolded Maggie. "I think we can agree on why Kratos is here but also where he comes from, so we shouldn't be so flippant about him."

Stuart then came trailing in after locking the door.

Though she had calmed down a bit and now paid attention to Riley's pale complexion and bloodshot eyes, Maggie feared the worse. "Tell me," she said in a softened tone.

Uncrossing his arms and looking down, Riley answered in a rough voice, "Just before you came in, I suffered some sort of coughing fit that left me completely unable to breathe. After I woke from blacking out, I found Kratos bouncing up and down on my chest. A moment later, I clearly heard someone's voice— I'm assuming it was the Devil—telling me how he had just caused Jonathan to commit the fourth deadly sin."

Maggie gasped. "How much time do you think Jonathan has?"

Riley shrugged his shoulders. "Jonathan has only been in Hell for a little more than twenty-four hours, and Lucifer has already caused him to commit four sins—not just any four sins—four of the seven deadly sins. So, I'm guessing he has maybe one more day. Then again, I'm just guessing and running on zero rest."

"Well, I know you don't want to hear this, but you can't leave right now," said Stu, earning a quizzical look from Riley. "You both need to be a little more alert to drive anywhere, let alone journey into the unknown to try to rescue your friend."

"Stu has always been the voice of reason," said Maggie.

"That has to get annoying," said Riley, looking at Maggie.

As a sheepish grin played at the corners of his mouth, she jokingly replied, "It did for the first twenty years of my life. Now I just take it in stride and smile when prompted."

Stu chuckled and spoke in an outlandish voice, "And that's why you pay me the big bucks, see!" This earned genuine smiles from both Maggie and Riley.

"I will wake you both in a few hours," Stuart said in a serious tone. "Meanwhile, is there anything more you need me to do?"

"Actually, yes," said Riley. "We didn't bring anything other than the two guns for protection, besides Kratos, of course."

"Say no more," said Stu. "I'll take care of it. Do you have any sort of preference in firearms?"

"And just where are you going to get guns on such short notice?" asked Maggie.

A mischievous grin formed on Stu's face. "Well, I have been meaning to tell you, I've been stockpiling a small arsenal for quite some time. I knew the day would come when you would inform me that you were tired of the business world and our next adventure would involve overthrowing Hell!"

Despite how funny the comment was and how adorable Stu and Riley looked laughing next to one another, Maggie felt uneasy at the seriousness of their situation, causing her cheeks to redden. Seeing she was the only one not enjoying the moment, Stu and Riley's laughter faded as they settled back down.

"No, for real, I inherited a few rifles and handguns when my father-in-law passed. I'll go get them."

Stu leaned down and kissed her on the forehead, then gave Riley a hug and showed himself out.

After he was gone, Maggie looked at Riley, who shrugged his shoulders in an apologetic way.

"We better make the most of the time we have until Stuart gets back," said Maggie. "Especially since this is the last real rest we will get for a while. I haven't had a sleepover since high school and don't have much in the way of family or I would have had added a guest room. So, I guess you can just take my room and I'll take the couch."

Riley paused, his eyes giving away that he knew something he wasn't going to say. "Couch is fine with me," he said, walking past Maggie as he made his way to the couch. Then he tried to situate himself by attempting to cover his feet with the bottom of her robe.

Going to the hall closet and retrieving her largest throw blanket, Maggie handed it over, all the while wondering just how they were going to rescue Jonathan, and what would happen to any of them if they weren't quick enough.

"Riley, what do you believe will happen if . . ." His exhausted and sad expression stopped Maggie from continuing the question. "Sorry. We'll deal with it if we have too."

"Maggie, your guess is as good as mine. I'm flying blind here, too, and having to put my trust in God and Kratos."

"Guess we'll find out in a few hours," said Maggie.

"Guess we will," said Riley, pulling the blanket up and snuggling in. He instantly fell asleep, putting an abrupt end to their conversation.

Letting out a yawn of her own, Maggie started for her room when she noticed Kratos at the front door on guard duty. "You can sleep on the couch by Riley or in the bed with me. I think we'll be okay for a few hours."

Kratos briefly looked at her, then turned to face the door once more, as if to tell her he was staying exactly where he was.

"Okay, well, I'll see you in a few hours."

When Maggie turned off the lights, she saw a pair of red glowing eyes staring back at her in the darkness. Startled by the sight, she immediately flipped the lights back on, only to see Kratos cocking his head in confusion. Then, as if figuring it out for himself, he walked over and allowed Maggie to pet him before returning to his post in front of the door.

She turned off the lights again, ignoring Kratos's red eyes staring at her, and made her way to her room, all the while feeling like a little kid who was scared of the dark. Maggie quickly closed the door behind her and jumped into bed, choosing to leave the lights on. After snuggling under the covers and fortifying herself with several pillows around her, Maggie trembled for a moment. *I will never ever get comfortable with seeing that, especially right before bedtime.*

CHAPTER 39

J ameson gently slapped the side of Barbados's face to wake him. He couldn't believe how easily they had been outwitted by someone who had been playing a fool. The time, planning, deceit, and overall dedication to stay the course—Jameson couldn't help but marvel at how brilliantly Gideon had played them. At the same time, he wished for a redo so he could pound Gideon's useless ass into the ground. At the very least, he'd be more observant instead of allowing Barbados to distract him with his endless, useless jokes. With this last thought, Jameson slapped Barbados much harder than he needed.

"What in the hell do you think you're doing?" screamed Barbados.

"Better question: How in the hell did we not see through Gideon's bullshit persona? Answer me that, you fucking worthless shell of an elder demon!" Jameson snapped.

His blood boiled as they glared at one another. He wanted nothing more than to end their agreement, finishing off what Gideon had started. Unfortunately, he would need Barbados now that it was just the two of them.

Jameson tried to get control of his temper. "We have a job to finish, and we won't succeed if we're constantly at each other's throats. Agreed?"

Barbados stepped forward, reaching out his hand, and Jameson thought he was going to take a swing at him. Instead,

Barbados offered his hand in a sign of truce. Taking it, Jameson further questioned how he had allowed himself to be so naïve about Gideon.

"Guess there's no honor among thieves," said Barbados. He then spat in the alley several times to clear his mouth.

Ignoring the attempt at humor, Jameson looked up and down the alley to make certain no one else had seen them. He took charge of the situation and ventured toward the street. After looking up and down the street, he located a bus stop a few hundred yards away. Jameson started walking in that direction when he was stopped dead in his tracks by the sound of a gun being cocked behind him. Slowly turning around, Jameson saw Barbados standing just a few feet away, pointing a gun directly at his chest.

"I know what you must be thinking," Barbados said. "How did this simple-minded moron get a gun? And how did this situation go so badly before it's even began?"

True, Jameson was sharing those exact thoughts, but he was too confused and shocked to voice them.

"Let's go back into the alley," said Barbados, motioning with the gun barrel to make certain Jameson understood what was expected.

Unable to comprehend how Gideon and now Barbados had bested him, Jameson stood motionless for several seconds until Barbados fired a shot over his head.

Jameson threw both hands up in surrender and hurriedly did as he was instructed. He paused only to look up and down the half-lit streets, hoping to see someone else, but found no one.

"Where did you find the gun?" Jameson asked Barbados as he walked deeper into the dark alley.

Barbados followed several steps behind him. Jameson was distracted by thoughts of how he was going to get out of this current situation. Then something hard slammed into his right temple, sending him down to the ground onto all fours. Then Barbados followed up with a hard kick to his left side, cracking several of his ribs, and then flipping him over onto his back.

"The bitch had it stuffed in the back of her waistband," said Barbados. "Even surprised the hell out of me when I found it. Just think if she had been even a little bit more coherent." Barbados laughed and sighed. "Well, there's really no use in speculating now."

Holding one hand to the side of his head and raising the other in a sign of surrender, Jameson's mind raced with how to save himself. He had been reduced to pleading with another demon he thought of as an idiot.

"We need to help one another if we are going to succeed," said Jameson.

"Jameson, we're fucked even if we do pull this off. Are you too dumb to see that?"

He knew Barbados was correct, but Jameson couldn't help but hold on to the belief that if they were successful, just maybe Savior would show them a little mercy and not sentence them to an eternity in the pits.

"At least I can take a little satisfaction knowing it was me who got the best of you," said Barbados. "Someone you've always looked down on, the same way you did Gideon. It's all kind of comical when you stop and think about it. Wouldn't you agree?"

Jameson wished his vision would just focus for a moment so he could at least attempt a weak lunge for the gun. Knowing his time was out, Jameson finally gave in, closed his eyes, and waited for the chain of events to play out like a bad dream he couldn't awaken from.

"Freeze!" cried a woman's voice.

Opening his eyes, Jameson saw Barbados turn his gun on the

unwelcomed visitor. He did an odd shuffle as two shots rang out, and Barbados was hit directly in the chest.

The red mist clouded Jameson's vision as the overwhelming taste of iron filled his mouth. Blinking, spitting, and giving several shakes of his head to clear the cobwebs, Jameson saw Barbados's lifeless face looking back at him. His mouth attempted to form his last words, yet no sound came out as the light faded from his eyes.

Jameson smiled and whispered to the corpse, "See you in Hell, asshole." He wanted to laugh at how fortunate he had been, but the pain in his side threatened to flare back to life if he did.

Attempting to push himself into a seated position, Jameson stopped when the woman said sharply, "Freeze. I won't say it again."

Jameson put his hands up in surrender. A piercing pain broke through his ribs. Unable to stop himself from crying out, he dropped his arms and fell to the concrete, taking shallow breaths to keep the threatening blackness from consuming him.

When he was finally able to focus, Jameson thought of the consequences that awaited him if he failed to find and kill Riley. It was too late for Barbados, and maybe even Gideon, but Jameson still clung to the hope that if he acted quickly and succeeded, his punishment wouldn't last for all eternity.

"Sir, I want you to roll over to your stomach and keep both hands visible as you do. Do you understand the orders I've just given you?"

So, it was a police officer who had entered the fray. Jameson felt both relief and a sense of urgency to make sure his current predicament didn't involve him being handcuffed and stuffed into the back of a police cruiser.

The officer repeated her order, and although her voice was

unsteady, she left no room for doubt that she had complete control of the situation.

"I understand," he said. "Just be patient with me, as I was being beaten by the man you shot only moments prior to your arrival, and I am a little dazed and in a great deal of pain."

The officer didn't offer anything more. Jameson began to shift onto his stomach, doing everything possible to keep the pain at bay. His right eye instinctively closed as the blood from his scalp wound found its way down the side of his face.

"I can see you're injured, and I'll get you taken care of once my backup arrives," said the officer, now standing a few feet in front of him. "Do you have anything on you that poses a threat to me?"

Resting his head on the concrete, Jameson took in several small breaths before responding, "No, I have nothing on me."

"Uh-huh," said the officer dismissively. "Would you like to tell me what you were doing in an alley at night and what exactly was going on before I arrived?"

You have to come up with something, Jameson thought. *You're running out of time before backup arrives.*

Looking up the alley, Jameson found his answer, as the red and blue lights from the officer's car had revealed it to him.

"I heard a woman screaming, so I came running into the alley and tried to stop this man from assaulting her, but he overpowered me. He hit me in the head with something and knocked me out. I don't know what happened to her, but just before I blacked out, I'm pretty sure I saw her take off in that direction."

He pointed for emphasis but remained face-down to ensure he didn't pose any sort of threat.

Instinctively, the officer turned for a split second to look in the direction where Jameson was pointing. That second was all the time Jameson needed to get away.

Jumping to his feet and pushing the officer into the wall, using his forehead like a battering ram, Jameson quickly overpowered the officer, leaving her unconscious at his feet. Retrieving her gun, Jameson sprinted toward the opposite end of the alley. Before turning onto the next street, he gave one last look down the alley. Several more shadows now danced in the glow of the red and blue flashing lights.

Not daring to run, Jameson instead kept a hurried pace across the street. He then entered another alley and, once out of sight, began sprinting. He was weakening much faster than he believed his mortal body should.

Locating a glass-enclosed bus stop, Jameson hobbled over and collapsed under the weight of his body, finding solace on the hard metal frame. His mouth was as dry as a desert, and sheets of sweat poured off him. He soon discovered the reason why his mortal body was failing him so quickly. He had a gunshot wound just below his right nipple, which left blood remnants on his shirt and down the front of his jeans.

"Fuck me," Jameson uttered

Jameson rested his head against the glass enclosure at the back of the bus stop, still in disbelief at how bad everything had gone. He looked out at what he assumed to be his final resting place when a large granite plaque on the wall across the street caught his eye. It read: "Gregory Portal Provider corporate headquarters."

"Fuck me," Jameson uttered.

He could not comprehend how Lady Luck appeared to be on his side one moment and then the next tried to kill him. If this pattern continued, Jameson knew he would be dead soon, whether it was from blood loss or something else.

Unsteady but getting to his feet, Jameson tucked the stolen gun into the back of his waistline and proceeded clumsily across the street into an underground parking garage.

CHAPTER 40

Having made the ten-minute drive back to his house in record time, Stuart couldn't wait to sit down with his wife, Alyssa, and tell her everything.

It was all so bizarre that Stuart still had a hard time wrapping his mind around everything. He shuddered, recalling how the hound's eyes had pinned him to his seat and sniffed him out as soon as he entered the room.

Opening the front door, Stuart called out, "Hey, sweetie. I'm only going to be here for a minute. When I get back, I have the most insane story to tell you."

The smell of his wife's baking stopped Stuart from popping in and out like he planned. Detouring to the kitchen, he found her putting the last finishing touches on some blueberry scones. She was a petite woman with a booming personality that brought out the best in Stuart's outlook on life. They met at a small coffee shop she owned, and although he was now biased, Stuart believed it produced some of the best pastries he had ever tasted. However, in the end, she was forced to sell, which later turned out to be a blessing in disguise, since she was going to be a stay-at-home mom. She became pregnant with their first of two girls shortly afterward, something every fertility doctor they had met with deemed to be impossible.

The day after Maggie first met Alyssa, she'd asked the board members for a quick ten-minute recess to discuss the details regarding the new merger with Stuart.

After everyone was gone, Maggie had asked in a serious tone, "When is the wedding?"

Stuart remembered laughing at the question, since he and Alyssa had only been dating for a few months. "You stopped a meeting with a multi-million-dollar deal on the table to ask me this? There is something wrong with you, and I mean seriously wrong with you!"

"All right, bring everyone back in. Just remember this exact moment when someone else swoops in and woos her away. Because I'm telling you, Stu, in a few years you won't even be able to recall this meeting or the money that was attached to it, but you will recall missing out on what could have been. This wouldn't need saying if you weren't so bull-headed and actually listened to me for once in your life."

Needless to say, later that morning with Maggie in tow, they'd sought out the perfect ring. It was the first impulsive decision Stu had ever made, and now, with his and Alyssa's ten-year anniversary just around the corner, it turned out to be the wisest decision.

Stuart stood in his kitchen watching his wife. He smiled, wondering how he had ever gotten so lucky to get to spend his life with Alyssa by his side. "Care to give me a brief synopsis of this insane story?" Alyssa asked without looking up from her task.

Although she was a stay-at-home mom, Alyssa continued working full time, refusing to give up on her culinary skills. She maintained a steady stream of clients from several local stores, as well as catering wedding parties, birthday parties, and other type of events.

"Trust me when I say you will not believe me, but you will also think that I have gone crazy. I only stopped by to retrieve the guns your dad left us."

Alyssa finally stopped what she was doing and gave him a questionable look. She then slapped his hand away from the scones.

"Ow!" Stuart exclaimed.

Alyssa smirked. "It's gotten that bad at work?" She placed both hands on her hips in mock curiosity. "Because if I have to choose a side, then I'm choosing Maggie's."

Although having known Maggie for most of his life, Stuart kind of felt like an outsider when the three of them were together. Not only had Maggie convinced him to marry Alyssa, but she also later convinced Alyssa to take up baking once again. Maggie had even helped transform their once ordinary household kitchen into one that would make most bakeries envious.

"Okay, mister, you have to give me something to satisfy my curiosity now that you have it piqued."

Pulling her into him, Stuart gave her a brief kiss, which quickly turned into one of passion. If it hadn't been for Alyssa giving his chest a soft push, Stuart wouldn't have returned to the office until late afternoon, if at all.

"Damn," said Stuart. After all these years she still had complete control over him. "Uh, sorry, sweetie," he said, trying to quickly atone for his slip-up, knowing how his wife felt about even the slightest of foul language.

"Actually," she said, "in this case, I think that word is the perfect way to describe our rushed state at the moment. Nevertheless, I'm still curious."

Stuart looked at his watch and frowned. Alyssa picked up a scone, placed it on a napkin, and handed it over. "I guess I can deal with the suspense leading to your story, for the time being. But if you hurry home, the kids have after-school activities until six and we can pick this back up."

Accepting the scone and settling for a kiss on her cheek,

Stuart quickly began calculating everything he had to accomplish before he could leave the office for the day. He decided to give Alyssa a shortened version of the story to hopefully curb her curiosity until he returned and could explain in more detail. He thought of Kratos and again couldn't help but shiver.

"It involves the paranormal and supernatural," he said.

This time it was Alyssa who laughed. "My goodness. I didn't know we were at that stage of our sex life. I would never describe us as the Hallmark Channel couple, but apparently, I have been reading the wrong supermarket magazines."

Both now laughing, Stuart embraced her once more, then went and retrieved the guns out of the bedroom safe. "Love you," Stuart called out as he left the house with a scone in one hand and the duffel bag of weapons in the other.

CHAPTER 41

S taying out of the path where the cars came and went, Jameson found a corner of the parking garage where he wouldn't be noticed and sat down. He hadn't intended to fall asleep. He only want to catch his breath and muster up his remaining strength to finish what he had come to do. However, sleep unexpectedly found him.

The slamming of a car door, followed by someone whistling, brought him back to his senses. Disoriented from the bright sun pouring through the concrete slits of the parking garage, Jameson wondered just how long he had been out. The day hadn't fully stretched itself awake when he had first entered the parking structure, but now it felt like mid-afternoon.

Pushing himself upright, Jameson leaned heavily on the nearest car and scanned the parking lot. He saw a tall, slender Black man retrieving a duffel bag from the back of an SUV. The sign in front of the parking spot read, "S. Branch, Vice President."

Giving the parking area another glance before deciding it was either now or never, Jameson began to move with as much speed as he could muster, while at the same time retrieving the gun out of the back of his waistband.

"Mr. Branch?" called Jameson, causing the man to turn just as Jameson slid the barrel of the pistol under his chin. "I will blow your goddamn head off unless you do exactly what I tell you to."

Stuart felt the hairs on the back of his neck rise as the man shoved the cold barrel of the gun harder into his chin. Disoriented and confused, he realized the man had addressed him by his last name.

Judging by the man's outer appearance, Stuart concluded that he was not affiliated with any type of law enforcement. However, he also didn't appear to be a drug-addled thief looking to secure his next fix. The man was dressed in casual business attire, minus the wound in the chest area.

It was the look behind the man's hazel eyes that was somehow more threatening than the actual gun. They were lifeless, as if a soul didn't exist inside the man's mortal body. Stuart had seen this same cold, vacant look before in the expression of a dog.

"You're going to take me to Ms. Gregory, or I'm going to put a round in that simple head of yours and I'll just figure out another way inside," said the man. "Don't bother playing games, either, because we both know she's in there."

Wishing there was something he could do to intervene, Stuart scanned the parking garage for someone who might help, but it was empty. Staring helplessly back at his assailant, Stuart reluctantly nodded his head.

"Smart choice. Now move," said the man, pushing Stuart in front of him.

Walking over to Maggie's private elevator, Stuart stopped in front of it. Like a little kid, he raised his free hand, asking for permission to speak. The barrel of the gun once more pressed into him, except this time it was at the back of his head.

"This is Ms. Gregory's private elevator. I have a keycard attached to my belt that operates it. May I retrieve it?"

"Slowly," said the man, pressing the gun barrel harder into the back of Stuart's head.

Stuart swiped his badge, and when the doors opened, he was

shoved by a foot into his lower back, sending him crashing into the elevator, releasing his hold on the bag of weapons to stop his head from bouncing off the elevator wall. The air forced out of his lungs as the butt of the gun rammed several times into his right side, and he dropped to his knees.

"What floor!" the man screamed. He pointed the gun at Stuart's forehead.

"Top," Stuart wheezed. "Thirteenth floor."

As they began to ascend, Stuart knew he had served his purpose and could do nothing more to stop the inevitable. He was going die in this elevator.

"Will we encounter anybody else when the doors open?"

Thinking once more of Kratos, Stuart wanted to smile at the thought of the Devil hound.

"So, help me, I will kill you right now—"

"The entire floor is Maggie's own personal suite. As far as I know, it's just her and Riley waiting for me to return."

Seeing the small trickle of hope enter the man's eyes, Stuart immediately realized his mistake of mentioning Riley. The gunman positioned himself in the back of the elevator. He motioned for Stuart to stand in front of him. "If anything, unexpected comes through those doors when they open, you die first. Understood?"

Stuart prayed Kratos would show him mercy and be quick enough to save his life. He whispered, "Amen." As the elevator dinged, the doors opened.

CHAPTER 42

Startled awake by what seemed to be the sound of a tornado passing over Maggie's suite, Riley caught a glimpse of the back of Kratos smashing through the front door and leaving what remained of it hanging loosely on the hinges.

Riley fussed with the blanket as he got to his feet, then froze at the sound of a single gunshot echoing from the corridor, followed by Stuart crying out, then silence.

Forgetting all about the need to be cautious, Riley ran into the hallway, closely followed by Maggie. Then both immediately froze.

Stuart was lying motionless, half in and half out of the elevator. A small red patch began to spread in the middle of his back where the bullet had penetrated.

The noise coming from Kratos at the back of the elevator sickened Riley as he momentarily glimpsed Kratos tearing into the intruder's lifeless corpse.

Sucking in several sharp breaths to calm his stomach, Riley knelt down next to Stuart, located his pulse, and pressed both hands over the gunshot wound to stop the bleeding.

"Maggie, call 911."

When Maggie didn't move, Riley repeated himself a bit more harshly. He gasped when the intruder's body disappeared right in front of them. Kratos immediately began to leave deep scratches in the white tile before giving up and turning his blood-covered face toward them. His red sinister eyes craved more from the dead. Haunted by the look, Riley repeated his order.

"Maggie, call 911!"

Just as she turned to run into the suite, Stuart's voice caused her to freeze. "I can't feel a thing below my waist. I know I've been shot, but I'm not in any sort of pain. Just discomfort from being in this position and not being able to move my legs."

"Stuart, I need you to remain calm until we can get some help," said Riley. Then, with a new desperation in his voice, he pleaded with Maggie, "Would you please call 911?"

"No," interjected Stuart. "How would you even try to explain this? Besides, we just cleared Maggie. If you contact the authorities, they'll have more questions than she has answers, which will only further diminish everything I've been able to pull off for her in these last few months."

Riley was stunned by Stuart's control and forward thinking under such distress, and he didn't know what to say. But he was thankful when Maggie knelt down and positioned Stuart's head onto her lap. "Riley, go make the call. My phone is on the kitchen counter. Stuart, I don't care about—"

Without having to say a word, Stuart snorted and smiled at Maggie, silencing her. "The last thing I saw as the elevator doors opened was Kratos knocking me out of the way. From the look of the now empty elevator, I assume it was a demon who was pulled back to Hell."

Riley exchanged a quick glance with Maggie, and it was clear from her expression that they were both confused.

"Truthfully," said Stuart, "everything I thought I knew about religion has changed in the past few hours. I guess I do know one thing for certain, and it's that demons aren't allowed to physically walk freely amongst us." He looked over at Kratos and then back to them. "Okay, on second thought, maybe not, because why is he still here?" Grimacing, Stuart held out a hand to Kratos, coaxing the hound over to him.

"Thank you for saving me."

After everything the hound had done, the compliment was more than deserving.

Maggie stroked the hound as well, giving Kratos a brief hug before returning to the matter at hand. "Stu, you need medical attention. What do you expect me to do? Am I just supposed to leave you here and hope for the best? How do you expect me to explain that my best friend and acting CEO was shot right outside my suite?" Maggie waved emphatically toward the elevator to drive her point home.

Then Maggie gasped and pointed, causing both Stuart and Riley to look. The elevator had transformed back to normal. Even the deep scratches left behind by Kratos were gone.

After everything Riley had lived through and thought he knew about the paranormal, it still surprised him. He cautiously stepped into the elevator, feeling compelled to touch where the claw marks had been, just to prove to himself they were no longer there. He ran his hand across the smooth cold tile and searched for the smallest trace of blood, and he wasn't surprised when he couldn't find anything.

"You will need to wipe the security footage of me and that demon meeting in the parking garage," said Stuart.

"What about you, Stuart?" Maggie angrily interjected. "You seem to have everything figured out, except that you are shot, bleeding out, and I will not just leave you. So shut up. And Riley, go make the damn call!"

"God, I love you, Mags. Always will," said Stuart. "But you are the most stubborn woman I have ever known."

Too concerned with Stuart's wellbeing to appreciate the humor, Riley remained silent, not caring in the least about anything other than getting Stuart help.

Stuart sighed. "Maggie, I know you don't believe as I do. But I do have faith in a higher power, and it's telling me that my life was spared for a reason. My God is always at work, especially in our darkest hours. Now I can't explain why my being shot is part of His design. Other than maybe this is my trial to have to overcome. Same for Riley, Jonathan, and even you, Maggie. My only hope is that maybe, just maybe, you will see the hand of God work miracles in your life before it's too late."

Defeated, Maggie took one of Stuart's hands and kissed it. Tears trickled down her cheeks as she kissed it again and again, until finally allowing Stuart to pull her into his embrace. Maggie was overcome by loud sobs that shook her body.

"Keep her safe, Riley, but make sure you also come home," Stuart said. "I look forward to hearing the rest of your story and all about this next part of your journey. The duffel bag should have everything you need just in case Kratos isn't enough."

"You can count on it," said Riley.

A bizarre thought raced through Riley's mind. *If Kratos could teleport himself into unlocked vehicles, much like Jonathan could, then could Kratos also teleport others?* He would never forget the day he had been shot in Paul's grocery. Jonathan had teleported him back to the lake house to get help from the local town doctor, Josh Hardin.

The pain now seemed to be setting in, and Stuart let out several sharp breaths. He shut his eyes and moaned.

"Stuart," said Riley. "I have an idea about how to get you help. I don't know if it'll work, so just bear with me."

Instead of explaining himself, Riley knelt down next to

Kratos. "Do you think you could get Stuart to the closest hospital and return without being noticed?"

Without hesitation, Kratos bowed his head, then walked over to Stuart. Maggie looked as though she was about to argue until Stuart cut in.

"I love you, Mags. I will always love you."

Stuart's face relaxed. His eyes rolled back in his head before regaining their focus. Then, as if in a trance, he said, "You can't travel with the Ferryman as a non-worshipper. If you try to, your parents will find you, and you will be forever trapped in a place where my kind is not permitted to go."

Stuart's words caused the hairs on the back of Riley's neck to stand on end. Without another word, Kratos leaned forward and gave Stuart's face a single lick, and they both disappeared.

CHAPTER 43

The further Jasper, Brian, and Tamara worked their way into the cornfield, the more the light pollution from the town left the night sky, making it impossible for Tamara to navigate where she was. Fear began to edge itself into her subconscious with each hurried step, causing her breathing to intensify.

Tamara was uncertain of how long it had been since Brian last stopped to inform her that they were finally going to start making their way across the field. She felt a bit relieved in assuming it wouldn't be much longer until they were in Jasper's fallout shelter. That felt as though it had been more than an hour ago.

It wasn't until she heard Brian's soft voice directly ahead of her that she was able to calm down and take in her first full breath. "Not much further, but we need to be really quiet for this next part," said Brian. He took her hand and led her back to the edge of the cornfield where the town began.

The distant ripple of the creek returned its soft, rhythmic sounds as they drew closer. They heard the sound of people shouting in the distance, which Tamara assumed must be the diggers.

"Tricky part," whispered Jasper next to them, peering to the other side of the creek. "We're open targets, so we can't all go at once. I'll go first and will make a bird call after I make sure that no one else is around."

With that, the elderly man made his way down the side of the bank and began tiptoeing across some large rocks that stood barely visible in the creek. Accomplishing this task, he made his way up the other side of the embankment and over to a secluded house that was half illuminated by a distant streetlamp. Tamara lost sight of Jasper when he disappeared around the back of the property. Several long minutes later, Tamara heard what she thought was an owl calling out.

"Coast is clear," said Brian. "It's a little slippery. but after we cross the creek, there's nothing to it."

Taking her hand, they proceeded down the same path, and before long, they were all back together. Pulling open a storm door which lay directly on top of the ground, Tamara followed Brian down the tight, steep staircase, jumping when the door closed behind them with too much force.

"Sorry 'bout that," Jasper quietly said.

After the last step, they stood directly in front of another door that Brian knocked on twice, paused, then knocked three more times. Moments later, they were welcomed by a small petite woman who worked part-time as an athletic trainer at the high school.

"Tamara!" Javanna excitedly said, quickly wrapping her in a strong embrace. "I can't believe you're here, but I'm so thankful you're okay."

The woman knew what kind of state Tamara's mother was in and had made it a welcomed habit of stopping by a few times a month to check in on them.

"Thank you, Javanna," said Tamara, unsure of what else to say.

The young woman then gave her hand a soft squeeze. Her expression told Tamara she already had come to suspect what had happened to her parents. Looking away to stop the tears from filling her eyes, Tamara took notice of Jasper's large and well-equipped fallout room.

There were half a dozen bunk beds lining one wall, a small, well-stocked kitchen in the far corner, and a large, black, metal gun safe off to one side. The doors of the safe were wide open, displaying the contents of a small arsenal.

"Let's see if we can find you some dry clothes," said Javanna, leaving Tamara among the town's refugees.

Some she recognized but didn't know by name. Each individual she made eye contact with gave her a sincere smile before returning back to their conversations.

There were just over a dozen who remained behind to help the less fortunate. Most of them were in their later years. However, they didn't show signs of weakness, but rather a will to fight and a desire to help those who'd been left behind.

"Here you go," said Javanna, handing Tamara a pair of sweats. "I was still working at the high school when everything went sideways, so I borrowed a few items I figured would come in handy. Thankfully, Brian found me when he had, as I was oblivious to the evil that came to our town."

"Thank you," said Tamara, accepting the offered items. "Brian spoke of the women and children who were left behind."

Javanna dropped her head for a brief moment before gathering herself. "There were four other women, but they went out on a patrol to see if they could assist in rescuing others. When they didn't return, we didn't bother sending anyone else out. Brian and Jasper were the last two, and thank God . . ."

Saying nothing more, Javanna wrapped Tamara once more in a hug before drawing back. "As for the children, there are just the one-year-old twins from the Misk family. Horrible to believe that their parents would just abandon them like they did."

Tamara recalled the Misk family. The dad was her high school English teacher, and his wife, if she remembered correctly, worked nights at the hospital in Deadwater. The only distinct memory she could recollect of them all being together was at a basketball game she had played in last year. Other than that, they were very unsociable, which Tamara chalked up to the twins being a handful to manage.

"They're sleeping peacefully in the other room," said Javanna.

Despite the Misk family being, for lack of a better word, outsiders, Tamara thought it odd how Javanna would presume they would just up and abandon their children.

"It's true," said Javanna, reading Tamara's expression. "Whoever this strange man is, he somehow has the ability to control people's minds. I know how bizarre it sounds, but Mr. Hastings"—Javanna motioned with a hand to point out the large, burly man—"watched from a distance as people we once thought we knew turned on one another, just because they'd been ordered to. Mr. and Mrs. Misk assisted the innocent to the town square, only to be used as martyrs to show what will happen to anyone who doesn't fall in line. Mr. Hastings also said that all the willing participants had a blank stare, as if they were in some sort of trance. After he found the twins, he brought them back here, and we've all sort of pitched in to take care of them."

Only when Tamara began to sob did she realize her mistake. Javanna tried to embrace her, but Tamara took a step back and held up her hand.

"Dammit! Tamara, I am so sorry," said Javanna.

Tamara felt sincerity in the apology, but it had stripped away the last bit of hope she clung to and confirmed her worst fear: her father was gone.

Doing her best to keep her emotions under control, Tamara searched the fallout room for a place to change and be alone for a few minutes.

"Right through that door," said Javanna, already anticipating Tamara's needs. "It's small, but it'll give you a bit of privacy."

Tamara gave Javanna's hand a brief squeeze, then closed the door softly behind her. The room's only light came from the lamp on a nightstand next to a large bed, where two small bundled-up individuals lay resting peacefully without a care in the world.

Walking over and peering down at the sleeping twins tucked safely away under the covers, Tamara reminisced about the times her father had purposely embarrassed her in front of her friends when she had sleepovers. He'd tell her friends stories of how she used to creep into her parents' room late at night when she had bad dreams. At the time it had been infuriating, but now Tamara wished those days would come again.

Taking a seat at the end of the bed, Tamara broke under the weight from the realization of all the precious memories she would never see come to fruition: her parents watching from the audience as she graduated from high school and eventually college, talking her through her heartbreaks and trials and errors as she entered her adult life and started a profession of her choosing. Her father would never escort her down the aisle on her wedding day, only after reminding her fiancé that he loved her first and how she would always have his heart. The grandkids who would never know just how kind and giving their grandparents had been. She continued to sob and rock back and forth from the strain of all the what-ifs and could haves until a soft knock came at the door accompanied by an elderly voice.

"Tamara? Could you join us for a quick moment?"

Getting herself under control and wiping the tears off her

face, Tamara breathed in several quick breaths before responding, "Be right out."

Hurriedly, and albeit a bit clumsily, she pulled on the sweats before opening the door to find Mr. Hastings's solemn expression housed behind a long graying beard.

"My apologies for the interruption, but we need to get on the move," he said. Giving her a brief hug, Mr. Hastings led her to where the rest of the group was already waiting.

"Friends, this town is no longer our home," said Mr. Hastings, his bottom lip beginning to quiver. "I'm afraid if we stay any longer, we won't make it through the night. The diggers will eventually find us, and even if they don't, once they've completed their takeover of our town, we'll be trapped down here for who knows how long."

The group, having formed a small circle, exchanged knowing glances with one another, all silently agreeing in unison.

Mr. Hastings continued. "Since there is a total of fourteen of us, excluding the twins, I think it would be wise for us to leave in two groups, unless there are any objections?"

When no one spoke, Mr. Hastings said, "The first group will consist of Javanna and Tamara, so they can carry the Misk twins, while the rest of the group watches over them. After the first group makes it to Jasper's property line, they will signal the second group, which I will be in, to let us know that it's safe."

Before Mr. Hastings could continue with the rest of the plan, thunderous knocks came from the outside door.

They had been found.

As she watched the terror spread across everyone's faces, Tamara's only thought was how a similar scenario had played out earlier at her house. Her father had sacrificed himself so she could live. This time she was on her own, or so she thought. The twins began crying in the other room. Their cries flooded Tamara with both feelings of relief and shame, knowing this group of people were going to sacrifice their own lives to protect Tamara and Javanna as they attempted to get the babies to safety.

CHAPTER 44

After leaving Jameson and Barbados sprawled out in the alley, Gideon aimlessly walked the streets of downtown Taupe City for over an hour, just taking in the architecture of the large office buildings. He enjoyed the feeling of not having to rush to get everything accomplished in under a minute, as he had to do while collecting the souls of the dead in Tristan's region.

His only purpose, and his only desire, was to know how Tristan and Legionaries were able to stay out of Hell for so long without the fear of being pulled back. Gideon just wanted a little time for himself to cherish this sense of normalcy, especially knowing it might not last once he was face to face with Tristan and Legionaries.

Gideon stopped to peer into a large glass window displaying different types of pastries. A memory of when his daughter was younger flooded into his mind and sprang to life. They'd gone to a nearby donut shop every Saturday morning, just the two of them. His wife opted to stay in bed since it was her only time to sleep in.

However, Gideon cherished these daddy-daughter dates, no matter how exhausted he was from the workweek. Their order was always the same: a pink donut with sprinkles and an orange juice for his daughter; and a black coffee, glazed donut, and several sausage and cheese kolaches, which he would later take home and split with his wife.

His eyes found the coveted, pink-glazed sprinkled donut in the display. Gideon's first instinct was to walk in and purchase it, except he couldn't because he didn't have the means to.

"Next time, sweetheart, I will get you a whole dozen," said Gideon, imagining his daughter there next to him.

"Promise?" his daughter asked as her small frame suddenly appeared in the reflection next to him.

Unable to speak, Gideon closed his eyes, wishing there were something he could do for a second chance at life. *Promise, my love,* he thought, feeling his throat tighten from the strain of the imagined scene.

"Excuse me, but do you have some change I can borrow?" asked a man behind him.

Opening his eyes, Gideon saw two very skinny men in the reflection of the glass. Turning to face them and judging them by their dirty clothes and scabs on their arms, Gideon deduced that they were probably homeless.

"You say 'borrow' knowing full well that is a lie. You could never repay me," said Gideon with an edge rising in his voice. These two had spoiled one of his most precious memories, and now they would pay for it. "Your question should've been, 'Can I spare some money?' This way we both have the understanding that you're a lowlife, scum-sucking, worthless piece of filth who shouldn't be allowed to continue breathing my air. You can't even afford the drug habit that has a stranglehold on you."

The men pulled small dull blades from their pockets, which pleased Gideon. He knew once he got ahold of them, he could slowly torture them with their own blades. He would start by removing their tongues so no one could understand their screams for help.

"Into the alley," demanded the man who had asked for the money.

Doing as instructed, Gideon said over his shoulder, "I'm learning to really hate alleys, but I do seem to do my best work under the shroud of their darkness."

After leading the men far enough away from the street to where he was sure they wouldn't be seen, Gideon abruptly turned and, his demonic speed still intact, broke the first man's wrist and took the knife from his hand. Gideon silenced the man's short-lived scream, dragging the dull blade all the way through the throat and neck muscles, feeling a slight pause as the blade made contact with bone before finally becoming stuck.

Leaving the knife dangling from the man's throat, Gideon turned to face off with the other man. An evil smile formed on Gideon's face, terrifying the other assailant, and causing him to turn in an attempt to run.

Gideon pounced, driving the man's head into the concrete, causing the knife to fall from his grasp. Grabbing a handful of the man's greasy hair, Gideon felt overwhelming pleasure as he pressed his head into the concrete and dragged his face back and forth across it as if he were painting a canvas.

Feeling justified for taking retribution against the two men who broached the memory of his daughter, Gideon searched the lifeless corpses for money and came away with a little over forty dollars.

Exiting the alley, Gideon hurriedly made his way from the crime scene and found relief at the sight of a Greyhound station a few blocks away. Entering the bus station, he went straight to the bathroom, making sure to keep his head down. After thoroughly washing his face, neck, and hands, he turned his attention to the blood splatter on his clothes, scrubbing until they appeared to be no more than dark smudges.

Stepping back from the mirror to judge his appearance, Gideon decided it was passable enough to not draw any unwanted attention. He exited the restroom and proceeded to a ticket counter.

"One ticket to Broken Falls, please," said Gideon.

The elderly woman behind the counter looked Gideon up and down. "Unfortunately, we can only get you to the town of Deadwater, which is about an hour outside of Broken Falls."

"That'll be just fine," said Gideon, giving the woman a sincere smile.

"Do you have any bags that you need to check?"

"No, just a one-way trip to see family."

"Twenty-seven-fifty," said the woman.

After the exchange of money, and while waiting on the printed ticket, the woman pointed at a bus. "It leaves in the next twenty minutes. There is plenty of room, but you'll need to hurry, as the driver won't wait."

Gideon walked swiftly over to the awaiting bus and held out his ticket for the driver to scan. Once aboard, he chose a seat at the back of the bus away from the rest of its occupants. Locating the lever to lean the seat all the way back, Gideon immediately slipped into a deep, peaceful sleep. The memory of his daughter licking the topping off her pink sprinkled donut flooded his dreams.

"Thank you, Daddy. This is the best donut ever."

CHAPTER 45

L
ooking out from his perch atop the town square, Legionaries stared at the expressionless faces of his followers, who were awaiting his next order. From the corner of his eye, he saw Tristan had now joined the group and was dressed in clothes that were far too small for him. He gave a nod of his head to confirm he had completed his task.

Legionaries knew the subordinate demon must have had questions about how and why he had come to be here instead of being forced back to the depths of Hell. He felt appreciative of his alter ego, Legion, who had put all of this into motion. Tristan, being his first in charge, would fit perfectly into his plan. It was time to introduce him to the group.

Motioning for Tristan to join him, Legionaries said, "Slaves, this is my first-in-command, Tristan. He was the leader of the largest region of Hell until I plucked him out of that miserable existence. He will now assist us in the taking over of the remaining parts of the town."

Legionaries turned to face Tristan and smiled at the demon. "We are not brothers, nor do we share any type of special bond, beyond having spent time in Hell. I want you to hear me clearly when I say if you ever confuse your role here, I will finish what I started at Riley's lake house. Understood?"

"I'm only here to serve. Nothing more," replied Tristan.

"Good," said Legionaries.

Listening in on Tristan's thoughts, Legionaries heard no ill will or underlying intent. He found only confusion mixed with bouts of happiness. Tristan wanted to serve Legionaries and was ready and willing to do whatever was asked of him.

"Tristan, we have three more neighborhoods to clear. First, I want you to take a few of my followers over to the gun store." Legionaries pointed at one of the buildings surrounding the town square. "Then have them execute the rest of the martyrs. We'll deal with their bodies later. For now, I'll watch over them until you return from getting the weapons."

Legionaries shook his head at Tristan's outer appearance. "Change into something more fitting for someone who is now my first-in-command."

Tristan nodded and went to carry out his duty. Legionaries walked to the pleading martyrs, motioning for Miranda and two other men to accompany him. He stood directly in front of them, feeling neither pride nor pity as their desperate faces stared helplessly back at him. The group of martyrs whispered quietly, to be shown mercy, all except for the man named Bob, who Legionaries personally escorted to the square. He did share the same helpless expression as the others, but his demeanor was different. He looked worried, but not for himself, which only made Legionaries feel annoyed.

"Bob," Legionaries called flatly.

Despite how close they were in proximity, Bob sat stoically, looking out into the nothingness as if having not heard Legionaries. This only annoyed Legionaries further.

Legionaries stepped over a few of the martyrs, who hurriedly moved out of his path, and knelt so he was eye to eye with the man who still paid him no attention.

"I had your wife murdered by one of my associates while you were unconscious."

A few tears sprung to life from Bob's eyes. The news about

his wife wasn't as detrimental as Legionaries had hoped for. If the man's thoughts weren't so jumbled, Legionaries would just tap into them. However, they were still jumbled as before, as if there were another paranormal being at play here, one whom both Legionaries and his alter ego, Legion, feared.

"Miranda," said Legionaries, still kneeling and staring at Bob. "Does Bob have any children?"

Before she had time to answer, Bob looked directly at Legionaries, then looked immediately away, telling him all he needed to know.

"How many children?" said Legionaries, pressing the issue.

"He has a daughter, but I don't know her name, only that she's a teenager."

Legionaries stepped just out of Bob's reach. The two followers who had positioned themselves on either side of Legionaries had intercepted Bob and quickly silenced him with several hard blows to the face.

"Save him until after we have located his daughter," said Legionaries, directing the order to the man now standing over Bob. "I can't wait to see this little family reunion."

The follower pulled Bob's limp body away from the other martyrs, then secured him with a rope to a metal fencepost.

Minutes later, Tristan walked up, now dressed in all dark-fitted clothes with a rifle slung over one shoulder and the rest of the followers in tow.

Taking the rifle, Legionaries handed it off to one of the nearby followers. Leaning in, he whispered, "You won't be needing this. Or did you forget we aren't allowed to kill any of the believers who oppose us?"

Not expecting an answer, Legionaries sent out a pulse, ensuring his hold over his followers, excluding Miranda and Tristan.

"Take as many as you think you will need to finish securing the town. Don't bother bringing back any who oppose me except for a female teenager. Be on the lookout for her. Her I want. Anyone else, you are to kill on site. Send a few of the followers you won't need to guard the only entrance into this town and have the rest dig graves on either side of the main road. They will serve as a warning of what will happen to anyone who dares to enter."

"What about them?" asked Tristan, motioning toward the group that remained huddled together in search of safety.

"Who else did you think would be occupying those newly dug graves? Just make certain you don't harm the man I have tied up. I'm saving him for later."

Saying no more, Legionaries took Miranda's hand and escorted her toward a house that had already been cleared. When she rested her head against his arm, Legionaries was unable to contain his smile, now realizing he could indeed have it all. Power and companionship. Something his predecessor had longed for but had never obtained.

CHAPTER 46

R iley was mystified, though a bit relieved that Kratos was actually able to transport Stuart to the safety of a hospital.

His smile was quickly removed by Maggie's scolding tone. "Where did Kratos just take Stuart?"

"I'm pretty sure he took him to the closest hospital, like I asked," answered Riley. When Maggie's frown deepened, Riley quickly added, "Stuart is fine, Maggie, I promise. Besides, don't you agree by now that Kratos is here to help us?"

Still frowning, Maggie walked past Riley and back into her suite without responding. Following her, Riley noticed Maggie had picked up her phone and appeared to be texting someone.

"Stop," said Riley. When she didn't, Riley took the phone out of her hands.

"What in the hell is wrong with you?" screamed Maggie.

"You can't tell anyone about what's happened here," said Riley. "You must appear to be in shock when you learn about Stuart, which is not going to happen for a good while, especially if you're still planning to come with me."

Before she could lunge at him in anger, Kratos materialized between them.

"Where did you take Stuart?" screamed Maggie.

Kratos looked at Riley as if confused by the question, then back to Maggie.

"Kratos, did I tell you to take Stuart away?" Maggie snapped.

Before Riley had a moment to register what Maggie's intentions were, she slapped Kratos with everything she had, taking out her frustration in one violent act. Instead of reacting violently, Kratos merely dropped his head, submitting to whatever came next. Jolting himself out of his state of shock, Riley caught Maggie's arm mid-swing before she could do it again.

"Stop it!" snapped Riley. He grabbed Maggie's other wrist and pushed her back against the kitchen island. "Stuart told us to handle the situation in this manner because he wanted to protect you and because he loves you. Hell, I love you, but I won't allow you to act this way just because you're hurting! If you want to be mad at someone, then be mad at me. I gave Kratos the order! But don't you ever do that to our dog ever again! Do you hear me?"

When Maggie calmed, Riley released his hold, shaking his head in disgust. He turned to apologize to Kratos for not acting quicker and was stunned and saddened to see actual tears running down the sides of the hound's muzzle. His heart broke at the sight of this great beastly hound, who had literally come from Hell to protect them, now enduring unjust punishment from those who had sworn to protect him.

Maggie began to cry. She pushed past Riley, fell to her knees, and embraced Kratos. "Forgive me?" she said, burying her face into the side of Kratos's neck. "I swear to you, I will never physically harm you ever again."

Kratos leaned forward and licked the side of her face several times. Accepting the given kisses, Maggie took hold of Kratos's head and kissed him on the nose. "I love you, Kratos, and I promise that I will never hurt you again." She then looked at Riley. "He may have been one of the Devil's hounds, but you were right. He is ours now."

Riley nodded his head in agreement at Kratos.

"I'm sorry, Riley. I—"

Before Maggie could further reprimand herself, Riley cut her off. "Everything is happening so quickly. I don't expect us to always keep a level head. Just earlier I was the one threatening Kratos, and now I feel like he is ours. There is no way I will just leave him behind. It's weird how quickly our bond has formed. However, if we continue to give in to our anger, I'm certain we will fail in rescuing Jonathan."

Nodding her head in agreement, Maggie stood and began to pace. "I do wish I could be there for Stuart. He has done so much to ensure I'm taken care of. I honestly feel as though I'm turning my back on him when he needs me the most."

Amazed at the clarity and determination in which Stuart had handled everything, Riley thought about the last thing Stuart had said: *You can't travel with the Ferryman as a non-worshipper. If you try to, your parents will find you, and you will be forever trapped in a place where my kind are not permitted to go.*

Shuddering at the thought, Riley wondered if Maggie had even registered what Stuart had said. Since Riley believed in the same God as Stuart, the only thing he was able to interpret from the seemingly prophetic message was that Maggie would not make it out of Hell since she wasn't a believer in God. It was a risk Riley was uncomfortable with. They were about to embark on a dangerous venture, and it wasn't a risk that he was willing to allow Maggie to take.

"You're right," said Riley, earning a curious look from Maggie. "What kind of friend would you be if you left so unexpectedly? You just cleared up everything with the FBI, and if you now went missing after your best friend was shot . . . Well, I don't care what story Stuart tries to spin, you'll be right back under the public's scrutiny. At least if you are here, you can do some damage control."

Maggie stared long and hard at him, and Riley had to look away, still hoping she hadn't seen through his intentions.

"Riley, I'd ask where this sudden concern for my well-being came from, but if I had to guess, it was because of what Stuart had said about my parents."

Remaining silent, Riley refused to look at Maggie.

"Stuart didn't know what he was saying. He was suffering from blood loss and in extreme pain. Besides, a ferryman? Really? For someone who considers themself a Christian, how can you even entertain such nonsense?"

Riley could not contain his silence. "Nonsense or not, the threat is real, Maggie. I don't even know if we can get into Hell, but I do know if you come with me, you won't be returning. So, as my friend and someone whom I care deeply for, I want you to stay here."

Maggie turned away, ending the discussion. Riley and Kratos followed her through the suite, stopping at the locked door they had encountered earlier. Maggie typed in a code on the keypad. The door made an unlocking noise, and they entered.

With the high-tech lock on the door, Riley anticipated something of great value residing on the other side. He was completely dumbfounded when Maggie opened the door to a sparsely furnished home office.

As Maggie situated herself behind the desk, Riley wondered why this room was off limits when all her dumb, precious, and overly priced rocks were out in the open.

While Maggie typed away at the keyboard, Riley busied himself by petting Kratos, jumping a little when Maggie let out a loud sob. He came around the desk and saw the reason for the outburst. On one of the two computer monitors was footage of Stuart exiting his SUV, smiling broadly, completely unaware of what was about to happen to him. While retrieving the duffel bag out of the cargo space, the stranger quickly closed the distance between them. Just as Stuart turned, the demon pressed the gun barrel under Stuart's chin.

"Show me how to delete this. We don't need to watch anymore," Riley said.

Maggie typed a few commands, which brought up a prompt menu. She pressed Enter, deleting the video and replacing it with live footage of the parking garage.

"I'm going to change," said Maggie, leaving Riley and Kratos alone in the room.

Still dressed in only Maggie's robe, Riley thought he should have asked Stuart to borrow something of his to wear. As he made his way to the living room, he found a brand-new set of clothes for him folded on the couch. He quickly got dressed and wasn't surprised to find that everything fit.

Maggie reentered a moment later, gave him a quick once-over, and nodded approvingly. "Everything fit all right?"

"Yes. I'm just surprised you had time to buy this stuff."

"I just ordered them from a nearby store and had them delivered. I'm glad they fit," Maggie said. "Have you given any thought as to how we're going to locate our rogue demon?"

As though having the exact same assumption, Riley and Maggie looked over at Kratos, who stood several feet away.

"Wait. Where's the duffel bag?" asked Maggie.

Realizing it was still in the corridor, Riley went and retrieved it. Walking back over to them, Riley watched Maggie perform a simple kind act by rubbing Kratos behind his ears. Riley smiled to himself, hoping and praying that their lives would return to this type of normalcy. With Jonathan.

Stuart's last words broke into Riley's thoughts once more, spoiling the scene that was playing out in front of him and in his head, creating fear. This could be the last time they'd be together in Maggie's suite. Riley needed to make one more case as to why she should remain behind.

"Maggie," he said.

Maggie slipped her hand into his and kissed him. She then looked down at Kratos and nodded.

Riley felt the sticky warmth from Kratos's tongue on the back of his hand that Maggie was holding. They were transported in a blink of an eye to the middle of a vacant street overlooking what appeared to be the outline of a deserted town.

CHAPTER 47

T ristan watched as Legionaries disappeared with Miranda into an empty house. He couldn't comprehend how carefree his leader appeared to be behaving, especially since he knew firsthand the consequences that awaited them if they failed. And yet he walked off, leaving Tristan in charge, fully confident in his decision.

What Tristan was now taking part in was completely unheard of in the world of the damned. Legionaries was starting a rebellion which, if successful, would start a new way of life for all demons. Tristan was determined more than ever to make this work so he would never have to return to the pits to be tortured for the rest of eternity.

Tristan looked boldly at the followers. "Slaves, draw near."

As the group of followers formed a semicircle around him, Tristan knelt and began pulling single blades of grass from the ground. He allowed the wind to take them, fascinated by not only the feeling of the grass between his fingertips, but how he no longer had to worry about the minute time frame.

"We have three more neighborhoods to search through," said Tristan as he continued pulling methodically at the grass. "I will be taking most of you with me. The rest of you will dig graves along the main road's entrance." Without looking, Tristan pointed to the person standing directly in front of him. "What's your name, slave?"

"Clara," came a woman's voice.

Tristan looked up to find a petite middle-aged woman with a swollen mouth. He thought it strange that during his time as Region Leader he had never worked with a female demon.

Without having to count, Tristan glanced around at the followers, estimating a little over three hundred of them.

"Clara, I want you to take a hundred followers to the town's entrance to dig graves on either side of the main road for all the dead martyrs . . . including them." Tristan pointed at the remaining captives. "All are to be buried there, except for the man tied up. Legionaries does not want him harmed. After you've finished, set up a perimeter around the town to make certain no one can enter or leave. You have five minutes to gather your group. Now go."

Walking away from the group, Tristan heard Clara shouting directions. He was impressed with how quickly she took to her new leadership role. The town was blanketed by darkness. The only illumination came from a few remaining streetlights. Tristan looked up at the night sky and its endless stars. It was the first time since his previous life he had the opportunity to appreciate their beauty. A painful memory wormed its way in, which was very odd given all his time in Hell.

It was a camping trip at the Big Bend National Park for what promised to be a spectacular meteor shower. "Sure, are a lot of stars, Daddy," said his five-year-old son, Troy, lying next to him atop the makeshift blanket they had spread out on the ground.

His wife, Charlotte, lying on the other side of Troy, reached over and gave Tristan's hand a squeeze. "This was a great idea. Thank you for making the time for us."

She was referring to the number of hours Tristan had been putting in at the law firm. What Tristan hadn't informed his wife was that earlier in the week he had been chosen to assist in a big wrongful death case against a pharmaceutical company that would soon be consuming all of his time. Not wanting to spoil the moment, Tristan just kissed the back of her hand and looked back up at the stars.

Troy pointed with emphasis to the sky. "I see one!"

"Good job, buddy," commented Charlotte. "Keep watching because there will be a lot more."

People suddenly began screaming, followed by several shots of gunfire, tearing into Tristan's memory, spoiling one of the last peaceful times he had shared with his wife and son.

As the smoke from the guns began to dissipate, Tristan irritably watched as Legionaries's slaves probed the corpses of the captives with the barrels of their rifles. Clara, the woman he had placed in charge, walked over to a man who was attempting to crawl away. She placed her rifle against the back of the man's head and pulled the trigger without any form of remorse, then continued with the task of checking the rest of the group.

Tristan had only ever seen this type of brutality from other demons in the confines of Hell as they fed on one another. Now, a small part of Hell had taken up residence in this small, secluded town of Broken Falls.

Tristan only knew the name of the town by listening in on the thoughts of Legionaries's slaves when they had raided the gun store. This was a new ability for Tristan, one which he only thought Lucifer and Legionaries possessed, until now. Tristan had no real idea why he was able to do it now. He assumed it had something to do with being Legionaries's first-in-command.

As Clara's group began loading the dead martyrs into the back of a large flatbed truck, the followers who would now accompany Tristan to the other three neighborhoods formed a semicircle around him.

"You," Tristan said flatly, singling out an overweight man to the left of him. "Master Legionaries has informed me that you have already cleared one neighborhood, but there are three more to go. Correct?"

The man sharing the same blank look as the rest of the group gave a single head nod in response, which angered Tristan. During his time as Region Leader, his Elders and slaves knew they were to verbally answer him when he spoke to them.

Tristan walked slowly in front of them, examining them. They all had a red hue to their eyes. It would appear for only a moment, then be gone the next, like the flicker of a flame.

"When I speak, you verbally respond," said Tristan.

"Yes, Tristan," the group responded in unison.

"Fifty of you will begin patrolling the streets in groups of two. The rest will come with me."

Needing no further instruction, a group stepped back, paired off, and headed in different directions as instructed. The rest stayed put, awaiting his next order.

It was eerie how the group appeared to share the same thoughts, as if reading each other's minds, an ability Tristan wished his former Elders—Jameson, Barbados, and Gideon— had shared. *What has become of them?* he thought. *And, more importantly, which of the three low lives have taken up my previous role as Region Leader?*

Dismissing the intrusive thought, Tristan pointed again to the same overweight slave, but before he could give an order, the group immediately spanned out, cocking their guns and pointing them down the dark road ahead.

Staring into the dark empty street, unable to see what the followers had, Tristan slowly advanced. He held a hand in the air for the group to wait. As moments passed, Tristan focused more intently into the blackness. Finally, the outline of what appeared to be a single individual came into focus, accompanied seconds later by a male's voice.

"Don't shoot. I am unarmed and have journeyed farther than any of you could even fathom just to be here. That is, of course, except for you, Tristan. You know me, just as I know you."

CHAPTER 48

Gideon was startled awake by the bus's air brakes. Still groggy and dazed, he stood and stretched before following a few other passengers off the bus.

"Just a quick thirty-minute pit stop and then we're back on the road," said the driver. "Folks, I do mean thirty minutes exactly. It's nine fifteen now, so I expect you back at nine forty-five because I will not wait any longer or come looking for any of you."

Gideon mentally agreed with the couple standing next to him when they called the driver an asshole loud enough for the man to hear it.

It had been morning when he boarded the bus, and now it was late into the night. Gideon couldn't believe he had slept for as long as he did. Walking over to the driver, who was checking to ensure that the cargo compartments were still secured and locked, Gideon noticed the man's name badge read "Cliff" and not "asshole" as the couple had so delicately put it.

"Excuse me, Cliff. This is my stop, but I need to get to the town of Broken Falls."

"Okay," said Cliff dismissively, not bothering to look up from his tedious task and ignoring what Gideon was implying.

"Well, could you help me out?"

Cliff stopped what he was doing, eyed Gideon, and then laughed. "I'm not heading in your direction. Besides, I can't just drive an hour out of the way because this here bus"—he slapped one of the windows several times to drive his point home—"has a tracking device on it. This way the company knows where I am at all times, which means you are shit out of luck, no matter how much you beg!"

Without hesitation, Gideon slammed Cliff against the side of the bus and slapped the man over a dozen times in just a few seconds. "I used to feed on your kind in Hell, sucking the very essence and arrogance out of their soul as they screamed and begged for their mommy to save them."

Cliff, too stunned to speak, struggled under his grasp. Gideon leaned closer to Cliff's face, noticing the hue of his red eyes reflecting in Cliff's. It was something all demons shared, no matter what their natural eye color was. It lay just dormant inside the pupils, distinguishing them from those who weren't of their kind.

The sound of liquid hitting the pavement filled the silence, followed by a stench that could not be confused with anything else.

"We are at a truck stop," Cliff said shakily. "You'll be able to find a long-haul trucker who will gladly give you a ride. Just, please, don't hurt me anymore."

Gideon gave Cliff a final shove, then turned and headed to the truck stop. After twenty minutes, he found a ride with a trucker named Wanda, and a little more than an hour later, mixed with polite conversation, she dropped him off on the side of the highway a mile outside of Broken Falls.

"Sorry, I can't take you all the way, but I'd have a helluva time trying to get turned around since there's only one way in and out of that town."

"I appreciate you getting me this far," said Gideon before closing the door.

As Gideon walked toward the town, he began to feel something supernatural drawing him forward. Each quickened step informed him that he was on the verge of finally getting his answers. If the Ferryman was telling the truth, maybe it was possible that Legionaries was just as powerful as Lucifer.

Gideon hadn't realized that he had been in a flat-out sprint until the sign "Welcome to Broken Falls" was directly in front of him. He stopped to take in his surroundings; all the town's lights were out. The only light coming from the full moon exposed the outline of some house's rooftops, as well as silhouettes of more than a dozen individuals appearing to dig holes on either side of the main road entrance.

Gideon wanted to avoid confrontation until he had a better understanding of what he was walking into, He quickly passed to the other side of the road, then tediously maneuvered himself down a steep enclosure that led to a slow-moving creek.

The creek, although no more than twenty feet across from either side, presented him with a new set of problems. A series of large rocks stretched from one side to the other, covered in thick green algae, which promised to dump him directly into the water with one misstep. The second problem was the creek's sandy bottom. If he tried to just tread through, he would wind up making more noise if he got stuck.

Gideon cautiously executed his way across the rocks. When he was on the other side, he gave a quick look around, making sure he hadn't been noticed, then moved with haste to the top of the embankment.

Slipping in between two homes, making his way to the front yard, Gideon crouched down behind a large oak tree and waited. He expected to hear distant voices telling him where to proceed, but he was surprised when he heard several gunshots go off in the distance, informing him of his destination.

After walking only, a couple of hundred yards, Gideon began

to vaguely make out a man's voice. When he drew closer to where the sound was coming from, Gideon recognized who the voice belonged to. It was the voice of a fool. However, fool or not, this individual held the secret to what could be his new life.

At the sound of guns being cocked and knowing they were being aimed blindly in his direction, Gideon raised both hands in surrender, proceeding with his steady pace.

"Don't shoot, for I am unarmed and have journeyed farther than any of you could even fathom just to be here. That is, of course, except for you, Tristan. You know me, just as I know you."

CHAPTER 49

Legionaries was curious to know if his powers were still growing or if they had finally reached their full capacity. He did notice a new ability emerge after the last time he emitted a pulse to ensure his slaves weren't a problem for Tristan. Now he was able to see through the eyes of every one of his followers, which unexplainably excluded Tristan and Miranda.

Leading Miranda away, Legionaries felt unsteady as his distorted vision became too much to process. It wasn't until his alter ego, Legion, whispered, "Calm yourself, for I am here and will always protect you." He was then able to find control once more.

He walked the rest of the way to the nearest house without further incident. He entered the living room and took up occupancy on the sofa. Miranda, as if somehow able to read his thoughts, remained quiet as she sat in a recliner opposite him.

Closing his eyes, Legionaries took a deep breath. Legion spoke inside his head. "I have yet to show you everything you are capable of, Legionaries. This is just another taste of what you once could do before a God cast us into a herd of pigs, and thus ending our existence with a death plunge. The longer we are free from Hell's grasp, the more powerful you will grow. You see, Legionaries, there was a time when you could control a person's actions and then you watched through their eyes as they did what you asked. Now, I want you to focus first on only the followers around Tristan. Then narrow your focus to one individual and tap into their synapses to control them like a puppet."

Doing as instructed, Legionaries thought of where he had left Tristan, and from a bird's-eye view, he saw his followers had formed a semi-circle around him.

Before Legionaries could ask how this was possible, Legion answered, "Yes, my love. You even have control over the beasts of the land, water, and air. For instance, I took the liberty of searching this town through various animals' viewpoints without you ever even knowing. I wanted to sharpen this ability before I shared it with you. The town is practically all yours now, except for a few stragglers who have joined up in some futile resistance. They are currently hidden in a fallout shelter that's a few blocks away from the town square. When the time comes, I will reveal the exact location so we can start our next phase."

"Yes, Legion," answered Legionaries, not feeling odd about basically answering a part of himself.

Legionaries focused on one of the followers who was standing in front of Tristan. His view became limited to that individual. He listened to Tristan explain to the group what was expected of them.

"You," Tristan said flatly.

Tristan then pointed aimlessly to an overweight man who stood to the right of the person Legionaries was now occupying.

"Master Legionaries has informed me that you have already cleared one neighborhood, but there are three more to go. Correct?"

Taking up residence in the fat man's body, Legionaries had to stop himself from smiling as he gave a nod of his head in response, knowing how angry it would make Tristan.

On cue, Tristan walked slowly in front of the group, making

eye contact with every one of Legionaries's followers. "When I speak, you verbally respond!" yelled Tristan.

Legionaries pulsed, ensuring the group replied in unison, "Yes, Tristan."

Tristan paused for a moment before continuing. "Fifty of you will begin patrolling the streets in groups of two. The rest will come with me."

Further testing himself, Legionaries touched the synapses of the fifty followers, and had them take a step back from the group. He then paired them off into groups of two before releasing them in different directions.

"Playtime is over," said Legion. "Someone you'll recognize from your past is approaching."

Fearing the worst, Legionaries released his control of the group over to Legion, who then immediately caused the followers to span out and aim their guns in the same direction down the dark street.

Disoriented after being snapped back to his own body still sitting on the couch, Legionaries stood and quickly left the house, with Miranda following. Again, she didn't speak a word, which made him appreciate her all the more.

As they made their way through the town square, his followers halted their task of loading the dead martyrs onto a large flatbed truck and quickly knelt. Ignoring them, Legionaries stretched out his awareness to locate the unwelcome individual's thoughts. Moments later, the name *Gideon* came to fruition. Searching his own memory, Legionaries placed the name and knew exactly who this demon was and what his former role had been.

Legionaries walked up and stood next to Tristan, who hadn't noticed because he was still focused on the form taking shape in the dark where the voice had come from. Legionaries gave a single wave of his hand, ordering his followers to stand down. "This stranger is one of ours. In fact, he used to work for you."

He leaned into Tristan as he said this. Tristan briefly looked at him, then continued staring down the dark street until Gideon finally came into focus.

"You are amongst friends, Gideon," said Legionaries. "If you were here for any other reason than to find refuge, you would already be back in Hell!"

Stopping several feet away, Gideon looked confidently at Legionaries's followers before dismissing them. He then looked first at Legionaries and then at Tristan. "I come with no ill will, only questions."

The comment had been directed toward Tristan, but Legionaries stepped forward. Again, giving a wave of his hand, he dismissed his followers, except for Tristan and Miranda.

"This conversation is best suited for indoors," said Legionaries.

Not waiting for a reply, he turned and went back to the vacant house, with the rest following. After Tristan and Gideon were seated, Legionaries leaned over to Miranda and whispered, "Wait for me upstairs. I shall be up after my business is concluded."

Saying nothing, Miranda nodded and excused herself.

Entering the living room, he found Gideon and Tristan sitting on opposite ends of the couch. Legionaries sat in the recliner across from them, listening in on their private thoughts.

Tristan's thoughts were swirling with questions about how Gideon had successfully escaped. Gideon's thoughts, although for the most part jumbled, begged to learn how to stay on Earth so he wouldn't have to return to Hell. For good reason, the two demons loathed one another and longed for the opportunity to take retribution for how they had been wronged.

"First of all," said Legionaries, interrupting their thoughts, "if either of you ever step out of line under my watch, I will reach inside your mortal body, rip out your souls, and eat them."

This immediately cleared up any ill will that Tristan had felt toward Gideon. Gideon, however, gave Legionaries a look of defiance.

"So be it," said Legionaries.

While now pinning Gideon to the couch with one large cat paw, Legionaries was surprised by how quickly he was able to morph into the beast, Legion. The transformation was so abrupt, Legionaries's clothes laid shredded on the floor.

Tristan pulled his legs from the floor, pressed his body as far into his end of the couch as he could, and tucked himself into a ball to keep as far away from Legion as possible. Gideon could only stare back in horror as Legion opened his eagle's beak, revealing a serpent tongue. The room fell into an intense silence until Legion put his serpent tongue to work. He struck Gideon in various places across his face, causing the demon to cry out in dismay and pain.

Transforming once more to his mortal body, Legionaries was again astonished at how fast he was able to perform this feat, when only hours earlier it had taken several minutes for the painful process to be completed.

Kicking his shredded clothes out of the way, Legionaries sat back in his chair, crossed one leg over the other, and waited until he had both demons' full and undivided attention.

Gideon, having finally stopped screaming, clumsily began feeling at the sides of his face, grimacing at the various inflicted puncture wounds. Meeting Legionaries's piercing gaze, Gideon held up both hands in a sign of surrender.

Tristan, too, had somewhat relaxed now that Legionaries was back to normal, placing both feet firmly on the ground. However, he didn't bother making eye contact with Legionaries.

"Clearly, I'm not what you remembered, am I, Gideon?" Not wanting a response, Legionaries continued. "I'm aware of the reason you've come and the answers you seek. I was once forced to be a servant, beaten into the role of lackey so that I could no longer remember what I really am. That was until the false God Lucifer made a critical mistake by casting me into the depths of Hell where, amidst the pain, I found peace within my agony. I found solitude. That was when I met my true self, Legion. So, I ask you, Gideon, when you look at me, what do you see?"

Tristan and Gideon exchanged brief looks before responding in unison.

"We see God."

CHAPTER 50

Fear was a feeling that Gideon had never experienced throughout all his time in Hell. No matter what he was forced to endure, he was always able to escape into one of his past memories and block everything else out. Now he was unable to stop his hands from trembling under Legionaries's cold glare.

Gideon hadn't believed the Ferryman when he said Legionaries had been forced into the role of lackey and was actually more than what he appeared to be. Now that Gideon was seated directly across from Legionaries, he could attest to it not only being true, but Legionaries was, without a doubt, a god. At this revelation, Gideon unconsciously looked up to find Legionaries's piercing gaze had softened into a demonic smile.

"Thank you," said Legionaries. "I find myself in wonderment of you as well, especially with how you were able to find us. I can hear your thoughts. However, come kneel before me so I may get your complete backstory."

Having nothing to hide, Gideon did as he was instructed. When Legionaries placed a hand upon his head, Gideon's entire body, including his mortal lungs, froze in place. His past memories poured forth, from not only his time in Hell but also his previous life.

Powerless to control what Legionaries was able to access, Gideon's intentions changed from wanting to protect his sacred life memories to entering survival mode. His lungs burned with the desire for one more taste of fresh air. The dark spots which had previously threatened the outskirts of his vision took up further residence as his state of consciousness slipped further out of grasp, until at last darkness overtook him.

Several slaps landed to the side of his face, pulling Gideon out of the blackness. Gideon coughed so violently tears filled his eyes. Wiping them away, Gideon pushed himself up to his knees. He wouldn't dare try to stand.

"So, a woman by the name of Esperanza has been appointed to my previous role," said Legionaries without concern. "It appears at first that she was doing a splendid job, which is until that idiot, Lucifer, finally learns of what she's been attempting to cover up. Then it's back to the pits for her. I'm quite surprised he left her in charge of Hell. His blind desire to unlock the abilities of the guardian angel, Jonathan, will be his undoing."

Getting clumsily to his feet and falling back to the couch, Gideon began clenching and unclenching his hands to help loosen his taxed forearms. His whole body had gone so rigid from the strain of what Legionaries had done to him that he could feel his muscles beginning to cramp. When he caught Legionaries looking at him, Gideon stopped what he was doing, hoping Legionaries wouldn't perceive it as any form of threat.

"Permission to ask a few questions of my own?" asked Gideon, still unable to look directly at Legionaries.

"Tristan will never be pulled back to Hell unless I do it myself," said Legionaries, answering Gideon's unasked question. "As for you, I'm actually going to give you a choice."

Gideon wanted to speak, but he knew it was time to remain silent and hope for Legionaries's mercy.

"You are actually quite fascinating," said Legionaries. "No other demon can access their past. Not even when I was Lucifer's lackey could I do this. It took being banished to the depths after

I struck Lucifer to learn what I actually was. He kept me close so he could keep me ignorant of my past, torturing me constantly to ensure I always feared him. Which makes me question why you were allowed this ability. Or was it just an oversight by Lucifer?"

Gideon also wondered about this, but he never told anyone out of fear that his gift—and curse—might be taken from him. Yet he carelessly made a deal with the Ferryman for his memories in exchange for the answers about Tristan's whereabouts.

"Ah, the Ferryman," said Legionaries. "That old relic is still around?" He grinned at Gideon, who for a quick moment had made eye contact with him. "He's the least of your worries, depending on what you choose."

Somewhat aware of what the choice might be, Gideon forced himself to look directly at Legionaries. "I'll assist you in whatever way you ask of me. I will pledge my allegiance to you, and all I ask for in return is that you don't cast me back."

When Legionaries didn't answer, Gideon felt compelled to strengthen his case. "You've seen my past and know what I've been through. Furthermore, did any of my memories give you pause for doubt about any objective other than what I've already told you? As for working alongside Tristan, I will heed your warning and will shelve my contempt toward him."

"Good," said Legionaries. "You two will share leadership roles. We're almost done clearing this town of anyone who opposes me. The last of these non-worshippers are in a fallout shelter a few blocks away. I'll temporarily allow you both the use of the gifts of my sight. This will allow you to find the fallout shelter more quickly. However, remember the rules: You aren't allowed to harm the non-worshippers. Only the mortal followers still possess that capability, having not yet tasted the fires of Hell."

Legionaries stood. He pressed his thumbs gently on both Gideon's and Tristan's closed eyes. Opening his eyes, Gideon found he could see through the walls of the house all the way to the followers working in the courtyard.

"Now leave me, and do not return until the job is finished. Tristan will explain what else needs to be accomplished."

Leaving the house, Gideon anticipated Tristan would come across as entitled and overbearing since it had been his personality when he was Region Leader. Instead, he spoke in a tone that would suggest they were close friends. "Things sure are different here. Especially for me and my plans for the future."

Gideon remembered how goal-driven Tristan had been with his region, the constant plots and schemes to overthrow another Region Leader in order to expand his own. The difference now was that Gideon had the power to say no and would refuse to help Tristan in any way, especially if it meant jeopardizing what Legionaries wanted.

"I can't read your mind," said Tristan, "but after our previous lives, I know what you must be thinking." Making their way over to the followers who were waiting where Gideon had first encountered them, Tristan clarified his intentions. "Same as you, I just want to stay out of Hell for as long as possible and will do absolutely anything to make sure that happens."

For once, Gideon agreed with him. He had been truthful when he told Legionaries he would shelve the contempt he had for Tristan. "Likewise," said Gideon. "What's the sudden change in your character about? Is it just about no longer being an occupant of Hell? Or are you just telling me what I want to hear?"

"Nothing like that at all. I don't expect you to believe me or for us to ever be friends. When I was sent out on that mission to bring down the guardian, I was humbled. Not by the guardian but by Legionaries. Legionaries wasn't making an idle threat when he said he can reach inside your mortal body, rip out your soul, and devour it."

Needing to know more, Gideon put a hand on Tristan's shoulder and stopped him. Studying Tristan's face, he could see that the once prideful and overzealous demon was truly terrified of Legionaries's capabilities.

"Yes, Gideon, Legionaries tore my soul out of my body and then swallowed me. As powerful as I believed myself to be, I was completely powerless to stop him. I was stuck inside Legionaries with no way out and no way to know how long I'd remain in my prison. I was only released a few hours ago when he spat me out. I can't even describe the agony I felt, but I've never felt that kind of pain before. It wasn't a physical pain but a psychological one, which, in my opinion, is far worse. I had no concept of time. Little by little, I began to lose the ability to even think for myself. There's not a doubt in my mind I would have just ceased to exist if Legionaries hadn't brought me back. Like I had never even been born."

Trying to comprehend what Tristan was saying, Gideon understood one thing for certain: he never wanted to cross Legionaries. Of all the horrific, torturous acts he had witnessed during his time in Hell, the thought of being fully consumed by another demon made Gideon shudder.

"Since I've been back, I'm beginning to remember my past life. Just bits and pieces here and there, but they are my reasoning for not wanting to do anything to upset Legionaries. They're painful, but they're worth it. They make me feel almost—"

"Human," said Gideon.

Tristan offered a sad smile and resumed heading toward the awaiting followers. "I don't expect us to be friends, either. But I will work with you, without any friction on my part, because I, too, feel the same as you do. I never want to return to Hell. Ever again."

They made the rest of the way to the followers in silence. Gideon wondered if this could be a start to a better life, one actually built on trust between demons all working to achieve the same common goal. Ironic as that sounded.

A wheelbarrow of dead martyrs passed in front of them. The lifeless eyes of several victims seemed to be casting judgmental stares up at Gideon, as if telling him in one deafening silent voice, "Your kind will never be welcomed where I'm going. My reward is an everlasting life of peace and hope for the choices I made when I was alive. Your choices and your eternity are already in motion. You're just looking for ways to postpone the inevitable."

CHAPTER 51

A s the knocking outside the fallout shelter continued to grow more intense, accompanied by more shouting to open up, Mr. Hastings took Tamara by the arm and led her into the room where the babies were crying.

Javanna had already pulled on and fastened a heavy backpack to herself and began assisting Tamara with hers. Mr. Jasper hurriedly placed the twins in individual baby carriers, walked to a section of the wall, and gave it a hard shove with his shoulder, causing it to open. Prying it the rest of the way open, he looked at Tamara and gave her a sad smile.

"Hopefully, we can keep the diggers occupied long enough for you two to escape with the babies."

Four more men entered the room, rifles in hand. "How can we help?" said one man.

"Jasper and Brian are going to stay behind with a few others to create a diversion," said Mr. Franklin.

Tamara personally knew Mr. Franklin because he lived down the street from them, and he was also a regular at her father's store. At the neighborhood cookouts, he had always brought what he called his "world-winning salsa," which was always too spicy for anyone to eat. This memory made Tamara's eyes fill with tears.

Javanna handed her one of the twin's carriers, then gave her shoulder a light squeeze.

"You two will accompany me up first," said Mr. Hastings,

pointing at Mr. Franklin and the man standing next to him. "We need to move quickly, and I want you to span out once we're outside so that we aren't all lumped together. Then I want Tamara and Javanna to exit next, followed by Dennis and Roy." He looked to the last two men. "Understood?"

The small group nodded, exchanging sad smiles, as this was more than likely the end for them.

"I love each and every one of you," said Mr. Hastings. "Let's make our final act on this Earth one of defiance so these children have a chance to grow up and live a long life." Saying no more, Mr. Hastings walked boldly up the stairs and waited for Mr. Franklin and the other man to join him. "I'll see you on the other side," said Mr. Hastings to the two men.

The three men shared a final embrace. Mr. Hastings turned the handle on the outside door, which released a loud screech in protest. Exchanging one last look with the group, Mr. Hastings smiled, then charged out into the dark night, accepting his fate.

Quickly ascending the steps, Tamara stopped just outside the door as someone slammed into the back of her. Before she could fall, a firm grip tightened around her free arm, steadying her and in the same moment pulling her along. "We have to keep moving," Javanna said sharply.

After what felt like a full minute had passed since leaving Jasper's safe house, Tamara had an overwhelming feeling that they were going to be okay. As she continued to put distance between her and the diggers, the sounds of gunfire erupted behind her, replacing her inner peace with terror. The chilling sounds of screaming filled her ears.

No longer feeling Javanna's hand on her arm, Tamara panicked and began sprinting blindly into the night. A few strides later, she twisted her ankle on the uneven ground. Feeling the pop in her right ankle, Tamara instantly released and dropped the baby carrier to the ground as she clutched at her foot. The loud shrieking cries coming from the baby carrier were quickly accompanied by the sounds of bullets whizzing over Tamara's location.

Fumbling around in the dark until she could locate the upside-down carrier, Tamara pulled the baby out and pressed it gently into her chest. Making certain not to smother the infant, she ignored the painful protest from her ankle, got to her feet, and set off. She increased her pace with each agonizing step, all the while praying she wouldn't be shot in the back.

When she was unexpectedly slapped in the face by something, Tamara let out a loud cry. It was only a tree branch. She pushed through the rest of the outstretched tree branches until she was free of them, then froze, uncertain as to what to do next.

"Tamara, I'm over here," said Javanna to her left.

Something in Javanna's voice didn't sound right. Managing to find Javanna seconds later, now that the moon was no longer hidden behind the clouds, Tamara saw that her friend had been shot. She quickly put the one twin down, who immediately went back to screaming. Tamara pulled off her backpack and rummaged around in it until she located baby wipes. She tore several out and pressed them into the wound in Javanna's chest.

Javanna stared helplessly back at her. "Follow this tree line. It'll take you to the road," she said, then turned her head and spat. Thick, gooey strands of blood dripped from her chin. She looked at the twin she had been responsible for and said in a weak voice, "Do everything you can to give them a chance."

Tamara took Javanna's hand and gave it a squeeze. Javanna then reached down to her side, retrieved a handgun, and handed it to Tamara. Having never held a gun in her life, Tamara awkwardly accepted it.

"I can carry you," said Tamara, realizing only after the words had left her lips that it wasn't true.

"Go," said Javanna. "You haven't much time." The woman shuddered several times, followed by a loud wheeze.

Tamara felt numb. It all felt overwhelming and impossible. Her family and friends were surely now dead, and soon she would suffer the same fate because there was no way she could make it safely to the town of Deadwater, especially with two infants in tow. For the first time, Tamara seriously considered ending her own life right then. Just press the gun to the side of her head and end it all before anyone else could. The sounds of the twins crying brought her back to sanity.

"I will do everything possible to keep them alive," said Tamara. But Javanna's lifeless eyes seemed to plead with her to get moving.

Putting the gun inside the backpack, Tamara leaned down and kissed Javanna lightly on the forehead. She slipped the backpack on, then picked up the twin lying next to Javanna.

Fucking impossible, thought Tamara as she positioned the baby inside her sweat jacket.

Retrieving the baby carrier Javanna had been carrying, Tamara was amazed to find that Javanna, although mortally wounded, had put the baby's needs first, as the infant was now asleep with a bottle in its grasp.

Tamara found several more bottles in Javanna's open pack. She pulled one out and placed it into the cold hands of the twin tucked inside her jacket, who gladly accepted it.

Although she was wearing baggy sweats, the cuff on her right ankle was stretched from the swelling. She knew it was from either a bad sprain or a small break, but she couldn't worry about it now.

Following the tree line and moving as quickly as she possibly could, Tamara could hear distant cheers of victory, which could only mean everyone who had been in Jasper's fallout shelter was dead.

At the end of the tree line was the road that led out of town. Looking both ways to ensure there was no one else insight, Tamara disobeyed the direct order her father had given regarding the road and began a fast pace, walking away from the town she had once called home.

As she came over the peak of the first rise overlooking the town, Tamara froze at the sound of a growl.

CHAPTER 52

Exchanging a confused expression with Maggie, Riley released her hand to look around and make certain they were alone. Seeing only cornfields on either side of the road, he blew out a breath of relief because no one had witnessed them simply materialize into existence.

Riley could see why the rogue demon had chosen this location. It was secluded, and when the distant lightning lit up the night sky for a second, he could see the town tucked away at the base of a mountain range.

He was about to voice his thoughts to Maggie when he was distracted by a multitude of gunfire echoing off in the distance. He grabbed Maggie and pulled them both to the hard pavement. Riley covered Maggie with his body until the shooting ended. When he was positive that they weren't the intended targets, he jerked Maggie to her feet and led her into the closest cornfield.

"Are you hit?" asked Riley. Without giving Maggie a moment to answer, Riley began checking her clothes for any holes. Then he abruptly turned Maggie around, running his hands across her back in search of any warm or wet spots.

"I'm all right," said Maggie, shaking and turning back to face him.

Wrapping Maggie in a tight embrace, Riley shuddered at how close Kratos had gotten them to whatever chaos the rogue demon had begun. He wanted to scold the hound, except Kratos was still standing guard in the middle of the road, his red eyes seeing everything that had just transpired off in the distance.

Taking some solace in the calm demeanor of the hound, Riley still began to worry about the safety of Kratos just sitting out in the open in the middle of the road.

"Kratos, come."

For a long moment Kratos held his ground, still focused intently on the unfolding events in the distance, which Riley and Maggie weren't privy to seeing.

As his fear for the hound's safety grew, Riley took a step toward the road and called once more. "Kratos, please come here."

The hound turned his glowing red eyes at him, as if reading Riley's thoughts of concern for only his safety. Kratos finally acquiesced.

"Good boy," said both Riley and Maggie.

Then, in the same chaotic manner he had checked Maggie, Riley ran his hands all over Kratos's body to ensure he hadn't been injured either. This earned him several licks to the sides of his face.

"What in the hell is happening around here?" whispered Maggie.

Sharing the same concern, Riley stepped halfway out of the cornfield, straining his eyes for any sign of an answer. He instead noticed that he had left the duffel bag of guns out on the road. He considered making a run to retrieve it, but when Kratos issued a deep, threatening growl, he strained to see what Kratos could see. Riley was taken aback when he heard the sound of what appeared to be babies crying. The sound was coming toward them.

"What in the hell is that?" asked Riley.

Leaving their cover of the cornfield, Kratos walked into the middle of the road and readied himself to attack. As the sound of babies' crying grew louder, a figure began to appear. As the figure came into view, Riley could see it was a teenage female holding a baby carrier. She froze at the sight of Kratos, who was now advancing toward her.

"Kratos, stand down," said Riley.

With Maggie following, Riley hurried over to Kratos and placed a hand on his back.

"We won't hurt you," said Riley.

When the teen didn't respond, Maggie took the initiative by stepping in front of both Kratos and Riley. "My name is Maggie, and this is my friend Riley and our dog Kratos. I assure you we will not hurt you."

Instead of responding in words, the teen broke into loud sobs before falling helplessly to her knees in a sign of surrender. "I'm sorry, sweet babies. I did the best I could."

Without hesitating, Maggie rushed over and dropped down next to her. "I will not let anyone hurt you. You can trust me."

"Trust?" The teen practically spat the word in disgust. "We're not on the same side. You are with that group of killers I'm trying to get away from. You can deny it if you want, but no normal dog looks like that!"

She pointed an accusatory finger at Kratos, then attempted to back away by scooting on her butt. The teen kicked helplessly at the ground before relenting, but still had the presence of mind to keep the baby carrier behind her, offering as much protection as possible.

Kratos pushed past Maggie's outstretched hands, sniffing the young woman several times. He licked her arm once and slowly backed away, taking a position next to Maggie.

"Like, I said," Maggie spoke softly, "we are not here to hurt you. I know my dog is scary looking, but I promise you, he will not harm you."

The young woman looked up at them from her huddled

position, fear laced in her eyes. Then her expression softened from
Maggie's reassurance and from Kratos's single lick. The babies
had also stopped crying, making Riley further believe that Kratos
possessed some sort of calming ability, similar to what Jonathan
had done when he sent out large amounts of peace.

However, Jonathan was a guardian angel and Kratos was
one of the Devil's hounds. Jonathan had told him once that it
would be fatal if he ever attempted to heal someone by passing
some of his power into them. But Kratos showed up moments
after Jonathan had been pulled into Hell. Riley started to put it
together in his head. Had Jonathan encountered Kratos at some
point and somehow forced a piece of his abilities into him? If
that were the case, then Kratos possessed not only what a hound
of Hell could do, but also what a guardian angel could do. This
was how Kratos could move faster than even Jonathan.

"Oh my God," Riley gasped.

Maggie had been hugging the teen, but now frowned at him.

"Sorry for my outburst," he said. "Here, let me help you with
your things. We need to hide in the corn stalks so we can talk for
a bit. Afterward, Kratos can take you far away from here so you
will be safe from anyone who is trying to harm you."

When they had gone far enough into the cornfield, ensuring
they couldn't be seen from the road, Riley pushed several stalks
over, forming a four-foot perimeter so they wouldn't have to
sit in the dirt. Once that was completed, Maggie and the teen
changed the two babies, made them each a bottle, wrapped them
in blankets Riley had pulled from the pack, and laid them next
to one another.

"My name is Tamara," the girl said, offering her hand out to
Riley.

"Pleased to meet you. Just wished it was under different
circumstances."

Now as they were all seated, with Maggie and Tamara next to one another holding hands, Riley wanted to know what was happening inside the town to be a little better prepared. Unfortunately, to start firing question after question would not only be wrong of him but would also earn him a harsh reprimand from Maggie. Seeing Tamara's weary expression, he couldn't even imagine the hell she must have gone through to escape, all the while protecting those babies.

"I can't thank God enough that you found me," said Tamara. "I wouldn't have made it much farther." She broke down into Maggie's arms.

Riley felt ashamed for only thinking about what Tamara could tell him instead of immediately getting her to safety. He looked at Kratos standing next to the road. Although Kratos had been facing away from them to watch the road for any more signs of life, he immediately turned his head and locked eyes with Riley, informing him that he missed nothing.

"Tamara, I think it best if Kratos took you and the babies far away from here. It's hard to explain how Kratos can do this. Just know you were right with your first assumption: he isn't just a normal dog. Besides, it gives Maggie and me time to figure out what we need to do next."

Wiping her tears, Tamara looked at Riley. Her face was pained, and it was clear she had been through so much. Fear washed over her expression, not for herself, but for them.

"Riley, we all need to leave here together. The town that I once thought of as home is cursed. What remains behind is what nightmares are made of."

Thinking of Jonathan and knowing the answers of how to rescue him were just within his grasp, Riley shook his head. "Nightmares are the least of my worries. I've come to rescue my friend, and I'm not leaving without him."

CHAPTER 53

Tamara could certainly sympathize with Riley about wanting to save his friend. She had also wanted to save her parents from the evil which now resided in their town. However, that all changed after watching loved ones and neighbors be ordered to kill one another and doing it without hesitation or remorse. Tamara had to be brutally honest about the whole situation if she wanted to save Riley and Maggie from the same fate she had narrowly escaped.

"I'm sorry to tell you this, but there's no one else left alive," Tamara blurted. "I mean, there are, but they now serve some stranger who arrived yesterday morning. Honestly, I don't believe he's even human, just an evil entity who is masquerading as a man. The group I was with told me there was no one left to be rescued. The 'diggers' have already captured or killed those who had stayed behind.

"Diggers?" asked Riley.

"It's just a nickname given to those who now serve the stranger. Guess it's as good a name as any. They will be digging a lot of graves now that no one else is left alive."

Under different circumstances, Tamara would have felt like a foolish teenager telling a ghost story in a weak, half-hearted attempt to impress the celebrity now holding her hand. She had introduced herself as Maggie. However, Tamara knew she really was Mary Allison Gregory. Tamara couldn't help but smirk when she realized that "Maggie" was obviously a play on her initials,

M.A.G. It had taken her a moment to figure out where she had recognized Maggie from, but her gorgeous looks and warm smile could not be mistaken for anyone else. She owned Gregory Portal Provider, a streaming service her father raved about because he no longer had to have multiple subscriptions to watch his favorite shows.

Tamara remembered visiting her dad at work the day George jokingly told her that he could have been set up for life. If only Gregory Portal Provider had agreed to the merger of his old tech company.

It was bizarre how these old memories so easily surfaced, when only an hour earlier Tamara was being shot at. She assumed that was how the rest of her life would be. Thoughts of what could have been flooded Tamara's mind. What could have been was destroyed by the evil tearing Broken Falls apart. Everything and everyone in her entire world had been destroyed.

Feeling Riley and Maggie watching her, waiting for her to continue, Tamara cast a side glance at Maggie, who was holding out a baby wipe to her. Not realizing she had even been crying until now, Tamara accepted the wipe and dabbed both eyes.

"Thank you," she said quietly, feeling safer when Maggie pulled her into a side hug and positioned her head onto her shoulder.

"So, you've met this strange man?" asked Riley.

Before Tamara could answer Riley's question, Maggie cleared her throat in disapproval at his question and glared at Riley. It was almost comical how Riley immediately looked away like a scolded child.

"No," said Tamara. "I've never met him. Me and my father had just come back from our yearly hike when we learned of his presence. Our neighborhood had turned into mayhem in the few hours we had been gone. Belongings spread out all across lawns, while people were making quick getaways. Our neighbor across the street, Mrs. Cafferty, told me what was happening. She said a strange man had broken up the Catholic church service and issued a warning: Whoever remained in town after midnight would suffer his wrath."

Oddly, Tamara thought they wouldn't believe her. Instead, Riley nodded for her to continue, which made Tamara suspect they quite possibly knew this stranger.

"You know this individual, don't you?" asked Tamara, unable to hide the anger in her voice.

If they expected her to open up about what she had experienced, while secretly keeping her in the dark about what was really going on, then Tamara refused to placate them. She did not want to be treated like an adolescent teenager.

"You have every right to be angry with us," said Maggie. "Time is not in our favor, or I would tell you everything. However, I will confirm the stranger is not human, but in fact a demon. A very powerful demon we crossed paths with right before our friend was taken from us. Which is why we have come. We hope he will be able to tell us how to find our friend."

Tamara, having been a Christian most her life, wasn't completely shocked by this admittance, but she was confused as to how this was even possible.

For the most part, Tamara believed in spiritual warfare, regarding angels and demons battling over lost souls. However, coming to terms with the fact that a demon could take human form and overtake an entire town was stretching her reality. She then looked at the dog they had called Kratos. When it looked back at her, its red eyes were glowing. Tamara felt goosebumps rise over her entire body, causing her to gasp and look away.

She wanted to run until Maggie firmly took her by the shoulders. "Tamara," said Maggie, making certain they made eye contact. "You can trust us. Kratos, although also not of this world, is on our side. He's the reason we're here."

Gaining her composure, Tamara looked once more at Kratos, who went back to his post, vigilantly watching the road.

"Our friend that we are looking for is also not from this world," said Riley. "I don't know if you have any sort of religious background, but—"

"I was raised in a Christian home," said Tamara, cutting Riley off.

One of the twins began to fuss, putting an end to the conversation and the questions Tamara knew she would never get answers to.

"Kratos, come," said Maggie.

Tamara, now holding the twin, rocked back and forth until it calmed. She peered down at the small, fragile little one. The baby reached up and took hold of Tamara's hair.

Tamara's mind raced with thoughts of getting to safety, of what would happen to her and the twins once they had. As thoughts swirled in her head, she was saddened by the realization that once they reached safety, the twins would most likely be put into foster care. They would never know what had really happened to their parents or how Tamara had saved them from the evil that had taken over Broken Falls. Tamara untangled the hand from her hair and kissed it. Looking up, she found Maggie giving her a sympathetic smile.

"When I get back," said Maggie, "I will make certain the three of you are taken care of and, if you'd like, to remain together."

Tamara smiled and took Maggie's hand in hers. "You are much prettier in person, and even kinder than I thought you'd be."

Tamara could see her comment had caught Maggie off guard. Her face flushed and she flashed Tamara a genuine smile. With that, Tamara kissed the back of Maggie's hand, same as she had done with the twin.

"This next part I won't even attempt to explain, but Kratos has the ability to take you far away from here. I recommend he take you to the hospital where he took my friend earlier, back in Taupe City. Unless you have somewhere else in mind? Where you know you'd be safe?"

Tamara looked at Kratos's red eyes, which were now a dull brown. She thought about asking how this was possible but knew it would be a foolish question since Kratos wasn't from this world.

"That would probably be best," said Tamara. "I was separated from my family when all of this happened." Fighting back fresh tears, she took several quick breaths to calm down before continuing. "My mom is sick and couldn't be moved, which is why my family didn't leave when everyone else had. The last I saw of my parents; they were still alive. My father made certain I escaped, but he remained behind to stay with my mom. I know this is a lot to ask, but could you ask that demon, when you see him, what happened to my parents? My father's name is Bob Madison. No matter how much the truth hurts, I must know with absolute certainty so I can have some closure."

Maggie nodded and hugged her, followed by Riley, who handed her the other sleeping twin. "You won't need your backpack, unless you have any keepsakes you would like to take with you," said Riley.

"No, just the baby stuff, but since I'm going to a hospital, I won't need anything. I just don't know how I'm going to explain any of this once I get there."

Maggie began rifling through Tamara's backpack, tossing items out of it at random before withdrawing a white cloth and a crayon. How or why a crayon was even in the pack puzzled

Tamara, but if Maggie could use it to help her and twins, she was grateful. Maggie began writing on the cloth, then folded it and pushed it into Tamara's left front jean pocket, her own hands being occupied with the twins.

"When you get to the hospital, I want you to ask to have Alyssa Branch paged. She's a very dear friend of mine, and her husband, Stuart, is being treated there. Stuart is my best friend. Alyssa will be under a lot of stress, so just hand her the note and everything else will be taken care of."

Despite what she had been through, Tamara felt like she could trust both Maggie and Riley.

"Everything is going to be okay," Maggie said. She gave Tamara's shoulder a light squeeze before looking down at Kratos.

Tamara watched the hound in curiosity as to what it would do now that it had been given a silent order by Maggie. For a fleeting moment, Tamara noticed a small hue of red come to life in the hound's eyes, but before she could comment on it, Kratos licked her hand, transporting her just outside of a hospital emergency room entrance.

Tamara looked around to see if she had been noticed by anyone, then jumped when something nudged her in the back. Turning, she saw Kratos staring up at her.

Still somewhat afraid of the hound, Tamara slowly knelt anyway, feeling the strong need to thank Kratos for bringing them to safety. Peering into Kratos's dull brown eyes, Tamara thought that under different circumstances the hound could be confused for just an oversized dog. Except Kratos's colossal physique was much larger than any living canine and would be the first dead giveaway.

"Thank you for saving us," said Tamara, closing her eyes and bowing her head as a sign of respect.

Tamara wished to pet or hug Kratos, to further express her

gratitude. Kratos seemed to have picked up on her thought, and he leaned forward and placed his head to hers before licking her face several times. Then, in the blink of an eye, he disappeared.

CHAPTER 54

Esperanza was watching the events unfold with Jameson, Barbados, and Gideon from Savior's theater room. While in the theater room, anyone could see anything that had happened or was happening anywhere in Hell and on Earth. No matter how many times Esperanza watched the scene play out between the three Elders—Jameson, Barbados, and Gideon—she just couldn't comprehend how Gideon had outwitted not only Jameson and Barbados, but her as well.

With no alternative on how to right this wrong, Esperanza remained in the small theater, wondering just how everything had gone wrong so quickly, and what would become of her after she informed Savior of everything that had transpired in his absence. He would surely cast her back into the pits of Hell, where Jameson and Barbados had already returned to after their mortal bodies had been killed.

Esperanza had been worried about Hell taking Barbados's corpse while humans were in the vicinity of it. She was thankful when Hell waited until the officer who killed Barbados was unconscious from Jameson's attack before doing so.

Jameson had been returned to Hell with much less stress to Esperanza, since only Riley and Maggie had been there when it happened. That was another thing Esperanza still couldn't figure out: who or what had killed Jameson. He was alive, standing in the elevator one moment, then on the ground the next with his throat and chest cavity ripped completely open, without so much as a trace or shadow of who or what had done the killing.

The only other person in the elevator was the man named Stuart Branch, an employee of Maggie's. However, he had been facing away from Jameson at the time.

It wasn't until the elevator doors had opened that the violent act had occurred. For whatever reason, no matter how many times Esperanza watched the footage, it revealed nothing. Jameson was standing, the doors opened, then he lay dead in the back of the elevator. It was unexplainable.

As for Gideon, he had left the alley, then boarded a bus, and again the footage for whatever reason didn't reveal his destination. When the footage did pick back up, Gideon was stepping out of a large truck, saying something to the driver only she was privileged to.

Gideon then turned and proceeded down a desolate road with cornfields on either side of it, and then nothing. He simply vanished and the screen went dark.

Nothing about this whole ordeal made any sense. Esperanza wished that she had the power to pull Gideon back the moment he turned on Jameson and Barbados, but only Savior and Hell itself had the power to do that, and Hell was limited to only taking the dead.

Leaving Savior's theater in a daze of confusion, Esperanza stopped and stood outside the viewing room where Lucifer and Jonathan were. Before she could analyze the situation any further, Lucifer exited, smiling broadly at her.

"Summon all the Region Leaders to my cathedral. I have an announcement."

As Savior turned to go back in the room, Esperanza stopped him. "I'm sorry, Savior, but I have made a critical error."

Turning to face her, Savior held up a hand for silence. He

then placed a hand under her chin and made her meet his eyes. Seconds later, Esperanza could feel her memories being pulled from her. When Savior had seen Esperanza's memory of her, Jameson, Barbados, and Gideon overstepping their roles to correct the Tristan situation, his eyes went so black that Esperanza could see her burning soul reflecting back at her.

Releasing her, Savior stepped back and smiled sadistically. "So, you failed me and now must be wondering, what happens next. Tell me, Esperanza, what do you believe I should do?"

Trembling uncontrollably, Esperanza stood there silently waiting for the pain to begin. She knew there was nothing she could say in her defense.

"Silence is exactly the correct answer," said Lucifer. "You will absolutely be punished, just as soon as I decide the timing is right for it. This will allow your thoughts to fester, causing yourself trepidation and distress while awaiting your punishment. For now, go summon the Region Leaders as I've asked."

Turning again to leave, this time Savior stopped on his own accord. "Esperanza, do not ever mistake my kindness for any sign of weakness. I only show you this mercy because I'm on the cusp of getting what I have been after for over two thousand years, and I haven't the time to deal with you."

When the door closed and she was once again alone, Esperanza shook from the worry and fear that filled her after hearing Savior's threat. She proceeded toward the front door, which led to Hell, where she would take a wormhole to each Region Leader's territory to summon them.

Esperanza became acutely aware of the danger beginning to unfold, as each door she walked past would open and a hound would exit. The door would then slam closed behind them, increasing Esperanza's concern. As the rest of the doors on her path continued to open, releasing more hounds, and adding to the multitude already on her heels, Esperanza quickened her pace until she was in a flat-out sprint.

She paused at the front door, her hand resting on the handle. Esperanza finally built up the courage to turn and see at least a dozen hounds staring at her, their mouths open to reveal the sinister rows of razor-sharp teeth.

Dropping to her knees and closing her eyes, Esperanza waited for the feeding to begin. One minute seemed to pass. Then two. Followed by countless more, until Esperanza at last opened her eyes, wishing now she hadn't.

She was face-to-face with one of the hounds, its deadpan eyes were boring into hers. When it partially opened its mouth, an exhale of warm air hit her in the face, along with the smell of decaying meat from its last meal.

Esperanza let out a blood-curdling scream as several teeth sunk into her extremities just before they began tearing her apart, and her last coherent thought was for mercy.

CHAPTER 55

W hen Kratos materialized, Riley gave him a thorough rubdown, thanking the hound for his loyalty.

"That poor girl," said Maggie. "She's so fortunate to still be alive. I just hope we are able to locate her parents . . . alive."

Riley was preoccupied with his thoughts of finding the best strategy to go about entering the town as safely as possible. He was fairly certain Tamara's parents were already dead and didn't want to upset Maggie. Instead, he wondered what the chances of actually being able to sneak into the town would be. They didn't know the layout. They couldn't just walk through the main entrance, or they would be killed instantly.

"Riley," said Maggie, now standing next to him, taking one of his hands in hers. "Since the town is now overrun by a group Tamara referred to as 'diggers,' how are we even going to get inside?"

He looked into Kratos's dull brown eyes and could still see a soft hue of red glowing behind them. This gave Riley an idea. Whether it would work or not, he hadn't a clue, but it was the only real chance they had.

"I guess we should stay off the road and try to make our way as far into the town as possible. Hopefully without being seen," said Maggie. "Unless you have something else in mind?" Worry was written all over her face, and her body was trembling.

"That rogue demon is too smart, and by now he has fortified the town and left nothing to chance regarding anyone being allowed to enter or leave. If we so much as try entering, we will end up dead. However, I have thought of something that might just work." Seeing the skepticism in Maggie's expression, Riley pressed onward. "Remember how I'd told you I met the Devil's hounds before Kratos ever came into our lives? Jonathan once told me if he ever attempted to heal someone it could immediately kill the recipient because they weren't made to handle even the smallest amount of his abilities. I had asked him this because I was curious as to why he hadn't just healed me when I was shot that day at Paul's grocery."

Maggie's expression changed from skepticism to confusion.

"Sorry. I know I'm rambling, but I have a point. Kratos entered our lives right after Jonathan was pulled into Hell. For a while, we debated whether Kratos was on our side, or if he was secretly setting us up for failure. I'm certain I now know the truth. You see, I believe Kratos must have come in contact with Jonathan, even for a short amount of time. Jonathan had to have known that Kratos could handle his powers and healed him, passing on some of his abilities so Kratos would be able to protect us. This means Kratos not only possesses the capabilities of the hounds of Hell, but also that of a guardian angel. You see, the demons and the damned are not only terrified of the Devil, but also his hounds. Because to the hounds, they are food."

Maggie looked briefly at Kratos. "I think you may be reaching a bit, but let's just say, for argument's sake, I believe you. This still doesn't help with our current predicament of getting into the town without being murdered!"

Giving Kratos a few more rubs behind his ears, Riley took both Maggie's hands in his. "Kratos will stay here for the time being. Once we're inside the town and have met with the demon and declared our intentions, which I'm sure will be answered with mocking amusement, I want you to whistle as loud as possible. I have no idea how the rest will play out. I just hope it's in our favor."

Maggie studied him for several minutes before reluctantly nodding her head, agreeing to go along with the plan. She then knelt next to Kratos, taking his head in her hands. "We are putting all our trust and faith in you, big guy. I meant what I said before. You belong to us now, and we belong to you. We most definitely won't let you go without a fight."

She kissed the top of Kratos's head and received several kisses in return. Then she looked at Riley with uncertainty. "You know, Kratos could probably just transport us directly in front of that demon and we wouldn't have to go through all of these 'what if' scenarios, right?"

"Maybe," said Riley. "But if he could have transported us directly to the demon, don't you think he would have done that to begin with? If he could have just transported us directly to Jonathan, that would have made this all the easier. Unfortunately, for whatever reason, Kratos is no longer capable of simply entering Hell anymore. Which is why I firmly believe he was healed by Jonathan. Angels aren't able to journey into Hell. They can only be forced."

Without responding, Maggie retrieved their duffel bag. She then handed Riley one of Stuart's handguns and took two out for herself, tucking them in the back of her waistband.

Although Riley wasn't good with a pistol and preferred a shotgun or rifle, he followed Maggie's narrative. He tucked the gun into the back of his waistband for easy access, hoping their arrival wouldn't come down to a shootout.

Taking Maggie's free hand, Riley looked down at Kratos. "I will die before I ever allow you to be stuck in Hell again."

Kratos licked his outstretched hand several times, then sat back on his haunches.

Without feeling the need to give any further instructions to Kratos, Riley led Maggie out of the cornfield and back onto the road. He paused when a light sprinkle of rain landed on the sides of his face.

"Riley," said Maggie.

Looking out from their vantage point atop the road, he tried to make out the rooftops in the distance. Storm clouds moved in. Riley felt Maggie squeeze his hand with a little more urgency. He stared at her in the sparse moonlight and noticed a different side of her. Although fearful of what lay ahead of them, there was a sudden vulnerability in her eyes.

"I love you, Riley. I know my timing couldn't be worse but—"

Riley pulled Maggie closer and kissed her. She had entered his life because Jonathan had asked her to watch over him. In that short span of time, their relationship had transformed from strangers to a rare friendship where they were forced to rely on one another to stay alive. Now he realized he couldn't imagine going through life without her by his side.

Stepping back, Maggie smiled at him. "Just remember, I said it first!"

Riley chuckled at how Maggie always seemed to make him smile. Even under the direst of circumstances, she found a way. Riley took her hand, and together they walked slowly toward the town of Broken Falls.

THE END

VOLUME 1 IN
THE RILEY SERIES

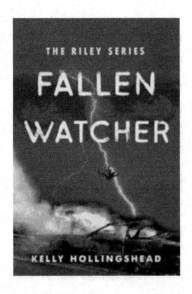

A paranormal suspense that brings good and evil into different perspectives.

Riley's world is torn apart on his wedding day when he and his wife, Allison, are involved in a hit-and-run accident and Allison doesn't survive. When Jonathan, Allison's guardian angel, chooses to fall to Earth to remain by Riley's side, the evils of Hell are unleashed to destroy both Jonathan and Riley. A ferocious battle of good and evil surrounds Riley as Jonathan tries to save him and the ugliness of Hell tries to consume him.

VOLUME 2 IN
THE RILEY SERIES

"One way or another the dues of the past must be paid."

Mysterious forces are driving a deadly wedge between Riley and his best friend, a fallen angel named Jonathan.

A year ago, Riley had come to put his trust and his very life in Jonathan's hands, but something is happening to Jonathan—something very dark—and it's putting Riley at risk. He was once Reiley's most trusted friend, but now Riley is beginning to fear him . . . and for good reason.

They will both face impossible decisions, and only one of them will survive as the forces of evil once hunt them down.

ABOUT THE AUTHOR

Kelly Hollingshead is an avid reader who prefers books over music. He found entertainment in books as a child due to growing up in a large family where money was always tight. However, the library was free, and entertainment was endless, simply waiting between book covers.

From an early age, Kelly has approached writing as an enjoyable pastime until his wife convinced him to try to publish at least one story. This is his third published novel in the Riley series.

Kelly has been married for thirteen years to his wife, Melissa, and they have a sweet daughter, Brynn. When not working on the Riley series, Kelly enjoys spending time with his family and friends, and meeting new friends and fans at book signings.